The World-Eel's great coils poured up out of the ground and Tua-Li was rearing, swimming up the smoke-tree with impossible strength, like a monstrous fish fighting its way up a mountain cascade.

Coming after her.

"Faster!" Rafti screamed at the ghost stallion, knowing he was already climbing as fast as his eight legs could fly. They were closer to the stars than the eel was to them, but fast though the horse was, Tua-Li was faster. The eel's endless coils looped up from the Inner Ocean, and Rafti saw how truly terrifying he was, how unprepared she had been for the dangers she was confronting.

For Tua-Li was guarding the Mother's Inner Ocean, where the dead went . . . and Rafti was stealing the souls of Moth, Tramu, and her other self.

Souls that belonged to the Mother.

Souls that the eel wanted back.

SCOTT BAKER

A TOM DOHERTY ASSOCIATES BOOK

This is a work of fiction. All the characters and events portrayed in this book are fictional, and any resemblance to real people or incidents is purely coincidental.

FIREDANCE

First printing: September 1986

A TOR Book

Published by Tom Doherty Associates, Inc.
49 West 24 Street
New York, N.Y. 10010

Cover art by Boris Vallejo

ISBN: 0-812-53145-0
CAN. ED.: 0-812-53146-9

Printed in the United States

0 9 8 7 6 5 4 3 2 1

Part One: Rafti

Chapter One

She had been beautiful once, but that had ended three years ago, in the burning pit, when she'd lost an eye to one of the dead and herself lain three days dead before being summoned back to life. When she slept half shadowed, she was beautiful still, but in the daytime, her once flame-bright hair now mostly gray, the dead eye staring milky and accusing from the purplish-red mass of scar tissue that ringed it, she knew she was hideous.

Her name, though it no longer fit her, was Rafti Shonraleur's-Daughter, and she was fifteen years old. Tomorrow she was to be given in marriage to Kalsanen Touminor's-Son, an old man with failing eyes and strength, for it was the Earth Mother's will that all young women, even such as Rafti, be given and taken in marriage, and Kalsanen Touminor's-Son was the only man in the village who would take her willingly, scarred and bitter and marked by strangeness as she was.

But she didn't want him, she hated him as she hated the dead eye and the leathery purple half-mask that disfigured the face around it. Kalsanen Touminor's-Son wasn't her husband, he would never be her husband: he was bridegroom to the dead eye, willing to take it to wife in return for someone to do the work his first wife was too weary and his twin twelve-year-old daughters too lazy to do; in return also for Rafti's slim strong body beneath him at night in the stinking darkness of his hut, where he wouldn't have to see the dead eye, his true wife, staring up at him out of Rafti's face.

Tomorrow night. Unless tonight she could convince him, make him believe that the price he'd have to pay for her was too great, the dead eye too fearsome to be worth the unwilling drudge and bedmate she'd make him.

It had been different then, on that day three years ago when she'd first found herself part of the silent crowd of villagers huddled together in front of the Temple watching the two Nomad shamans slowly leading their shaggy, scrawny black horses down the broad stairway the Ancestors had cut in the jagged black basalt of the volcano's slope. Rafti had never seen horses before, but she knew what they looked like from the Temple friezes showing the Ancestors' flight from their ancient homeland in the south. The steps the shamans were descending led straight up the slope from the Mother's Temple to the rim of Her Burning Mountain, deviating from their course only when they had to twist around the huge irregular blocks of stone and obsidian scattered without apparent order up and down the mountainside, then down inside, through the sound of belching magma to the lake of fire within, and they led nowhere else: the two could only have entered the Valley as the Ancestors themselves had, by making their way across or through the molten lake. There was no other way to pass the steep mountain walls that sheltered and trapped the village, held its twelve families in as they held in the warmth that was the Earth Mother's gift of life to the Children of Raburr here in their exile in the frozen north.

Rafti knew that other such shamans had come before, many others over the long generations, to watch the fire-walking and take with them the occasional girl who showed the promise of becoming a firedancer, the even rarer boys the shamans chose to raise as shamans like themselves. The two horses looked heavily laden: the shamans always brought goods and messages from the other valleys around the Mother's Burning Mountain, where the rest of Her people had found refuge in their exile; brought metal tools from the peoples still living in the south, tools that Rafti's people had long ago lost the skill and wisdom to manufacture for themselves, so that the Ancestors' forge had stood cold and silent now for uncountable generations. Sometimes they would bring with them a young woman from one of the other valleys and leave with another for the next valley to be visited, though these two were alone. And they always brought their herbs and healing arts, though the price of their aid was such that only the village's most important families had ever been able to pay it. Yet the last Nomads to visit the valley had come before Rafti had been born, and she had never seen one.

"Their horses," Manmoutin Manlaiteq's-Son, the village's Tradition-Master, said somewhere off to her right. She looked for him, located him talking with her older brother Teltinor, whom he was training to take his place as the village's memory. Beyond them she saw Valinor, her eldest brother, and her younger sister, Lashimi, standing silent, listening.

Rafti caught Manmoutin Manlaiteq's-Son's eye, asked, "What about their horses?"

He nodded back at her as though pleased with the question and said, "Not even the Ancestors were able to force their horses to cross the Earth Mother's Burning Lake. They finally had to slaughter some for meat and free the rest."

"But the other Nomads, the ones who've come here before?" Teltinor asked. He was three years older than Rafti, but still too young to remember the last shaman's visit. Perhaps Valinor had been old enough, but he was four years older even than Teltinor.

"No. Perhaps in some other valley, but never here."

Rafti pushed her way through the crowd. Men and women moved aside for her as soon as they saw who she was: Rafti Shonraleur's-Daughter, eldest daughter of Shonraleur Valinor's-Son, who was First Speaker for the Council of Elders, and of his wife, Rafti Rafti's-Daughter, the Earth Mother's Priestess, and as such the only woman in the Valley permitted to speak in Council and to bear her mother's name instead of her father's or husband's.

At the front, just before the low tanglethorn hedge separating the smooth circular expanse of black basalt on which the Temple stood from the profane world in which the people of the valley raised their children, worked their fields, and tended their groves and animals, she found Manlaiteq Manmoutin's-Son. He glanced down at her and smiled without saying anything as she squeezed in next to him, then took her hand and held it tight as he turned back to watch the Nomads.

"Are Mother and Father in the Temple?" she asked him.

"Yes. Shhh."

The younger shaman led the way. He looked eighteen or twenty years old and not particularly tall, but he was broad-shouldered and powerfully muscled, though almost unnaturally gaunt. Tired as Rafti could see he was, he still moved with a surprising, almost gliding grace. He wore loose breeches of smooth red-brown leather gathered at the ankle, and over them a long wide-sleeved and open-necked caftan made from what Rafti thought might be the skin of a bear: other fur-bearing animals she knew only from the Temple friezes and Manmoutin Manlaiteq's-Son's tales, but there had been bears in the Valley when the Ancestors first found it, and one of them had left the skin that still hung on the wall of her father's hut. The shaman's cap was a strip of dark hide wound many times around his head and held in place by a band of red copper, with a copper moth attached to the front, over his forehead. From cap and caftan hung myriads of tiny gold and copper mirrors and other ornaments that caught the light with every step he took; from his back hung numerous long wide ribbons of black and white fur, and around his neck was some sort of complicated silver chain from which hung a single bright silver blade, a dagger with neither hilt nor the tang by which a hilt could have been fastened to it, a blade like the flattened metal fang of some great beast.

His long, thick hair was braided in a profusion of tightly twisted separate strands, some the same red as Rafti's own hair, others a glossy black unknown in the Valley, the whole tied behind his head with a shiny amber-golden cord, and his sparse beard was a mottled confusion of the two colors. His dark, yellow-brown skin glistened as though oiled or coated with grease, and his face was strong-boned but weary, prematurely lined.

He kept his gaze on the stairs in front of him, as though he was so tired he was afraid he'd fall if he let his attention wander from them for so much as an instant. Just once he paused to stare down at the massed villagers, and when he did, Rafti saw that the eyes in that dark, hard face, beneath the mismatched brows, were a startling yellow, clear and bright as the sun.

He seemed to be staring right at her, or past her at someone he knew. Rafti almost turned to see who he could have recognized, to avoid his too-bright eyes, but then he looked back at the steps and continued on.

He had been looking at her, not at anyone behind her. Something about him frightened her, made her want to turn away and hide from him, yet there had been none of the obvious cruelty, none of the greed and contempt, that she would have thought to be what she'd fear in a shaman's face.

He passed from her sight for a moment behind a towering block of pink-flecked granite, and she looked away from him to the older shaman following with the horses. He was darker—eyes, skin, hair—and grimmer despite the almost dancing lightness of his feet on the stairs and the white fur caftan he wore in place of the other's black. The amusement plain even from this distance on his long angular face was harsh and cold, sardonic. Yet he was gentle with the horses, often pausing to whisper to them, occasionally beating out short messages to them on the stretched and painted hide of the oval drum hanging from his waistband.

His costume was much more complicated than his companion's, with perhaps a little less metal on it but with a multitude of fur and cloth ribbons, bright-winking stones that might have been jewels or fragments of rock crystal, shiny black obsidian disks. On his head he wore a cap made from the body and feathers of some small black hawk—the hawk's head with its cruel black beak staring out from above his own dark features; the bird's long graceful wings outstretched, caught in a rigid down beat as though immobilized in the very instant it took flight; the tail fanning out to cover the back of his neck. Yet the hawk's eyes were bright gold and the gold ornaments on the shaman's white caftan gleamed their proper color in the sunlight, and many of the ribbons that hung from his costume were shiny and bright, beautiful as the breeze played with them. He looked hard, yes, and dangerous, but though there was little kindness evident in his face, neither was there any gratuitous cruelty there, at least not that Rafti could see.

And it was vital to the whole valley that neither of them be too cruel, because one of the shamans who had visited the valley in Rafti's great-grandmother's time had been as ruthless as he was powerful. Only one, out of the many who had come over the generations with their goods and messages and healing arts, with the brides that helped make of the separated families in their closed valleys still a single people, but that one the Valley would never forget, for now there were only twelve families where once there had been thirteen.

The shaman had come for a firedancer. He had offered

twice the customary price, but he had refused to believe Rafti's great-grandmother when she said there were no girls suitable for his purposes. And when she had prepared the burning pit and shown the shaman that those villagers whose grace in the Mother's eyes would let them pass unharmed over the coals were either men or boys, or past the age to become the dancer the shaman sought, he had forced the widower Shulteurtas Jattasteq's-Son's four handsome but timid daughters to attempt the crossing. After he'd had to watch his three eldest daughters burn, Shulteurtas Jattasteq's-Son had tried to stop the shaman from forcing his last daughter out onto the coals, but the shaman had struck him down with a gesture, so that he died screaming without a hand having been laid upon him. Yet before the shaman could make Shulteurtas Jattasteq's-Son's final daughter follow her sisters, she had thrown herself facedown into the pit, to burn and die and be reunited with her family, thus cheating the shaman of his last hope of getting what he'd come for.

But even that most ruthless of shamans had not been able to bring his horse with him across the Earth Mother's Burning Lake, and perhaps his cruelty had been the reason, his lack of that very kindness the hawk-faced shaman was even now showing to the horses.

The shamans vanished behind the Temple. In any case, Rafti herself had nothing to fear from the burning pit. She was her mother's daughter and would someday be the Earth Mother's Priestess, Rafti Rafti's-Daughter instead of Rafti Shonraleur's-Daughter or even Rafti Manlaiteq's-Wife; she had walked the coals four years now, ever since that first time when she'd been eight years old.

The strangers were spending too long in the Temple. They'd brought no brides to trade, and none of the boys Rafti's age or younger showed the signs of a developing shaman. Had it been a matter of messages from the other villages or of trade, Manmoutin Manlaiteq's-Son and the three remaining members of the Council of Elders—Telsal

Telsal's-Grandson, Karmin Silsinour's-Son, and Kalsanen Touminor's-Son (whom Rafti suddenly glimpsed, arguing in half-senile fury with his wife and daughters)—would have been summoned within. Trade, like war, was the responsibility of men, and it was for the Council to set its terms.

So the two shamans could only be here in search of a firedancer. And Rafti knew she was the only girl of her generation who had the strength and beauty and skills, the grace in the Mother's eyes, that would allow her to become the kind of firedancer they'd come for.

"Why can't they finish?" she demanded, only realizing that she'd spoken aloud when Manlaiteq Manmoutin's-Son squeezed her hand tighter and said, "It won't be much longer."

"You don't understand," she said, but it was hopeless, he was grinning at her, happy, almost laughing. She was the only one and they'd come to take her away from her people. But she didn't want to go, she wanted only to stay with Manlaiteq Manmoutin's-Son and have his children, bear him sons and herself a daughter who would succeed her as the Earth Mother's Priestess just as she herself would succeed her own mother.

Her mother appeared on the Temple steps, called to the Council members in the crowd. Manmoutin Manlaiteq's-Son and the others made their way through the gate out onto the smooth black basalt expanse surrounding the Temple, crossed it and disappeared into the Temple after Rafti's mother.

"You don't understand," Rafti said again, but he was still staring expectantly at the Temple and didn't even hear her.

Chapter Two

When at last they came back out again Rafti's mother, as befitted the Earth Mother's Priestess, led the way, followed closely by her husband, and after him the four other elders in single file. She held her head high and her back straight; she was dressed in the long blood-red ceremonial skirt that left her torso bare. Her heavy breasts were still firm, just beginning to sag despite the five children she'd borne, the four she'd nursed until they were old enough to feed themselves after her first son had died in the cradle of the choking sickness, and her nipples had been accentuated with red ochre paste. She wore a green mask to show that she was not there as Rafti, the wife of Shonraleur, a woman who had been born and been subject to father and husband and who would inevitably die, but as Woman, all women, faceless, the undying vessel for the Earth Mother's infinitely greater and more mysterious fecundity.

Rafti hadn't seen her father since she'd left to work in the barley fields at the other end of the valley early that morning (for all agricultural work, save only the cultivation and preparation of the ibjeq plants, which were grown on land apart and used only for purposes of trade, was the Mother's work and forbidden to men, just as war and trade and the work of the forge were forbidden to women). He was carrying his gold-inlaid elder's staff and wearing the vest of forged copper links that had passed from First Speaker's son to First Speaker's son since the time of the earliest Ancestors, but while some of the links still gleamed their proper warm orange-red, too many others were greening and corroded, and some links were twisted and broken or missing altogether, their repair and replacement beyond the knowledge of anyone in the village now that her people's forge was so many generations dead and cold.

Always before Rafti had thought the vest a thing of wondrous wealth and history, but now, looking at it as if she were seeing it for the first time as it really was, dull and ragged and clumsily patched, slowly being eaten away, generation after generation, by the green sickness, she suddenly knew that the vest's very existence was an accusation, a condemnation, the proof that none of her people for generations upon generations had had the wit or the courage to see that their greatness was long lost and that they were unworthy of the long, proud lineage that their possession of the vest symbolized to them now.

She felt ashamed for her people, their poverty laid out so proudly for strangers to see. The Ancestors, Raburr's First-Born Children, had crossed the lake of fire in the Earth Mother's Burning Mountain with all their children and possessions and animals, everything but their horses; they had won from the Mother Her promise that so long as they continued to honor Her and keep to Her ways, She would keep Her Burning Mountain's wrath from them; they had cut their broad stairway into the living basalt of the volcano's flank, and with the stone taken from it erected a Temple to the Mother on the newly solidified lava. They had killed the bears that had held the valley for their own and taught their crops and animals to thrive in the black soil and steamy sulfur-scented air.

They had been heroes, for all that they had come to the valley fleeing for their lives from some unimaginable enemy. And now there was no one remaining among their descendants with even the strength or the courage to try crossing the Burning Lake to regain the outside world. Her people were trapped here for all time, dependent on the Nomads' infrequent visits for what little they knew of the other families that had survived the exodus with them, for all they knew and needed of the world beyond thc Rcf-uge's impassable walls. The Earth Mother sheltered and protected them, true, but they were like children who'd lost the courage to leave their mother's womb, who would finally die there unborn. And yet the yellow-eyed shaman—he couldn't be more than twenty years old but he'd brought a horse across the burning lake and already he wore more copper in his headband, in the mirrors and chains and charms that dangled and shone from his robe and cap than had gone into the vest of which her father was so proud, more copper perhaps than all that which her people still hoarded from their years of greatness.

That two shamans should have so much wealth and obvious power when her people had been reduced to so little (and they were *hers*, just as she was the Earth Moth-er's: if she could keep the shamans from taking her, she'd be married soon, and then it would be only a few years until she succeeded her mother as the Earth Mother's Priestess, as her mother had succeeded her own mother, and so take for herself the name Rafti Rafti's-Daughter; then *she* would be the one to intercede with the Mother when the village angered Her, then it would be Rafti who held the Burning Mountain's fires from the Valley) . . . that the shamans had come to buy *her* for a pittance from her people when they needed her but dared not defy the shamans who were the last surviving link to the other villages and the world they had lost, that they'd come to take her away and turn the gifts granted her by the Mother for the good of her people to *their* private use, and make her dance for the amusement of strangers—

No. It was impossible, intolerable. She would not let it happen, she would not do it.

The shamans had still not emerged from the Temple. She looked away from the slow-moving line of elders, up at Manlaiteq Manmoutin's-Son. He felt her gaze on him and smiled briefly back at her, then turned from her to watch for the shamans. After a moment she looked away from him.

Tradition-Master's son, Tradition-Master after his father, she knew him well enough to be certain that he was thinking of nothing but the messages that the Children of Raburr in the other villages had sent his father, unless it was of the message that his father would in turn compose and send. Her father, her brothers, Manlaiteq Manmoutin's-Son: she could count on none of them to help her. If she had been born into one of the lesser families, perhaps, or destined as bride for any but the village's future Tradition-Master, then perhaps one of those who loved her would have defied custom for her, but they were who they were, and for all their love she could expect nothing from them: she would have to find her own way to save herself.

Her own or the Earth Mother's. Her own mother could do nothing without a sign from the Mother: she served the Earth Mother, and though she was not bound in the same way by the straight lines of lineage and law that bound the men, though it was her duty to nurture and contain her people, yet it was the Mother who made firedancers and perhaps even shamans, so without a clear sign her mother's duty to the Mother would be to follow custom like the others.

Help me, Mother, Rafti pleaded, not sure whether what she was doing was right or wrong. Please help me.

Nothing came to her, no sudden certainty or knowledge. She would have to do what she could, hope the Earth Mother would help her when the time she would need Her help came.

The only way through the barrier that surrounded the Temple precincts was through the labyrinth gate, a waist-high tanglethorn maze that a man with his sense of sight to guide him could negotiate without difficulty, at least by day, but that would confuse and trap those spirits that might wish the Earth Mother's Temple or Priestess harm. Rafti's parents and the Council members following them had already made their way through the labyrinth and were waiting just outside it (the crowd of villagers had given way to make room for them and Rafti felt herself jammed up against whoever it was who was behind her) by the time the shamans finally emerged from the Temple, each now leading his own horse. The older shaman had removed his caftan and cap and replaced them with an open vest of red-brown leather, but the younger shaman still wore his entire costume and Rafti could see now that the metal bars on his sleeves and chest imitated the pattern of the bones beneath his flesh, as though he wore his skeleton on the outside like a tortoise. And there were other bones, even what might have been the golden skeleton of a small bird, hanging and swinging and clashing against one another as he moved.

But the sound of all that jangling metal had distracted her a moment, kept her from realizing that with the two shamans was Cama Namleteq's-Daughter, the village's ancient shamaness, dressed in her rancid red rags. She must have been already waiting there inside the Temple before Rafti had arrived. The hawk-faced shaman was talking to her in a low carrying voice while the younger shaman looked on and seemed to be listening intently, and the old woman was nodding and giggling and grinning toothlessly at them, every now and then sneaking a glance at the villagers watching from the other side of the tanglethorn maze to make sure they were all still watching her. And that, somehow, was the worst of it, the final insult, that her mother and father had been reduced to leading the way for Cama Namleteq's-Daughter, who was a shamaness in name only, whose only skill was that of counterfeiting pleasant dreams for those too poor in spirit to find their dreams in themselves, and whose half-remembered herbal lore was little better than Rafti's own. Who had let Rafti's eldest brother die and who for five years now had been too lacking in the Earth Mother's grace to dare the burning pit at Her yearly Festival.

The elders were still huddled just outside the labyrinth gate, perhaps waiting to make sure that the shamans and their horses could traverse the maze without help and so show themselves to be what they seemed and not malicious spirits in disguise. The shamans came to a halt before the labyrinth, and Rafti could feel the sudden tension in the Council and crowd, but it was only a moment's delay so they could unburden their horses and make it easier for them to negotiate the maze's narrow corridors. Another few moments and they were through the labyrinth and strapping their bulging leather sacks and baskets back onto their animals.

Only then did Rafti realize that her mother and father and even Manmoutin Manlaiteq's-Son were grinning as broadly and as foolishly as Cama Namleteq's-Daughter. They wouldn't have been joyous and excited like that at the thought of losing her, no matter what custom decreed or how great a price the Nomads were offering. This had to be something else, something different and unexpected, and Rafti felt the strength her determination to defy the shamans had given her only an instant before leave her, and then there was only the sudden hope caught in her throat as her father raised his inlaid blackwood elder's staff for silence.

"Sulthar and his nephew Moth have come to us from our people's ancient homeland, which they tell us has become part of the Empire of Chal. They are both Masters of Fire. Moth is of the blood of the Children of Raburr and he has been tested and proved by the fires of the Harg. He has come with his uncle to ask us the use of our forge, come to ask our permission to kindle fire and life where for too many lifetimes there has been only cold and emptiness. In return he has vowed to teach us the lost art of keeping the

Hearth-flame a fit home for Raburr, so that Raburr will again have that home among us which is His by right and which He has lacked for so long.

"The Mother's Priestess and the Elders have examined Moth. We have found him to be truly of the Children of Raburr, truly a Master of Fire. We have given him our consent, and Raburr will have his home amongst us again."

It was only much later, after her father and the other elders had taken the young shaman to examine the forge while his grim-faced uncle, surprisingly, juggled for the younger children and made them squeal with delight by plucking bright fragments of rock crystal from their ears and eyes and mouths, that Rafti thought to ask herself why the two had come to her tiny valley, her tiny village, instead of remaining among their own people to do whatever they intended to do in the forge, and whether, for all that her mother seemed to have given them her consent, their plans would truly be pleasing to the Earth Mother.

She would ask her parents and whoever was chosen to learn the Hearth-secrets. If they couldn't, or wouldn't, tell her she'd ask the shamans themselves. But if they lied to her or refused to tell her she might never learn what they'd come here to do. Forge law was clear: no one not already an initiated and tested Master of Fire could enter a forge once its fires had been lit and Raburr had entered into them. And there was no one in the village, not even her father, despite the ease with which he led the villagers across the coals every Festival, who could call himself a true Master of Fire.

She could demand that she be the one taught to tend the forge fires (for women could tend the forge and become Masters of Fire, even though they could not learn to work metals, just as men could help clear the land without for that having the right to participate in the sowing), but she was afraid to do anything that would bring her to the shamans' attention. Because even if they did nothing here to offend the Earth Mother or bring Her Burning Mountain's wrath down upon the villagers, even if the shamans had not come to the valley because they were searching for a firedancer, there had still been that shock of recognition or desire in Moth's yellow eyes when he'd stared down at Rafti from the mountain stairs, and there was still nothing to prevent the two from exercising the right custom gave them to buy whomever they chose to take with them as a firedancer after the Festival, now less than a month away.

And if that firedancer were her people's only Master of Fire, so much the better bargain for the Nomads, so much the worse for her people.

Chapter Three

It was the night of the full moon, the night of the Festival. At dawn all the hearth-fires and time-candles in the village had been extinguished and lit anew from the undying flame in the Mother's Temple, and the day had been spent in rites of thanksgiving and renewal. Rafti was dressed in her long sheer red Festival skirt, her torso and feet bare, her flame-red hair hanging scented but loose around her shoulders. The sun was gone but the moon was not yet up. When it appeared, the time would be come to climb the steps to the top of the Earth Mother's Burning Mountain, prostrate herself there in silence on the rim of the cone, then descend the mountain to cleanse herself in the cold-water lake in the grotto at the far end of the valley, where the fat blind white fish swam, and then at last return to the Temple, where the old women were even now finishing preparing the coals for the burning pit.

The pit was ten bodylengths long and three wide, cut from the basalt that floored the Temple yard and lined with thick slabs of black- and pink-flecked granite. It would be filled to a depth of a little over the length of one of Rafti's arms with white-hot coals, and all she had to do was walk barefoot across the coals from one end of the pit to the other. The burning pit had never frightened her before—

she had walked the coals four times now and each time the Earth Mother had held her safe and kept the fire from her, as Rafti had known she would, so that there had been only the ecstasy of her total surrender to the Mother's love, the joy and the trust that had taken her unhesitatingly across the pit. Then last year the Mother had entered into her as she stepped onto the coals and taken her feet and hands and body, and danced with them a song of praise and joy and life there in the center of the pit, and it had been as though she were a bird of living fire dancing weightless and free like the moon in the sky, and yet she had been neither moon nor stars but the Earth beneath her feet, dark and warm and wise, the Mother whose love held and protected all that She had given life even as this valley that She had given to Rafti's people held and protected them from the icy cold around it, from the unknown enemy that had driven her people from the south, and it was then that Rafti had first known with all her being that she would be the Earth Mother's Priestess after her mother, that it was she whose destiny it was to shelter and protect these her people even as the Mother was sheltering and protecting *her* from the killing heat of the coals beneath her feet.

But that had been last year, before the shamans came, and though she had done everything she could think of to avoid attracting their attention, even to putting aside her need to find out what they were really doing in the forge, and accepting as a fact that they wouldn't reveal their goals without herself trying to confront them and confirm what the others had told her, still only yesterday Moth had sought her out and spoken to her.

Manlaiteq Manmoutin's-Son and her brother Teltinor had been the two chosen to assist the shamans in the forge. They spent their days there from dawn to dusk, hidden from their fellow villagers behind the wall surrounding the outer compound, or else out searching the valley for the proper woods and grasses and clays and other substances the shamans needed for the work already in progress in the inner forge, to which the two from the valley were still refused entry.

But though Moth and Sulthar still refused to tell anyone exactly what it was they were making in the forge, or why they had chosen to come to this valley to make it, there was no suspicion in either Teltinor or Manlaiteq Manmoutin's-Son, and they had obviously talked freely with the shamans, must have answered all their questions and told them whatever they wanted to know about the valley and its people. Because Moth had come to Rafti, his mirrors and charms and metal bones jangling and clashing, the copper moth, his totem, gleaming from his forehead in the late afternoon sun as though it were still reflecting the forge fires.

"Your brother tells me your name is Rafti," he said.

"Yes," she told him, because it would have been pointless to deny it.

"He told me that last year the Mother entered into you at the Festival and that you danced for Her on the coals."

"Yes," she said again, because there was nothing else she could do. For that moment she hated Teltinor for his stupidity and selfishness, for his craven willingness to do anything, say anything, if he thought it would please the shamans. There was nothing obviously threatening in Moth's face or voice; if anything, he sounded as though he were trying to keep from frightening her, and his expression was sad and even almost vulnerable. But she was too afraid of his attention to want to see the person he was trying to force her to see in him, and she stood there staring at his face but avoiding his eyes, trying to let whatever he wanted to create between them die stillborn, trying to kill it with her silence, offering him nothing. But he just stood there looking at her, his face open and unguarded and twisted with some sort of pain until finally she said, "Why do you ask me that?"

"Because . . . five years ago, when I was still living in Kyborash—" The name meant nothing to her, as he seemed to realize, because he explained: "Kyborash is one of the cities of the Chaldan Empire, where your people originally came from. Or at least it was before it was conquered. I was betrothed there to a girl named Rafti. She was a smith's daughter, of the Tas Sil, which is what the Children of Raburr became there when they submitted to the King of Chal. She had hair like yours, and you have her eyes . . . and there's something else about you that's her, she didn't really look like you, but there's something about the way you move or maybe about the way you look at things when you're not moving—"

"What happened to her?" More to stop him, make him get it over with than because she wanted to know.

"Her father had her killed. To keep her from marrying me. Because I was unable to keep my shaman's vocation hidden, and the people of the Chaldan Empire have no love or understanding of such things. They take us for madmen, lock us in cages and either stone us to death or sell us to the Nomads for slaves."

"You were—?"

"No." He didn't let her finish. "But my uncle was."

"Why are you telling me all this? About her?" She knew she shouldn't ask him anything, should just stand there stupidly, passively, listening but offering him nothing, no sympathy, not even the opposition or denial that would prove that she cared, that she could be made to care, but she couldn't stop herself.

"She's dead, I never knew her. I don't want to know anything about her. All I want to do is stay here and serve the Mother. I don't care about anything else."

"But you bear her name, Rafti. The Earth Mother gave you her name. And she was of your people. She too was of the Children of Raburr."

"I bear my mother's name, shaman, and *her* full name is Rafti Rafti's-Daughter. Did my brother tell you that while he was telling you all the rest, that my mother and grandmother and great-grandmother before her were Rafti too? If the name was a gift from the Mother, it was given us long before your Rafti came into existence. I share a name with her, perhaps, but I am not alone in doing so, and that name is all we share. *All.* My soul is my own. *Your* Rafti was still alive when I was born and named; nothing passed from her to me when she died; there is no connection between us. I am myself and myself alone. You will never find her in me."

"Perhaps." He hesitated. "Yet—I saw something of her in you while I was still coming down the steps, when you were only another stranger in a crowd. So perhaps it was that there was something of you, of your long heritage, that came to her with your name."

Rafti shook her head, denying him, her face closed and angry.

"I'm sorry if I have offended you, talking about her," he said. "I mean you no harm."

Rafti turned from him to go, but there was something more she had to know. She fought it, told herself she didn't need to know, but she had no choice, and after she'd walked perhaps a dozen steps, she turned back to him and asked, "How did she die, your Rafti?"

"Her father sold her to be buried alive in Prince SarVas's Necropolis, as one of the handmaidens attending the dead prince's bride. The Warriors of the Voice dressed her in red and painted her face and hid her red hair with a headdress of lapis lazuli beads. Then they tied a gold ribbon to her arm and made her drink something to forget who she was, so she'd be just like all the other handmaidens. And she was: I was watching when they all went beneath the earth together, and I couldn't even tell which one was her. Then the warriors sealed the tomb with stone, and left them there to suffocate beside the dead prince and his dying bride. But I think the drug they made her drink kept her from any pain."

Rafti hadn't understood everything he'd said—too many of his words were strange to her, or came oddly twisted from his mouth and seemed to mean something different to him than they did to her—but she'd understood enough.

"I'm sorry for you," she told him. "That you hurt for her. But it's your pain, not mine: there's nothing I can do to help you with it." She left him then, and he didn't try to stop her, he didn't make any effort then or later to speak to her again, though she was aware of his bright-burning yellow eyes on her whenever she was near him.

But though she no longer feared to find him cruel like the shaman who'd destroyed Shulteurtas Jattasteq's-Son and his four daughters, she now had a new fear—that he'd force her father to sell her to him, not because he wanted the firedancer he had the right to demand, but because he wanted someone to take the place of his dead Rafti. And that would be worse than anything she'd imagined, because a firedancer at least danced with the Earth Mother's grace, it was the Mother who danced through her. But to be forced to replace that dead girl whose name she shared—that would be to lose not only her people but the Mother and even herself, to lose the meaning of her name and find herself reduced to the accident of the sounds it shared with the dead girl's name.

No matter what happened, what she felt, this year she dared not surrender to the dance, not there in the burning pit, where he would be watching her with his uncle, perhaps only waiting for an excuse to take her.

But the moon was rising at last and the drummer had begun to beat the great drum that was used for the Festival alone. A beat and then a long silence, another beat: the steady throbbing of a giant's heart.

Her mother first, and then her father, wearing his copper vest but without his elder's staff, began to ascend the mountain stairway. Rafti had danced with the Goddess in her body at the last Festival; her place in this year's procession was the place of honor, third, behind the Priestess and First Speaker, before all the other villagers, even the other elders. She began to climb, matching the rhythm of her steps to the slow beating of the giant drum, one step for every beat and then, a pause, another step, desperately trying to put aside her fear and ignore the growing heaviness in her legs, desperately trying to open herself to the Earth Mother and Her healing love.

Behind her came the girls and women, and behind them the men and boys led by Manmoutin Manlaiteq's-Son, all those who were fit enough to make the climb and not needed elsewhere.

It was a long way up to the black-gleaming obsidian platform at the crater's rim, and the moon was much higher in the sky by the time she finally reached it. Out of breath and so tired she had to fight to keep from falling as she knelt in her place at the sheer edge and looked out and down into the huge crater bowl, into the red-lit smoke and clouds of drifting ash, she was still afraid, still unable to find her way back to the inner silence she sought as she felt the first vapors from the lake of fire so far below brush against her hair and skin, creep into her nose and throat. Her eyes were beginning to water; she blinked back tears, forced herself to trace the stairway's spiraling descent down the interior wall of the cone. Then she had to look away, dizzy, but the movement made her head spin even more and she grabbed the smooth sheer edge in front of her to steady herself. The obsidian was burning hot, hotter by far than she remembered it from the year before; the air parched her face and throat, caught in her lungs, and made her cough. And far below her, there where the spiral stairway lost itself in the smoke and the glow, she could hear the lava's liquid gurgling, its slow infrequent belching, as though the cone opened into the scarlet-burning entrails of a giant baby for whom Rafti's days and years were only moments. Yet Moth and Sulthar had led their animals down into that burning and then through or across it, up again to where she was kneeling now; if they brought her, they'd take her through it somehow, the same way they'd brought their horses. Perhaps blindfolded and tied to one of the horses' backs to keep her from panicking and dying: Teltinor had told her that the animals had been blindfolded for the crossing. But Teltinor and Manlaiteq Manmoutin's-Son were already talking about how soon they'd be able to cross on their own, leaving the valley not for slavery but for freedom, to rediscover their lost kin and reunite their separated people.

The heat was blistering her knees, burning her hands where she clutched the sheer edge, but she was forbidden to call on the Mother for help. She was not here to resist or to triumph over anything, but rather to endure and accept, to know that alone and separated and without the Mother's strength within her she was nothing, less than nothing, helpless.

When at last she could endure it no longer she rose and made her way down the stairs, still keeping rhythm with the Festival drum. Her parents were long gone, as were many of the girls and women who'd followed her, and some of the older men, but that meant nothing: the longer she'd resisted the crater, the more complete her submission when it came, the easier it would be to surrender herself at the burning pit.

Her grandmother, Rafti Rafti's-Mother (who had been Rafti Rafti's-Daughter before Rafti's own mother and who now that her husband was many years dead lived alone in a tiny cell hollowed out of the volcano wall behind the Temple) was waiting for her, as she waited for all those who descended, at the bottom of the stairs. She tied the garland of waxy scarlet flowers and soft green leaves around Rafti's neck, then fastened grass-green orchids, the sign of the Mother's special favor, in her hair.

Rafti went from the Temple precincts to the grotto lake by way of the path that was reserved for this journey and this journey alone. It was the most beautiful path Rafti knew, avoiding the village and fields entirely to take those who walked it through the valley's wild places, through groves and meadows, alongside the valley walls at times, past pools both steaming and fresh, between the twin geysers. And for each place there was somewhere to pause and stand and watch, a spot where you could sense the strength of the mountain wall without being pressed in too uncomfortably close beneath its overhanging mass, where you could feel the peace and solitude of the grove or smell the night-blooming freshness of the moonlit meadows and watch the twin geysers come bursting from their squat cones of half-dry mud, silver and mysterious and unexpected in the moonlight until they retreated beneath the earth again a few moments later.

At the entrance to the grotto she shed her skirt, hung it on a branch of the ancient silver-leaved tree where all the villagers who had preceded her had left their clothing. Save for her father's robe and vest there were no men's garments hanging from the tree yet; the other girls' and unmarried women's skirts were a cloudlike, almost invisible green, those of the wives and matrons a more substantial dark green, on which the embroidered leaves and flowers, fruit and tubers and stalks of grain were difficult to make out in the semidarkness unless you stared long and hard at them, but only Rafti and her mother had red skirts.

She bent to enter the grotto. Inside, it opened up, a great hollow gourd-shaped cavern stretching away and back under the mountain, all but a narrow strip of beach filled by the cold-water lake. Her mother stood by the water's edge, her face hidden by her green mask, though she was otherwise unclothed, and she was holding a burning torch. She had been the first to ascend and descend the mountain, the first to purify herself in the lake's waters, but she would be the last to leave the grotto, and though the fire-walking would not commence without her, she would be the last to cross the coals.

Rafti followed the narrow strip of shore to the left until she was beyond the light cast by her mother's torch. There in the darkness she waded out into the lake until the water reached her chin, took a deep breath, and continued wading until it was over her head and her hair was floating up around her face. The water was shockingly cold. She opened her mouth, sucked in water, swirled it around seven times to clean her mouth and throat and purify her speech, then blew it out again and started over. A cloud of blind cave fish, tiny but fat and fearless, clustered around her, nipping lightly at her skin, tasting her for the Mother as others tasted the leaves and flowers of her garland and the orchids in her hair. Rafti stayed submerged and still until her lungs could take it no more, then kicked off to gasp for a lungful of air and made her way back to shore.

Most of the girls and matrons were already waiting for Rafti outside, dressed once more in their Festival skirts. They had had to await Rafti, but the men and boys just beginning to arrive would be free to return to the Temple as soon as they'd cleansed themselves: they had only needed to wait until her father returned to the Temple, and his clothing was already gone from the tree.

She made sure her garland and orchids were still securely in place, then knotted her skirt back around her and led the women down the return path, keeping silence. Her fear was a faraway thing now, buried deep or washed away in the grotto lake; perhaps the blind fish had eaten it. She was conscious of the honor, the responsibility, she held, conscious also that it was not she who was being honored but the Mother through her.

Her father and the old men and women were waiting at the burning pit, the old women standing to the left of the pit holding the long wooden rakes with which they stirred the coals to make them burn more fiercely, the old men either to the right of the pit but back a ways, witnesses to the ritual rather than participants in it, or else carrying the heavy wooden buckets of cold water with which they doused the old women, their rakes, and one another every few moments.

The children, those too old to be carried by their mothers across the coals but not yet old enough to walk them in safety themselves, were seated at the far end of the pit, far enough away to be spared the worst of its heat, though the old men splashed the youngest ones with cold water every now and then anyway to keep them comfortable. Rafti saw Lashimi among them, sitting in the front row.

To the right of the children sat the shamans, dressed in their heavy leather and fur garments and wearing their caps, though their feet were as bare as those of the villagers. Mallente Manmoutin's-Daughter, Manlaiteq's youngest sister, was sitting next to Sulthar, trying to get him to pluck rock crystals from her eyes and mouth and ears again, but he just smiled at her without saying or doing anything, and after a while she gave up. As soon as Rafti realized that she was staring at the shamans, she looked away from them, though the fear she'd felt earlier was still too far away to trouble her now, was perhaps even dead.

A few of the women who'd followed Rafti from the grotto—those who did not feel the Mother's grace strong within them this year—sat down behind the children. Rafti saw Cama Namleteq's-Daughter among them, sitting just behind the shamans, and had to suppress her anger: the woman was old enough now so she should have been helping rake the coals if she didn't dare walk them.

Some of those sitting with the children, like some of the children themselves, would be visited unexpectedly by the Mother during the course of the night and would join the other villagers on the coals. That was how it had been for Rafti four years ago, when she'd been only eight and sitting without expectation of doing anything but watching with the other children.

And some of those who dared the coals for the first time, like some of those who had never doubted their ability to walk them, would find their faith failing them and would be horribly burned. Everything possible would be done for them, the whole village would grieve for those who died, but the responsibility for their fates would be theirs and theirs alone: the Mother forced no one to prove his or her love for Her on the coals. She only demanded that those who wished to do so did so in love and honesty, and those who tried to lie to Her or to their neighbors or even to themselves by pretending to a faith and a love for the Earth Mother that they did not have were punished for it.

Rafti put all thought of failure from her. The last of the men had arrived, and after them her mother. She still wore her green mask but she had put her skirt back on and her hair floated free and richly red down her back. The old men and women were beginning the Festival song, their voices weaving in and out of the great drum's ponderous heartbeat. The singing went on and on, monotonous yet powerful, the words so ancient that no one even remembered a time when their meaning had been known.

Rafti's mother prostrated herself to the fire pit, then rose again and, still facing the pit, began to sing. Her long song of prayer and thanksgiving wove in and out of the song the old men and women sang, complementing and completing it, though the meaning of the words they sang had been lost long before anyone now living had been born, while the words that Rafti Rafti's-Daughter sang were born within her at this very moment, a song never before sung bursting from her heart in a language that even the youngest of the village's children could understand.

And then her part of the song was over, though the old men and women continued their chant unfalteringly. Rafti's mother knelt to the white-hot coals, reached in, and with her naked hand took one from the pit. She straightened with it, turned, and held it high so that all those watching from the four sides of the pit could see it in her hand, then handed it to her husband. He took it from her, held it an instant—a small trial, another instance of the Mother's mercy, this last test so that those unfit to walk the coals unharmed would have every chance to know their unfitness and withdraw before they committed themselves. He handed it back to her, smiling, and she put it carefully back in the pit with the other coals.

Slowly, proudly, Rafti's father walked the length of the pit, never pausing, never ceasing to smile, his robe brushing the white-hot coals without catching flame. At the far end of the pit he turned back and knelt on the coals, giving thanks once again to the Earth Mother, then rose and stepped from the pit onto the surrounding stone.

Turning back yet again, he took the flower and leaf garland carefully from around his neck and tossed it as far as he could out over the pit. He threw it high, so it would take a long time to fall back to earth, but before it had dropped much lower than the height at which it had hung around his neck while he was crossing, it burst into flame and burned, leaving nothing but a fine rain of gray-white ash to settle to the coals.

The old women stepped forward, stirred the coals with their wooden rakes, stepped back. The old men doused the old women and their rakes with water. Rafti's mother knelt to the pit and took another coal from it, straightened.

Rafti stepped forward to take it from her hands.

Chapter Four

The coal was warm, not hot, in her hand, with a heat more that of flesh than of fire. As though it were a tiny coiled embryo the size of one of the pinkish-white plums from the groves Rafti helped tend, hairless and smooth and self-contained as any fruit, yet alive with a human warmth.

She clutched it, on sudden impulse brought her clenched fist up in front of her face, as close as she could get it and still keep her eyes focused on it, twisted her wrist around so she could look at the back of her hand. It glowed a bright transparent copper red, as though the flesh of which it was made had become some strange heavy liquid compounded of equal parts fire and melted tallow, and through that transparent flesh she could still see the burning coal, a bright-burning silver moon in a cage of spider-leg shadows: the bones of her clenched fist.

She opened her hand and gave the coal back to her mother, who took it from her, knelt to place it carefully back in the burning pit, then straightened to face Rafti again. She was staring directly at Rafti, smiling at her, and yet the smile was not her smile, not the smile of Rafti Rafti's-Daughter who was wife to Shonraleur: it was the Earth Mother's smile and the love that Rafti could see clearly in her eyes was the love the Earth Mother had for all those whom She had created from Her own flesh, the love that She had for all those who cherished Her in themselves.

Rafti stood silent and unmoving a moment, not seeing the people around her, not hearing the song the old men and women were singing, but letting it all wash over and through her without trying to seize or understand it, and then she stepped out onto the coals. Onto the Mother's orange and white burning flesh. Everything else faded, was not: there was only the ever-changing mosaic of brightnesses and burnings that filled the long rectangle that was the burning pit, that she had to walk, its bright shifting surface soft and uncertain beneath her feet, the heat rising from it like a sunlit breeze. She took a first step forward and the breeze caught her up, lifted her and whisked her weightlessly as thistledown on across the shifting surface, as though she were being carried through the flesh-warm depths of a living sea by a gentle but irresistible current that was playing now with her feet, now with her hands, now with the muscles of her face and body, even as it played with her floating, streaming hair so that now at last she was dancing, floating, flying, faster and faster like the wind she'd become, the wind that blew not over but through the Earth's living density, through all that lived and bred and died on its surface and in the shallow depths of its oceans, through the trees and flowers and grains and tubers, the wild beasts and fishes and the animals kept by men, through the men and women of these the Mother's twelve valleys and of the vast world beyond them, through Rafti Rafti's-Daughter there behind her and through Shonraleur Valinor's-Son there waiting for her at the other end of the pit, through those two men seated there beyond him by the children, and they were of both the world beyond and of this, *her valley*—

Memory clutched, grabbed, and twisted in her as she realized who she was and who they were and what she was doing, remembered that she couldn't let them see her dance, she had to stop. She tried to fight the currents carrying her through the glowing depths, fight the wind dancing through her, and she stiffened her body against them and refused their demands.

Refused and was only Rafti Shonraleur's-Daughter, herself alone, there in the center of the pit, on the bed of burning coals, and even as her long red skirt burst into yellow flame, as her hair, her feet, her skin and eyes caught flame and she felt rather than heard the scream caught stillborn in her throat and she fell, burning—even as she saw Lashimi, who had never before dared the burning pit, dashing for her across the coals, behind her the yellow-eyed shaman Moth with his copper ornaments jangling and clashing as he ran, and only after them her father, his mouth gaping open with shock and surprise—even then there was no pain. Only the surprise she felt at her sudden knowledge that this was the Mother's answer to her prayer, that Lashimi would be the Mother's Priestess in her place, the place that must always have been Lashimi's, for all that Rafti had imagined it hers. It could only have been her pride, her greed, that had allowed her to believe that Rafti Shonraleur's-Daughter was the only woman in the valley who could hold and nurture and protect its people, when in truth it was the Earth Mother and the Earth Mother alone, working through whomever She chose as Her instrument, who contained and sheltered them.

The coming of the two shamans had been a test for her, an ordeal as the burning pit was an ordeal, and she had failed it, yet the Mother had been merciful and held from her the pain that she had merited.

Lashimi knelt beside her on the coals, touched her forehead, and the flames went out, the flesh of her body ceased burning. Then her father and Moth were there with Lashimi, the three of them lifting her dead body, carrying it from the pit. Its legs were blackened stumps and most of its flesh charred meat, the heart had given up trying to force blood through it, and the scream caught in its lungs had died there, while the pain of her burning sat astride the still chest like a twisted and deformed animal the color of soot and cinders, raking the unresponsive flesh again and again with its gray metal claws. But Rafti herself was still lying there stretched out on the coals where she had fallen, watching them carry the body she had lost from the pit, and that was how she finally knew she was dead and a ghost.

A great lassitude came over her. She lay there where she had fallen, ignoring the villagers whose paths across the coals took them through her spirit-body. Somewhere far away the body that had burned and died was being laid out on a blanket on the floor of her father's hut, but though she knew it was there and could find it if she wished, it was of no interest to her and she let it slip from her awareness. She felt soft as melted tallow, boneless and heavy, as she began to sink slowly down through the soothing warmth of the white-hot coals. She knew that if she wanted to stop sinking and remain where she was, floating there on the surface of the world where all created life lived suspended above the Mother's Inner Ocean, she would have to teach herself to fly or swim somehow in the next few instants, but there was nothing there to keep her; she was too tired, too languid, too heavy to even try to resist as she slid gently, so gently down through the coals, through the thick slabs of granite that floored the pit into the close-grained black basalt beneath, then down through the smooth homogeneity of the basalt into the lava lake still burning a thick murky red below.

Chapter Five

There was no burning, no pain, no pressure, no fear, only the slow drifting descent. Like a dead leaf steadily sinking ever deeper into the absolute stillness and peace of a bottomless lake, a bottomless sleep. A dead leaf: the Mystery of the flowering plant, the stalk of grain, that was the Mystery of all created life—the plant dies but from its death comes a seed to be quickened in the Earth Mother's womb, and from that quickened seed the plant that had died is born anew.

Rafti was a seed, dead and sleeping, sinking toward rebirth. Around her now the burning depths of the Mother's Inner Ocean, a sultry red-orange that was slightly more transparent than the magma of the lake she'd passed through: the same color as her hand had been when she'd looked through it to see the burning coal imprisoned within. The Ocean's red-orange was cut by languid swirls of scarlet and crimson, thick drifting russet clouds, quick sharp flashes of bright yellows and oranges, occasional blue-white flares. And in the light of those flares, when her vision was no longer limited to the half dozen or so bodylengths closest to her, she could see the veins of ore like great floating waterweeds, like stone trees or flowers taller than mountains, broader than the valley in which she had passed her life, yet still not mature, still growing, floating rootless and unanchored here in the burning depths yet reaching with inconceivable slowness (the slowness somehow visible to her, as visible as the veins of ore themselves) ever farther upward, ever closer to the skin of the world where the ores would at last attain their maturity and flower into metals and precious minerals: lead ripening into silver, silver into gold, gold into copper, bridesmetal, diamonds, rubies, emeralds, turquoise, and lapis lazuli, all that came most precious from the Earth Mother's womb.

Far, far above her Rafti began to hear drumming, sharp staccato sounds that disturbed and hurt her, threatening to pull her from her sheltering languor: two stretched animal-hide drumskins being beaten with sticks of once-living, once-human bone. The drums were speaking to her, but their voices hurt her, demanded that she awaken to time to understand them, and she didn't want to awaken. Now the pain the Earth Mother had held from her had found her, was following the drumming to her, gray metal claws unsheathed as it leaped from drumbeat to drumbeat after her through the red-burning depths, and there behind it, following it to her, were the two shamans riding on their drums.

Then the blind fish from the grotto lake were all around her, a soothing shimmering cloud of flashing bodies and fins that was all chill white silver and icy white flame, beautiful and silent, that demanded nothing of her and allowed her to let all memory of that painful partial reawakening to time slip from her again, that hid her from the pain pursuing her and let her give herself up again to the timeless solace of her drifting descent even as somewhere immeasurably distant the drumming died away in confusion.

Until at last the fish left her in a flurry of flashing silver fins and scales and eyes, and she found herself settling feet-first to the featureless plain of burning yellow mud that was bottom to the Mother's Inner Ocean, there where the Mother (mountain-huge, thousand-armed, heavy-breasted and legless, growing like a stupendous tree from the Ocean floor, Her skin patterned with browns and greens like the bark of a mottle tree, Her eyes brown also and infinitely gentle for all that Her great black-lipped mouth was filled with thousands upon thousands of jagged and discolored tusks) awaited Rafti, and She was beautiful beyond human comprehension.

Rafti knew the Mother, had known Her all her life. Her preparation for this moment had begun when she was five years old; she had been taught to understand what was happening to her now, what the Mother expected of her, and how to do what was needful, but nothing in those years of devotion and training and belief had prepared her for the absolute terror of the Mother's presence, for the total paralysis of her will that was part of that terror and that made it so hard now to do what had to be done.

Her bare feet were just beginning to sink into the sucking yellow mud. She let herself fall slowly to her knees, bent forward, and with what seemed infinite slowness extended her right arm out in front of her, pushed the longest finger of her right hand into the burning mud until the whole first finger joint was buried, then pulled her finger out again with the same agonizing slowness.

The blind fish hovered over her, a shield of ice and silver, but despite their protection she began to hear the drumming again. It was fainter now, much farther away than it had been before, as though it had lost her and the pain that rode it was searching for her somewhere she was not.

The Mother gestured with one of Her many exquisitely tapering hands and the fish streaked away upward, were lost almost immediately in the thick flesh-red overhead. A moment later the drumming stopped again.

Rafti stared down at the impression her fingertip had left in the mud: a rounded hollow marked with the fine lines and whorls she'd been made to contemplate on the tip of her finger every day since her fifth birthday, when her Temple training had begun. Her personal labyrinth.

She wanted only to turn, run, burrow into the mud, do anything to escape the Mother's unendurable presence, but her panic was irrelevant, only part of that frozen paralysis that gripped her will and left her spirit-body to repeat the sequence of actions her grandmother had trained into her physical body back in the Temple. She straightened, regained her feet, backed slowly away from the tiny hollow her fingertip had left in the smooth sucking yellow mud, her every movement impossibly deliberate.

Seven steps back and she stopped again, waited for the Mother's response. It came. The Goddess reached forward, the rapid movement of Her many arms more like the imperceptible growth of a tree's limbs somehow rendered visible than like any movement that could have been made by a man or an animal, or even by a fish: beautiful and perfect in itself, but something no man or woman should ever be forced to see. The long tapering hands dug into the mud on all sides of the tiny hollow, grasped the sea bottom like a woman grabbing dough she was kneading to stretch it flat for baking, and pulled it away from the hollow, so that the sea bottom stretched. Yet the hollow Rafti's fingertip had left in the mud was not pulled flat or out of shape, was not effaced or distorted in any way but was itself stretched larger along with the sea bottom around it until it had become a spiral whorl pattern the diameter of Rafti's right forearm. It was now perhaps four times as deep as the hollow Rafti had pulled into the mud, as though while the Mother's many visible hands had been stretching the sea bottom containing it wider, other, invisible, hands had been gently tugging the hollow itself downward, so that now the grooves between the ridges of the whorl pattern were themselves as deep as the original hollow had been.

The Mother lifted Her many hands from the sea bottom, held them hovering over the labyrinth design an instant so as to give Rafti a last chance to contemplate the pattern and fix it in her mind, assure herself that it was, indeed, the same as that which she herself had pressed into the mud. Then the Mother patted the left side of the design flat.

Rafti had no need to look at the tips of her fingers to know that the whorls on them, too, were now half effaced. Her panic was gone, and with it many of her memories: she felt light and empty, like a soft-skinned hollow gourd. Yet the memories she would need were still there, intact, and with her panic had gone her paralysis: she belonged here now, she could act as she was meant to act without hindrance, and the expectation of her impending birth filled her with a sudden hunger, an excited anticipation unleavened by fear or doubt.

She knew what she had to do to be reborn: with the tip of the first finger on her right hand retrace the effaced channels of her labyrinth from memory, without error. If her reconstruction was perfect, she would be reborn with all her memories not only of her previous life but of this interval between lives. But if she altered in any way the design, she'd be condemned to find her way through the new labyrinth she would have brought into being to the body of that unborn child whose inner and outer whorl patterns would be those of the design she'd created, for the coiling entrails in the belly and the convoluted brain in its skull-box of bone took their form in their own hidden ways from the birth labyrinth. If the labyrinth she so created was too aberrant, the embryo she followed it to would be monstrous or deformed; if she lost or trapped herself in the labyrinth's altered turnings, Tua-Li, the World-Eel, who lived in the mud beneath the Mother's body, would pluck her from it and eat her, destroying her soul forever, while the child whose whorl pattern mirrored that of the altered labyrinth would be stillborn, and soulless.

It was the way things were, had always been, would always be. There was nothing strange or frightening about any of it, not here, on the featureless plain of burning yellow mud that was the Mother's Inner Ocean's floor. Rafti knelt again, settled back on her haunches a moment to regard the remaining half of the design, then leaned forward and began sketching the missing channels into the yellow mud, working rapidly and without hesitation, in perfect confidence.

A hand, all dry bones and withered tendons and shrunken peeling flesh attached to a mummified forearm that faded away into nothingness halfway above the wrist, leapt from nowhere to grab her own right wrist, yank her hand from the design she'd almost finished reconstructing, and hold it there above it while a second skeletal hand appeared and began rubbing out not only many of the channels Rafti had restored to the design but also some parts of the original that the Mother Herself had left untouched. It was Rafti's life that was being effaced, all her hopes for any future existence, and she tried to twist free of the hand that held her wrist imprisoned, pry it from her with her own free left hand, but the skeletal hand was rigid as stone or metal and her own flesh seemed soft as overripe fruit, her strength nothing in comparison to the hand's, and all the while she was struggling to free herself of the hand holding her wrist the other hand was adding new lines and linkages to what remained of Rafti's birth labyrinth, creating from it a strange new closed pattern with neither beginning nor end.

She didn't understand what was happening, what the hands were or why they were doing what they were doing to her; she only knew that it was wrong, horribly, impossibly wrong, that nothing new or different or unexpected could ever be allowed to happen here where all was as it always had been, as it always would be, and as it always had to be, here where any change whatsoever could only be a falling away from the universe's one possible perfection. Rafti was dead and she accepted her death. It was right and proper because she knew what it meant and what she had to do and what would happen to her when she did it, even what the consequences of any failure would be, but the hands had no part in any of that, could never have had any part in that, and she knew even as she struggled against them that she was lost forever, caught up in something utterly beyond her comprehension, utterly evil, that she was beyond all hope.

The drumming that had threatened her earlier was suddenly back, louder now, closer, the pain that rode it almost upon her. The hand that had mutilated her labyrinth leapt from the sea bottom to clasp itself tight around her left wrist, hold it prisoned as the other hand held her right, and even as it closed on her the blind fish were back, a swirling chaotic turbulence of ice-flashing white fins and silver-scaled fire all around her. One of the maddened fish struck her a glancing blow on the forehead, another caught in her hair an instant before freeing itself by yanking the strands of hair in which it was tangled from her head. And that, somehow, shockingly, hurt her as nothing had hurt her since she'd knelt to the fires in the Mother's Burning Mountain feeling the exhaustion in her muscles, the heat on her skin and in her throat and lungs, as neither the fires of the burning pit nor the death of her body nor her spirit's descent through the burning magma of the lava lake to the hotter fires of the Mother's Inner Ocean had hurt her.

The hands yanked her to her feet, pulled her stumbling forward through the maddened cloud of fish. She had no time to think or decide: the labyrinth was there in front of her, she was going to drag her feet across it and destroy it, the only way to save it was to lift her feet free of the yellow mud and pull them in tight to her body.

As soon as her feet lost contact with the ocean floor she began to shrink, the labyrinth expanding before, then beneath her as the hands carried her out over it, and all around her the maddened silver fish rushed and collided with one another in their frenzy, all of them massed confusedly together above the labyrinth as though trying to shield it from her, but the fish were so huge and slow-moving and she was so tiny, the hands so quick, that she found herself darting effortlessly between the sluggish giants, being carried farther and farther out over a labyrinth grown so huge that its furrows had become steep-sided canyons and all but a tiny fraction of its immensity was lost in the red-burning distance. The Earth Mother too was gone, lost on the far side of the labyrinth, far beyond the limits of visibility.

She was over the heart of the labyrinth now, and the hands pulled her swooping and weaving down through the thrashing colliding mass of fish into the labyrinth, then through it, faster and faster between its steep canyon walls until everything was an incomprehensible blur around her and she could no longer distinguish between the yellow mud of the canyon walls and the burning red honey that was the Inner Ocean itself.

Then it was gone, all of it was gone, and she was in a place where the Mother had no dominion, and it was dark and silent and dry there in the tomb, where she lay twisted in an agony she had never felt, that she still didn't feel but that she was beginning to remember, her ghost's flesh wrapped tight around another's dead, hungry bones.

Rafti's bones. The *other* Rafti's bones.

Chapter Six

She could have remembered it all if she'd let herself, remembered how it had been to be Rafti, daughter to Tas Gly the ferret-faced goldsmith and Kytra his wife, remembered growing up in Kyborash, the time she'd spent as a hierodule for the Siltemple, remembered Tramu, Moth's cousin, and how she'd hoped to marry him before he'd been sent as a tongueless slave to the lead mines in Nanlasur . . . remembered, even, what it had been like to be betrothed to Moth himself, but there were too many memories, none of them simple or neutral or separable from the others, and to take even one of them into herself and let herself understand it would have been to open herself to a whole other life and be devoured by it. And yet all these alien, threatening memories were her memories now.

Why? she demanded of the other Rafti, because asking questions was less terrifying than searching out the answers for herself in the intertwined complexities of the other's past. Why, Tas Gly's daughter?

Because you are who you are, Rafti Shonraleur's-Daughter. Because of the name we share, and because Moth saw me in you, so that trying to call you back he awakened me instead.

She lay there on her side, one arm twisted beneath her,

surrounded by crumbling skeletons in the low, dark airless chamber, and though her ghost's flesh felt nothing, her bones ached with the memory of her dying.

I don't understand.

I was in Sartor's Royal Realm, but I was frozen there, Shonraleur's-Daughter, no longer alive but not yet dead either, trapped between the two and unable to continue on to my next rebirth. Like a small animal caught out of its burrow high on a mountain face at night in one of the cold months, and in the morning when you find it it's dead and cold, as hard as a piece of wood until the sun gets to it and melts it back to flesh again.

Sartor's Royal Realm? Sartor?

It would be easier if you'd let yourself remember. There's nothing to be afraid of. I'll help you, keep you from losing yourself; I won't devour you any more than you devoured me when I remembered *you*—

She had no real alternative, no other way she could think of to learn what had happened to her, what was going to happen to her. She let herself remember.

Remembering, she knew herself daughter to Tas Gly and his wife Kytra, betrothed to Moth, the only son of Ri Tal the potter and his wife Kuan (who was herself daughter to Tas No, who before his disgrace had been Tas No Sil, the Sil Smith). Yet though every smith's daughter was required to serve the Siltemple as a hierodule for her appointed time like all the other women of Kyborash, smith law nonetheless demanded that she wait two years before her marriage to Moth could be finalized and consummated, and when Tas Gly discovered that Moth suffered from fits (Rafti had been there when he learned, had seen Moth go rigid and start to spasm, his every muscle fighting every other muscle, threatening to tear him apart, his eyes rolled all the way back in his head so that only the whites showed, and the smell of the urine staining his clothes sharp in the air of the house), he had seen the opportunity to revenge himself on Tas No, Moth's grand father, for the arrogance Tas No had always shown him. He had taken Rafti from Moth in the only way he could, selling her to King Tvil as one of the forty-nine handmaidens who were to attend the Princess Daersa and accompany her into death and beyond, to Sartor's Royal Realm, just as the Princess herself had been chosen to accompany her husband, Prince SarVas, to whom she had been given in marriage after he'd been killed by a lion:

She is dressed in a long robe of shiny red silk, her hair hidden beneath an elaborate headdress of lapis lazuli beads; her face has been painted to a green and gold mask, and a golden ribbon is wound tight around her left arm. Earlier she had been afraid, but before the ceremony she'd been made to drink some dark, bitter-smelling liquid and now she is calm, numb; even her painted face has stopped itching. She stands surrounded by her fellow handmaidens, indistinguishable from them, watching as the six Warriors of the Voice in their yellow and white siltunics carry the golden boat that is the Prince's coffin, which will carry him safely to Sartor's Royal Realm, down the ramp of fire-hardened brick. The Sil Herald chants their progress through the Necropolis.

Soon the four harpers, tall, dark-haired men in brown, descend the ramp, carrying their bull-headed harps. When they have taken up their positions in the Prince's chamber and been sealed in with him, the six Warriors of the Voice emerge, to be joined by a seventh, who stands at the head of the ramp. Now the Warriors of the Hand, who are to form the Prince's retinue in the Royal Realm (strong-looking, tall young men in blue siltunics, with breast-plates, helmets and swords of that wondrously hard copper the secret of which is known only to the weaponsmiths of Chal), drink from the copper cup the seventh warrior holds out to them and make their way below, each carrying something that was precious to the six-year-old Prince in life.

Everything is going faster, accelerating. King Tvil kills

the white bull with his hands, and within what seems no more than instants it has been dragged below and the Prince's tomb sealed, earth heaped over it. Princess Daersa, ten years old, dressed in cloth of gold and covered with lapis and jewels, her face proud and unafraid, walks down the second ramp and is sealed into her chamber.

One by one the handmaidens follow her, accompanied to the top of the ramp by the Warriors of the Voice. Rafti's turn comes almost immediately; the Warrior of the Voice takes her arm and together they glide decorously across the ground to the ramp; she tastes the green-tasting liquid from the copper goblet and sees the Roads of the Dead gaping open like hungry mouths all around her even though she is still in life. She makes her way down the ramp, stoops to enter the low chamber, crosses it hunched over in the torchlit semidarkness to her appointed place, and curls up on the cushions, her head touching the feet of the handmaiden in front of her, waiting. She can see the dead warriors whose powdered bones had been used to prepare the clay from which the bricks for the Necropolis's walls had been made; they surround her, a wall of ghosts, bound to the defense of the walls containing their bones. The next handmaiden curls up behind her, touching her in the same way Rafti is touching the girl in front.

Then the torches are extinguished and the dim light from the entrance is gone. She knows that the chamber has been walled up. She lies still, one arm twisted uncomfortably beneath her; by the time she decides to straighten it, she finds she cannot. Her lungs are burning, her chest is straining for air; all around her she can hear the other handmaidens gasping, choking, as they asphyxiate.

A great mouth opens in the tomb, closes around her.

Light. Golden yellow, thick as honey or clotted cream. A sea of golden light, and she and the other handmaidens are at the oars of the great copper-scaled barge that had been Princess Daersa's bier. They are crossing the golden sea to Sartor's Royal Realm. Rafti pulls the massive oar to her, lifts its blade free of the golden sea, and pushes it away from her again as she bends forward: her motions are effortless, the oar weightless, the golden sea unresisting and without substance. A little ahead of their barge she can see the Prince's ship, his warriors, in their blue siltunics and shiny breastplates and helmets, rowing—and coming closer now ahead of them is an island, a single sheer peak jutting from the sea, and both peak and palace are the same shimmering gold as the sea.

They dock in silence, leave their boats, and climb the spiraling path to the palace. There are no plants or animals, no birds or insects, only the silent stone, the Prince and Princess leading the way, the warriors and harpers and handmaidens following. Their feet make no sound on the path. No one speaks.

They reach the palace, enter it, follow its long winding corridors to the throne room. There the Prince and Princess ascend their separate daises, sit in state on thrones facing not each other but open windows, through which they can gaze upon the featureless, unchanging, empty golden sea. The harpers, warriors, handmaidens, all take up their positions. Rafti turns to one of the other handmaidens, as if to ask or tell her something.

And everything stops. Nothing moves, nothing changes, nothing happens. Rafti remains frozen there like a dragonfly in amber for all eternity, caught in mid-gesture, unable to do anything but remember, unable to stop remembering, stop longing for the life she's left behind, hungering for it with a hunger that grows ever stronger, ever more painful as the ages pass.

A frozen tableau, a display ready for Sartor's viewing, but no eyes appear in the sky, no footfalls resound in the corridors, Sartor never appears. Nothing moves, nothing changes, nothing happens. Until the sound of drumming breaks through the stillness and Rafti awakens to find herself dead dry hungry bones in an airless tomb, to find that her death has been too long delayed and that the child as whom she'd been destined to be reborn has died still-born, so that her death has now become as much of a trap to her as her dying had been.

But the drumming continues, distracting her from the tiny child's skeleton moldering in its unmarked grave, pulling her free of the tomb so she can see and suddenly understand what her bones had been learning for themselves during the years of her absence, the years in which they'd lain chittering softly to the other skeletons in the Necropolis, learning from the earth they were beginning to rejoin. And before the drumming fades again she realizes that this time she has a chance to escape.

One chance. The other Rafti, the one Moth was trying to summon back. Dead, as dead as she is, but with her chance for rebirth still ahead of her.

And Rafti Shonraleur's-Daughter heard the drumming start up again in the distance, coming after her yet one more time.

Chapter Seven

They want to take you back, Shonraleur's-Daughter. Your family has paid them to put your ghost back in your ruined body, bring it back to life again. So you can live out your life crippled and hideous and useless, while I remain trapped here as the centuries pass, until finally I fade. Or until you die and free me and I steal your rebirth from you.

What is it you want from me?

Take me with you. Share your body with me while you live, give me a part of it for my own use. Give me an eye, only one eye, so I can see color again.

And when I die?

We can share your rebirth. Be reborn as twins, since your people let them live, or merge to become a single person who will remember both of us the way people sometimes remember more than one of their previous lives, without conflict.

Why should I do all that for you? What can you offer, what can you be for me that would be worth the loss of one of my eyes, worth a stranger in my soul for the rest of eternity?

I can take the pain of your resurrection from you, take it all upon and into myself and guard you from it, so that only that part of your body that is mine will be crippled and hideous.

I can survive the pain without you.

Survive it, yes, but I can help you with it and make things easier for you. The pain, and other things as well. It's going to be different for you when you return to life; your people will know that you died on the coals because you lacked faith in the Earth Mother, and that the shamans brought you back to life anyway. It's not going to be easy for you with them, Shonraleur's-Daughter. But I can offer you my memories and experiences, all the skills that I gained when I was alive, and that I've spent my ages in the Royal Realm going over and over again until now I can call back the slightest detail, the most trivial incident. I can offer you my strengths and knowledge as a ghost, everything that my second self learned here in the tomb while I was trapped in the Royal Realm, the powers that enabled me to defy the Earth Mother and bring you here, and that you'll have no chance to learn for yourself before you're restored to life. And remember, even if you agree to house me in your body and soul and give me the use of one of your eyes, my second self will still be here with my bones, and with the skeleton of that stillborn child who was also me. Perhaps a time will come when you will be glad to have a ghost to do your bidding. And I can offer you the assurance that if you help me now, I will not be awaiting your death here, festering with bitterness and anger and resentment until my hunger for your life has grown so overwhelming that at the end of this life or one of those to come I take your rebirth from you and leave you trapped in this tomb in my place.

I have only one more thing I can offer you, but that, perhaps, the most important: my friendship, the friendship of someone who already shares with you not only your name but the inner substance that that name reflects. Remember, I am already so like you that it was I whom Moth found while seeking you, not one of your ancestors, or anyone else with whom we might share our name.

And you're here with me, Rafti Shonraleur's-Daughter, you've shared my memories of my death and of the Royal Realm, you know how much like being you it is to be me, for all the differences in the lives we've lived. You know that I need your help, and what it would be like for me to be trapped here forever.

You said you defied the Mother to bring me here, Rafti told the ghost. I worship the Mother; I have no wish to defy Her.

In a sense I defied Her, yes, just as Moth and that other one will be defying Her when they rescue and resurrect you. Just as they defied Sartor when they awakened me, and as Sartor Himself defied Her to put me in His Royal Realm. But my second self has come to know Her well as it's lain here moldering in this tomb, come to know Her and Her will better than we knew them back in Kyborash, or than your people know them in their valley. She doesn't care whether any of us live or die, whether we change anything that has to do with what we do between birth and death, so long as we are born and we die. All that matters to Her is that the world continue, day after day, season after season, year after year, that She draw Her labyrinth for every dead soul as She's always done. We and the things we do aren't real to Her, not the way the Earth and the seasons are.

The drumming was almost upon them now, circling closer, following the pain to her.

Why should I believe you—believe all this?

Because my memories are open to you. You can take them and enter them and remember everything I'm telling you for yourself even as I remember it anytime you want to. Then you'll know whether or not I'm telling you the truth. Because the only reason we're talking to each other like this is that you're afraid to learn the truth directly, afraid to find out what my second self remembers, what it's really like to be dead. But I've hidden nothing from you, I'm hiding nothing from you, and for that alone you should trust me, even if you refuse to examine the truth for yourself.

If I let you into my body, let you take one of my eyes, will you leave if I demand it of you? Return here to your bones and leave me in peace?

Yes. I promise you that, Shonraleur's-Daughter.

But how do I know that I can trust you? Know that even if you mean it now, you won't change your mind?

Have Moth bind me to an oath.

He was pledged to you, almost your husband. I can't trust him.

The other one, then. I've never met him. Have him bind me, so that I can keep your eye only so long as you allow me to.

I make you no promises, Tas Gly's daughter. But I will try it for a while.

She felt a tension go out of her then, a wall she hadn't realized the other was maintaining with their combined strengths go down, and the drumming was suddenly all around her. The pain that had been hunting her came hurtling through the walls of the tomb and threw itself upon her, rending her ghost's flesh with its gray-metal claws, ripping her from the other Rafti's bones, and yet once again the agony she should have felt was held from her, though this time it was Tas Gly's daughter who took it into herself and endured it.

She knew that if she tried to enter the other Rafti's memories now to verify for herself that all she'd been told was true, she'd feel the pain that had been meant for her, and that was more than she could force herself to do.

She would have to trust the ghost, trust to the oath the other Rafti had promised to swear.

Chapter Eight

The beast had her against one of the walls; she could see its red eyes and how it was ripping her with its claws and teeth, smell its hot breath on her face, but that was all: no pain, not even any sensation of movement when it took her in its jaws and shook her, or battered her against the wall and floor.

Ignored by the beast now that she'd been ripped free of it, the other Rafti's skeleton was trying to repair itself. Yet even while the disjointed and splintered bones were crawling slowly back together, chittering softly to one another as they began to mend, the shamans arrived, riding on their drums.

But their drums had changed, become great eight-legged white horses with the blank-eyed, staring faces of gulls; Moth and Sulthar sat cross-legged in oval depressions in their mounts' backs as though in shallow canoes, guiding their horses by striking them with the long batons of carved bone they held in their left hands. And the shamans too were different, totally changed, for all that Rafti had no more trouble recognizing them than she'd had in recognizing their drums.

Sulthar was naked and hawk-headed, hawk-winged; and the hollow in his mount's back in which he sat was overflowing with small, furry, bright-eyed, and sharp-fanged animals, while a cloud of birds of all kinds great and small accompanied him. But Moth . . .

There were three or more of him in a constantly shifting relationship to one another, and two of those were dead. The three were constantly merging and separating, vanishing into one another only to reappear alone or in combination with the others, so that sometimes he had only one, at other times two or even three bodies growing from his lower torso, sometimes two, four, or six arms, and once, when all three heads sat together on his impossibly broad shoulders, Rafti caught a glimpse of yet another head, a fierce-eyed hawk's head like that which Sulthar wore.

The Moth who was alive was taller than Moth had appeared in the flesh, older and crueler-looking, with yellow flames burning in his eyes, and his long red and black hair tied back with an amber-scaled serpent; and where his right forearm should have been he had a great curving blade of burning red copper.

And then the second Moth, a boy, perhaps Moth as he'd looked when he'd been five or six years younger, but with short-cropped brown hair and wide, trusting black eyes in a face that looked as though it had been open and generous in life—but the skin was leather-dry and creased, covered with a fine powdery white dust, and every part of the body and head save only the face around the eyes and mouth had been pierced over and over again with some small triangular blade: the triple-lipped wounds were desiccated, curling slightly at the edges.

The third figure was a naked man, older than either of the others, stocky and powerful, his hair a flaming red. He was writhing in final agony on the long polished black-wood stake that protruded half a bodylength from his right shoulder; his nose and ears had been hacked off and pink foam dripped from his mouth, but his eyes were open, fierce and black and staring, and his lips were moving, struggling with words he could no longer force them to shape.

As the three figures shifted and merged, the stake protruded now from the boy's leathery shoulder, now from that of the man with a burning blade for a forearm, and all three figures were splotched and running and smeared with the impaled man's blood, the bloody foam from his mouth.

Rafti recognized the dead, knew them from the other Rafti's memories: Moth as he'd been when he was still a potter, before he'd become a smith (though his hair had been red and black then, not brown, and his eyes golden), and Tas Et, Moth's uncle, Tramu's father, as Rafti had seen him when her father took her to watch him die on his stake in the Great Square, with his wife and son tongueless in the cage at his feet. But when Rafti reached further, trying to make sense of the little she remembered, understand how Moth's uncle and former self had become part of the triple being coming after her now, she began to feel the distant agony that was the gray beast's claws and teeth in her flesh, and she retreated in panic back to her familiar self, her ignorance, though she hated herself for her cowardice.

The two shamans had slipped past the Necropolis's guardians and were only four or five bodylengths away from her now, riding hard, their gull-headed horses eight-legged blurs beneath them. Rafti could see them yelling to each other and to their mounts, striking them frenziedly with their long carved bone batons, yet the only sound was the drumming everywhere around her; the shamans came riding through the drumming in utter silence, without disturbing the dusty bones and jeweled headdresses, the once-bright silks whose beauty she still remembered from the day when they'd sealed her into the tomb to die. In all the time she'd been watching them—how long?—they couldn't have advanced more than a few handspans toward her, toward the other Rafti's skeleton still struggling to knit itself back together, toward the gray beast still worrying her insubstantial, unfeeling flesh with its claws and fangs.

As the shamans continued their infinitely slow progress across the tomb toward her, the drumming seemed to fade and their horses' movements slowed until at last she could see the graceful movements of their many legs clearly. And now at last, the drumming fading almost below the limit of audibility, she could hear them, hear the faint brushing and scraping sounds their hooves made sliding through the other handmaidens' chirping and whispering skeletons without so much as disturbing the dust on them . . . and then, much later, handspans closer, beginning to disturb them, rocking the skulls with their lapis-beaded headdresses still on them, the loose piles of jeweled bones, as they passed through them, as though the bones had been touched an instant by a breath of wind.

Moth! The other Rafti's voice as clear as it had been when Rafti'd first heard her, despite the beast now gnawing at her entrails.

Their entrails.

Moth, stop! Listen to me! I'm Rafti—Rafti who was killed to keep her from becoming your wife! I mean none of you any harm!

She could hear the horses' many hooves striking the floor now, somehow very far away, and nearer hear the bones cracking and breaking beneath them, see the disjointed skeletons drawing slowly together, groping for the intruders with futile anger, unable to touch them or their mounts, and then, from even farther away than the sound of the hooves, she heard the dead boy's voice, softer and more patient-sounding than that of the living shaman had ever seemed.

I recognize you, Rafti. But let her go.

Then, his voice harshening as the dead boy gave way to the older Moth with the copper blade where his right forearm should have been: Whatever our debts to you,

you have no right to her. Free her to return to her body and we will leave you in peace.

Tell them, Shonraleur's-Daughter. Tell them. They'll believe you where they might never trust me.

She hesitated an instant, then: Moth, Sulthar, can you hear me? Me, Rafti Shonraleur's-Daughter?

We can hear you. Sulthar's voice, harsh as a hawk's scream.

I have— The two of us have struck a bargain. Tas Gly's daughter is . . . to return with me. To my body. I'm giving her my left eye to share with me, so I can free her from this tomb. But only so long as I want her in me, and only if you can bind her by an unbreakable oath to leave me without harming me if I demand it. If you can bind her, Sulthar, not Moth, since he was once betrothed to her.

They were only handspans away from her now and the sound of their horses' hooves on the fire-hardened brick floor was deafening. The gray beast lifted its head, snarled at the shamans, and drew back, left Rafti for an instant. She tried to get to her feet, found that she could. Her flesh was ripped and shredded, hanging in loose tatters, her exposed and mangled entrails already beginning to slip from the hole the gray beast had opened in her belly, but the wounds seemed to have no effect on her ability to use her ghost's body.

She hesitantly touched the dangling entrails, felt nothing. Pushed them back inside her, held her left hand over them to keep them from sliding out again.

This is truly your will? the Moth who had a gleaming copper blade for his right forearm asked finally.

You have not been forced or threatened into saying this against your will? Sulthar asked. We can protect you if you need protection.

Their horses were standing quietly next to her now, feathered flanks heaving, the air whistling in and out of their bone-white beaks. She could have reached out and touched their heads if she'd wanted to. And all she had to do was tell the shamans that, yes, she'd been forced or threatened or lied to, and then they'd free her of this tomb and the ghost and take her back to her valley and restore her to life so she could be herself again.

Free her of Tas Gly's daughter's ghost, who was even now suffering the pain that should have been Rafti's, so she could return to a life where there would be no one to hold the pain from her and where she would no longer be the Earth Mother's favored child, Her next Priestess. Free herself by betraying that other self whose memories she'd shared, whose pain she knew and understood, whose father had already betrayed and killed her—and do so knowing what this further betrayal would mean to her, what it would be to her to be trapped forever in this tomb.

And knowing that if she did betray the other Rafti, she might find herself one day trapped in this tomb even as the one she'd refused to help had been.

Yes. It's truly my will, she said at last, not knowing if she was consenting out of honor and generosity, or only to keep the pain from her and not have to fear what would happen when she died again. Sulthar leaped from his horse and had the other Rafti swear to her oath on her second self, on the skeleton she would leave behind in the tomb. Then Sulthar helped her mount behind Moth, and the two shamans took them back through the ways beneath the earth to her body where it lay three days dead.

Chapter Nine

They emerged from the Underearth in the Mother's Burning Mountain, Moth with Rafti on his horse's back behind him leading the way, Sulthar following. The air, even the hot smoke- and soot-filled air inside the mountain's cone, was too thin, too cold for Rafti, but it took only an instant for the eight-legged horses to climb the spiraling stairway up out of the cone, and then a single impossibly slow and graceful leap for each horse to span the distance between the volcano's rim and the valley floor.

It was night: dark, clear, moonless, the stars burning cold above them. They came to earth on the far side of the river, landing gently in the dry grasses, a short ways from the forge. The drumming was all around them, but through it Rafti could hear birds calling to one another in the nearby trees, hear the insects in the grass, and all their voices were so cold and sharp and clear that the sound of them hurt her.

A fire was burning within the forge. Rafti could see through the thick walls of both the outer and inner compounds to the flames in the hearth, hear them hissing and crackling, feel their reassuring warmth, just as she could feel the cold malignancy of the great broken copper sword she could see lying in two pieces beside its exquisitely worked jeweled scabbard on the low stone bench to the right of the hearth. A second, cooler, fire smoldered in the shallow fire pit that had been dug in the hard-packed earth floor of the felt tent that had been erected just outside the entrance to the forge.

Within the tent Rafti's charred body lay wrapped in a rug of scarlet wool. Perhaps two handspans from the body a copper dagger had been stuck in the ground so that only a few fingerwidths of the gleaming blade were visible; the blade and wire-wrapped hilt seemed faintly blurred, as though vibrating too rapidly for the eye to perceive their movement.

A little farther away Moth sat on a small rug of white fur, wearing his shaman's costume and beating out a single monotonous pattern of sounds over and over again on his drum. His eyes were open but rolled all the way back in his head so that only the whites showed, and a slow trickle of blood had forced its way out through the unbroken skin of his forehead and was making its sluggish and congealing way down his nose and face to clot in his sparse beard and moustache.

Why is . . . why are you bleeding like that?

Because of me, the dead boy said, somehow separating himself from or emerging from the other two figures and turning his dry dusty wounded face with its gentle, trusting black eyes to face her. Because I'm part of him and he needs my strength to travel the ways beneath the earth, but I'm dead.

Beside the two figures Sulthar danced and leaped, bare-chested beneath his caftan with its heavy ornaments jangling and clashing as he moved, beating out complex and constantly changing rhythms on his drum and accompanying himself with a harsh, loud, wordless chant.

The tent's entrance flap had been tied open and a red silk thread led from its center pole to a birch sapling that had been stripped of its bark and set up upside down with its seven naked roots in the air. The shamans' black horses had been tied to the birch with red silk cords, and Rafti's sister, Lashimi, sat cross-legged on the ground beside them, half asleep and nodding but still watching the horses as best she could.

As Moth and Sulthar approached on their eight-legged steeds, the horses began quivering and making small anxious noises. Lashimi seemed unaware of the approaching riders but noticed the tethered horses' anxiety and awakened immediately. She stared wildly around, then squeezed her eyes tightly shut and started yelling, "They're here! They're here!" in a voice more terrified than excited. Sulthar's drumming changed instantly, slowed until it matched Moth's.

As the drumming slowed, the eight-legged horses began to shrink, and with them their riders, until they were smaller than the tiniest insects. Another great leap, as long and as slow and as graceful as that which had taken them from the volcano's rim to the valley floor, and they were on the red silk thread, galloping silently along an unimaginably long crimson bridge, whose far end was lost in the vague distance.

Yet another leap and the palm of Sulthar's hand stretched away beyond the limits of visibility all around them, a mottled translucent brown and pink landscape all huge slowly shifting ridges and valleys, beneath whose surface Rafti could see the shaman's blood rushing, an uncountable number of tangled red and blue and purple subterranean rivers and streams twining around the underlying bones.

Moth came to a sudden halt on top of one of the ridges. Sulthar—the tiny hawk-headed and hawk-winged Sulthar—drew in close beside them.

Climb off and mount behind me, Shonraleur's-Daughter, he told her. I have to take you to the sky if I'm to heal you.

The dead boy helped her off Moth's horse. Holding both hands to her opened belly, she crossed cautiously to

Sulthar's mount, and the shaman drew her up behind him, in with the birds and animals. Something small and furry, with red eyes and sharp teeth, climbed into her lap and licked her entrails where they bulged from her belly despite her efforts to hold them in, then, its curiosity satisfied, curled up and seemed to go to sleep.

Not knowing what else she could do, Rafti decided to ignore it. She looked back, saw that the other Rafti, all dry ragged skin and sharp bone beneath her bright silks and jewels, her skull's face masked with green and gold paint, was still sitting behind Moth.

The pain . . . ? she asked Sulthar.

She still bears it for you, and will until you've been healed. Rafti thought she could hear approval in his voice.

Moth's horse leaped again, landed on her dead body's forehead. The other Rafti climbed stiffly off Moth's horse, lay down in the vast hollow of Rafti's blackened and empty left eye socket, and curled up like a starving child going to sleep, then grew until she filled the hollow like an unborn child in its mother's womb.

The tiny Moth on his eight-legged horse leapt from the dead Rafti's head for the drum his greater self was still methodically beating. Horse and rider hung suspended an instant over the pattern painted in the drumskin's center—

And a gray hawk with eyes of burning darkness swooped screaming from nowhere to rake horse and rider with its talons and send them spinning away to hang bleeding in the air, the horse making frantic swimming motions with its eight legs, just short of the drum. Outside of the tent Moth's physical horse screamed.

The gray hawk banked, disappeared through the wall of the tent. The blood dripping from horse and rider evaporated before it could hit the ground. Moth—the dead boy now—leaned forward and whispered something to the horse. It made spasmodic swimming motions, as though trying to pull itself through the air to the drum.

Just as it began to move, the gray hawk came diving

down on them through the tent's felt roof. The dead boy and the impaled man tried to grab hold of it while the older Moth, whose right arm ended in a copper blade, struck with it at the hawk's right wing.

The blade slid through the wing without so much as dislodging one of its feathers. The hawk shook free of the other arms with which the threefold shaman sought to restrain it and, reaching back with its great hooked beak, ripped the arm ending in the blade free from Moth's shoulder.

Beating its wings fiercely to regain its lost momentum, the hawk tried to escape the tent with the severed arm in its beak, but before it could do so arm and blade dissolved into copper-red mist. Screaming its frustration, the hawk continued out through the tent wall.

The tiny eight-legged horse was floundering in the air, desperately trying to regain its equilibrium. Moth, clinging grimly to its back, was only the dead boy and his older self now; the impaled man was gone.

The mist into which blade and arm had dissolved congealed into two dense clouds. One darted to the copper dagger stuck in the dirt and was absorbed by it; the other made its way more slowly toward Moth's physical body. Before it could reach its destination the gray hawk was back, diving on Moth and his horse from behind. Yet even as the hawk's talons closed on him, he and his horse billowed outward in a sudden explosion of thick blood-red smoke that grew ever more diffuse until it filled the tent. Hidden by the smoke, the hawk screamed its frustration again.

The smoke condensed, drew in upon itself to form three separate clouds. One darted to the drumskin and was absorbed by it; the second drifted purposefully out through the tent's open door flap. Outside the tent Moth's physical horse made a long, satisfied snorting noise.

The third cloud became a hawk, black with golden eyes, but far smaller than the gray hawk. Even as the gray hawk swooped down upon it, talons outstretched, it rose to meet its adversary—and then, somehow, just before the gray hawk could seize it, it had shrunk, darted between the closing talons and past the larger hawk, was racing toward the seated Moth.

Hovering impossibly stationary in the air, the gray hawk gave another harsh scream as the tiny hawk darted in through Moth's right nostril, but this time the scream was of satisfaction. It shrank to a point and disappeared.

Moth shuddered, then collapsed unconscious to the floor of the tent, bleeding from his ears and nostrils. A single great gout of half-clotted blood burst from his forehead as he fell, then the blood welling through the skin there stopped altogether.

He'll be safe until we return, Sulthar said. We can go now.

Sulthar's mount leapt from the shaman's greater self's palm to the crimson thread, galloped along it. Behind them Sulthar's greater self resumed his wild drumming.

Safe from what? Rafti asked.

From Casnut, our master. That was him, the gray hawk. Remember this, Shonraleur's-Daughter, the time may come when your life depends on understanding it: as soon as Moth masters something new, Casnut attacks him and forces him to use what he's learned to keep Casnut from killing him. And this will continue until either he kills Casnut or Casnut kills him.

Why?

Because Casnut has chosen Moth to succeed him. And no one would ever willingly suffer what you have to suffer to become a Great Shaman. Not unless the only other choice was to be killed.

Why tell me all this?

Because you have been opened to the spirit-world now. It is part of it, you cannot escape it. And you too have a choice: you can learn to be a spirit-master, a shamaness, and rule the spirits with which you will come in contact, or you will be possessed and destroyed by them.

By the ghost?

No. She is bound to you by her oath. But you are open to the other dead, to all the spirits of sickness and disease now. The ghost can help you learn to recognize and resist them, to heal yourself and others, help you discover what it lies within you to become. Use her wisely, for your own sake.

Rafti thought about that for a moment, asked, And you?

A minor shaman. A healer, a juggler for children, a talker-to-animals. Nothing more.

They could see the birch trunk ahead of them now, a vast slippery-smooth tree trunk with its roots in the sky, its branches beneath the earth: a pillar joining all three levels of creation together.

Close your left eye, Sulthar said, turning back to her. She closed it and he touched it with a fingertip. When she tried to open it again she found she could not. Sulthar turned away from her again and their mount climbed the tree to the sky.

Rafti could never again remember much of the trip they made through the seven heavens until they came to the place beyond them all where Rafti's third self, her truename, awaited her, perfect and serene, there where her ripped and mangled ghost's flesh was made new again and without flaw, though she was still unable to open her left eye. Nor could she ever remember much of her return to earth, but only how it had been when she'd awakened to find her body healed and well again without flaw.

How it had been when she realized that there was no depth to anything she saw, that for all its movement and color the world around her was flatter than the Temple friezes.

How it had been when they showed her her face in the silver mirror Sulthar held up and she first saw her left eye, not black like the right, but milky and swollen and translucent like a great fever blister, the other Rafti's skeletal form curled half visible inside it like a jointed worm in a rotten fruit.

How it had been when she'd stumbled from the tent to confront her terrified family and friends and she'd seen Manlaiteq Manmoutin's-Son turn away from her, unable to meet the dead eye's accusing stare.

Chapter Ten

It was well past midday when Rafti finished her field work and was free to return to the hut she shared with Cama Namleteq's-Daughter, away from the rest of the villagers, there to eat and begin preparing herself for Kalsanen Touminor's-Son.

Cama should be awake by now, though she was likely to still be too confused to be of much help with anything. She'd rubbed herself with the yellow-gray salve she made from the forbidden roots of the ibjeq plant the night before in search of a vision that would help Rafti, but her visions had turned dark and empty on her and Rafti had had to spend most of the night holding her in the darkness of their hut as she shuddered and choked, screamed with what could have been either fear or rage, or perhaps the two together.

Not that there'd been anything unusual or unexpected about that. It was what almost always happened when Cama Namleteq's-Daughter tried to shamanize. Almost always, but Rafti had hoped for the rare exception.

The old shamaness was sitting up on her pallet, still dressed in the ragged red robe she'd fallen asleep in the night before, but though she was awake, she seemed even more confused than Rafti'd feared she'd be: she was rocking slowly back and forth, muttering or crooning to herself and twisting and untwisting her hands, her eyes watery and unfocused.

"Cama?" Rafti asked, but the old woman just kept on rocking and blinking. Rafti couldn't even tell whether or not she'd recognized Rafti as herself, or if she was even aware that there was someone else in the hut with her. In any case, she'd be of no further help for tonight.

Which was what Rafti had assumed would happen all along. Even Cama's rare successes at shamanizing usually left her in a doddering trance that lasted so long that she'd forgotten anything she might have learned before she was coherent again. The surprising thing was that she kept on trying.

Rafti took some barley and dried beans from the unglazed jars at the back of the hut, crushed them together, and ground them fine, then added spices and let the mixture soak in the clay pot they used for cooking while she fed dried grass and slivers of bark and wood to the coals left over from the previous night's fire. When everything was ready, she put the pot on to cook.

But Cama was still unaware of her when the food was ready, so Rafti took it outside and ate it alone and in silence, sitting on a flattish granite boulder and dipping the thick stuff from the pot with folded pieces of flatbread while she went over what she was going to have to do.

The wedding was set for tomorrow night, but the preliminary ceremony—the presentation of the bride and groom to their respective families—would take place at dusk tonight. She already knew what she had to do—Cama had been teaching her to fake spirit possession for two years now, ever since Rafti had first come to live with her as her apprentice—but Rafti was afraid to let her performance go too far. Cama Namleteq's-Daughter convinced those who paid her for shamanizing—inasmuch as she was able to convince them at all—that she really was in contact with the spirits she claimed spoke to and through her by convincing herself, at least for the duration of a séance. But Rafti knew that if *she* convinced herself, if she allowed herself to *believe* she was possessed for even a moment, she might open the way for the other Rafti, Tas Gly's dead daughter, to escape the eye where Rafti kept her walled off from her proper self.

And that was something she'd do almost anything to avoid, because of the way the ghost had already cheated her, for all that it was still bound by its oath to her, for all that she could order it back to its crumbling bones and imprisoning tomb anytime she chose to do so. She had already tried it once and succeeded, and that was how she knew the choice was impossible, that what happened to her when the ghost left her was far worse than enduring its presence.

It had been at the end of her first year back among her people, with the Festival less than a month away, when she'd been unable to bear her isolation any longer, unable to bear the difference that had lost her Manlaiteq Manmoutin's-Son, as it had lost her her chance to ever become Rafti Rafti's-Daughter, as it had lost her her family, her friends, her hopes. It had been night; she'd been left alone in her father's hut; what exactly she'd hoped to do was no longer clear to her, if it ever had been—something confused about returning to her earlier self in time to walk the coals as she'd done in previous years, and thus show her people that she still was really one of them, that they had no reason to continue to avoid her—but what she'd done was order the other Rafti out of her and back to her tomb.

The ghost had gone, taking the dead eye with her, as Rafti had hoped she would. But in its place she'd left not the healthy eye Rafti had expected but only the blackened and empty socket that had been Rafti's as a corpse, and from that empty socket the purple scar tissue had begun to spread, creeping out and threatening to engulf her entire face.

With the loss of the dead eye the pain the other Rafti

had been holding from her all that year had come at last. But it had not been as overwhelming as Rafti in her cowardice had been afraid it would be, and she knew she could have conquered it, withstood it, and learned to live her life in spite of it, just as she could perhaps have learned to endure her new and accentuated hideousness.

But what she could never have learned to endure was that with the other Rafti gone she could *see* with the empty socket. And what she saw was the darkness of the tomb where the other Rafti lay wrapped around her twisted, hungering bones, listening to the murmuring of the earth and to the other skeletons whispering among themselves. There was no way to shut out the tomb, to look away from it or close her eyes to it, to look at anything else without seeing it there too, and when at last that night she fell asleep, she dreamed that it was she who was back there, trapped for all eternity. So in her sleep she had asked Tas Gly's daughter to return to her, had even apologized to her and said she'd been wrong to banish her, and when she'd awakened, the dead eye had been there again in her face, and she no longer had to look out into the tomb. But the scar tissue that had spread from the charred hole was still there, ringing and emphasizing the dead eye in a way that made its hideousness inescapable, impossible to ignore, as it had never been before.

But though that horrible and inexplicable change had completed her isolation from her people, from everyone but Cama Namleteq's-Daughter, who, envying her her strangeness, and perhaps even her hideousness and the way the villagers shied from her unconsciously and fell silent when they saw her, had taken her in and tried to be a friend to her when all those whom Rafti had loved had done their best to forget her very existence. Yet now it would be useful, now it would help her rid herself of Kalsanen Touminor's-Son.

Two years before she might even have been desperate enough to have welcomed him, taken the contemptible place in his family and in the village that marriage to him would have given her, and thought herself content with it. No longer. Not now that she'd learned how much less painful it would be to live away from the others as Cama did, what it would be like to become the village's shamaness herself after the old woman died. She'd be isolated and alone, true, but no more so than she'd have been trying to live among them as Rafti Kalsanen's-Wife, there with her dead eye to mark her strangeness for all around her to see. Outcast, but without the unceasing humiliation that would be hers as his drudge, and able at least to use her hideousness, her difference, her memories of the time she'd lain dead, to convince the others that she had those supernatural powers that Cama had so much difficulty faking.

She should have gone with Moth and Sulthar when they'd offered to take her with them and train her to become a firedancer and a real shamaness. She could have returned to the valley when she was older, demanded a place of honor among her people, or gone to one of the other valleys if she still found herself an outcast here. But she'd blamed Moth for her death and disfigurement, even screamed at him once in front of her mother and father that he could cure her anytime he wanted to, that he'd planned the whole thing, even her death, to get her from her father without having to pay the customary price for a firedancer, and that he'd be able to restore her beauty as soon as it came time to sell her again.

She'd stayed by Moth during his long convalescence, at first because she was unwilling to let him out of her sight for fear that she'd miss something she could use to force him to cure her. But as more than a month went by and he was still too weak to stand unaided, though Sulthar chanted and drummed and danced over him from dawn to dusk and sometimes through the night, she'd been forced to realize that he had almost died rescuing her, that he was still close to death because of her, and that rendered all her accusations absurd. She couldn't believe that Moth would have been willing to risk sacrificing himself, willing to suffer as he was suffering, merely to avoid paying a price that he could have paid with the least of the metal ornaments from his costume.

"Why doesn't he get better?" she'd asked Sulthar. "You said I'd be able to heal people if I became a shamaness. Why can't he heal himself? Why can't you heal him?"

"Because Moth has two souls, and the soul of the person in him who could have become a healer or accepted healing from another is already dead," Sulthar told her, and she remembered the dead boy she'd seen when the shamans had brought her back from the other Rafti's tomb through the ways beneath the earth.

When at last she'd believed them, finally accepted the fact that they could do nothing to cure her disfigurement, she'd begun to feel ashamed of the way she'd accused Moth in front of her father. Though her pride kept her from admitting to Moth that she knew she'd been wrong, then or ever, she'd done what she could to help Sulthar care for him and she knew that he'd understood what she was unable to tell him in words. Yet when at last Moth had regained enough strength to leave the valley again and he and Sulthar asked her to accompany them, she refused again, though she would have gone with them gladly if the same guilt and twisted pride that had kept her from apologizing had allowed her to.

She'd been a fool, a fool twice over. They could have taught her to control the ghost, forced it to obey her. But it was too late now.

Rafti finished eating, went back inside the hut, rinsed her bowl out with sand. Cama was still confused, unaware of her surroundings. Rafti got together her clothing and few belongings, took them to her father's hut. She was his to dispose of again, until Kalsanen Touminor's-Son refused her. Then he'd have no choice but to allow her to return to Cama's hut and become her assistant, accept the pitiful sum that would be all that Cama could offer him: Kalsanen Touminor's-Son was her father's last chance to obtain for her a bride-price and a husband, and with that chance gone and the necessity of paying the much higher bride-price that Teltinor's eventual bride's family was sure to demand when *he* married, Shonraleur Valinor's-Son would be only too glad to rid himself of the extra mouth to feed that was all Rafti could ever be to him now.

Three years earlier, before he'd promised everything he had to pay the shamans who were bringing his beloved daughter back to him from the dead, Rafti's father had been wealthy, rich in gold and grain, in dried ibjeq leaves and flowers and roots, in promises owed him. He'd never forgiven Rafti for the loss of his wealth, never forgiven her for having returned to him disfigured and strange, nor for the way she'd refused since her resurrection to be even so much as a spectator to the Mother's Festivals—and he'd never forgive her now for the loss of even that trivial contribution toward the price he'd have to pay for Teltinor's marriage that her own bride-price would have brought him.

He'd be right to hate her for it. He'd given her more than any father owed his daughter, and she was returning him less than the worst of daughters owed her father. But painful though that knowledge was, it changed nothing: she had not come back from the dead to cook for Kalsanen Touminor's-Son, support his flabby flesh at night, and endure his wife's and daughter's insults during the day.

The ceremony took place in the Temple at sunset: in Rafti's valley, as in the land her people had been driven from so long ago, the setting sun marked the beginning of the new day, a day born in darkness and reaching like a green plant toward the light, only to die again as the sun itself died, to be reborn once more from the womb of night.

The chamber was oval, high-ceilinged, hot. It was lit only by the coals smoldering red in the deep, round fire pit in the center of the smooth stone floor. Clumped together on the right side of the chamber were the bridegroom and his family: Kalsanen Touminor's-Son himself, sleepy and half-senile; Malsenth, his squat and squinting wife, and her two equally ill-favored daughters; and Sammetq Touminor's-Son, Kalsanen's younger brother, generous but stupid, there with his wife and two sons.

On the opposite side of the pit Rafti stood with her family: her father, wearing his vest of copper links and carrying his elder's staff, face dignified and hard; Lashimi, so conscious of her new role as the Goddess's favorite that she could see in Rafti's coming marriage only all women's sacred destiny; her brothers, Valinor and Teltinor, both despising Kalsanen Touminor's-Son and sympathizing with Rafti, both accepting the marriage as right and proper and inevitable anyway; and Valinor's young wife Setla, herself only a little more than a year older than Rafti but with her infant son cradled in her arms, her only concerns her husband and child.

Facing the two family groups were Manmoutin Manlaiteq's-Son and Rafti's mother. They were both there as witnesses—Manmoutin Manlaiteq's-Son, as the Tradition-Master, the witness for the village, Rafti's mother, as the Earth Mother's Priestess, there for the Mother—rather than as participants. Their faces were closed, impersonal, the faces of strangers.

Rafti's father swore to Kalsanen Touminor's-Son (who as the eldest surviving member of his family was representing himself) that Rafti was virgin and had been promised to no other man, that she'd been properly instructed at home and in the Temple, would be a faithful wife to him and respect and obey him in every way, that she would bear him children.

He too was impossibly distant, reciting his words by rote. For an instant, listening to him, despite everything he'd done for her and all she owed him, Rafti hated him far worse than she hated Kalsanen Touminor's-Son.

Who in turn swore that he would feed and clothe and protect Rafti, that he would worship the Mother, whose mortal embodiment she was, in and through her, and that he would raise any children she bore him as his own sons and daughters. He detailed the list of gifts to be given Rafti's father and family to console them for the loss of their daughter: a small, clumsily fashioned gold ring, five pots of ibjeq leaves and one pot of ibjeq berries, twenty storage jars of barley, two goats. Nothing, or next to nothing.

Rafti's father said that the gifts were more than satisfactory and that his family would be honored to accept alliance with Kalsanen Touminor's-Son and his family. He handed the future bridegroom the small gold-chased bone flask containing the musk to be poured on Rafti's hair.

Rafti rolled her eyes back in her head as Cama had taught her to do, so that only the whites showed. She screamed, pretended to choke, flung her arms wide, and went into faked convulsions, muttering unintelligibly to herself as she flopped back and forth on the smooth stone floor. But Kalsanen Touminor's-Son and Malsenth just laughed at her efforts, and her husband-to-be poured the perfume over her there where she lay writhing and mumbling, while Lashimi turned away from her, ashamed.

Her mother was there as the Earth Mother's witness: she kept her face impassive as she watched Rafti, made no comment then or afterward. But after Kalsanen Touminor's-Son and his family were gone, Rafti's father dragged her from the Temple, told her, furious, as soon as they were out of the sacred precincts, that if she continued trying to lie to her husband that way after her marriage was completed, she could only expect to be beaten for it—or at least that's what he himself would do to a wife who tried to shame him like that in front of family, village, and Goddess.

Which left Rafti with only two real choices. She could banish Tas Gly's daughter's ghost to her tomb once again and hope that the sudden appearance of the charred hole there in her face where the dead eye had been, the purple scar tissue lapping outward from the empty socket to cover more and more of her face, would be horrifying and terrifying enough to scare Kalsanen Touminor's-Son away from her. Or she could attempt to make peace with the ghost and hope that with the other's help she could force her husband-to-be to renounce his claims to her.

But that choice, finally, was no choice at all, because Malsenth—herself squat and sagging, rough-skinned, beginning to lose her teeth—would have liked nothing better than to see Rafti stripped of even what little of her former beauty remained to her, nothing better than to see her so hideous that she'd never threaten the toadlike older wife's domination of her husband and would never be anything more than someone—something—to do the work that Malsenth would otherwise have to do herself.

Sooner or later Rafti would have to ask the ghost for help. Ask, and hope that Tas Gly's daughter would demand nothing more of her than she'd be able to give, nothing worse than the vision of the tomb she'd been forced to share that time she'd tried to banish the other.

She'd been taken back to her parents' hut for the night, was lying stretched out on the pallet that had been hers before she'd gone to live with Cama Namleteq's-Daughter, when she came to her decision. Everyone else was asleep. She started to get to her feet so she could go outside and find someplace where she'd be alone and secret for her conversation with the ghost, then sat down abruptly on her pallet again: she didn't know if there'd be anything to her conversation that anyone else would be able to perceive, much less that would awaken her sleeping family, but if there was, so much the better.

She closed her eyes, bit her lip. "Tas Gly's daughter," she whispered. And then, louder, almost defiantly, and for the first time, "Rafti?"

Yes, Rafti, her other self answered.

Chapter Eleven

She spent the next day acting the obedient daughter, the submissive bride-to-be. Malsenth and her mother painted her body and breasts with red ochre, stained her lips scarlet, emphasized the good eye with blue-green malachite, dressed her in her grass-green bride's robes, and wrapped her with garlands of white flowers.

They'd tried to hide the purple scar tissue ringing the dead eye with more malachite, had only succeeded in accentuating the eye's pus-whiteness, the unclean accusation of its stare.

Rafti's mother had been distressed, though she'd done her best to keep her distress from her daughter, but Malsenth had been well pleased, for all that she too had done her best to keep what she felt secret.

As pleased with Rafti's mother's distress as with what she imagined to be Rafti's own, Rafti realized after watching Malsenth covertly for a while, surprising the anticipatory half smiles the older woman allowed herself when she thought no one was looking, hearing the satisfaction so poorly masked in her voice whenever she offered sympathy or advice.

It was as though Rafti had been blind all her life, was only now beginning to glimpse the reality of what had always gone on unperceived all around her, and that knowledge was as bitter in its way as the look on Manlaiteq Manmoutin's-Son's face had been when he'd first seen her after her resurrection.

She could never allow herself to realize that she hated either of you before, her other self said. When you were the Earth Mother's favorite, because hating you would have been to defy and deny Her. But she's always envied and resented your mother, hated her own daughters for not being more like *your* mother. So that now that you're no longer the Mother's, she can tell herself that all your claims to be better than her were lies, she can allow herself to feel the hatred she's held within herself for so many years.

But if Malsenth had been pleased with the way the malachite accentuated the dead eye's pussy stare, so had Rafti, though she'd been more successful in hiding her feelings than the older women, perhaps only because her reaction was something neither one expected. She'd told them that her real reason for having tried to repulse Kalsanen Touminor's-Son had been the shame she'd felt at the knowledge of how ugly and undesirable she'd appear to him on her wedding night, how unsuited she'd become for the role of bride. They'd both believed her unquestioningly, each for her own reasons.

Let them think you've surrendered, her other self had advised the night before, after they'd concluded their pact. You've already done far too much to frighten your village: remember how my father had Moth tortured, and how easy it would be for them to convince themselves that the uneasiness they feel around you comes from some great evil in *you*.

But they know me, Rafti protested. They know I've never done any of them any harm—

They knew the Rafti who died in the fire pit, not the one who returned to them after three days dead. The Earth Mother's next Priestess, not the one-eyed girl who spent so much time with that shaman while he was recovering and then went off to live with Cama Namleteq's-Daughter. You came back to them different, and they have no way to be sure you're really who you claim to be and that you haven't been possessed by some evil spirit. . . .

Such as yourself.

Such as myself. So save your efforts for your husband alone, for your marriage bed. There I'll do everything necessary to make it seem he's the one refusing you, and not you him.

After that refusal, as soon as she and the other Rafti were alone again and sure to be undisturbed, the first part of the payment she'd pledged: she would have to let herself remember not just those few memories that had already shown her that the ghost's pact with her had been sincere, that the other had known nothing of the healing awaiting Rafti in the heaven beyond the heavens and had not known that her presence there in Rafti's left eye socket would keep the healing from being complete or that her continued presence would somehow become necessary to Rafti . . . not just those few selected memories but the whole of the other Rafti's life as she'd re-created and remembered and analyzed and understood it in that eternity out of time she'd spent a prisoner of Sartor's Golden Realm, and with that remembered life her memories of the grave as well, her brief stay there and all that her second self, her skeleton, had learned while she herself was trapped in Sartor's Golden Realm. With everything, finally, that the ghost had come to understand watching the way Sulthar slowly restored Moth's strength to him while Rafti screamed accusations at them both.

And then, with the ghost to show her the sicknesses in people, to help her drive them forth or locate the victims' straying souls, she could become a true shamaness, a healer such as this valley had never known. Perhaps in time she might even learn to heal herself.

If Kalsanen Touminor's-Son refused her.

He will, the ghost reassured her, giving Rafti a glimpse of her memories from the brief time she'd spent as a hierodule in the Siltemple at Kyborash, her body at the disposal of all who paid the Temple's price. Trust me: I know men well enough to know when he'll be most vulnerable.

Later that afternoon Malsenth and her mother walked by her side as she delivered the passis, the sticky nut, honey, and barley sugar sweets given as presents to those guests invited to the wedding as gift-givers. Normally, not only the gift-givers but everyone else in the valley managed to end up at a wedding, those uninvited coming by for a few brief moments to wish the couple luck and accept a tiny cup of barley beer from the bride. But this time there would undoubtedly be few if any people except Cama there uninvited, and there were less than a dozen leaf-wrapped passis on the wicker tray Rafti carried.

She tried to make herself believe that she was really glad when she saw people turn from her and pretend they hadn't seen her so as to avoid the necessity of offering her the ritual congratulations that the men—and the teasing that the women and girls—owed her as a bride, tried to tell herself that their reaction augured well for her attempt to repulse Kalsanen Touminor's-Son. Tried and failed: each time someone turned away, hesitated, or changed the way he or she was going to avoid confronting her, it hurt, hurt worse than she'd ever imagined it could. She wondered how many of them had always resented her secretly, the way Malsenth had, how many of them would be secretly pleased to see her humiliated.

The only consolation was that Manlaiteq Manmoutin's-Son wasn't there to see her, to turn from her or force himself to congratulate her with shame on his face and a voice full of lies.

It was over quickly enough and they returned to the hut. Her mother's face was a mask, with the same impartial expression she'd worn at the ceremony the night before.

Malsenth talked on and on until finally she realized that neither Rafti nor her mother had spoken to her for some time and that neither was paying any attention to her. She fell silent then, watching them but looking away when they glanced at her, never quite meeting their eyes.

About a half time-candle before dusk Lashimi entered hesitantly, embraced Rafti, then began dressing herself for the ceremony. She took herself very seriously now that she'd become her mother's successor, moving with a dignity and an attempted authority that would have been ridiculous or irritating in anyone less sincere.

The ceremony took place once again in the Temple. Both her parents were there in their official capacities, so Valinor, as her eldest male relative, accepted the presents the guests brought and answered for her when the time came for her to respond to the ritual questions. Rafti had only to stand there unspeaking and unprotesting, her head bowed submissively, as her father and family relinquished their claims to her and transferred them to Kalsanen Touminor's-Son.

The ceremony went on and on around her, interminable for all that she dreaded its finish. Every now and then she had to prostrate herself or make some sort of gesture, once or twice she was allowed to signify her assent to everything Valinor had said and accepted in her name, but mostly she just stood there and watched.

At last it was over and she was Rafti Shonraleur's-Daughter no longer but Rafti Kalsanen's-Wife, bound to honor and obey her husband and his senior wife in all things.

The time had come for her to thank her invited guests for their gifts. She did so distractedly, then, suddenly afraid that Manlaiteq Manmoutin's-Son would feel it his duty to come and accept a cup of barley beer from her, told her new husband that she felt the time had come for them to retire to the marital chamber behind the Temple.

Malsenth accompanied them back to the chamber, which

had been cut into the living rock of the Mother's Burning Mountain next to the honeycomb of cells in which Rafti Rafti's-Mother and the other widows lived. By custom newlyweds spent the night there, while family and guests remained in the Temple feasting, waiting for the old women to examine the bride at daybreak and verify that the marriage had been consummated so everyone could return home.

Kalsanen Touminor's-Son had a sick, sour old-man's smell, hair curling from his nostrils and ears. Malsenth ushered them in past the hanging curtains that blocked the entrance, lit the lamps within from the one she was carrying.

"I'll be outside if you need me," she said, speaking not to Rafti but to her husband. "If you need any help."

He just grunted in reply. Malsenth looked around the chamber one last time, stared tightly at Rafti, and left.

Now, the other Rafti said, and Rafti gave the ghost her body to use as her own.

Chapter Twelve

She was watching herself from some point that was both within and outside her body, that kept shifting back and forth between reality and memory, between the yellow-lit marital chamber and the airless darkness of her other self's tomb. As though she were dreaming, or had somehow taken refuge in a dream and, hidden within it, was spying on the waking world around her.

Kalsanen Touminor's-Son was blinking slowly and nearsightedly at her, licking his slack lips, fumbling determinedly with the complicated folds and fastenings of his elaborate wedding costume. She was glad he didn't try to say anything to her. He was far away, ridiculous, amusing; she had to keep herself from laughing at him as she helped him out of his clothing, laid it out for him, as she shed her own clothes with a stylized grace and slow provocation that she realized her other self must have been taught when she'd been being prepared for her time as a hierodule.

"Do you need any help?" Malsenth called from outside as he reached for Rafti.

"No!" He was breathing hard, angry at the interruption. Sweating. "Go away!"

The pallet in the center of the floor was covered with a red cloth on which elaborate depictions of couples making love had been embroidered. Rafti—the other Rafti—avoided Kalsanen Touminor's-Son's outstretched arms, slipped deftly past him to the pallet, knelt down on it facing him, and waited.

He blinked again, confused, then followed slowly, a ponderous mass of sour mottled sagging flesh, hairy and quivering as he moved, his erect penis almost hidden between his massive thighs, between the drooping folds of his belly. He would have been pathetic were it not for his hands, strong, blunt, grasping, the hands of someone both powerful and utterly selfish.

"Over here." Her other self speaking softly so as to make sure that Malsenth couldn't overhear her. Rafti found herself imagining that she had Kalsanen Touminor's-Son pushed back against the chamber's wall the same way the gray beast had had her, that she was eviscerating him, slashing his belly open with clawed fingers so his entrails spilled from it, came slithering out to tangle at his feet and fill the marital chamber with their slimy coils—

Her other self was helping him down onto the pallet, whispering something in his ear. He held himself back for a moment, glaring at her in suspicion or protest, but then the other Rafti whispered something more and he lay on his back, gave a satisfied grunt, and, putting his hands behind his head, closed his eyes. She began touching him, stroking his skin, teasing him, avoiding his hands whenever he reached for her.

It went on and on, interminable as the wedding had been. Rafti found herself getting bored. She took refuge in the other Rafti's memories for a while, sampled the training Tas Gly's daughter had been given to prepare her for her season as a hierodule, relived her experiences with the men who'd paid the Siltemple for her company. Somewhere in the back of her mind she was aware of Kalsanen Touminor's-Son wheezing and panting, aware of the way his whole body quivered with abject, flabby eagerness as she straddled him, lowered herself slowly onto him, the pain as she took him within her so like that other pain she remembered from her first time in the Siltemple that it was without importance. . . . Even as she turned from memories of the Siltemple and her time there in general to pursue the memory of that single time that Tramu, whom she'd wanted for her husband and whose family had scorned her father's offers, had paid the Temple for her services and how she'd hated him for it . . . even as she went from that remembered humiliation on to other, happier, memories of Tramu from the period before he'd started mocking her for thinking the daughter of as inept a goldsmith as Tas Gly could hope to marry the Sil Smith's grandson, and those happy memories were overshadowed by that last, unbearable memory of having seen him there with his mother in the cage with their tongues cut out, beneath the impaled body of Tas Et his father, all of them being punished—and Tramu and his mother eventually to be sent as slaves to the lead mines at Nanlasur—for having allowed the Sword That Was King Asp (the same sword, Rafti suddenly realized, recognizing it from Tas Gly's daughter's memories, that Moth and Sulthar had been reforging when they'd had to interrupt their work to bring her back from the dead) to be stolen from them by Nomads . . . even as she lost herself in her other self's memories she still retained a distant awareness of her husband's sweaty flesh bucking and shaking beneath her, rasping within her, as the other Rafti brought him closer and closer to his climax while still contriving to deny it to him—

Until at last she was snapped back to full consciousness of her physical self as the other Rafti let Kalsanen Touminor's-Son have his orgasm at last, his whole body spasming helplessly with the force of it, the last of his strength and will spurting from him into her to leave him helpless and open, empty and vulnerable:

As Rafti's flesh melted from her bones, dripped and ran in rivulets of putrescent slime down over him to pool on the pallet around him, and he found himself being straddled by a grinning skeleton, his flaccid penis trapped in the pelvic girdle that was closing tighter and tighter like a pair of fleshless jaws while the skeletal fingers scurried over his body in mocking imitation of their earlier caresses, found his neck and there began, ever so gently and playfully, to squeeze—

His face went a mottled, angry red; he was gaping, staring, his eyes wide, wider, bulging insanely from his head. Rafti took her hands from his neck, dropped the illusion she'd created for him.

Too late. He made a strangled, choking sound, his face all bluish-purple now, his hands clenching tight then releasing as his body spasmed one last time within her, and then he was still.

You killed him!

I— She could feel the other's confusion. I just wanted to scare him . . . make him leave us alone. . . .

Can you bring him back?

Not without my second soul . . . my skeleton . . . to allow me access to the Earth Mother's domain. I'm sorry.

Rafti was still straddling the corpse, but her body was her own again. She freed herself of her dead husband, was just getting to her feet when Malsenth burst into the room and started screaming that Rafti was a witch who'd murdered her husband with magic.

Rafti said, "Be quiet," and took a step toward the older woman. She had no clear idea of what it was she intended to do, but Malsenth shrank away from her, terrified, then spun around and pushed her way out through the curtains, still screaming as she ran.

Rafti picked up her grass-green bride's robes, began winding them back around herself.

Cover his body, the ghost suggested. Make as much of a show as you can of respecting it, try to look like you're grieving over it.

Rafti hurriedly straightened the corpse's limbs, then covered the body with a scarlet wall hanging on which idealized men and women demonstrating the various positions for lovemaking were stitched in green and white thread.

What now?

When I was in the Siltemple, there was an old Warrior of the Voice who came from one of the smaller cities downriver to buy the services of one of the other hierodules and prove his manhood on her. . . .

While she listened to her other self and experienced the ghost's memories for her own, Rafti rubbed her eyes to redden them, then seated herself on the mat beside her dead husband's body, tucked her legs under her, and sat with her back straight but eyes lowered, in what she hoped would seem a convincingly respectful and modest posture.

And despite everything that had gone wrong, despite the danger the ghost's miscalculation had put her in, Rafti found an unexpected sense of relief almost overshadowing her anxiety. Not only was she free of Kalsanen Touminor's-Son, but the ghost had proved herself fallible—and that meant that Rafti wouldn't have to consider herself so hopelessly ignorant and inferior that for her own good she'd always have to accept and obey the ghost's orders.

Meant that she hadn't exchanged an outward and superficial servitude for a far more humiliating and profound slavery.

Chapter Thirteen

Listen.

The sound of Malsenth's voice, soft footsteps approaching, then silence. They were just outside the chamber.

They're watching you through a gap in the curtains, the ghost said. Rafti forced herself to keep her head down, did nothing to indicate that she was aware of their presence.

She heard the curtains being drawn aside, twisted her head around to look. Her mother and father were standing there, flanked by Manmoutin Manlaiteq's-Son and the other surviving members of the Council. Behind them were the two families, the rest of the wedding guests, Cama, Malsenth. Cama alone was looking at her with what might have been sympathy. Rafti's mother and some of the other women—though not Malsenth—had weapons in their hands: the long sinuously curving and recurving daggers that had been forged in that almost forgotten age when women as well as men had been smiths, that could only be used in the defense of the Mother's Temple and Priestess.

That they were ready to use against *her*, against Rafti who'd for so long been one of the Mother's chosen.

The silence went on and on as they stared down at her and past her to Kalsanen Touminor's-Son's corpse with its purple face and bulging eyes, its scrawny ankles sticking out from under the scarlet hanging. Then Rafti got to her feet, moving as slowly and with as much deliberate grace as she could force from her cramped and aching body, so as not to startle them into attacking her.

She turned to face them, said, "Father—" and took a step toward him.

He retreated a little and held his elder's staff up in front of him, brandishing it at her as though to ward her off.

"No farther. Malsenth Kalsanen's-Wife has accused you of having killed Kalsanen Touminor's-Son by witchcraft."

His voice was cold, distant, thin with what was either fear or suppressed anger, perhaps both. The voice of her executioner.

Rafti saw Malsenth sheltered behind him, the same look of satisfied malice that the older woman had been trying to suppress earlier in the day now clearly visible on her face. As though her husband's death meant nothing to her, was just one more weapon she could use against Rafti.

Don't let them see how angry you are.

"Malsenth's mistaken. I swear with the Earth Mother as my witness that I didn't kill him, by sorcery or by any other means."

Then she repeated the story her other self had furnished her with, adapting it when necessary to her situation: Kalsanen Touminor's-Son had told her that he was still as much of a man as anyone half his age and that he was going to prove it to her; he'd refused to stop making love to her and rest even after he'd totally exhausted himself but had demanded she continue on; she'd obeyed him and tried to please him in every way until suddenly his heart had burst from his unaccustomed exertions and he'd died, there on top of her. . . . She'd been praying to the Mother for guidance when they found her. . . .

Manmoutin Manlaïteq's-Son had been nodding slowly throughout most of the story, and when Rafti finished he said, "It's possible. . . ." Malsenth said, "No!" but the Tradition-Master ignored her and continued, "There was a similar history here once before, and in the same family, six generations ago, when Teltinor Touminor's-Son took to wife a girl of fourteen, Shina Straglin's-Daughter, though he himself was at the time almost seventy and the oldest man in the village. He too proved incapable of surviving the excitement of his wedding night, though his wife conceived a child by him that was born after his death. . . ."

Rafti's mother had lowered her ceremonial blade a little while the Tradition-Master spoke, though her expression remained that of the Mother's distant and impartial Priestess. Even Rafti's father was staring down at Kalsanen Touminor's-Son's body as though struck by the contrast between the scrawny legs sticking out from under the hanging, and the youthful and indefatigable couples lovingly embroidered on its scarlet cloth.

"No! She's lying!" Everyone turned back to Malsenth. "I was watching through the curtains, in case my husband needed me—"

She's lying, the ghost said. She was sitting against the wall, about three bodylengths away.

"—and I saw her, she was on top of him, taunting him on—and then she turned into some sort of horrible *thing* that wasn't Rafti at all, and it ripped his heart out of his chest and *ate* it!"

That wasn't the illusion I created, but she must have sensed me in you anyway. Stop her, quick, before she's had a chance to accuse you any more!

Rafti said, "She's the one who's lying, not me!" To the ghost: Can you keep me safe in the fire pit?

Yes. If you can learn to trust yourself as you once trusted the Mother.

"I call on the Mother to witness my innocence! I demand the right to have Her judge me in the fire pit!"

"But she's always been able to—" Malsenth began.

Rafti's mother cut her off. "Her faith failed her once, and the Mother punished her for her presumption as none of the rest of you have ever been punished. If she's lying, the Mother will know, and will punish her for it again."

"So you can save her the way you did the last time?" This not from Malsenth, but from one of her daughters.

"No!" Rafti's father. "If the Earth Mother finds her guilty, we will accept Her judgment."

"But I saw her!" A despairing wail from Malsenth.

And then suddenly Rafti saw her chance, knew what to do.

"If anyone killed Kalsanen Touminor's-Son by sorcery, it was Malsenth! That's why she's trying to tell you I killed him, so no one will suspect *her*. If she's innocent, let her prove it in the same way I will, in the fire pit. Let the Mother decide between us."

Malsenth said, "No, no . . ."

Rafti's father looked at the older woman, then back at Rafti. He stepped past her and pulled the hanging from Kalsanen Touminor's-Son's body. Stared down at the corpse a moment, then covered it again and looked to his wife. "What does the Mother say?"

"Let Malsenth prove her innocence in the burning pit. But only if Rafti can prove her own first."

Chapter Fourteen

Sunset.

Rafti closed her eye, found the thread-thin canal of smoldering red flame the ghost had taught her to ignite in her spine.

Take a deep breath.

She breathed in, felt the flames pulsing with the current of air.

Feed the flames.

She pushed the dead air out, took another breath, fed the flames with her anger and her hatred and her fear until they burned a bright yellow-orange, until they danced through her hotter than the coals in the burning pit and consumed her utterly.

Now. Open your eyes.

She opened her eyes and stepped lightly out onto the burning coals, stood there a moment unharmed.

The villagers lined both sides of the pit, watching her in silence. Rafti began walking, stopped halfway across the pit as she'd been instructed to, turned back to face Malsenth and the Council of Elders, there where they stood clustered together.

Her mother was wearing a green and black half-mask, the same colors that wound in tight bands around the robes

Rafti and Malsenth wore. She asked, "Do you swear before the Earth Mother that you are Rafti Kalsanen's-Widow who was Rafti Shonraleur's-Daughter, and not some spirit who has taken possession of her body?"

They had rehearsed both question and response with her before the trial. She said, "As the Earth Mother is my witness, I swear that I am Rafti Kalsanen's-Widow who was Rafti Shonraleur's-Daughter, and that no evil spirit of any sort has taken possession of me or has replaced me in my body. If I am lying, or in any way guilty of this or any other crime before the Earth Mother, may She strike me dead here and now and eat my soul."

She stood there unharmed, facing them, laughing inside, and the Mother wasn't there with her. Only herself, Rafti, and the other Rafti, who'd shown her how to do consciously what she'd always been able to do, but in ignorance of the fact that she was doing it herself.

Malsenth was standing beside the Council members, terrified. Rafti took another deep breath, felt the flames within her flare white-hot as she fed Malsenth to them, waited for the next question.

"Do you swear before the Earth Mother that you did not kill your husband, Kalsanen Touminor's-Son, by sorcery or by any other means, and that you did not use any sort of witchcraft whatsoever against him?"

Rafti swore that she had not, and was about to continue on across the coals when her father surprised her by asking, "And do you also swear that you have not accused Malsenth Kalsanen's-Widow of having murdered her husband by witchcraft out of a desire to use the Mother as instrument for your private vengeance, but rather because you think the accusation is worthy of being brought before the Earth Mother for her decision and judgment?"

For an instant Rafti's control slipped and she felt her inner fires fading, but the ghost steadied her and she closed her eye again, brought the fires back under control.

Now none of them can ever accuse you of having

plotted her death. And when her turn on the coals comes he can ask her the same question.

Rafti swore that she'd accused Malsenth of having killed Kalsanen Touminor's-Son only because she thought the accusation worthy of the Mother's judgment, and not because she wanted to use the Mother for her personal vengeance, then continued on across the flames to safety.

The people standing near her began edging away from her, so that in a few moments only Cama Namleteq's-Daughter was left with Rafti at the far end of the fire pit. Rafti let the inner flames die away, so that there was only the smoldering heat of the canal waiting in her spine to remind her that she could summon the burning back whenever she chose to do so, and she felt the exaltation that had held her in its grip while she'd been on the coals drain from her.

Malsenth was trying to escape now, but Rafti's father had caught her, was holding on to her while Rafti's mother said something to her, tried to calm her. In another moment they'd force her out onto the coals.

She was still struggling, had begun to scream. Rafti suddenly found she couldn't watch any longer. She turned away and started walking, didn't turn back when she heard Malsenth's screaming become agonized shrieking or even when, instants later, it stopped altogether.

She didn't realize where she was going until she found herself climbing the stairway the First Ancestors had so long ago cut into the jagged black basalt of the volcano's flank.

My second soul, the ghost said. There in the tomb, outside Kyborash. And the skeleton of that child I should have been, born dead because I was trapped in Sartor's Golden Realm. Perhaps with their help we can find a way to heal you.

Rafti hesitated a moment, remembering Cama waiting for her beside the burning pit, then continued on. The half-moon gave her just enough light to see the steps in front of her.

When at last she reached the black-gleaming obsidian platform at the crater's rim, she paused only long enough to catch her breath and glance up, once, at the moon and stars, then summoned up the flames the ghost had taught her to ignite in herself and continued on, down into the red-lit smoke and the clouds of drifting ash.

By morning she'd have crossed the crater and be descending the steps on the other side of the mountain.

Part Two: Moth

Chapter Fifteen

Timor came beating rapidly out of the sunset, summoned by the sound of Moth's spirit-drum. A few Nomad warriors saw him as he came winging low over their concealed camp, a great black hawk with a wingspread of well over a bodylength and eyes of the fiercest gold; their eyes followed his flight an instant before they went back to their tasks, all but one, a Teichi who went to report the hawk's return to Ravnal, the raid-leader, and to the Taryaa who remained hidden with him in his tent.

The spirit-hawk found the shaman sitting cross-legged and alone by a fire in a hidden half canyon a short ways from the other Nomads. Timor circled the fire twice, finally allowed Moth's drumming to coax him down onto the perch of polished bone the shaman had waiting for him.

Where is he now? Moth's drum asked.

In the high pass. He plans to spend the night there; I saw him making camp.

He's still alone?

Yes. And frightened, though he knows that neither he nor the contents of his cart would interest bandits.

There's no one else nearby? No Warriors of the Hand or Voice?

A village of farmers a day's ride back. Two Warriors of the Hand accompanying a trader's shipment of gold and silver from Nanlasur, but they won't cross your path for two more days.

No one else?

No.

Then I have no more need for you. Go now and come back tomorrow night.

If Casnut permits.

Moth took his hand from the drum and the spirit-hawk took flight. Returning to Casnut, its master.

Their master.

Moth put the drum aside, stood, and stretched his legs. He was exhausted, would have to sleep as soon as he'd told Ravnal where to find the trader with his oxcart full of pots and funerary vases.

He dreamed that night of fallen Kyborash, of Rafti and Tramu, of his father's potting compound and his grandfather's forge, where he'd fashioned the golden blade with which he'd killed his potter's soul, and with it his father's son. But the dream was elusive and confused, fled him whenever he tried to grasp it and wring from it its meaning, and in the end he could make no sense of it.

When he awakened, the day was warm, the sun already high. The others had the trader waiting for him.

Tall, powerfully muscled, with skin gone prematurely gray though he was younger than Moth, his face heavily tattooed and his chest and back covered with ceremonial scars, Ravnal was standing watching as Moth struggled awake. Behind Ravnal stood his young brother Tjei, face twisted into a contemptuous sneer. Only fourteen years old, Tjei adored Ravnal, followed him everywhere, did his best to imitate his every action and gesture.

And hidden in their tent, its sexless body swathed in loose robes, its toothless mouth concealed behind a mouth mask of bright fluttering silk, the Taryaa who advised and deferred to them. Who with its fellow Taryaa ruled them, as Casnut, the Royal Eunuchs' sworn enemy, ruled Moth.

Moth drank the fermented mare's milk mixed with powdered horse's blood as he tried to clear his head and comprehend his dream. He pretended to ignore the raid-leader, made the Teichi chieftain wait while he carefully unwrapped the cloths binding the deep, festering wound in his left calf, where he'd been gored by a broken tree branch while riding in a semitrance a few months earlier. Ravnal kept his face impassive, but Tjei's sneer gave way to an angry scowl.

Moth cleaned the pus from the wound as best he could, packed it with soft, waxy red-brown snarl leaves and honey grass, wrapped the cloths tight again. He could have done more with the Deltan herbs the Taryaa was certain to be carrying, but even if the eunuch could be persuaded to give them to him, there was no way he could accept its aid without shaming himself before the others.

"Why not just heal yourself and be done with it, shaman?" Tjei asked. Taunting him, showing off for his brother. "If you really have any of those powers you claim for yourself . . ."

The Teichi had killed or exiled their shamans years ago, soon after the attack on Kyborash, when their shamans had tried to force them to return to their herds in the parched northern plains and stop hiring themselves out to the Taryaa as mercenaries. The Royal Eunuchs had no desire to commit themselves to an open war against the Chaldan Empire, and little use for the wealth to be looted from the Empire's cities, so with the Taryaa as their advisers the Teichi priests and chieftains had grown rich on the spoils of conquered Chaldan cities. They professed contempt for the tribes still accepting their shamans' authority, and opposed them in council.

Moth stood, putting his weight on his injured leg. He relaxed the discipline that kept the pain from him. It was worse than it had been the day before, as he'd known it would be—it was worse every day than it had been the day before—and the pain was beginning to creep up into his thigh. He walled it off again.

"Well, shaman?" Ravnal asked.

"Because the spirits demand something in return for their aid. They gave me the power to kill; in return they took from me the power to heal myself."

It was a half truth: Moth was twin-souled and one of his souls was dead, had been forced to commit suicide in order to save the other, leaving Moth himself half dead, a necromancer, a crippled shaman who was able to travel the ways beneath the earth at will, who could pluck souls from the Mother's grasp and defy the Nine Hells but who was unable to ascend the Tree of Creation to the sky and the heavens beyond, who was unable to free himself of either his uncle Tas Et's blind frozen vengeance or of his own hatred.

Sulthar had always been able to heal him, but Sulthar had returned to his northern forests, and without his help Moth was slow to mend, slower still every time he used his powers. His vitality was so depleted that even now it took months for a bruise to heal, so depleted that any trivial flesh wound would eventually kill him, as the wound in his calf would kill him in time despite all his skill with herbs unless he found Sulthar to heal him first.

And every time he put on animal form or was forced to defend himself against one of Casnut's attacks, every time he confronted Tua-Li, the monster eel whose coils wrapped the roots of the Cosmic Tree and who alone could grant Moth entry to the ways beneath the earth . . . every time he killed with his hand or spirit or put on the ghost of King Asp to wield the sword he'd reforged in that northern valley where the other Rafti lived, he lost more of that exhausted vitality and brought himself that much closer to his own death.

"The power to kill." Ravnal sneering at him now, mocking him in front of the other warriors. "So you say."

"Are you challenging me to prove my spirits' power on you?"

"Sometime, perhaps, shaman, but for the moment save your strength for those who can appreciate it. Like this defenseless Chaldan."

"As you wish, raid-leader."

The trader was young, no more than seventeen or eighteen, with black hair cropped short, a scraggly beard, frightened green eyes. The Nomads had stripped him of his green siltunic and gray linen undertunic, then tied him naked to one of the wheels of his loaded oxcart.

Moth picked up the trader's intricately carved staff, hefted it. It had been a long time since he'd carried a staff of his own. He put it down, took the trader's cylinder seal out of the man's belt pouch, examined it. A man driving an oxcart between two stylized palm trees, with a prayer in wedge-shaped cuneiform characters beside one of the trees. He put the seal back in its pouch and the pouch down again, picked up the dagger housing Tas Et.

"Your name, Sklar?" he asked the man politely in his own language. The trader stared at the copper blade but said nothing. Trying to be courageous. Moth repeated his question, as politely as before.

When the trader continued to refuse to answer, Moth sent Tas Et into him, let the man writhe with his uncle on the stake on which he'd been impaled, share for a moment Tas Et's frozen and eternal death agonies.

For the benefit of the watching Nomads Moth waited until the man began to scream before pulling Tas Et back out of him and into the dagger again. The Nomads were all watching in silence now; even Ravnal had lost his mocking smile, and Tjei looked frightened. Moth put on a smile of his own, repeated his question yet again.

"Sklar Dest."

"And your city, Sklar Dest?"

"Erac."

"Chal," Moth corrected him softly. "You left Chal

with a load of funerary vases, half for Erac, half to go to Nanlasur. In Erac you took on some more pots to replace those you'd delivered. Or have I made a mistake somewhere?"

He sent Tas Et into the trader again, pulled the smith's spirit back before the trader had had a chance to gasp.

"No." A whisper.

"Good. You've tried to lie to me once now. Don't do it again. You came from Chal, you stopped in Erac, you're going to Nanlasur. Have you ever been to Nanlasur before?"

Sklar Dest started to shake his head no, caught himself, but by then it was too late.

"No, then," Moth said. "Do you know anyone there, anyone who'd recognize you?"

"Yes."

He's lying, Tas Et said.

I know.

"Who?"

"The Sklar Nanlasur-Sil. Sklar Marj Nanlasur-Sil."

Kill him now if you're going to kill him, Moth's potter's ghost said. He's told you all you need. There's no reason to make him suffer anymore.

Yes there is. For Ravnal and his Teichi. To frighten them and their Taryaa.

"No one else?" Letting the trader hear his disbelief.

"Yes, maybe . . . I don't know. Maybe some of the other traders or people from Chal. Or Erac or one of the other cities."

"But the only one you're sure of is Sklar Marj Nanlasur-Sil?"

The Sklar hesitated again. Moth said, "Don't lie to me."

"Yes. No one else."

Moth took the sword from its sheath, held it up. "Do you recognize this sword?"

"No . . . I—"

Moth cut him off. "This is the Sword That Is King Asp.

The sword that Asp broke at the Seven-Year Festival in Kyborash but that was stolen before it could be reforged and Asp's broken life restored to him. Do you recognize it now?"

"I . . ." Sklar Dest stared in horror at the gleaming blade.

"The blade has been reforged. You've seen the Seven-Year Festival?"

"Yes." An unwilling, terrified whisper.

"Then you know that this blade *is* King Asp. That King Asp, King of all Chal, Sartor's husbandman, your master, lives on within it. Will you touch it now, Sklar Dest, touch it for me and swear in King Asp's name and before Sartor that you know Sklar Marj Nanlasur-Sil, and that he'll recognize you?"

"I . . . No. I can't. He . . . never saw me. He won't know me."

Moth reached into the blade, found Asp's cold malignant spirit. Put it on and made it his own.

The Nomads saw him straighten, alter. Physically he remained unchanged, but the spirit animating body and features, looking out of his eyes, was different. Was King Asp, Sil of Sils, Sartor's husbandman, the man for whose delight the warriors of Chal had conquered so many cities, killed so many people.

Was King Asp and yet was no less Moth, was Moth become Asp, altered and transmuted, not replaced.

Asp-who-was-Moth, Moth-who-was-Asp, killed the trader with the sword that was himself. It took a long time, but there was no blood, not even when at last he beheaded the corpse. The sword had drunk it all.

He turned back to face the watching Nomads, grinned at Ravnal, and the thirst was in his smile, in his eyes. Tjei took an involuntary step back, stopped half hidden behind his brother.

"Remember this the next time you think to mock or

doubt me,'' Moth told the Teichi raid-leader. His voice was deeper, totally arrogant, with a different accent.

Ravnal stared back at him, meeting Asp-who-was-Moth's yellow eyes despite his fear, refusing to lower his gaze or look away. Angered, the King ordered Tas Et into the Teichi chieftain so that Ravnal too could know what it was to die on Tepes Ban's stake.

As Tas Et had died, impaled for having lost the blade that was Asp by command of Asp's son, King Tvil, on whose person and family the dying smith had vowed his death curse.

Tas Et refused Asp, struggled against his former King's dominion. Wrenched Moth free of his fusion with him.

Together, they forced the dead King back into the blade. Moth sheathed the blade and picked up the dead trader's clothes and staff, put the Sklar's pouch on his own belt. He started to turn away, then, struck by a sudden intuition, turned back to the Sklar's cart and used the dagger housing Tas Et to pry the seal off one of the baskets of pots from Chal.

He recognized the pot as his father's work immediately. It was delicate, slender, made from the finest white clay (the same clay Ri Tal had taught Moth to find high in the mountains above Kyborash) then glazed a delicate green, its long, tapering neck wound with brightly dyed nettle fibers. Almost exactly like those first vases Moth had made after he'd been sealed to both the Ri and Tas Sils, though as a RiTas—a potter-smith—Moth had had the right to wind the necks of his vases with fine gold wire in place of his father's nettle fibers.

Potter? he asked, but the potter's ghost was gone, had accompanied the dead trader's spirit on the first part of its journey to the Mother and rebirth.

Moth felt someone's gaze on him, looked up. The Royal Eunuch was standing outside of Ravnal's tent, staring silently at him with its great, pink, rabbitlike eyes. Showing itself to the other Nomads in the party for the first time since they'd left the plains. As if to say, The shaman may command certain powers, but we are with you and we—with our mouths no living man has ever seen, our strange eyes, the cities we rule and the power we wield—we are more mysterious than he and his kind, we are more to be feared than he is.

Moth met the Taryaa's stare, then turned away and, with what remained of his strength, limped back to his separate fire and waiting drum.

Ri Tal had been the potter's father, not his: when Moth had killed his Ri soul, he had killed his father's only son. But there was satisfaction nonetheless in the knowledge that the old Ri was still alive. The ghost would be pleased.

Moth collapsed by the fire and slept until night came, and with it Timor. He roused himself long enough to show the spirit-hawk where he'd hidden the sheathed sword and the dagger housing Tas Et's spirit, retaining for himself only an ear stud he'd cut from the dagger's tang and coated with gold leaf to conceal its true nature. Timor agreed to guard them for him, and left, leaving Moth to sleep again until morning.

At dawn one of the warriors—a Tlantlu, a member of the tribe to which Casnut had once belonged and not one of Ravnal's men—shook Moth respectfully awake. Moth thanked him and roused himself, cleaned his wound, and dressed it with fresh leaves and grasses, then sewed tiny pieces of metal and bone from his shaman's costume onto the trader's undertunic and siltunic in places where they'd go unnoticed, finally put on the man's clothes, hung the purse with its cylinder seal around his waist, and picked up the carved staff.

Leaving his horses with the Tlantlu, he climbed onto Sklar Dest's oxcart, took the reins, and left for Nanlasur.

He was too weak, too exhausted, too drained to remain conscious long, or awaken often. Whenever he fell asleep his uncle's spirit would prod the oxen for him, keep them on the road and moving in the right direction.

Sleeping, he dreamed of Casnut and Kyborash, of Rafti and the Royal Eunuch who'd once pretended to save Moth and Tramu from abduction by the Nomads, but the dreams were without clear form or meaning, were only random memories reunited by chance and desire.

Chapter Sixteen

Wake up, Tas Et told him, breaking the dream. They're coming, the ones the hawk told you about.

Moth opened his eyes, rubbed sleep from them, and picked up the reins. He looked around. It was late afternoon and the road led upward through the mountains; he must have already passed most of the foothills. His leg ached despite everything he'd done to wall off its pain, and he had a headache. He needed more sleep.

The other oxcart was just coming up over the crest of the mountain ahead of him. It was larger than his, heavily laden, with four oxen instead of two straining to pull it. He could see two Warriors of the Hand in silver breastplates over faded blue siltunics sitting beside the trader in his grass-green siltunic.

Who are they?

Syrr R'nay, Syrr Tebtil, Sklar Brin. From Nanlasur. No one who would know either you or Sklar Dest.

The road twisted back and forth down the mountain slope. Moth pulled his oxcart off to the side at one of the turns, leaving room for the larger cart to continue past. But the Sklar who was driving, a middle-aged man with a small, hairy nose and bushy eyebrows in a broad complacent face, halted beside Moth. They exchanged Sklar greetings and identified themselves, then the trader asked, "How's the road?"

The two Warriors of the Hand accompanying the Sklar were eyeing Moth with bored suspicion. Moth said, "It's all right until Erac, but part of the way's been washed out just north of Chal. It'll be hard going if you're as heavily laden as you look to be."

"We are, but we're only going to Erac. You didn't see anybody on the road between here and there?"

"No . . . A few field slaves and freeholders in their fields before I got to the mountains, but that's all."

The Sklar was studying Moth. "You have Tas blood, don't you?"

"My grandmother was a smith's daughter."

"Of Nanlasur?"

"No, Chal. I've never been to Nanlasur. Why?"

"Because Sartor has granted the Nanlasur Tas Sil an immense lode of silver where before their mines yielded only lead. I'm carrying sixty sixty-weights of silver ingots myself, and they're sending a kailek downriver to Chal with twelve times more! That's all I know, but maybe they'll tell you more about it."

Moth shook his head. "I'm only a Sklar, even if my grandmother was Tas. They don't share their secrets . . . or their wealth. I'm not even carrying smith work this time, just a load of pots from the Ri Sil."

"You'll probably be given a load of silver like mine to take back to Erac . . . and a cargo worth more than pots the next time you make the trip to Nanlasur. Sartor's luck, young Sklar."

"Sartor's luck, elder." The trader flicked his reins. His oxen started sluggishly forward again. The Warriors of the Hand returned their gazes to the road ahead of them.

Moth hesitated an instant before continuing on, tempted to summon Timor. The Nomads would undoubtedly capture the Sklar and his cargo, but it might be worth informing Ravnal that there'd be a kailek loaded with further silver to be intercepted at the Singing Straits, where the Thys—Nanlasur's river—debouched into the Nacre a ways above Kyborash. . . .

No. Even if there was still enough time for the Nomads to reach the straits before the kailek, he owed them nothing. When the other cart was at last distant enough, he gave the oxen back to Tas Et and slid down into sleep.

Not Timor but Casnut came to him in his dreams as a gray hawk with burning eyes. He reached into Moth's sleeping body with his beak, pulled him from it, and made him a hawk with shiny black feathers and an ivory beak, hooked and cruel. Then the master shaman breathed the strength Moth needed to animate his hawk's body into him and led him up into the sky, where they wheeled together among the cold stars—each gleaming ball of ice the frozen soul of an enchanter or Taryaa who had refused death and change for the timeless stasis of existence as Sartor's Nighteyes.

You've lost the ability to heal yourself, Casnut told Moth. You're dying.

Then heal me.

No. You must learn to heal yourself if you're ever to be of any use to me or to the Mother.

How, then?

As long as your potter's soul remains dead you yourself can never be more than half alive, as futile and frozen as your uncle's vengeance, as the Taryaa themselves. To make yourself whole again you have to resurrect Sartor-ban-i-Tresh and make him part of your living self again. Only then will you be able to climb the Tree of Creation to your truename and the healing beyond the heavens.

How? Moth asked again.

Find what remains of your dolthe and wed it to the blade with which you killed your potter's soul. Construct for yourself a new and living soul from their union.

Moth's dolthe: the clay soul-talisman that Ri Tal, his father, had fashioned for him when he'd received his name and that Ri Tal had buried somewhere in the hills outside Kyborash. And the triangular golden blade with which his potter's soul—his Ri soul—had committed suicide, in which the Ri's ghost had chosen to remain for a time after its death. Moth had left the blade buried by the Necropolis, where Rafti was entombed, because his Ri soul had loved her and wanted to stay with her, there where it could bleed slowly from the golden dagger into the earth around it and so, with Rafti, rejoin the Earth Mother. But though the bones that were Rafti's second self had remained in the Necropolis, the soul the potter had loved had been absent, stolen from the Earth Mother and potter's ghost alike, trapped for what could have been all eternity in Sartor's Royal Realm. So that when Sulthar had first guided Moth back through the ways beneath the earth to the Necropolis, Moth had found the Ri's ghost willing to relinquish blade and earth and rejoin his surviving self.

Casnut was ordering him to wed his soul-in-clay to the blade his smith-self had forged for one purpose alone: to kill the Ri soul whose essence the dolthe had shared, reflected, shaped. The blade the smith had not even found the courage to use, which the potter had been forced to use on himself.

It was ironic, bitter, almost funny: Moth's father had dreamed of making Moth the first RiTas, the only man in all the Chaldan Empire sealed to the mysteries of both the potters' Ri Sil and the Tas Sil of the smiths. Moth too had dreamed of one day being able to create from the union of clays and metals things both new and beautiful. But he had failed: sealed to both Ri and Tas, his soul had been ripped apart, so that Ri he was Sartor-ban-i-Tresh, Tas he was Sartor-ban-ea-Sar, and though both had been Moth, they'd been too fundamentally opposed to have ever existed in harmony . . . would have eventually torn Moth apart with their struggles even if his uncle's spirit had not intervened, forcing the potter's soul to suicide so as to leave Moth Tas only, and thus free to become the weaponsmith his uncle needed as instrument for his vengeance.

And now that Moth had lost family, friends, both the Sils to which he'd been sealed, now that he'd lost Kyborash, Chal, even Sartor . . . now that it was all meaningless, he was at last to fulfill his father's dreams for him. Resurrect the potter who was Ri Tal's true son, only to make of that resurrected son the most potent enemy possible for everything his father had ever been or loved. Of his father himself, there in Chal, where he'd gone to live just before Kyborash had fallen.

The potter's ghost would perhaps have objected to that union, had it been there to hear, would perhaps still object. No matter: Moth was too cold inside, too dead to care, except in those rare moments when his potter's ghost sparked his emotions to remembered warmth. He would convince the ghost, force it if he had to.

He looked to Casnut for confirmation of his understanding, but even as he did, hawk and sky melted into each other, faded, and were gone.

He came awake to the smell of river mud somewhere nearby, rocky ground scraping painfully across the exposed skin on his legs, realized he was being dragged from the trader's cart by two men.

Nanlasur, Tas Et told him.

He opened his eyes halfway, saw two Warriors of the Hand, tall stocky men with square-cut black beards, green eyes, swarthy skin, both wearing finely worked silver breastplates chased with copper and gold over their azure siltunics. They looked like brothers but not twins: one was noticeably older than the other, with a tinge of gray to his beard, and had the butter-yellow border to his siltunic that showed him to be a sixtyman—a leader of sixty other Warriors of the Hand—and thus probably soon to become a Warrior of the Voice.

The oxen had carried Moth the rest of the way through the mountains while he slept. He felt a moment's futile anger at Casnut, choked it back. Another of the shaman's ordeals: the dream had told Moth something he needed to know, but Casnut had forced it on him in such a way as to make sure Moth arrived at Nanlasur confused and unable to carry out the plans he'd made without last-minute improvisations, in such a way as to make what he had to do even more difficult and dangerous than it already was.

They know you're awake, Tas Et told him.

Chapter Seventeen

Moth moaned theatrically, opened his eyes wide, and stared up at the two warriors half carrying, half dragging him toward the city gate. The clouds above the city were red with the setting sun. His legs had been scraped raw by the rough ground, and the headache with which he'd started the day was worse, made it almost impossible to think. He'd probably hit his head when they pulled him from the cart.

Moth moaned again. The younger warrior said, "He's waking up." He sounded disgusted. The two dumped Moth in the dust, stepped back to watch him struggle to his feet. His left leg almost collapsed beneath him; he recovered his balance, stared wildly around. He was about a hundred bodylengths from the main gate. He did his best to look even more confused than he really was and make the warriors think he was almost out of his mind with fear.

"What's wrong, trader?" the sixtyman asked. "What happened?"

"Nomads, they—they, I saw them—" He broke off, caught his breath, and shook his head as though trying to clear it, only making his headache worse, then took another deep breath and started over, his words tumbling from him in a single uninterrupted flow: "A Nomad war party, they didn't see me but they might be right behind me . . . I drove as fast as I could but they had horses, that's how I knew it was a war party, they didn't have their carts, just their horses and—"

"Where?" The sixtyman grabbed Moth by the shoulders and shook him to make him stop. "Where'd you see them?"

"The mountains . . . the other side of the first high pass coming from Erac. They were camped for the night, I wouldn't have seen them at all if—"

"When was this?"

"Yesterday evening. Just after dusk. I drove all night, that's why I fell asleep, but the oxen must've kept on after I lost consciousness."

"How many were there?" the sixtyman asked, while at the same time the younger warrior demanded, "Did they see you?"

"Sixty . . . maybe a dozen more, I'm not sure. I don't think they could see me, I was most of the way up the trail and I wouldn't have seen them at all if it hadn't been for the light of their fires on the rocks, so—"

"Enough!" the sixtyman said. "You can tell the rest to the Syrr Nanlasur-Sil, if he wants to hear it. Come."

The younger warrior took Moth's arm and the two escorted him to the gate, waited while the Warrior of the Hand serving as the gate guard questioned him.

"Your name?"

"Sklar Dest, Reverence."

"What city?"

"Chal."

It was the wrong thing to say. "Your seal!" the sixtyman snapped. Moth took Sklar Dest's seal from his pouch, handed it over. The warrior examined it, turning it over and over in his hands and scowling at it, finally gave it to the gate guard for authentication.

The guard rolled it in the little trough of fresh clay he had ready for it, compared the resulting rectangular impression with the corresponding one on the official tablet for Chal, finally rolled the cylinder carefully in the official impression to make sure the correspondence was exact.

"It matches," he told the sixtyman, satisfied, and handed the seal to him.

"You're sure?"

"Yes."

The sixtyman in turn gave the seal to the warrior who looked like his younger brother, said, "Get the tablets his Sil sent and make sure the impressions match. Have a scribe read them immediately, and get the Sklar Nanlasur-Sil or anyone else who'll recognize a trader from Chal to meet us at the Siltemple." He paused an instant, then added, "And ask both Syrr Gerj Nanlasur-Sil and Tepes Sek to meet us there as well."

Tepes Sek. His name proclaimed him Nanlasur's torturer. Perhaps even a relative of Tepes Ban, who'd impaled Tas Et. But Moth no longer had the physical resources to survive even the mildest such questioning.

Especially since the Nanlasur Tepes would find on Moth's body the scars Lapp Wur, Kyborash's exorcist, had left there. When Rafti's father had denounced Moth, claiming that the fits he suffered whenever Tas Et's spirit entered him were proof of demonic possession, Moth had been given to the exorcist for questioning. Though he'd finally managed to convince Lapp Wur of his innocence, the scars the days of questioning had left on his body would be sure to rouse the Tepes's suspicion.

"I'm telling the truth, Reverence!" Moth protested as the young warrior nodded and left running. "I don't have any reason to lie to you. I saw them and came as fast as I could—"

"Then Tepes Sek will confirm your story. But I spent twelve years in Chal and you don't have the accent, I don't know your face. I'd remember a Sklar with smith blood and yellow eyes."

"I was from Kyborash before, Reverence." A risk:

there might be someone here who would know him from Kyborash, or know that there'd never been a trader named Sklar Dest there. "Before the Nomads."

"Enough! Anything you have to say, say to the Syrr Nanlasur-Sil."

"Please, Reverence! At least send someone to see if they're really out there! Then you'll know I'm telling the truth!"

"We'll know whether you're telling the truth or not soon enough."

Tas Et could have struck the man down for Moth, even killed him, but before Moth would have been able to flee, the bowmen watching from the walls would have filled him with arrows. And the potter's ghost could have done nothing useful, even if it had been willing to put aside its hatred of violence and of the Nomads' campaigns against the Chaldan Empire to try and help him.

Moth allowed the warrior to search him for weapons, then docilely accompanied him in past the guards and through the city gates.

Chapter Eighteen

The warrior who'd gone for the Syrr-Nanlasur Sil and the torturer was already waiting with them just inside the gates. The Syrr Nanlasur-Sil was an old, bent Warrior of the Voice in a clean yellow siltunic with the King's eye worked on it in silver and gold thread; he had a long scraggly gray-white beard, splotchy skin, and sharp, predatory eyes. He looked fierce but petty, the kind of man always flying into rages over trivia. Tepes Sek was short, stout, and clean-shaven, with brown hair and green eyes, his true expression disguised by the ceremonial crimson circles around his eyes and the soot with which the rest of his face was painted.

For an instant Tas Et succeeded in wrenching control away from Moth, and Moth found himself once again writhing in his uncle's death agonies on the stake on which Tepes Ban had impaled him, once again staring down at his tongueless wife and son and assistants in the cage at his feet as he uttered the smith's death curse, which had frozen him into something neither dead nor alive, neither man nor true ghost, but only this eternal instant of frozen agony, this blind will to vengeance on Chal and its King that was all that remained of what had once been Moth's uncle.

But Moth was shaman now, spirit master and no longer the helpless split-souled boy whom Tas Et had chosen as the instrument for his death curse. He regained control of his body before its momentary rigidity could have had a chance to betray him, forced Tas Et to look through the eyes they shared and see that before them was only a short man with a daubed and painted face wearing a reeking, shabby wool siltunic over a patched undertunic of crimson linen. A torturer, but not Tepes Ban.

The sixtyman prostrated himself to his Sil, repeated what Moth had told him, finished by stating that he'd never seen or heard of any trader from Chal with particolored hair and yellow eyes.

Then, turning to Tepes Sek, he said, "You came quickly." His voice was carefully respectful, but with a profound contempt in its depths where perhaps only Moth could hear it.

"I was already here, waiting." The Tepes's voice was surprisingly soft, almost apologetic. "For him, I think," he added, looking at Moth.

"Why?" the younger warrior asked.

"A dream!" the Syrr Nanlasur-Sil said. He sounded skeptical, but beneath his skepticism Moth could hear fear.

"Sartor sent me a vision last night," Tepes Sek said. "I saw Nanlasur attacked by hordes of Nomads on horses, saw them pouring in through our open and undefended gates and slaughtering us all. They left our severed heads in a rotting pyramid in front of the Siltemple—"

"I saw them too," Moth cut in desperately, trying to catch the Syrr Nanlasur-Sil's attention and change the direction in which Tepes Sek was leading the conversation. "The Nomads, I mean, I saw them, they're coming, but only about sixty of them, and I couldn't tell if they were coming here or going to Erac, they—"

"I saw your head there beside mine," Tepes Sek told Syrr Gerj Nanlasur-Sil, ignoring Moth's interruption, perhaps even smiling slightly though his soft voice remained as apologetic as ever. "I saw my children dead, your wife killed by Nomads when she tried to keep them from your daughter—"

"You had a dream, Tepes," the old Syrr said shrilly, the same contempt Moth had heard in the sixtyman's voice unconcealed this time, being used to cloak the Syrr's fear, his anger at the Tepes for having aroused that fear. "A dream, not a vision. Not unless we confirm it as an authentic sending. And then it would be for us and not for you to determine its meaning. Would it not, Tepes?"

"Certainly, Reverence."

"And what do your Nomad hordes have to do with him?" Gesturing disdainfully at Moth.

"Just this, Reverence. In my dream the Nomads were led by a man riding an eight-legged horse. A man with red and black hair and sun-yellow eyes, with a copper blade where his right arm should have been." To Moth then, with absolute certainty in his voice: "You."

"No! I'm no Nomad!" Knowing from the look on the Syrr Nanlasur-Sil's face that it was already too late, but hoping there was still a chance to gain more time by playing on the Syrr's will to deny the certainty he too had felt and believed. "I came in an oxcart, he saw me" —pointing at the sixtyman as if calling him to witness— "and I'm just a Sklar, I've got two arms"—he stuck his arms out in front of him, hands open to show they were empty—"and I don't even have a knife!"

"You have the face of the Nomad in my dream," the torturer said, almost apologetic, almost embarrassed, utterly sure of himself. "My vision told me I'd find you here today."

Casnut. Casnut, not Sartor, had sent him that dream. Forcing Moth into yet another situation where he'd have to use his shaman's abilities as Casnut wanted them used, or die for his refusal. Forcing Moth to continue the process of making himself over into the person Casnut wanted him to become until, finally, Moth would be ready to kill the

Great Shaman and take his place, since by then Moth would have become so like Casnut that the change would be no change at all, the Moth replacing the man he killed, no different from the Casnut who'd once killed and replaced his own master.

"What if the Nomads sent him his dream, Reverences?" Moth asked, directing his question to the Syrr Nanlasur-Sil. "To keep you from believing me?"

"You said they didn't see you," the sixtyman said.

"I didn't think they did. But I might have been wrong."

"My sons are waiting in my rooms," Tepes Sek said, ignoring the scowl with which the Syrr Nanlasur-Sil had been following Moth's exchange with the sixtyman. "Waiting, Reverences, for you to grant my vision's authenticity so we can question this supposed trader. Because if Sartor did send me a vision, then we have to learn what we can from him at once."

"If it wasn't just a dream," the old Syrr said.

"It was a vision, Reverence."

"That decision is ours, not yours, to make, Tepes."

Moth would have to kill them all, and with them the Tepes's sons and anyone else who might have heard his warnings. As soon as he was alone with them somewhere where he could go into a trance without danger of being seen or surprised, where he could kill them without alerting the rest of the city. In a way the whole thing was a matter of total indifference to him: he cared nothing for their lives, and whatever he did they'd be dead before morning. But killing them would destroy any chances he might have had to betray the city without submitting himself to the Sword That Was King Asp, and his struggle with the King's spirit would drain him of even more of his dangerously diminished vitality, bring him that much closer to his own death.

Casnut could only be trying to force Moth to return to Kyborash for his dolthe as soon as Nanlasur fell, abandoning his search for Pyota and Tramu. Moth's aunt and cousin had been sent to the Nanlasur lead mines when Tas Et died, and Moth had vowed to rescue them if they were still alive. Now it seemed that Casnut was trying to make him break that vow.

Unless the shaman intended to use Moth's vow to force him to an ultimate effort. Casnut's mind was impenetrable, his actions complex and ambiguous. With him Moth could never be sure if what he saw and understood was the truth or merely something the old shaman wanted him to believe for reasons he kept concealed.

Tas Et, Moth demanded, can you find them for me? Tramu and Pyota, in the mines across the river?

They're here with me in the Great Square. I can see them looking up at me through the bars of their cage—

Enough! Moth told Tas Et. It was useless. His uncle's spirit was frozen in the moment of its death, unable to comprehend anything contradicting the reality he'd known at that instant. Tas Et could perceive and learn, but what he learned was only added to what he'd known and believed at the moment of his death, without modifying it in any way.

I can show you where my dolthe is buried, his Ri ghost said, surprising him.

And the blade? Is it still there, by the Necropolis?

The blade has worked its way deeper into the ground, seeking to return to the Earth Mother. It lies just below the Princess Daersa's chamber now.

He would have to force his way into the Necropolis, overcome its guardians, traverse the labyrinthine tangle of the Roads of the Dead, all of which opened into the tomb. It would be harder in the flesh than it would have been if he could have sent his spirit alone, but not impossible if his strength held out until then.

What about Tramu and Pyota? he asked the ghost.

I don't know. The Nanlasur mines are not closed to me by Sartor, like the Harg, but the Earth Mother has little strength there. I am a potter, pledged to Her, with little strength of my own. But I will try.

Moth suddenly realized that the others were staring at him in silence. "Reverences, by your leave—" he began. "The Nomads, they're really there, but only sixty of them—" He broke off. It was too late, hopeless: he'd been supposed to lure as many of Nanlasur's warriors as he could away from the city into ambush, but the more he said, the less chance he had of convincing anyone of anything but his own guilt.

"Come." Tepes Sek took him gently by the left arm. "You can tell us the rest of your story at the Siltemple." With the young warrior clutching his right arm, the Syrr Nanlasur-Sil leading and the sixtyman behind, Moth was led through the narrow, interlacing, urine-smelling streets to the Great Square. It was smaller than the Great Square of Kyborash, but equally packed with a confusion of animals, goods, stalls, and men and women of all stations—Warriors of the Hand and Voice; more redheaded smiths than he'd ever seen gathered together in any one place, even at his Tas initiation; scribes in gray siltunics; field slaves in gray kilts; entrail readers in gray splashed with crimson . . . confectioners, boatmen, brewers, chisel workers, each dressed in the colors appropriate to his rank.

And among them a solidly built man a few years older than Moth, in the scarlet siltunic of a master potter: Ri Yeshun. He and Moth had been friends in Kyborash, when Moth was still Ri . . . but when Moth had been forced to kill his Ri soul and had become Tas alone, Yeshun had hated him for his betrayal of his natal Sil, hated him all the more because it had always been Yeshun who'd defended Moth's desire to become a RiTas before the Ri Council.

Ri Yeshun was arguing with a potter whom Moth didn't recognize. He had only to look up to see Moth and recognize his distinctive hair and eyes despite the Sklar's green siltunic he was wearing: the Nomads would have thought it unmanly of Moth to hide behind dyed hair, and without a certain minimum respect, even from those who considered him their enemy, Moth would never have been able to survive among them. But the potters were absorbed in their argument, gesticulating with their staves, and Ri Yeshun never even noticed the way the crowd fell silent at the sight of Moth and his escort, how they scurried out of their path, leaving their goods to be reclaimed later, only resumed their interrupted conversations when the torturer and warriors were past.

The potters turned into one of the streets leading from the square, were lost to view.

It would have made no real difference if Ri Yeshun had recognized Moth. It would have made Moth's task harder still, but he had not come all this way, done what he'd done and risked what he'd risked, to abandon Tramu and Pyota now. If they were still alive, he'd find and free them.

If it took the last of his strength to do so, and left him dead or too weakened to survive Casnut's next attack.

Rafti had died because Moth had let her father see him during one of the fits he'd at that time suffered whenever Tas Et's spirit entered him. Died because the only way to stop the fits was to house the spirit in the copper dagger now hidden in the mountains, and because Moth had had to kill his Ri soul before he could become a weaponsmith capable of forging it. Died, finally, because he had been too cowardly to do what had to be done until it was already too late to save her.

Yet his potter's soul had at last killed itself: Moth had already died once. And when Sartor-ban-i-Tresh died, all, or almost all, in Moth that was warmth and kindness, caring and joy—everything but his will and pride, his anger, and his hunger for what he had lost—had died with the Ri. With him, too, had gone Moth's fear, his cowardice: he wouldn't abandon Tramu and Pyota to their deaths as he had once abandoned Rafti, not to protect the empty half person he'd become.

I'll help you, his ghost whispered. Not because of your vow, but because I love them. You loved them too before we were sundered.

Before you died, potter.

They were almost to the Siltemple, were passing the shrines in which the men and women of the lesser Sils were worshiping the Aspects of Sartor appropriate to their stations, as Moth had once worshiped Sartor's Ri and Tas Aspects. The Siltemple was smaller and less impressive than any other he'd seen, though Nanlasur was rich and one of Chal's first conquests. The godhouse of enameled blue bricks atop its seven-storied step pyramid was barely high enough to be visible over the Temple compound's walls; the sky-blue enamel was old and weathered, flaking, and even the compound's walls looked badly in need of repair. But there were no gaps through which an escaping prisoner could flee, and the seven Warriors of the Hand stationed in front of the gate looked both dangerous and alert.

At a gesture from the Syrr Nanlasur-Sil they drew aside, let Moth and his escorts enter.

Closed in again behind them.

Chapter Nineteen

In through the gate, up shadowed gray granite steps, past the doorkeeper—a young Warrior of the Voice, perhaps no more than thirty, standing with drawn sword in his tiny alcove—then out through an arch and into the sunlight again: the Siltemple's outer compound. The godhouse was clearly visible now over the low wall of unbaked clay bricks separating inner and outer compounds; chisel workers were carving a scene—either war or hunting, it was too early to tell which—in bas-relief into a stone plaque set into the clay-brick wall alongside all the similar plaques showing the Kings of Chal killing lions and enemies, leveling cities, accepting tribute from subject kings, rising from the dead at the culmination of the Seven-Year Festival, prostrating themselves before Sartor, whose husbandmen they were. . . .

One of the chisel workers looked up, saw Moth and the others, glanced quickly away.

Tepes Sek's chambers were in the far corner of the low mud-walled building running the length of the right wall. The Syrr Nanlasur-Sil accompanied them as far as the doorslit, then turned aside, unwilling to enter.

"Question him," he told Tepes Sek. "But gently,

until such time as we reach a decision or the warriors sent to verify his tale return.''

''Certainly, Reverence. Shall I send one of my sons to attend you while we await your ruling?''

''Do so.'' Then, to the young Warrior of the Hand, ''Stay here with them until we send for you.''

''Yes, Reverence.''

The old Syrr turned away and left, followed by the sixtyman. Tepes Sek drew aside the many-layered hangings of thick, coarsely woven black wool that blocked the doorslit, revealing steps leading down into the reeking semidarkness. He gestured and the young Warrior of the Hand pushed Moth ahead of him down into a windowless room lit only by the light from the doorslit, the brazier of coals glowing red in one corner.

The warrior waited, alert but obviously ill at ease, though he tried to conceal his nervousness, while Tepes Sek's two black-kilted assistants—his sons, obviously, the elder perhaps twelve while the younger couldn't have been more than nine—stripped Moth of his green wool siltunic and gray linen undertunic. Moth made no attempt to resist, neither when they stripped him nor when they bound his hands behind him with nettle-fiber ropes.

''Father,'' the younger boy cried, ''look at him! He's covered with scars!''

''He's been questioned before,'' the elder boy said, certain and proud of his certainty. ''Look at his back and the backs of his legs. You can see what they did.''

''Those are just scars,'' Moth said as the torturer examined him in silence. Not so much because he hoped to convince the Tepes as for the benefit of the listening warrior. ''From Kyborash, when the Nomads took the city. I was hurt trying to escape.''

''The Nomads did that to you?'' the warrior asked.

''No, I was caught in my father's house when it burned. They thought I was dead but I had to stay hidden there until they were gone.''

"You're lying," the Tepes said. He turned to his younger son. "Tell the Syrr Nanlasur-Sil that he's been questioned, and not by Nomads. By one of us."

"Yes, Father." The boy left with the warrior. On their way out the boy paused to fasten the wool hanging behind him, leaving the room illuminated by the coals in the brazier alone.

Tepes Sek muttered something to his other son that Moth couldn't quite make out. The boy nodded, put a slender rod of some base alloy at the edge of the coals to heat, pulled it back a little at a sharp word from his father, then began arranging a series of stone knives and metal, bone, and polished wood gaffs and hooks on a stone slab by the fire. The instruments for that gentle questioning that was all Tepes Sek had been granted permission to proceed with for the moment.

The boy looked eager, excited, anxious to prove himself to his father. As Moth himself must have once looked, when the only thing in the world he'd wanted had been to become a potter like his father.

His eyes were adjusting to the semidarkness. The chamber was larger than he'd expected from his experience with Lapp Wur, completely subterranean, damp despite the coals burning in the brazier. Probably part of the old native temple that here, as in Kyborash and all the other cities the Chaldans had conquered, must have been razed to make place for the conqueror's Siltemple. The smell of damp clay and ancient mold mingled with that of the sweat from generations of terrified men, the reeks of carrion and burned blood, urine and excrement, the smell of hot metal and the harsh, stinging smoke from the brazier.

The rod was almost ready. Much hotter and it would melt.

The Warrior of the Hand? Moth asked Tas Et.

Standing guard outside.

The hangings blocking the doorslit were meant to muffle sounds from within: Moth could do what he had to without fear that the warrior outside would hear him and interfere, at least not before the Tepes's other son returned.

What about the boy?

Still waiting to see the Syrr Nanlasur-Sil.

Good: the Syrr wouldn't have learned about the scars yet.

And the sixtyman? he asked.

With the Syrr Nanlasur-Sil.

There was a narrow doorslit in the far wall, almost invisible in the shadows. Probably leading to another subterranean chamber, where Tepes Sek and his family slept. Like the entranceway, it was blocked with many-layered hangings of thick, dark wool.

There's no one inside, Tas Et told Moth when he asked. No sign of a wife, or that anyone but he and his two sons lives there.

Is there a way through to the outside that Timor could use?

No. The chamber is sealed.

Which meant there was no way Timor could reach Moth without passing the guard stationed outside and alerting him at a moment when Moth would be totally vulnerable. So he'd have to do without the spirit-hawk's aid, bring the Sword That Was Asp, the dagger housing Tas Et, back from the mountains himself. But he had neither his costume nor his drum, no way to put on animal form himself, no way to do anything except summon Tua-Li and travel the ways beneath the earth despite the cost.

But only one of the ways beneath the earth led from the Chaldan Siltemples: the Roads of the Dead, which the Chaldan dead traveled to the realms their Sils taught them Sartor had prepared for them. And the potter had been sealed to the Ri Sil, had never had a chance to gain that immortality promised potters whose work found favor in Sartor's eyes before they died: if the ghost traveled the Roads of the Dead without Moth, it would be destroyed.

The chamber is not totally sealed, the potter said suddenly. There's a weak place in one wall where you could break through into another room, one that was once sacred to the Earth Mother. With luck you'd be safe there long enough at least to get the sword and dagger.

But there's no way out to the open air?

No.

It would be harder to gain the Roads of the Dead from a place once sacred to the Mother, but he'd be able to make use of Her influence to separate himself from his potter's ghost, leave the ghost behind in comparative safety. At least, if—

Tas Et?

I can hold Tepes Sek for you. Nothing more, at least not until you return with the dagger.

Will you help me then, potter? For Tramu and Pyota?

To protect yourself, yes, but nothing more.

Then keep watch on the guard outside. Tell me if he becomes suspicious or tries to enter. And tell me if the other boy or the sixtyman returns.

The boy is still waiting to see them.

Good.

"The rod . . . that's right," Tepes Sek was telling his elder son, the same detestable pride in his voice that Moth had heard in his own grandfather's just after Moth had finally become a weaponsmith by killing a slave who'd been given his name for the ceremony.

"I'll tell you what you want!" Moth said. "Please, anything, all you have to do is ask! You don't have to—"

They ignored him, or pretended to, but his show of fear had ensured that they'd use the rod and not try something else first.

Moth closed his eyes, found his hassa: the narrow ascending column of slow-dancing red flame in the channel running the length of his spine. He concentrated, felt it quicken, expand, grow to fill his entire body as he fed it all his hatred for what it had been to be a weaponsmith, for Sartor and Chal and the way Tas Gly had made false accusations against Moth to Kyborash's exorcist, Lapp Wur, and had sent his daughter to her death . . . his hatred for Casnut and the Royal Eunuchs, for Tepes Sek and his cruel, innocent sons . . .

For his crippled self, whom he hated most of all.

His hassa danced ever faster, flared through yellow-orange to blinding white.

He opened his eyes, squinted out at the room through the dazzle.

"Pick it up with the forceps," Tepes Sek was instructing his son. "Now, lash it into place in that cleft stick. Quickly, before it cools. That's right. Now—"

Moth closed his eyes again, lost himself almost instantaneously in his hassa's serpentine dance.

"Did he faint?" the boy asked, disappointed, from somewhere infinitely far away.

"No. He's just pretending—and even if he wasn't, it would be easy enough to bring him awake. Now, stroke his skin *there* with just the tip of the rod . . . not where that other scar is but a little below it, along the inside edge of that open wound in his leg, where he'll feel it the most. . . ."

The rod touched Moth's wound and the boy screamed. Moth could smell him burning.

It was a good smell, rich and fatty, but not enticing enough to make him open his eyes. The room was silent, there was nothing to keep him there. He drifted away, lost himself once again in his hassa's dance.

Chapter Twenty

Pull yourself free! the potter's ghost was screaming at Moth through the white-hot dazzle. Now, before you burn away what little life you have left!

Is someone coming? It was hard to think.

Not yet. But you have to act now, while you still can.

Moth reluctantly stilled his hassa, opened his eyes, blinked in the semidarkness. Beside him the boy was a charred and blackened half skeleton, its right arm and shoulder missing. On the other side of the skeleton Moth could just make out the boy's ghost lying stunned on the floor.

Bring him back awake, he told the potter's ghost.

Tepes Sek lay moaning in the corner, blood dripping from his mouth and his eyes bulging from his head: he was with Tas Et on the stake, suffering the smith's death agonies for him.

The fires that had killed the boy had consumed the ropes binding Moth as well. He got shakily to his feet, had to lean against the wall to keep from falling. His body felt twisted and stretched, frayed thin; the room was too cold, too damp. He was beginning to shiver. It would have been so much easier to stay lost in the hassa's dance, let it shelter him until his body died and he could go on to a new, painless rebirth elsewhere. . . .

He waited until what little strength was going to return to him came back, then staggered across the room and got one of the Tepes's chipped stone blades, held it to the torturer's throat.

The potter had awakened the boy, had him sitting up, was explaining to him that he was dead.

Boy!

The ghost heard Moth's mental shout, looked up from his charred skeleton just in time to see Moth saw the crude stone blade back and forth across Tepes Sek's neck and watch his father die.

You're both dead now, Moth told the boy. But if you obey me, you can save yourself further pain.

He dragged the corpse to the spot where he himself had been tied, propped it against the wall beside the boy's skeleton in such a way that someone glancing casually in from the outside and expecting to see Moth bound there might be fooled.

The boy was sitting huddled up now, arms wrapped tight around his skinny legs as he stared at his blackened skeleton, his father's blood-soaked corpse, his skeleton again, moaning softly to himself.

Release the Tepes, Moth commanded Tas Et, and the torturer's ghost was suddenly lying writhing and screaming there on the floor where Moth had slit his throat. The boy heard his father's screams, looked up and saw him, ran over to press up against him.

You're dead, Moth repeated for Tepes Sek's benefit. Both you and your son. I killed you both, but if you obey me, I can spare you further pain.

He gestured at the corpse propped up against the wall beside the boy's skeleton, giving the Tepes a chance to study it long enough to realize that it was really his, and that it was really dead. Tepes Sek stared at it in silence awhile, summoning up his courage, then pushed his son aside and stood, walked unsteadily over to it, and stared down at it a moment longer, finally tried to touch it.

He jumped back when his fingers sank without resistance through the still-warm flesh. Put his hand to his throat, felt the unbroken skin, stared in terror back at the empty body that had been his.

I can conduct both of you safely along the Roads of the Dead to the realm Sartor has prepared for you, Moth said. Or I can put you back on the stake with my uncle, to suffer his smith's curse for all eternity. The choice is yours.

Who are you? The ghost's voice was flat, toneless: Tepes Sek was still too stunned by the realization that he was dead for anything else to seem real or important yet.

The one you saw in your dream. It was a true sending, though you failed to understand it. Sartor was preparing you to meet your own death, not telling you to interfere with His plans for Nanlasur's destruction.

Tepes Sek nodded, accepting the explanation.

But you're a Nomad! his son said.

Does your Sil teach that Sartor created men to fight and kill each other, because He delights in the spectacle of their slaughter? Moth asked the father.

Tepes Sek nodded again.

Without enemies for Chal to fight there could be no war, no suffering to delight Sartor. So I too serve Sartor in my way. Do you understand now?

Tepes Sek said, You're not Tepes.

No. But the Roads of the Dead are the same for all Chaldans, and I was born in Chal. I cannot enter the Tepes Realm myself, but I can guide you to it and ensure that your son is granted a place there even though he died before completing his initiation into your mysteries. I can protect you from the Earth Mother.

What do you want from us?

I want you to protect my body while I take your son on the Roads of the Dead. Kill anyone who tries to enter. If when I return I find that you've obeyed me, I'll grant your second son a quick, merciful death and take you both to rejoin your first boy in the Tepes Realm. But if you disobey me, I'll let the Mother eat both boys' souls and leave you to suffer my uncle's death curse forever.

Why?

Because I need to travel the Roads of the Dead. As for the rest, remember your dream.

If I ask you to let my son live? To save him from the others?

Then I'll spare him. The choice is yours. Now, will you swear on the knife that took your life and by your name that you will obey me in this?

Yes.

Pick up the knife and swear.

After the ghost had done so Moth put his trader's clothing back on, walked over to the charred skeleton, and wrenched a cervical vertebra free despite the skeleton's chittering protest, put it in his belt pouch.

I have your son's soul. Remember your oath, he told Tepes Sek. Then, to the boy: Come with me.

He pushed the hanging separating the two rooms aside, realized that the room beyond the narrow doorslit was even colder, even moister, than the one he was in.

Wait for me a moment, he told the boy's ghost. Making his way painfully back across the room to the brazier, he took some coals from it in his left hand to light his way, fed them with memories until they glowed yellow-orange.

The boy's ghost shrank away from him. Moth glanced around the room one last time, but there was nothing more in it he could use. He motioned the boy to follow him.

The second room was long, low, damp, filled with rotting heaps of clothing, piled with carved staves, sandals, ornaments, all the other things the Tepes and his ancestors had taken from the men and women they'd questioned over the generations. There was a low, continuous scuttling sound: rats, perhaps, or some sort of huge insects moving through the heaps.

Have you ever questioned a shaman?

I don't know what a shaman is.

Like me.

No.

Do you have a drum here? The boy looked at him blankly. Did you ever take a drum from someone you questioned?

Not that I— No.

Moth picked up a staff tipped with a beautifully carved jackdaw's head, used it to poke through the piles and heaps in search of the things he needed. He found a bow and a quiver full of arrows, but invaluable though they could have been in the open air, they were useless underground. Finally he came across an unfamiliar, long-necked string instrument with three of its many strings still intact. A cithern of sorts, like those the sellers of songs in Kyborash had used to accompany themselves, but smaller and more finely fashioned.

He put the staff down, disengaged the instrument carefully from the trash in which he'd found it. A rat scurried away, took shelter in a nearby heap of rags. Moth waited until he was sure the rat was going to remain there, then examined the instrument more closely. Its body was still sound, though brittle-looking: a brightly painted dried gourd to which the long wooden neck had been attached with tiny bone pegs, all of them holding firm. The neck was slightly warped, but it was still strong enough to keep the remaining strings in place.

Moth put his coals on a clear part of the mud floor, ignoring the boy, who was watching him fearfully. He cautiously tightened a string, then plucked it, getting a dull, flat, totally unmusical sound in response. He tried the other two strings with identical results. But it was good enough for his needs, more than good enough. He'd been lucky.

He put the cithern down again, picked up his staff. Kicked apart the pile of rags in which the rat had taken refuge, stunned it with a swift blow with the staff.

He had everything he needed.

Potter? he asked.

To your right, behind that heap . . . Yes, there. You see those worn bricks, just above the angle where the wall meets the floor? You should be able to knock a hole through them.

Moth took the jackdaw-headed staff, rammed it underhanded into the wall. The staff went right through, and before he realized what was happening, he found himself falling forward, unable to stop his motion in time.

The bricks had never been anything but sun-dried mud and straw, had been disintegrating in the moist underground darkness for generations. It took Moth only a moment's work with staff and hands after he'd recovered to make the hole large enough to crawl through.

He paused again to catch his breath, picked up the coals. Their warmth felt good in his hand but they were growing dim. He fed them memories of the Royal Eunuch, who'd once pretended to save him from the Nomads until the coals flared bright again with his hatred.

The floor beyond the wall was lower than the one on which he was standing, but not enough to make any real difference. He pushed the staff through, tossed the unconscious rat after it, took the cithern in one hand and the coals in the other, and went through the hole himself.

The air on the other side was as cold as in the room he'd just left and far staler, yet not as damp: it seemed somehow cleaner, as though Moth had passed directly from a rotting midden into one of the ways beneath the earth.

The boy was hanging back, afraid. Moth gestured to him, waited till the ghost had climbed reluctantly after him through the hole, then reached back through it with his staff and snagged some rags from a nearby heap, pulled them close enough to conceal the hole.

He held his coals high to examine the chamber he found himself in.

There was a headless image of the Earth Mother in the center: thick-bodied, with huge breasts and buttocks, made of some shiny black stone. At first he thought the statue was mutilated, its head probably knocked off by the Chaldan conquerors when they'd taken the city and razed the old temple, but a closer look told him it had been sculpted headless.

There was a shallow, oval-shaped depression between the massive, rounded shoulders where the head and neck should have been. Moth walked slowly up to the image, almost stunned by the calm power emanating from it. The boy was huddling back in the far corner of the chamber, as far from the image as possible. Perhaps the Chaldans had been too terrified of it to damage it. Moth examined the dark stone an instant longer, letting himself feel the power washing through him before deciding, then abruptly fed the coals one last time with his memories and his hatred, put them in the oval depression. They flickered twice, then flared turquoise, burning brighter by far than they ever had in his hand. The room grew warmer.

Moth relaxed. He'd done the right thing. The Mother was still here, and the Aspect of Her multiple and paradoxical being that the unknown Nanlasurian sculptor had captured for his people to worship was positive, life-enhancing, to be respected but not overly feared.

The potter would be safe from Sartor here.

Moth glanced back at the boy, still cringing in terror in his far corner, said, Come here.

The boy stayed where he was.

If you obey me, I can keep you safe. But only if you obey me. Now, come here and sit down next to me.

The boy came cautiously forward, finally sat down a little behind Moth.

No. Here, beside me.

The boy moved closer. From the hem of his siltunic

Moth took a sliver of the secret copper Chaldan weaponsmiths made from the marriage of ordinary copper and bridesmetal, then a curling horse's hair, a scrap of painted horsehide from the skin of his drum, finally a tiny sliver of wood he'd shaved from the drum's body, which was thus a sliver of the Cosmic Tree itself. With the copper fragment he cut his finger, then smeared the blood on the inside edge of the hollow-gourd body, stuck the metal, wood, hair, and horsehide scraps there.

While the blood was drying, he took from his pouch the dead Tepes's son's cervical vertebra, put it on the floor in a bridesmetal ring he assembled from sections hidden in his undertunic.

He was ready.

Taking a cross-legged position despite the way it hurt his wounded leg, he told the boy to imitate him.

As long as you remain where you are and say nothing you'll be safe, Moth told him when he was sitting correctly. No matter what you think you see happening to me, no harm can come to you unless you try to flee or interfere, or unless you speak. Do you understand?

In a frightened voice the boy said, Yes, but—

Then stay silent.

Moth took the cithern in his lap, closed his eyes, let the warmth the coals had not produced but only unleashed wash through him and soothe his weariness, the pain in his leg. Even with his eyes closed he could feel the boy watching.

As long as you do nothing you'll be safe, he repeated a final time, then let his breathing settle into a slow steady rhythm while his hands explored the cithern.

Finally, he plucked the first, cautious note from it. Far away, in the mountains where he'd hidden it, he heard his drum sound in resonance with the plucked string.

And in the burning yellow mud that was the bed of the Earth Mother's Inner Ocean, his gleaming coils of silver and ice wrapped tight around the Cosmic Tree's sunken roots, Tua-Li, the World-Eel, heard the drum's challenge as well.

Chapter Twenty-one

Even as he sensed the spirit of his drum approaching, felt it resonating louder in every colorless note he plucked from the ancient brittle cithern in his lap, Moth could hear the wet scraping that was Tua-Li all around him. The World-Eel was everywhere, inescapable, its great cold silver coils sliding over and over one another in the rock beneath his feet; he could sense the ground trembling nervously as, far below, the stone parted, then closed again behind the eel.

He felt the chill that meant that Tua-Li was almost upon him, opened his eyes, saw the eel thrust itself dull red and silver from the ground ahead of him: a great blind, questing, somehow horselike head on the end of a long serpentine neck, its grinning jaws lined with row upon row of gleaming triangular silver teeth. Moth chanted a single taunting word of power in the secret language Casnut and Sulthar had taught him as he plucked the final note from the cithern—

And the World-Eel, maddened, struck.

Moth kept chanting, kept the maddened eel from leaving him with his dismemberment uncompleted to return to its burrow in the mud beneath the Cosmic Tree's tangled roots. Tua-Li struck again and again, side-slashing the flesh from Moth's bones, ripping open the bony box of his skull, and spilling the wet brains from it, severing every tendon, slashing each and every bone free from all the others. As the eel ripped, sliced him apart, Moth used the pain to wrench himself free of his dying flesh . . . used it to retreat from skin, eyes, brain, muscles, from all his mortal organs, everything that would have left him vulnerable to Sartor. He took refuge in the immortal bone: in his second self.

When all that remained of Moth's former body was a pile of disjointed bones and a shapeless mass of already putrefying tissues heaped around his shadow-self (that false semblance that still sat, seemingly unharmed, plucking the cithern on the floor before the Mother's image), the World-Eel, blind to everything but the living flesh it had hated, which Moth's chant had forced it to destroy, forgot Moth, forgot its rage and the impulse that had brought it there, and returned to the Mother's Inner Ocean.

As soon as the eel disappeared Moth began to sing again: a clean, hard song in the secret language, burning air lashed to motion by his unbounded hassa, whistling over and through bare bone, without need of wet vibrating membranes or passages slimed with mucus or flabby lungs. Without need of his mortal flesh, though his shadow-self echoed his song as best it could. He chanted the names of power for every bone, for the copper sliver he'd attached to the cithern. Chanting, he took the substance of everything he named and made it part of his song, subject to his singing: his to use and control as he willed.

He fitted the disjointed bones together, bound them tightly to one another with filaments of copper wire. He made himself a new skeleton and named it, giving it life.

Calling Tas Et to him, he chanted the smith's spirit into a new body that he created from blood and metal, earth and fire, the cithern's monotonous music and the remembered pain of his dismemberment. All twisted fine metal filaments, slivers of bone, pain and music, coursing through fiery channels like blood through tiny throbbing veins . . . all hidden and contained within the dry bone, sheltered by it as its marrow had once been sheltered, as a beetle's soft inner parts are sheltered by its horny carapace: a body with which Moth could use the ways beneath the earth, with which he could travel the Roads of the Dead and emerge again to life.

A body over which Sartor had no dominion.

To this body, too, he gave a name in the secret language, and with that name, life.

He stood then, holding the cithern, leaving the illusion of his former self still plucking the cithern's outward semblance there before the Earth Mother's headless black image. He felt weightless, quick, volatile, yet infinitely strong, without weakness or vulnerability: another illusion, and one that he knew had killed many would-be shamans. Even the illusion of himself remaining seated on the floor was vulnerable, for all that it was a false-semblance only: any damage done it would find its way to the real Moth when the time came to use the illusion as the pattern for the re-creation of his mortal body, and the loss of the blood that was now beginning to force its way through the unbroken skin of his illusory self's forehead as well as through the cloths binding its wounded leg would weaken him dangerously on his return.

He remembered the boy, glanced over at him, saw him sitting with fists clenched and eyes squeezed shut.

It's all right now, Moth told him. The danger's over. You can open your eyes and move around again.

He could sense the spirit of his drum waiting impatiently for him to call it to him. In his hands he held the true cithern; he put it down in front of him, touched a string, pulled a note from it as he spoke the drum-spirit's secret name.

There was light in the distance, a pale flickering visible through the moist clay walls, red like a candle's flame seen glowing through the flesh of a cupped hand, but dimmer, less certain. It was coming closer.

Moth plucked the cithern again, repeated the drum-spirit's secret name.

They could hear the hammering of its many hooves. The boy opened his eyes, saw the skeletal form housing Moth's inner body, tried to retreat. Moth caught him by the arm.

It's all right, he said. The boy was trying to pull away. You're dead, Moth told him. Dead.

The boy slumped, remembering. Moth released his arm. Together they stared at the crumbling wall through which they could see the light of the spirit's coming.

Then it was there, in front of them.

A horse, or what had once been a horse. Dead staring eye sockets burning an unclean red, blunt teeth grinning through rotted lips. The flesh, puffy and swollen, slimed with mud and algae. Jagged wounds in the belly and sides, through which they could see fat green eels wriggling through its flesh, feeding on it.

It stank of the same sweet rot that had been eating Moth from within for so long, the approaching death he'd been tasting ever since Casnut had taken control of his life away from him.

The spirit came to Moth, entered the cithern, and the instrument changed, grew until it was a long slender eight-legged boat: rent and split horsehide stretched over a framework of articulated bones, with for the boat's prow the drum-spirit's horse's head on an arched and open neck, through which its vertebrae gleamed a damp, clammy white.

Potter?

I'll remain here until you return.

The potter's ghost left Moth: a dead boy six years younger than the shaman, every part of his head and body save only his face covered with small, dry, triple-lipped wounds. The ghost merged with Moth's seated illusory self.

The boy had been staring at the spirit-boat and the potter's ghost with mingled amazement and horror. Moth realized that the boy had been too confused when the potter's ghost had comforted him just after his death to realize that Moth and the ghost were different aspects of the same person.

Moth stroked the horse's neck, thanked the spirit for having responded to his summons, apologized to it for the state of the cithern with which it had had to fuse itself, then helped the stunned boy into his place in the back of the boat. Moth sat down in front, with the unconscious rat firmly held in his left hand, picked up the intricately carved bone baton lying on his seat, and touched it lightly to one of the exposed vertebra in the back of the horse's neck.

The boat began to run, circling faster and faster through the chamber, its walls, the Tepes's rooms and the buried ruins of the old temple . . . moving in an ever-widening spiral with the boy's cervical vertebra in its bridesmetal ring at the center, the boat's eight copper-shod hooves beating out an ever faster, ever more complex rhythm.

Moth chanted another word, one Sulthar had taught him, though his uncle had never made use of its power for himself. The young Tepes's vertebra in its circle of dull white metal was suddenly a jagged mountain of midnight blue lapis beneath a sky that had become a dome of gleaming white bridesmetal: the mountain through which they would have to pass to reach the Roads of the Dead.

A flick of Moth's baton, another word, and the eight-legged boat was racing up the mountain's almost vertical side. Then they had reached the top, and the mountain was a hollow cone beneath them, thick smoke rising from it like a great gnarled gray-green tree whose branches upheld the sky's gleaming dome, and they were out over the volcanic fires pulsing scarlet, yellow-orange beneath them—

The boy bit back a scream of terror and bewilderment, held himself rigidly erect as the boat shot down into the flames, through the magma and the burning into cold, cosmic laughter, into a sea of hate-filled faces, the faces of every man and woman Moth had ever betrayed, killed, or harmed . . . For an instant they found themselves soaring over what had once been the Great Square of Kyborash, the spirit-boat gliding on black leathery wings over the pyramid of ten thousand bleaching skulls the Nomads had left piled there when they took the city for the Taryaa . . . Then, before they could reach the city's outskirts and the Necropolis beneath the hills in which Moth's betrothed bride had been buried alive, that Great Square became another, and another, all these now cities that Moth himself had betrayed to the Nomads as he was even now attempting to betray Nanlasur to them, each city with its pyramid or pyramids of severed heads, bleaching skulls . . . For an instant Moth found himself staring into the eyes of a barely adolescent Sklar's son who'd come running to him begging for pity and shelter until a Nomad on horseback killed him with a spear . . . Then the fires were all around them again, licking hungrily at Moth's naked bones, though boy and boat passed through them unharmed. Moth had to use a word of binding to keep the flames from him, and the shock of its utterance sent him hurtling back to the shadow-self beneath the Nanlasur Siltemple, trapped him there as the shadow went into a violent coughing fit, began hacking up black blood. . . . He wrenched himself free, was back in the spirit-boat as it slid at last from the flames into a world of sweltering twilight, through clouds of swirling gray dust so thick Moth could barely perceive the river Nacre's noisome waters beneath the boat. In Ashlu, the Nacre was born in Lake Nal and flowed through Chal on its way to the Sea of Marshes; here it was fed only by the eternal tears of Sartor's dismembered mother, Neetir, and rivulets of Her blood coursed through it like great sluggish red worms on their way to the ocean.

Moth never knew when the Nacre had widened out to lose

itself in the bloody sea, only that the currents seething and twisting around them were growing ever more violent, until the spirit-boat was caught, yanked from its course, and hurled at the immense lapis lazuli Palace that was suddenly visible, rising stark and sheer from the writhing waters.

The Palace was as big as all Chal. It had eighty-four gates of gleaming black obsidian, like the gaping jaws of crouching beasts, set into its outer walls, each gate guarded by a dead Warrior of the Voice with faceted silver mirrors for eyes.

Above the Palace, like clouds of bruised purple shadow half veiled by the swirling dust, hung Sartor's Eighty-four Aspects. In every countenance gleamed the cold glaring stars that were His Nighteyes, each star the frozen soul of a dead sorcerer or Royal Eunuch.

As the spirit-boat neared, the Palace began to spin, languidly at first, then ever faster, the eighty-four black gates blurring into one another. Moth aimed the boat at the center of the spinning blue-black blur, ran the tip of his bone baton down the exposed vertebrae of the horse's neck on the boat's prow. The boat accelerated, its eight legs whipping frenziedly at the churning sea, pulling them from the currents' grasp and sending them hurtling directly at the Palace.

The boy cowered on the floor of the boat, covering his eyes.

Your truename! Moth demanded.

The boy tried opening his eyes, saw the spinning Palace rushing at them, screamed.

Your name! Moth yelled, slashing him across the cheek with the tip of the bone baton to get his attention. Tell me your truename!

Sartor-ban-i-Taur, the boy whispered, unable to tear his gaze from the Palace.

Moth spun to face the Palace, yelled the boy's truename at it as it filled the sky before them—

The Palace stood motionless. They were arrowing in through the jagged-toothed arch of one of the black gates, directly at the dead Warrior of the Voice who stood suspended on nothingness in their path, blocking the way with his great copper sword drawn and shining in the netherworld's burning twilight.

As they neared, the dead warrior brought his blade up. But even as he struck, Moth grabbed the unconscious rat and with a movement too fast for the boy to follow hurled it at the descending sword.

The blade sliced through the rat, splattered spirit-boat and dead warrior alike with the animal's sacrificial blood. The warrior froze motionless, his sword halted in mid-swing. He drew back, and the spirit-boat glided safely past him into the Palace and Sartor's Eighty-four Realms.

Chapter Twenty-two

As the boat slipped through the gateway into the Palace's interior, Moth had a confused glimpse of a tangled labyrinth of lapis lazuli corridors coiling and twisting around and through one another like entrails in starlit darkness.

Moth shouted, Sartor-ban-i-Taur! again. Everything came to a shuddering halt, reoriented itself around them.

The coiling corridors were gone. The spirit-boat was running with desperate speed through a jagged wilderness of splintered and fragmented bone, monstrous decomposing organs: all that remained of Neetir's dismembered body.

Tepes fled naked and wailing across knife-edged bone, burrowed like terrified grubs into the putrefying flesh, throwing themselves into the pools of hot lymph, anything to escape the terrible Face glaring down at them from the black cloud looming overhead.

The boy stared around him in incredulous horror as he realized the true meaning of the fate Sartor had reserved for the Tepes Sil. He shrank down in the boat, trying to clutch to its sides, hide from the Face, but unseen hands plucked him from the boat, and even as he screamed to Moth to help him, save him, he was fading, the whole Tepes Realm was fading until all that remained of it was the reek of Neetir's eternal decomposition, then even that was gone and Moth was alone in his spirit-boat in a world of swirling gray dust.

Moth was not an initiate of the Tepes Mysteries, had not known what kind of realm awaited the boy. Yet his fate seemed little worse than what he had been eager to help his father do to Moth, little worse, even, than much of what Moth himself had had to endure to become a shaman. If Sartor truly delighted in mankind's suffering, then perhaps the pain endured in the Tepes Realm would buy the boy rebirth as a warrior.

Perhaps, but Moth knew he would never fulfill his promise to Tepes Sek's ghost. Let the potter guide them to the Mother, where they would have to accept whatever destiny She chose for them. Not because Moth pitied them, but in memory of his grandfather Tas No, now suffering whatever fate Sartor had chosen for him in the Weaponsmith's Realm.

Sartor's Palace, the river Nacre, were gone. There was nothing but the dust, eternal, directionless, without gates back to the world of the living. The dust swirled through Moth's naked bones, coated them with gray. Moth could no longer sense his shadow-self bleeding in the chamber beneath the Nanlasur Siltemple; he was beginning to fade, lose himself in the dust's dry lifelessness.

Timor! he called, chanting the spirit-hawk's secret names, trying to call him, but the dust drank his words, stilled his chant.

He was fading.

Moth tried to summon remembered anger, make a fire of his hatred with which to burn himself free, but the dust drank his rage, as it had drunk his chant, leaving his soul parched and arid, empty.

Fading. He was too weak to free himself of the netherworld.

He needed his drum. If he had his drum, he could summon Timor, get the spirit-hawk to lift him free. But there was only the spirit-boat, drum-spirit melded to the ancient, cracked cithern, his last anchor to the world of the living.

He had no choice. Return to the Midworld, search out Timor, bring him back to me, he instructed the drum-spirit, beating out his orders on the exposed vertebrae of the horse's neck with his bone baton.

He sensed the spirit's assent, then the boat was gone, the image of a rotting horse with dead staring eye sockets burning red faded, and he was left alone with the ancient cithern in the hand that had been clutching the bone baton.

He tried to pluck a note from the cithern, summon strength to maintain himself, keep himself from fading. The cithern crumbled in his hands, was lost in the dust.

There was nothing but the waiting. He withdrew into his second self, curled tight like a skeletal fetus, trying to keep himself from feeling the dust drifting ever deeper over his exposed surfaces, collecting in the hollows within his open skull.

Then at last Timor was there before him: a great black hawk with eyes of furious gold, the beating of his powerful wings driving back the dust.

Moth tried to speak, force the words to whistle through the dust-caked bones, the clogged cavities of his skull.

Timor . . . I can't go on. Tell Casnut I don't have enough strength. . . . He has to heal me or send Sulthar back to me. . . .

You'll have to find your healing without his help if you're to be worthy of him. There was no pity in Timor's harsh voice.

Take me back. Back to the Midworld and my drum.

Do you swear the pact, service for service, a life for your life?

He had no choice: I swear—but only on the condition that the life I pledge you is neither Tramu's nor Pyota's.

Your condition is accepted.

Timor grasped Moth's skeletal form in his talons and began to climb, spiraling ever higher through what without

Timor had been only directionless immensity, colorless swirling. As they climbed, the dust solidified around them, became rock, the granite bones of the earth, until suddenly, with a mighty beat of his great wings, Timor carried them up and out of a vent in the floor of an extinct volcano and into the world of the living.

It was night. The cold outer air scoured the dust from Moth's exposed bones, washed the inside of his skull clean again. They climbed, the earth receding beneath them, and Moth began to feel a hint of strength growing in him: they were approaching the heavens he was unable to reach on his own, beyond which his truename—his third soul—and healing awaited him.

But Timor only circled there, in the chill upper air, then dived again, took Moth back down to the mountains where his horses were tethered, where he had hidden his costume and drum, the dagger housing Tas Et, and the Sword That Was King Asp.

The spirit-hawk dumped Moth contemptuously there, soared away without looking back.

Moth crawled to his cache, levered the rocks hiding it aside, pulled out his cap and put it on, pushed the red-copper circlet with the copper moth down over the bare bone of his forehead. He had barely enough strength to master the spirits of the cap and circlet despite the allegiance they'd sworn him. But when at last they admitted his dominion again, he was able to draw on their strength to master the other spirits of his costume. Dressing himself in it, he dressed himself in the spirits' power.

He carefully unwrapped his drum, caressed and soothed it, apologized for the hard use he was about to make of it. He sang to it until he was ready.

Now he could feel his shadow-self again, still bleeding though no longer coughing blood. He started drumming, and the shadow's eyes rolled back in its head so that only their whites showed. The few drops of blood that had been forcing their way through the skin of its forehead became a steady trickle.

Still grasping the drum in his skeletal fingers and beating out ever more complex rhythms, Moth began to dance.

He drew strength from the drum-spirit, from the Cosmic Tree, from which the wood for the drum had been cut. Used that strength to clothe his hands in protective flesh.

Taking the sheathed Sword That Was King Asp, he wrapped it in alternating layers of red and black silk before the dead King's malignant spirit could overcome the spirit-drum's protection and force Moth to conquer or submit to it again.

He put the sword aside, began to dance again. His tethered horses neighed with anxiety and anticipation. The roan he had chosen began to steam, mist rolling from it to enshroud Moth.

The mist condensed, congealed around the drum. Became an eight-legged horse with the head of a blank-eyed staring gull, an oval depression in its back where Moth could sit cross-legged.

Before the mist could entirely dissipate, Moth had plucked an ivory staff from it. Sitting in the hollow in his mount's back, the dagger holding Tas Et's spirit in his waistband, the Sword That Was King Asp resting uneasily in his lap, where he steadied it with his left hand while with his right he used the long ivory staff to guide his mount, Moth made his way quickly down through the skin of the world into the Mother's Inner Ocean.

He passed beneath the Nomad forces in position for the attack on Nanlasur, sensed Ravnal waiting hidden behind a hill. For a moment Moth forgot himself, let himself feel his hatred for the Nomad raid-leader. The Sword struck at Moth through his hatred, entered it and twisted it against him, until he forced himself back to dispassionate coldness, hid his hatred in the depths of his spirit where the Sword was unable to reach it and use it to attack him.

The lead mines were just beyond the city, on the other

side of the river. Even weakened as he was, he could have reached them in instants, found out whether Tramu and Pyota were still there, still living, but the shadow's pull was too strong and he could fight it no longer.

He emerged from the Mother's Inner Ocean into the chamber beneath the Nanlasur Siltemple, where his shadow-self and the suffering it had endured in his place awaited him.

Chapter Twenty-three

The coals still burned with unnatural brightness in the hollow between the Mother's rounded stone shoulders. In their light Moth could see his illusory self plucking monotonous notes from the cithern. The figure was drenched with blood: bright blood still welling from its forehead to trickle down across the closed eyelids and congeal in its beard; slow, thick blood draining from its leg wound; the dark gouts of blood that had been coughed up when Moth's spirit-boat traversed the barrier of flames separating the lands of the living from the realms of the dead now drying on the trader's green siltunic.

The illusion pulled at him, demanded he reintegrate it. He tried to resist, sensing the torturer's ghost struggling with the warrior who'd been standing guard outside the doorslit while a milling crowd of Warriors of the Hand and Voice looked on in horror and confusion. He would have been able to confront them better in his present form, but his false-semblance's need for reintegration was too powerful, and Moth had no choice but to merge with it.

He bit back a scream as the pain hit him, walled it off as best he could. Found himself sitting cross-legged on the cold floor, wearing his shaman's costume and holding his drum, the silk-wrapped Sword That Was King Asp vibrating angrily on his lap.

The shaman's costume was stiff with the blood that had covered his trader's siltunic, the cithern was gone.

Potter? he asked, wiping blood from his eyes with a trembling hand even as the potter's ghost relayed him an angry shout from the courtyard outside, showed him the other warriors pushing their way past the single warrior whom the Tepes had managed to immobilize.

It took them an instant to take in the torturer's corpse with its slit throat, the charred skeleton of what had once been the man's son, then the eldest Warrior of the Voice had ordered the others on to search the chamber in which the Tepes and his sons had lived amid their heaps of rotting treasures.

Another few instants and they'd discover the hole in the wall and the chamber beyond.

Hold them back as long as you can, Moth commanded Tas Et, and a man about to brush aside the heaped rags concealing Moth's hiding place suddenly screamed to find himself writhing impaled in Kyborash's Great Square. The smith's spirit abandoned his first victim, took another warrior, left him in turn for a third, a fourth . . . terrifying and confusing them, giving Moth the time he needed.

Moth tapped out a quick rhythm on his drum, felt strength answer his summons. He stood, attached the drum to his waistband with a practiced motion. Swayed there a moment, the spirits of his costume helping him maintain himself upright as he caught his breath, tried to clear his head.

He could delay no longer. Unwrapping the Sword That Was King Asp, he pulled it from its sheath and gripped it tightly in both hands. Fought the spirit's cold malignant eagerness, remembering how handsome and heroic King Asp had seemed to the potter's son he'd been when the King had broken the sword during the Seven-Year Festival and died, how King Tvil had impaled Tas Et for having allowed the sword sheltering his father's life to be stolen before it could be reforged.

Tepes Sek, Moth sent. Find your remaining son and hide him. Watch over him and keep him safe until I summon you.

He sensed the ghost's assent. There was nothing more to be done.

Moth put on King Asp's spirit and made it his own.

The pain was gone. There was only Asp.

Moth was too weak to resist. He was lost in Asp's need, Sartor's hunger.

When he regained consciousness of himself it was dawn and he was striding through Nanlasur's Great Square, the sword throbbing in his hands, people fleeing screaming from him.

Behind him a trail of bloodless corpses, the hacked and mutilated bodies of warriors, women, children, slaves, and animals mingled indiscriminately together.

An herb-seller reluctant to abandon the wares he'd been setting out lingered too long before fleeing, stumbled as he tried to make up for his delay with a desperate spring.

Asp was on the man in an instant, the great blade splitting him from head to groin. The sword thrummed with satisfaction as the dead king whose spirit Moth wore stepped over the pale, bloodless, still-quivering fragments of the herb-seller's body in search of further slaughter with which to delight its master.

Asp had been King of Chal, Sartor's husbandman. He had made war, conquered cities, razed temples in Sartor's name, faithfully providing his god with the slaughter for which Sartor hungered, in which He delighted. But Asp was only a spirit now, no longer King, unable to make war and denied the Royal Realm that should have been his reward for a lifetime of faithful servitude. All that remained to him was the bloodlust, the sacred delight in slaughter that he had learned to share with his god, and that he had made his own.

The gates, Moth whispered, tempting his former King with memories of the thousands upon thousands of men, women, and children slaughtered in the other cities Moth had betrayed.

Open the gates and let them in.

Moth's body hesitated, took a final stride toward a clot of terrified merchants huddled up against a wall, then turned toward the gate.

High overhead, black against the red of the rising sun, Moth glimpsed a circling speck: Timor, watching him for Casnut.

Are they in position? he asked the spirit-hawk.

They're waiting concealed near the gate.

Tell them to be ready.

The hawk swooped, clearly visible for an instant before it vanished over the wall, almost clipping one of the archers standing on the walkway over the narrow gate passage as it went.

The archer to the man's right turned to say something to him, suddenly saw Moth, and yelled a warning to the others. Bleeding, staggering, dressed as a Nomad shaman, and wielding the great copper sword, he was as effective a distraction as Ravnal and the others could ever have hoped for.

The archers nocked, shot before Moth could order Tas Et into them. Asp made no attempt to avoid the arrows. One struck Moth's body in the left side and he staggered. Moth readied himself to try to wrest control of his wounded body back from the dead King, but Asp ignored the pain, left the arrow protruding from Moth's flesh without even attempting to pluck it free as he continued inexorably on toward the gate. By now Tas Et had taken care of the archers, leaping from man to man, possessing each in turn just long enough to let him taste the smith's eternal frozen moment, panicking them as he had panicked the warriors in the Tepes's chambers.

One of the gate guards, a burly Warrior of the Hand,

fled. His companion, a scarred and stooped Warrior of the Voice, tried to stand his ground, but Asp killed him as easily as he'd killed the herb-seller.

Open the gates, Moth whispered, feeding Asp more memories of the tens of thousands massacred in the cities Moth had betrayed, tempting the dead King away from the pursuit of the fleeing gate guard with images of bright slaughter to come.

He had no strength left to command the spirit, could only buy its cooperation with promised bloodshed and hope for an instant when he could wrest his body away from it again. But at last Asp turned from his single-minded slaughter to yank on the thick ropes that opened the counterweighted inner and outer gates.

The Nomads came pouring through, whipping their horses on, screaming their triumph, with Ravnal and Tjei low on their horses in the lead.

Moth felt Asp tense, readying himself for slaughter, and frantically tried to wrest control away from him—only to see Timor diving at him, into him, grasping his spirit in its cruel beak and twisting it half free of his body, leaving Asp in total control for the instant.

As Ravnal galloped past, Asp struck.

A life for your life, Timor reminded him as he loosed his grip on Moth's spirit and let it regain his body. The pact you swore with me.

Chapter Twenty-four

Ravnal had no time to cry out or try to defend himself. The only sign that he knew what was happening to him was a widening of his eyes as the dead King's great copper blade swept out to cut through his leather armor, his ribs and spine, with a single clean backhanded stroke.

And in that timeless instant when the sword drank Ravnal's life, Asp's hatred for all life and Moth's hatred for Ravnal merged and were one. That single instant of union was all Moth needed. He wrenched control of his body away from Asp, forced the dead King back into the sword.

Ravnal's bloodless corpse came apart, head and shoulders falling to one side, legs and torso continuing on with his horse an instant longer before slipping off in turn. Yet luck was with Moth: Tjei was still bent low over his horse, urging it on, unaware that Ravnal was no longer behind him. The warrior following Ravnal, the only other Nomad who could have seen what had happened, died an instant later with a Nanlasurian arrow through the eye, while the warriors following *him* were too busy dealing with a charging mob of hastily assembled Nanlasurian defenders to worry about the fact that they'd lost their raid-leader from sight. They saw, had seen, only the shaman who had opened the city to them, standing swaying with drawn sword in his hands and a Nanlasurian arrow in his side.

Ravnal's panicked horse redoubled its speed and passed Tjei, who only then realized that something must have happened to his brother. He glanced back over his shoulder, but Ravnal's body was too far behind, already lost beneath the invaders' oncoming horses. Tjei's gaze met Moth's for an instant—but even if Tjei had been sure that his brother had been killed, and that Moth had been responsible, it would have been impossible for the young Nomad to fight his way back to Moth, equally impossible for him to pick Moth off with an arrow without taking the chance of killing a fellow Teichi instead.

Tjei turned away, whipped his horse on, vanished yelling down a narrow side street, heading for one of the lesser gates. But Moth knew that when Tjei had opened it to his fellow Teichi he would return to this first gate, find his brother's bloodless corpse, and accuse Moth of Ravnal's murder.

Unless Tjei died in the attack. Then perhaps no one would ever make the connection between the missing raid-leader and the bloodless corpse trampled almost beyond recognition just inside the main gates—

A shadow touched Moth's face. He looked up, saw Timor circling low overhead, knew with sick certainty that Casnut meant for Tjei to live to accuse him.

The Teichi had always opposed Casnut's plans when the tribes met in council, and Ravnal had been their spokesman. Now that he was dead, Casnut would have the respite he needed, but the Teichi and their allies would swear vengeance on Moth for the raid-leader's death. And that too, Moth realized, was vital to Casnut's plans: Moth had once again been manipulated so as to leave him no choice but to make the Great Shaman's cause his cause, Casnut's enemies his enemies, his very survival dependent upon the success of Casnut's plans.

Casnut claimed to be free, unpredictable, accountable to

no one. Claimed that it was his free choice to aid the Earth Mother against the Taryaa and the frozen stasis, the end to all change and growth, that the fulfillment of their plans would inevitably bring. He had told Moth that Moth, too, was free to choose, to act or refrain from acting as he so willed. But until now the situations with which Casnut had confronted Moth had always reduced to two simple choices: do what Casnut wanted or be killed for his failure.

He staggered back against the wall, let the cool sun-dried brick support him as he thrust the Sword That Was Asp into the packed earth and took his hands from it: he could grab it if he had to defend himself, but wouldn't have to waste his remaining strength fighting the dead King's spirit if he wasn't attacked.

Tas Et. Watch over me. Protect me.

He braced himself against the rough brick, reached across his body, grasped the arrow. Tried to wall off his pain, his weakness, everything but the need to yank the arrow from his side.

Nomads were still galloping through the gate in an unending stream, yelling and brandishing their short, reinforced bows, arrows nocked and ready. A horde thousands strong, nothing like the pitiful expeditionary force he'd warned the Nanlasurians against. The Nanlasurian warriors charged them again and again, suicidal attempts to take the gate back, only to be killed and trampled underfoot as the horde kept on coming, sweeping over them into the city.

The triple barbs were hooked into his flesh. He would have to cut the arrowhead out, or push the arrow the rest of the way through and out of his side.

He summoned what strength the spirits of his cap and costume had to lend him, braced himself. Shoved the head the rest of the way through, snapped the tough reed shaft, and pulled what remained of the arrow free.

His drum was hanging from his waistband, just below his wounded side. He stroked its head, tapping out a gentle rhythm. The drum was still part of the Cosmic Tree, which grew through the heavens to his truename and healing; it soothed his pain, helped him bear it.

Ripping a strip of cloth from his costume, he apologized to the spirits as he used it to wrap his wounded side. Then, propped up against the wall, he waited for the battle to end, the city to be taken, and its populace to be massacred.

It would be pointless for Casnut to cast him aside now. There would be a way to save his life, if only he could find it and bring himself to use it.

He was too weak. Betrayed by his body, too tired of killing and suffering, of standing by and doing nothing while men, women, and children whose only crime was to be what he himself had once been were slaughtered.

He felt the potter's presence, caught the ghost's excitement. Realized only then that he hadn't felt the ghost with him since he'd put on King Asp's spirit.

I've found Tramu, the potter whispered. In the mines. He's alive.

Moth felt a stir of returning purpose. What about Pyota? he asked.

Dead. There's a pit where they left the bodies of the slaves who died for the vultures. Her bones are there but her spirit is gone. There's nothing you can do for her.

Moth dismissed all thoughts of Pyota. He had never really expected to find either Pyota or Tramu still alive after so many years in the mines. But Tramu was alive.

Tramu. Moth remembered the Fair at which a Taryaa had had both Tramu and himself kidnapped, then rescued them itself so the eunuch could win their confidence and get from them the information about the sword Tas Et was then forging for King Asp for the Seven-Year Festival. He remembered the infusion the Taryaa had used to restore them to consciousness after they'd been drugged.

The herbs shamans like Sulthar used served primarily to attract and propitiate the spirits that did the actual healing and had little curative power of their own. But the Taryaa had no shamans: though there were sicknesses against which they were powerless, yet their medicines acted in and of themselves, and their knowledge of herbs and curative substances was the most advanced in all Ashlu. The Royal Eunuch who had been traveling with Ravnal would have the Deltan medicines that would give Moth the strength to save Tramu from the mines and get to Kyborash with him afterward.

And now that he'd killed Ravnal, and so made of himself the Teichi's sworn enemy, he had something to offer the Taryaa. They already knew he served Casnut, and that Casnut opposed the Teichi: Moth needed only to convince them that he was willing to betray the Great Shaman because he coveted Casnut's power and influence and wanted to supplant him, and the Taryaa would help him. That was always their way, to turn the conflicts of others to their own ends, keeping those who might someday become the eunuchs' enemies divided against themselves.

There were three great powers in Ashlu: the Taryaa in their cities in the southern delta, the Nomads in the northern plains, and Chal between the two. Chal protected the delta from the Nomads, but whenever Chal grew too strong or too avid for conquest, the Taryaa used the Nomads to humble it.

Moth knotted the cloth tighter around his wound, braced his back against the wall. He had killed his potter's soul, died a thousand times impaled with his uncle on Tepes Ban's stake: he could endure the pain, keep himself conscious, and defend himself until he had his chance with the Taryaa.

Was this betrayal, too, part of Casnut's plans for him? Casnut had allied himself with the Taryaa before even while working to destroy them; the Taryaa would be powerful allies . . . if he could betray them before they betrayed him. But the Taryaa had millennia of experience dealing with shamans, of playing the Nomads against the cities and the Nomad tribes against one another. They would know which oaths would bind Moth, which he could disregard.

High overhead he could see Timor circling, once more only a tiny black speck against the sky.

Chapter Twenty-five

The fighting had moved on into the city, leaving the ground just inside the gate littered with the dead and almost-dead, Nomad and Nanlasurian heaped indiscriminately together. Two bodylengths from Moth a black horse, its back broken, was still thrashing weakly as it tried to regain its feet. Ravnal and the warrior who had followed him through the gate had been trampled by so many horses that no one would have been able to recognize or distinguish their broken flesh with eyes alone. Moth could tell them apart because the other warrior's spirit still clung to what remained of his body, reluctant to begin its journey to the netherworld, while Ravnal's flesh was as empty, as spiritless, as it was without blood. Even the raid-leader's shattered and splintered skeleton was dead and soulless: the Sword That Was Asp had drunk Ravnal's second self as well as his first.

I've found them, Tas Et told Moth.

Moth looked around carefully, listened. There were only the heaped bodies, some few still twitching or bubbling red froth from their mouths, the broken-backed horse still struggling. Nothing that could threaten him.

Show me.

For an instant Moth was viewing a hillside overlooking

the city, seeing it, as Tas Et saw it, from all directions at once. The Taryaa was there, staring down at Nanlasur, its white robes and bright silk mouth mask concealed beneath a hooded cloak of gray wool. Two men dressed as Nomad warriors but wearing copper swords of Chaldan manufacture slung over their shoulders, as only Deltans wore them, attended the eunuch.

Then Moth was staring at the thrashing horse again.

Tjei? Moth asked his Ri soul.

He's on the far side of the city.

Watch over me. Call me back if anything threatens me.

Then, to Tas Et: Take me back there. Give me the larger of the two warriors to speak through.

The warrior jerked, strangled on a scream, his muscles locked rigid in the position Tas Et had held as he died on the stake. The Taryaa turned from its view of the city, studied the warrior.

"Moth?" it asked after a moment, its melodious voice calm, almost amused.

"Taryaa," Moth said. The warrior's voice was harsh, unnatural, as though the sound were being forced out between two rocks being scraped together. The other warrior clutched at his sword, was stopped by a motion of the eunuch's hand.

"I have an offer to make you," Moth said. "Meet me inside the main gate and we can discuss it."

"What kind of offer?"

"A weapon you can use against some of your enemies. One that they will think theirs, yet that will turn against them and destroy them when they least expect it."

"What would you wish in exchange for this . . . magical weapon, if indeed we could find a use for it?"

"Herbs and healing. Safe conduct for myself and one other to Kyborash."

"Safe conduct, Moth? When you are one of the conquerors?" A short, trilling laugh, inhumanly sweet. The great pink eyes staring moistly at him. "From whom should I protect you?"

"Ravnal is dead. When the Teichi discover his death, they may remember how he opposed my master Casnut in council."

"And accuse you unjustly?" A trilling laugh.

"Yes."

"Return my servant to himself," the eunuch said. "I will bring my medicines and meet with you."

"We have always had a great respect for Casnut," the Taryaa said. The eunuch's two warriors were standing some bodylengths away, as far from Moth as they could get while still remaining close enough to protect their master.

"He has great influence over many of the peoples of the northern plains," Moth agreed.

"Though not the Teichi."

"No. Yet perhaps now that Ravnal is dead—"

"The Teichi will find another Ravnal. But, tell me, you saw him die?"

"Yes. He came galloping in through this gate, a little behind his brother—only to take a Nanlasurian arrow in his eye."

"Did anyone else see him die?"

Moth gestured at the dead and dying, winced with the pain the movement cost him. "Some of them, perhaps. No one else."

"What about Tjei?"

"He was in front. He didn't see Ravnal go down."

"I see." Turning to the warrior through whom Moth had spoken earlier: "Examine the bodies. Find out if the raid-leader is among them. If he is, tell me how he died."

While the warrior studied the bodies, an expression of grim distaste on his face as he hunched down among them, using his sword to move the corpses around so he could better examine them, the Taryaa said, "So Casnut has named you his successor?"

"Not yet, no—his health is excellent and he will be a

power among the peoples of the plains for many years to come—but he is training me to succeed him.''

''He could have demanded any price he chose for the aid he gave us in taking Kyborash—yet you were all he took.''

The Taryaa was telling Moth that it knew who he was, his history, not just that he was a young shaman with Casnut as his master. That there was no way he could lie to it and expect to escape the consequences of his action.

''Casnut has few needs,'' Moth said. ''There is little you or anyone else could offer him that would mean anything to him.''

''It is said that he has become hostile to us.''

''With some truth.''

''Why then would he offer us this magical weapon—when he himself is perhaps our enemy?''

''I am acting not for him, but for myself.''

''Why? If you need aid, why not go to Casnut for it?''

''If Casnut had granted me what I desired, would I have come to you?''

''You still have not told me why he refused you.''

''I told you I wanted safe-conduct for myself and another person. My cousin Tramu. He's a slave in the lead mines, of no value to Casnut. Casnut won't do anything to help set him free.''

''You'll defy Casnut for him.''

''I have no choice. I swore a vow.''

''And you've sworn no vows to Casnut.''

''Many vows. But none that will prevent me from destroying your enemies.''

''Which enemies?''

They're coming, the potter's ghost whispered. Tjei and four others. They'll be here soon.

''Casnut,'' Moth said.

''Despite your vows to him.'' The eunuch's voice was ironic.

"Yes." Moth made it a flat statement. "The Teichi as well, should they prove too arrogant."

"At the moment the Teichi are your enemies, not mine. And you're only an apprentice shaman. Not yet your master's equal in either strength or influence."

"Not yet, but I will be. I will swear a vow to you now, one that will bind me as my oath to free Tramu binds me, that when the time is right you will have your weapon."

The Taryaa looked at the warrior who'd been examining the bodies and who was now standing waiting to be recognized. "Did you discover Ravnal's body?"

"I don't know. There are too many bodies and they've been too badly trampled. I can't even tell which are which."

"Nor how they died?"

"No."

"So I have to take what you tell me on faith?" the Taryaa asked Moth.

Moth forced himself to shrug. "The Taryaa have always claimed to be able to judge the truthfulness of a man's words."

"True." The eunuch thought a moment, then said, "My medicines cannot heal you. Only you can heal yourself, with time. What I can do is provide you with the means of stilling your pain, and with the strength to resist your wounds until they heal. Nothing more."

"Agreed," Moth said.

The Taryaa motioned the warrior away, then turned to Moth and asked, "Do you then swear on the Clay and on the Earth Mother, on Sartor and on your anvil, on both your Ri and your Tas souls, on the fire at the Heart of the World and the Tree of Creation, that you will turn upon our enemies and destroy them when we demand it of you?"

"I swear on the Clay and on the Earth Mother, on Sartor and on my anvil, on both my Ri and Tas souls, on the fire at the Heart of the World and on the Tree of Creation, that I will turn upon Casnut or the Teichi and destroy them when you demand it of me—if, in return, you give me the healing I need to survive and provide safe-conduct to Kyborash for both myself and my cousin Tramu."

"Agreed," the Taryaa said. It called to its two warriors, had them bring medicines and begin heating water. By the time Tjei and four of his Teichi cousins rode up, the Taryaa was daubing a thick, sticky brown poultice on Moth's wounded side and leg while Moth sipped an infusion against his pain from a nacreous cup fashioned in the shape of a horned beast from the Sea of Marshes.

"I'm looking for my brother, shaman," Tjei said. He was still a boy, with a boy's awkwardness, but there was nothing ridiculous about the menace clear in his voice.

"I saw him fall. Over there." Moth gestured. "An arrow, just after he came through the gate. It caught him in the eye."

Tjei stared down at the confusion of broken, trampled bodies, swallowed hard. For an instant he looked even younger than he was, a boy about to cry.

His face hardened again. He dismounted, knelt, and began methodically examining the bloody remains. One of the other Teichi tried to help, but Tjei gestured him away angrily. His face remained hard and closed as he found pieces of Ravnal's broken bow, a finger with a ring he recognized still on it. Even the tattoos and ceremonial scars that should have rendered the body recognizable had been mutilated by the horses' hooves. In the end Tjei had only his brother's weapons and personal ornaments, the finger in its ring, a few fragments of tattooed skin. Nothing to prove what had happened, how Ravnal had died, who had killed him.

The Taryaa had been watching and listening in silence. Waiting to see what Tjei would discover before it intervened.

"Tell me what you saw," Tjei said, after taking what he'd been able to recover of Ravnal's body and wrapping it in a cloak for a hero's burial.

Moth described the death of the warrior who'd followed Ravnal through the gate, how the Nanlasurian who'd loosed the arrow had himself been killed instants later. Tjei frowned, unsatisfied, convinced that Moth was lying but unable to put a reason to his certainty.

"What about you?" he demanded of the Taryaa. "What are you doing here?"

"Moth is wounded. He asked my help to heal himself."

Two of the cousins began whispering to each other. Tjei remained silent an instant, considering the situation.

"You said you couldn't heal yourself," he said finally. The cousins were still whispering. Moth knew that the tale of the shaman who'd had to ask the Taryaa to heal his wounds for him would soon be known to all the tribes of the plains. "You said you could only kill, not cure," Tjei continued. "That you'd demonstrate your powers on Ravnal if he doubted you. Perhaps you did."

"Are you accusing me of murdering your brother?" Moth asked. "Are you swearing blood feud against me?"

"If you killed him. I swear blood feud against whoever killed him."

"The man who killed him is already dead. I saw him die. And you do the Teichi's finest warrior no honor by claiming he was killed by a man so weak he has to ask his enemy's aid."

"You would never have been able to best him in battle, no, wounded or not. But you are a shaman."

"Tjei, you do not frighten me, but I wish no blood feud between your people and myself or my master Casnut. So I will take oath on my master's honor that I did not kill your brother—and more, that I would have prevented his death had it been in my power to do so."

It was true, all of it: Asp, not Moth, had killed the raid-leader, and Moth had tried to stop him.

I wonder what it thinks, Moth asked himself, catching the Taryaa's mild pink rabbit's gaze on him. If it thinks that because I can swear one oath it thinks is false, then the oath I swore to it will be false as well.

Yet the oath he'd sworn the Taryaa had not been false.

He was already oath-bound to kill Casnut. But that had been part of Casnut's plans for Moth for a long time, and was no treachery: the only way to succeed a Great Shaman was to kill him, and take his spirit and his spirit's spirits for your own. Moth would not be able to kill Casnut before Casnut was ready to die.

"You know we hear the truth in men's voices," the Taryaa told Tjei.

Tjei nodded unwillingly. "Swear, then," he told Moth. "If the Taryaa confirms your oath, I will accept it."

The other Teichi grinned, pleased at the double insult. Only a coward would let himself be treated as a man so lacking in honor that he needed another to confirm his oath; only a man without honor would ask his enemy to save him.

"I will swear on my master's honor, and on my own," Moth said. "Whether you are able to determine for yourself if I speak the truth or whether you need another's help to do so is no concern of mine."

One of the Teichi nodded again. Moth had been shamed by his need to accept the Taryaa's help, but he had not lost all honor.

"Swear," Tjei said finally, accepting the situation. Moth swore his second oath of the day, binding himself to the strictest truth as he denied having murdered Ravnal, and the Taryaa confirmed his words.

Tjei remounted, the cloak holding his brother's remains clutched tightly under his arm. He started to ride away, then halted, turned back. "I have an oath for you, shaman, to match that which you swore me. Here and now, by my brother's soul, I swear blood feud on any and all men who killed my brother or helped kill him, or who help to protect his murderer."

He rode off, with the other Teichi behind him. A boy with a boy's awkwardness and a voice that cracked when he spoke, and there was still nothing ridiculous about him or the threat he represented.

Chapter Twenty-six

The horse snorted, balked at the stream. Moth clung to it with his knees, using one hand to stroke it reassuringly on the neck, the other to speak to the animal through his drum, letting the drum-spirit soothe it and tell it what Moth wanted it to do. Moth had found it in the Nanlasur stables. It was docile enough, and had been well cared for, but had never been ridden before: there were few horses in the Chaldan Empire, and those were only used for drawing chariots and battle carts, as though they were only fleeter oxen or onagers.

The horse reluctantly yielded to the drum-spirit's entreaties, crossed the stream. A wide, deeply rutted path wound from the far side up into the mountains. Moth patted the horse's neck again, whispered encouragement to it as he urged it on with a further rhythm on his drum.

At the first crest he halted, exhausted, and concentrated on his breathing, keeping it slow and steady but deep despite the pain in his side every time he filled his lungs. The Taryaa's herbs and medicinals made it easier to wall off the agony from his leg and side, gave him the strength to keep his wounds from eating away any more of his remaining vitality, but nothing more. Moth would have preferred to have a Nomad escort for this trip to the mines, but the very weakness that made him need them also made it necessary for him to go alone: he had already shamed himself in front of the Teichi by accepting the Taryaa's aid; he dared not ask for further help, not even from those warriors whose tribes were still friendly to Casnut, nor let anyone know how weakened he really was.

He stared back down at the city, and at Nanlasur's turbulent river. He could just make out one of the Taryaa's Deltan warriors in the shipyard on the far shore, his identity obvious despite his Nomad dress because of the copper sword gleaming on his back. The Deltan was directing a group of Nanlasurian boatmen in blue-gray kilts who were readying the kailek Moth would be taking downriver to Kyborash: a rectangular wooden raft, six bodylengths long by three wide, of the sort customarily used for transporting heavy loads of timber or stonework.

Ashanorak, the Deltan Tas Et had possessed so Moth could speak to the Taryaa through him, and who would be accompanying Moth to Kyborash, was overseeing the work while his companion sat watching from the shade of a maro palm. The Taryaa itself was nowhere to be seen—hiding, most likely, in Tjei's tent, so that no one escaping the massacre would be able to say that he or she had seen one of the Royal Eunuchs with the Nomads.

Ashanorak knelt down, peered at one of the tightly sewn inflated ox hides that gave the kailek the buoyancy it needed to float its heavy cargoes. He straightened, drew his sword, and slashed it loose. The current carried it swiftly away, but before it was more than two or three bodylengths from the kailek, one of the boatmen was frantically lashing another in its place.

Ashanorak hadn't bothered to open his mouth, had merely glanced over at the men who'd rushed to replace the float. There were five boatmen. Only two would live to take the kailek downriver.

Moth lost interest. Ashanorak would be with him as much to watch over him and report what he did back to the

Taryaa as to protect him, but the Deltan seemed competent to get them to Kyborash, and Moth would be doing nothing he needed to keep secret from the eunuchs—or nothing, at least, that the warrior would be able to perceive.

The path wound on through light forest, second-growth cedars, and tangled underbrush. Beyond the next ridge Moth came upon a four-wheeled cart with a broken rear axle lying abandoned in the path. Three wicker hampers gaped open in the back of the cart, their seals broken: two were still filled with dull gray lead ingots, but the third was empty. It could only have contained silver, Moth realized: the Tas who'd been taking the cart back to Nanlasur must've abandoned the cart and its comparatively valueless lead to flee on foot with the silver ingots.

How much farther? Moth asked the potter, continuing on around the cart.

Not far. The next valley. I can show him to you.

No. Moth's refusal was instinctive, unreasoning, absolute.

Tas Et? he asked. Is there anyone here I need fear?

The Tas are all gone, and with them the Warriors of the Hand and Voice. The mines are deserted.

What about the slaves?

Those who were able to free themselves have already fled. The rest are chained or imprisoned, or too weak to pose any problem. You need not worry about them.

And Tramu? Moth asked.

Tramu? Moth felt Tas Et's incomprehension, found himself looking through his uncle's dying eyes yet one more time at Tramu and Pyota in the cage with Tas Et's assistants. He wrenched himself away, back to the mountain trail.

Tramu's underground, in one of the galleries, the potter's ghost told him.

He's still alive?

Yes, but he's been down there in the darkness without food and water for six days now. He can't last much longer.

A fine layer of gray ash coated the ground, the trees, and the underbrush. Moth could smell the mines now: the lingering smell of woodsmoke from the ovens in which the Tas had prepared their charcoals; sulfur and other noxious fumes from the roasting ores and from the furnaces in which the lead and silver had been smelted.

Closer still and he smelled the sweet rot of death and disease. The stench brought the Harg back to him: slaves scrabbling copper from the mountain rock with bare, bleeding hands; bodies piled high for the carrion birds while the Tas overseers wielded whips tipped with jagged metal; Moth himself killing the slave who had borne his name to make himself a weaponsmith like his grandfather. . . . At least Tramu was still alive. No matter how bad it had been here, at the Harg he would have been dead in a few months.

Moth remembered the peaceful northern valleys where the Children of Raburr had lost their forge lore, their mastery of fire. Had they been the same, before they forgot who they were?

But remembering the valleys around the Earth Mother's Burning Mountain brought back too many other memories: the Rafti whom Tas Gly had had killed to keep her from marrying Moth, the other Rafti who now shared her body and spirit with the ghost. . . . Sulthar had the freedom of the northern valleys, the forest villages. Moth could only act out the role Casnut had chosen for him in the Great Shaman's war against the cities and the stars.

Moth continued on past the huts in which the Tas overseers had lived, past the shrine in which they had worshiped Sartor's Tas Aspect. Everything was deserted, with clothes, tools, even weapons lying where they'd been abandoned when their owners had fled.

Potter?

To your right.

Moth guided the horse between heaps of broken rock, piles of ash and slag. The horse balked at a slave's mutilated body. Moth reassured it with his drum, urged it on. The boy had been as young as Tramu had been when they'd sent him to the mines, redheaded. A smith's son. The Tas Sil feeding upon itself, cannibalistic.

The stench of centuries of pain and disease and putrefaction was everywhere.

There, his Ri ghost told him. It was a vertical shaft like dozens of others, with the notched tree trunk that served as a ladder lying beside it, next to a pitch-coated bucket full of vinegar for fire-setting. The bucket was still tied to the rope with which it had obviously been about to be lowered into the shaft.

Moth dismounted, used the drum to command his horse to remain where it was. He dragged the ladder to the shaft, pushed and levered it into place.

The effort left him trembling. He forced himself to pause, sit down, and shake some curling shavings of dried, purplish-black root from a vial the Taryaa had given him, some powdered, reddish-brown leaves from another vial, out onto his hand and swallow them.

The vials contained only enough of the herbs for the journey to Kyborash, where the kailek would be met by other of the Taryaa's men and Moth's supplies would be replenished. Or so they had agreed, though Moth had no intention of letting the Taryaa watch over his actions in Kyborash.

When the trembling ceased, he started down the ladder, then hesitated and returned to the surface, where he unstrapped the sheathed Sword That Was Asp. He was forced to wear it Deltan-style now, slung over his shoulders, since the wound in his left side made it impossible to continue carrying it there as he always had before, but the sword would hamper him too much in the narrow shafts and tunnels. He set it on the ground beside the shaft.

Watch over the sword for me, he told Tas Et. Take possession of anyone who tries to touch it.

There is no one here you need fear.

Watch over it anyway.

Moth climbed slowly down the ladder to a tiny landing, where he found a supply of unlit torches waiting stacked beside a tunnel mouth. He took two of the torches and continued on, deeper into the earth, until, four ladders and landings later, the potter's ghost said, This one.

Moth turned his attention inward, found his hassa, breathed fire into the torch. He stepped into the tunnel. The ghost guided him through the fetid darkness, the labyrinth of narrow winding galleries with ceilings so low he had to scramble through them at a half crouch. To Tramu.

There, the ghost told him.

Three slaves lay bound together with leather thongs, and two of them were dead and rotting. The third was sleeping or unconscious.

He could only be Tramu, but Moth would never have known him. Less than a year older than Moth, he looked ancient. As pale as though he hadn't seen the sun for years, his wispy red beard tangled and matted, he was strongly muscled yet emaciated, almost withered-looking. His left arm seemed twisted, as though it had been broken and had not healed properly.

"Tramu?" Moth asked tentatively. There was no response. He reached over, grasped a scrawny shoulder, shook Tramu without getting any reaction.

He's too weak, the potter's ghost said. He needs water, food. Sunlight. You'll have to carry him out of here.

Moth summoned fire, used it to burn through the thongs binding Tramu to his dead companions, then pulled him out from under them and half dragged, half carried him back to the shaft and up to the surface.

Chapter Twenty-seven

Moth laid Tramu on a pallet in one of the Tas huts. He found water, forced a trickle down Tramu's throat, then mixed what remained of it with powdered horse's blood and fermented mare's milk—the ration all Nomads carried—and managed to force a little of the resultant thin paste down his cousin's throat.

Tramu was still unconscious, but Moth had no need to leave his own body to sense that his cousin's soul had been neither stolen nor forced to walk the Roads of the Dead, leaving his body behind. Tramu had none of that flaccid heaviness, aroused none of the instinctive disquiet that a man whose soul had been stolen would have aroused.

Moth sat cross-legged on the floor beside Tramu's pallet, grasped his cousin's pale, scrawny wrist with his left hand. The fingers of his right hand were resting lightly on the painted horsehide head of his drum, and he let the rhythm of Tramu's weak, faintly fluttering pulse flow through him to the drum.

The drum-spirit gave meaning to the rhythm he was tapping out, spoke to him through it, and let him know that no malefic objects or spirits had been introduced by chance or design into Tramu's body.

Relieved, Moth let go of Tramu's wrist, put the drum aside, and stretched out beside his cousin, let himself go to sleep as well.

Sleeping, he dreamed of Kyborash, of Tramu. Memories of the way he'd loved and envied his older cousin—of how proud he'd been to be with him and how he'd always hoped that people would look at him the same way they looked at Tramu—dissolved into one another.

He was remembering a time just before the Seven-Year Festival, when Tramu had been telling him about the part he was playing in decorating the sheath of the Sword That Was Asp, when the dream changed. Now he was Tramu, was squatting with the other blowpipers around Tas Et's forge and blowing through the hollow reed with its clay tuyere to bring the forge fire to the heat necessary to reforge the two pieces of Asp's broken life.

There was the sound of hooves in the street outside the forge compound, angry yells from within the house, where the Syrr Sil himself stood waiting with a select group of Warriors of the Hand and Voice to protect the forge compound. He heard a scream from the house, and suddenly four yelling Nomads burst into the compound.

Tas Et snatched up one of the other swords he'd been working on before the time had come to put everything else aside for the Sword That Was Asp, killed the first Nomad with it while Tramu and the other blowpipers were still trying to scramble to their feet.

Before Tas Et could pull the sword from the Nomad's body, it was all over: Tas Et and the two largest blowpipers had been knocked unconscious; the Nomads were holding Tramu and the remaining assistant.

Their leader was tall and gaunt, with hair so blond it was almost white falling over his scarred and tattooed face. He looked around the forge, found the Sword That Was Asp lying in its two pieces beside its jeweled scabbard, scooped them up and put them in a leather sack, tied it closed.

He said something Tramu didn't understand to the other

two. All three laughed. The leader knelt down beside Tas Et, forced his mouth open, reached in and grabbed his tongue, pulled it as far out as he could . . .

He severed Tas Et's tongue with his dagger, tossed it into the forge fire as he knelt by the first of the unconscious blowpipers, pried his mouth open, laughed again as he severed the blowpiper's tongue and looked up, staring directly into Tramu's eyes—

Tramu twisted free, ran screaming through the mines. But his feet had been hobbled together with a leather thong and he couldn't run; he could only hop and twist, hunched over, in the narrow passages as he stumbled toward the rock wall where he'd set the fire, dashed a bucketful of vinegar on it, and heard the rock crack, saw, in the last flicker before the fire was completely extinguished, the Nomad waiting with his dagger inside the rock, revealed now that it was cracking open. Tramu turned, ran as far as he could before the heat and the steam overcame him and he lost consciousness, to be dragged out again by the rope tied around his waist, given the flint hammer, and sent back to the rock he'd broken open, to chip the Nomad waiting inside it free—

Moth awakened terrified, running sweat. It took him a moment to regain control of himself, free himself from Tramu's fear.

Tramu was twitching in the darkness, moaning softly to himself. Moth lay down again beside him, warded himself against his cousin's nightmares, slept.

He stayed with Tramu two days, caring for him while he rebuilt his own strength as best he could with the aid of the Taryaa's herbs, before Tramu at last awakened.

"Tramu? It's me, Moth." Tramu's eyes focused on him, but there was no recognition in them, only an animal wariness.

Moth knelt beside him, still clutching the bowl of milk and blood he'd been carrying.

"Tramu, it's Moth! Your cousin Moth!" Still no recognition, only that wariness, the muscles tensed as if for flight. "Don't you remember me, Tramu?"

Moth put the bowl aside, reached for Tramu, saw Tramu cringe away from him. He got to his feet, backed up, trying to smile reassuringly.

"Is it because I look like a Nomad?" He lifted his cap from his head so Tramu could see his red and black hair. "I'm still Moth, still your cousin. I rescued you, Tramu. You're free, you aren't a slave anymore. You won't ever have to go back to the mines again."

His spirit has been damaged, the potter's ghost told Moth. He doesn't know who you are, who he is. He's lost his truename. He can't understand you. All he knows is the mines.

Tramu was eyeing the bowl containing the milk and blood paste with furtive greed. Moving slowly, so as not to startle or frighten him, Moth pushed the bowl closer to him with his foot, then retreated to the hut's doorslit and stood there, watching him.

"It's all right, Tramu." Trying to make his voice as soft, as soothing and gentle as possible. "It's all right, cousin."

When Tramu remained rigid and unmoving, Moth put his hand to his drum and spoke to Tramu through it the same way he'd spoken to the horse that had brought him to the mines.

Tramu glanced back and forth between Moth and the bowl of food, suddenly snatched it up and began scooping the mixture from it with his fingers and gulping it down, all the while continuing to stare at Moth.

Like a frightened animal. As though he weren't even human anymore.

He studied Tramu, trying to find the cousin he had lost in the man in front of him, tapping out questions he couldn't hear but could only feel on his drum, listening to the drum-spirit's equally silent replies.

Tramu's spirit was trapped between dream and waking,

between the life of his body and the Roads of the Dead. He must have retreated there, trying to escape the horror of the mines in his sleep, only to find himself unable to break the connection with his body and go free, unable to put himself back in his physical self again and return to waking life. Trapped there, with neither the material nor the spiritual realms to maintain him, his spirit had fallen in on itself, like a fruit left to shrink and wither in a cool storeroom in winter, until at last he had lost even his truename.

Moth thought of the Taryaa and their medicines that acted in and of themselves, rejected the idea. Their herbs and medicinals could do nothing for Tramu. His only hope of healing lay in restoring his truename to him, and that could only be done in the heaven beyond the heavens, by a shaman like Casnut or Sulthar.

But Sulthar was gone, and Casnut would do nothing for Tramu. There was only Moth, and he was unable to do so much as heal his own wounds so long as his Ri and Tas souls remained sundered. Moth's only hope of regaining the ability to heal himself lay in Kyborash, with his dolthe, his soul-in-clay, which he had to wed to the dagger that had killed his Ri soul. And then, perhaps, if he succeeded in resurrecting his lost wholeness, he would at last be able to make the ascent to the heaven of healing for Tramu as well as for himself.

Tas Et, he commanded. Let me look at Ashanorak and the kailek through your eyes.

The kailek was ready. Ashanorak sat in the shade on the shore, chewing a strip of dried meat and watching idly as a fat boatman looked the raft over carefully, hoping to find something he could do to improve his chances of being one of the men Ashanorak would pick to take the kailek downriver, but there was nothing remaining to be replaced, repaired, tightened, or lashed more securely in place.

Give me Ashanorak's body, Moth told Tas Et. *Let me speak through him.*

Ashanorak went rigid as Tas Et took possession of him. Moth felt an instant's total agony, dying with his uncle on the stake, then he was in the Deltan warrior's body.

"We leave tomorrow, at midday," Moth told Ashanorak, forcing the words out of the Deltan's throat. "Have everything ready by then."

Take me out of him but let me continue watching, Moth ordered Tas Et.

Ashanorak collapsed when Tas Et left him. When he got to his feet again Moth could see that he was trembling, his face working with fear. He would be no danger to them on the trip downriver, not even when Moth was asleep, or lost to his body in trance.

Ashanorak looked around, saw only the fat boatman who'd been looking for something to do and who was now watching him with slack-jawed amazement. The man seemed to remind Ashanorak of his dignity; he straightened, turned away from the kailek to bow in the direction in which he'd seen Moth riding off a few days earlier, and said in a tightly controlled voice, "Everything will be ready."

Straightening again, he turned back to the kailek, saw the boatman still gaping at him. Ashanorak's face tightened and his hand went to the sword slung across his back.

The boatman started to back away, shaking his head hopelessly. Ashanorak jumped onto the kailek's deck, started stalking him.

"I didn't see anything!" Ashanorak just grinned at the boatman, kept on coming. The man backed away farther, hands up in front of his face as if to ward off a blow, muttering unintelligibly . . . only to fall backward over the bulging sacks of foodstuffs lashed to the deck behind him and into the green, mucky water.

When he tried to stand up again, Ashanorak cut off his head.

Watching Ashanorak kick the headless body back into the water then stare after it with tight-lipped satisfaction as it drifted away, Moth knew he'd misjudged the man. Ashanorak was the kind of man who would react to the overpowering humiliation Moth had forced on him not with submission, but with unreasoning violence. The Deltan was still afraid of Moth, and he had undoubtedly been ordered to see that Moth reached Kyborash safely, but even so he might try to kill him if he thought there was a chance he could succeed, and then hope to justify himself to his Taryaa masters afterward.

This is a test, Moth realized. The Taryaa arranged to have Ashanorak accompany me to Kyborash so it could see what happens, how I'll handle him. How clever an ally or foe I can prove myself to be.

Ashanorak watched the body until it sank, finally turned away and went back to his place beneath the tree.

Bring me back, Moth commanded Tas Et.

It took Moth most of the next day to get Tramu to the river without having to hurt him or tie him up. Everything seemed to frighten Tramu: Moth himself, having to leave the shelter of the hut, the horse, even the unaccustomed heat of the sun on his unprotected face. Yet when at last the mines were lost in the forest behind them, some of Tramu's fear seemed to go out of him, and when they finally reached the kailek, he let Moth lead him aboard without protest.

The two surviving boatmen untied the kailek, pushed it free of the shore, came leaping after it through the green shallows, and scrambled on board. They began poling it out to the deeper water where the current would catch it, working with frantic eagerness, the memory of their companions' deaths still vivid.

Tramu found himself a place huddled between two stacks of lashed-down sacks of provisions. Ashanorak terrified him, and when the Deltan warrior approached, Tramu would huddle down farther, trying to hide, or scurry away to the other end of the kailek. Uncertain what to make of Tramu, unable to decide if he was merely the poor madman he seemed to be or if he was something else altogether—something important enough to justify this journey and the importance which both his Taryaa master and Moth seemed to place upon it—Ashanorak treated Tramu with wary contempt, in much the same way as Moth imagined he would have treated the half-witted son of a King Who Reigned But Did Not Rule in his native city.

Moth he avoided, making a great show of his deference and obedience, but watching him whenever he thought the shaman was unaware that he was being observed, and the expression on his face when he did was of pure hatred. Yet all Moth ever seemed to do was gaze idly out at the shore and water or up at the sky, do Tramu small kindnesses, eat, and sleep—sleep, in fact, for what was sometimes days at a time.

Ashanorak's terror gradually receded, until it was no more than wariness and caution—tinged, even, with a certain contempt for this shaman who was only able to sleep in the sun like an old man or hobble painfully around the kailek's deck like a cripple when he was awake, whose only interest seemed to be caring for a useless madman. And with Ashanorak's terror, though he did not realize it, went much of his fury, the determination Moth had sensed in him to avenge his humiliation whatever the cost.

The kailek moved steadily downriver, between willow- and shade-tree-lined banks, past occasional fishing villages, where men sat bare-chested casting their nets from the round coracles they'd made sewing fishskins together over wooden frameworks. As the days passed, the Thys narrowed, its banks becoming high, sheer cliffs of red and purple sandstone, white chalk, pink granite, the river alive with shoals of tiny red-scaled fish that leapt from the water in pursuit of flying insects almost as large as themselves, only to fall back to the kailek's deck and die. Sometimes, when Tramu didn't realize Moth was watching, Moth would see him snatch a fish up, twist it in his fingers to kill it, and swallow it whole.

Once Tramu looked up, caught Moth's gaze on him as he ate a fish. He froze, the fish still in his mouth. Moth smiled at him, said, "It's all right, Tramu," in as gentle a voice as he could manage, and after a long, fearful moment Tramu finally gulped the fish down.

From then on Tramu would eat the fish even when he knew Moth was watching him, though he would still leave them to flop and die on the deck directly in front of him if he caught Ashanorak or one of the boatmen looking at him.

Yet Moth's sleep was still contaminated by Tramu's nightmares. And in some of those nightmares Moth saw himself invading Tas Et's forge, yanking Tramu's mouth open while another Nomad held him, grabbing his tongue, holding it there an instant, grinning at him, before with a single motion he severed it, then threw it into the forge fire to burn.

Part Three: Necropolis

Chapter Twenty-eight

Lightning hammered the crest she'd just left and thunder exploded all around her. Already panic-stricken by the night and storm, by the steep, precarious mountain trails that the rain had turned into so many rushing streams, Rafti's horse reared, almost throwing her. She clung to its neck, trying to soothe it with her voice, but her words were lost in the thunder, and when the horse came down again, its right foreleg caught in a cleft between two rocks.

The horse screamed. Rafti leapt off, knelt beside it on the wet rocks, and carefully worked the leg loose. She ran her fingers up and down the leg, confirming what the dead eye showed her despite the near-total darkness, the masking flesh. Luck had kept the bone from snapping, but the horse would need a few days before it could carry her again.

There's a village over the next ridge, Rafti's other self told her. *We can shelter there until the storm's over.*

Rafti took the horse's reins, coaxed the animal slowly up the ridge into the wind and rain.

What kind of village?

Farmers and goatherds.

Chaldan?

In a way. The Siltemple in Kyborash used to take a third of their crops as tribute.

You've been here before? When you were still alive?

No. But all these mountain villages are the same.

Lightning flashed again as Rafti reached the top of the ridge, revealing a cluster of low oval stone buildings, like rounded mounds of clumsily piled yellow-gray rocks, huddled beneath a protecting overhang. Then the lightning was gone and all Rafti could see was a faint glow where one of the largest huts had been.

Who do they pay their tribute to now?

No one, probably. You're afraid they'll want to stay forgotten and won't welcome a visitor?

Yes.

They won't think you're a threat when you tell them that you're a firedancer and a healer.

Rafti picked her way slowly down the path toward the clustered huts, the ghost guiding her footsteps and the horse limping along behind. The village stank of goats, rotting vegetables, human excrement, like so many other tiny villages where she'd been forced to ask shelter after she'd left the three other firedancers with whom she'd crossed the Nomad plains and continued on south alone.

She twisted the band of bright silk that the forest people had given her and that she always wore dancing so that it hid the dead eye and leathery half-mask of scar tissue surrounding it while leaving the undamaged part of her face bare.

"Is anybody there?" she called.

There was no answer. Only a muffled cough from inside the nearest hut, the muffled bleating of a goat.

"I'm alone!" Rafti shouted. "I won't hurt you!" Still no response. "I can pay!"

She started around the largest hut, toward the hint of light she could still glimpse, stumbled over what seemed to be a heap of sodden branches.

Behind you, the ghost warned.

Straightening, she saw two men advancing cautiously toward her. One was young, a boy, though taller than she was, carrying a sputtering torch in one hand and a clumsily fashioned knife in the other. The older man, probably the boy's father, was squat and solid, with a thick staff that he held gripped like a club in both hands. Both wore the gray kilts her other self's memories told her Chaldan field slaves wore, but though the man wore the patched brown siltunic that was all his freeman's status entitled him to, the boy had on a chisel worker's black and green siltunic.

By the laws of Chal he had no right to wear a chisel worker's garments. The siltunic could only have been stolen or taken from the body of some refugee who'd died fleeing the destruction of Kyborash.

Father and son stared at her in silence, taking in the horse she was leading—such as only the richest Chaldan warriors had, and then only to pull their battle carts—as well as the blue silk concealing the left side of her face, the other bright silks visible beneath her sodden gray wool cloak.

"I need shelter for myself and my horse," Rafti said. "I can pay."

The boy grunted, stepped closer, and held up his torch so he could see her face better, grunted again when he realized she was young despite the gray in her hair, and beautiful.

"Who are you?" the older man asked. His words came half garbled from somewhere back in his throat, but he spoke so slowly that Rafti had no trouble understanding him.

"Rafti Shonraleur's-Daughter." In her valley, she would have been Rafti Kalsanen's-Widow now, but she had found that many of the people she met treated an unknown man's daughter with more respect than they would accord another, equally unknown, man's widow.

The boy started to say something, was silenced by an abrupt gesture from his father.

"You're not from Kyborash."

"No. I'm a firedancer and a healer, from beyond the Nomad plains."

He thought about that a moment, frowning, finally nodded. "My brother saw a firedancer once. At the Fair, when the Nomads and Deltans came to trade." He licked the corners of his lips. "He said that the firedancers were like the hierodules at the Siltemple, only instead of paying the Temple you paid them."

"People say a lot of things. I dance, and I can heal. Nothing more. Do you have anyone here in need of healing?"

"No." His voice hardened. "Is that what you meant when you said you could pay?"

"One of the things I meant. I can pay in Chaldan aubers if you want."

"You're alone?"

"Yes."

His gaze flickered from her to her horse, back to her again. "Twelve aubers."

Say three, the ghost told her. And he'll be cheating you at that.

They settled for five, with a meal as part of the bargain. The man and boy watched her avidly as she took out her pouch, shook five small lead coins from it, and slipped it back into her clothing.

She recognized that look, had seen it too many times before to mistake it. She kept her face from showing anything as she studied the boy in his stolen clothes. She could use the torch in his hand to frighten both of them, scare them enough so they'd leave her alone.

Wait until you're inside and have a better idea what they're going to do, her other self advised. Besides, if you scare them too badly, we may end up spending the night in the rain.

Rafti left her horse with the village's goats in a stone-walled enclosure sheltered by the overhanging cliff. The ghost would watch over it while she slept. Shouldering her saddle and the leather sacks holding her few possessions, she followed the boy back to his family hut.

He stooped low, hunched in through a roughly rectangular opening in the wall. Rafti hesitated before following him.

It's safe, the other Rafti told her. They'll probably wait until you're asleep to try anything.

Rafti worked her way in through the narrow opening. Emerging between two crude, smoke-blackened stone figures—one winged and male, the other exaggeratedly female—she saw the boy taking his place with his family around a shallow fire pit in the center of the refuse-strewn earthen floor. She looked at them: the older man and a woman obviously his wife, another man a few years younger—probably the brother—then the boy and his younger sister.

The girl had what looked like a huge wen on her neck. Rafti studied it through the dead eye, saw the wrongness within, the way it was starting to reach out from the growth to the rest of her body. The girl must be in constant pain, would die soon if the sickness continued to spread through her.

All the others were eyeing her with the same furtive greed. Once again she pretended not to notice, looked around until she found a corner where the angle would make it easier to protect herself if she had to, and dropped her things there. The family made room for her around the fire pit.

"A cold night to be caught in a storm," the wife said, her smile and the welcome in her voice belied by the darting glances she was giving Rafti's clothing and possessions. She handed Rafti a bowl full of watery broth with a few short lengths of tuber floating in it. "You've come a long way?"

"From Lake Nal." Seeing their look of incomprehension, she added, "In the forests beyond the Nomad plains."

"You came all that way alone?" the brother asked.

"Most of it."

"But you're only a woman," the wife said.

"A firedancer. We can protect ourselves." There was no reason to let them know that none of the other firedancers she'd encountered could have protected themselves as she could: where the others submitted to the fire as Rafti had once submitted to the Mother, gave themselves up to it and let it possess them, Rafti was a Master of Fire and the flames danced for her.

As she spoke, she stilled her thoughts, slipped into memory. Her heartbeat was the beating of the Festival drum, and she summoned up the Festival song, heard its monotonous, interweaving rhythms resounding within her skull. She fed the song to the flames that burned unceasingly in her spine until they danced through her in yellow-orange interlacings, then reached into the fire pit and picked up a smoldering branch, holding it easily in her naked hands.

They were all staring at her in paralyzed fascination. Holding the branch to her face, she blew on it for dramatic effect as she reached out with the currents of flame flowing within her. From the dead wood a tree of fire blossomed in her hands, its branches reaching up and out to lick at the mud-chinked stone roof overhead. Then, before the family had had time for more than an instinctive movement of recoil, she let the flames die away and tossed the blackened branch back into the fire pit.

They had felt the heat when the branch flared, knew that what they had seen was no illusion. It should be enough to keep her safe for the night, without terrifying them to the point where they would feel they had no choice but to attack her so as to save themselves.

"That was beautiful," the girl with the growth on her

neck said. She was the only one who hadn't cringed from the flames. "Can you dance for us too?"

"No. Your fire is too small and the roof is too low. Besides, I've come a long way and I'm very tired."

She saw the disappointment on the girl's face and took sudden pity on her. Anyway, she would probably be safer if they had reason to thank her as well as fear her.

"Come over here," she told the girl. "I have something else I can show you."

The girl's mother made a move to stop her as she got to her feet, but Rafti smiled at her and said, "I won't hurt her," and after a moment's hesitation the woman let the arm with which she'd been reaching for her daughter fall back to her lap.

Rafti gestured at the growth without touching it, asked gently, "Does that ever hurt you?"

"Sometimes, but it's going away. It'll be gone soon and then I'll be well again."

"Would you like it to stop hurting right away?"

"I told you we don't need any healing," the father said before the girl could answer.

"I won't ask you for anything in return," Rafti said. "As she said, it's going away. I'll just help her get well sooner."

"Why?"

"I'm a healer. Healers heal."

The father scowled, turning the idea around in his mind, finally said, "Go ahead. But if you hurt her—"

"I won't." Rafti turned back to the girl. "Would you like it to stop hurting right away?" she asked again.

"Yes."

"I'm going to touch your neck. When I do, I want you to close your eyes and think about your name. Don't tell me what it is, just say it over and over to yourself until you feel warm and all the hurt goes away. Do you think you can remember that?"

The girl nodded. "Then close your eyes." Rafti cupped

her hand over the growth. It almost filled her palm. "Keep on saying your name over and over to yourself," Rafti told her.

Rafti studied the girl through the dead eye, narrowing her attention, putting everything but the girl and her sickness out of her mind. As the ghost reached out and grasped the sickness, kept it from taking refuge elsewhere in the girl's body, Rafti drew on the girl's life-heat, summoning her sleeping inner fires against the sickness and burning it from her, driving it forth, out into Rafti's cupped hand.

There was a stench of putrefaction. Rafti snatched her hand away with the sickness clutched in it. The sickness struggled to escape into her flesh but the ghost held it prisoned in Rafti's clenched fist while she summoned her own vastly more powerful inner flames against it. When she opened her hand a moment later, nothing remained of the sickness but a coating of fine ash.

"Open your eyes," Rafti said. "How do you feel?"

"It doesn't hurt anymore," the girl said, hesitantly touching her neck. "But it's still there."

"It will be gone by the time you wake up tomorrow."

The girl nodded, accepting it all on faith. "Will you dance for us tomorrow, then?"

"I have to leave for Kyborash tomorrow." She smiled tiredly at the girl. "I'm sorry."

"Why are you going to Kyborash?" the brother asked as the girl went back to sit by her mother. "There was a flood, and then the Nomads attacked. . . . There isn't much left."

Tell them someone's waiting for you there, the ghost advised.

Rafti invented a Nomad warrior waiting for her in Kyborash.

"Does he know you're coming this way?" the husband asked. The greed was back in his voice, overcoming any fear and gratitude he might have felt. Rafti fixed him with a stare, and he added by way of belated explanation, "We don't get many travelers through here."

"He came through here a few days ago," Rafti said. "He taught me the route."

They didn't like that. "We didn't see anyone. . . ." the brother said.

"He would have ridden through at night, after you were asleep."

"We would have heard him," the brother insisted.

"Not if he didn't want you to hear him."

In the silence that followed the girl asked, "Why do you keep your face hidden like that? Is it because you're a firedancer?"

"In a way." Rafti swallowed the last of her broth. "But it's been a long day and I'm too tired to answer any more questions. I need to get some sleep."

She left the family still sitting around the fire pit and curled up around her things on her right side, leaving the dead eye, whose vision was not at all hindered by the layers of silk hiding it from the others, to watch over her.

Sleep came quickly, and with it the dream she had almost every night now: the forest village surrounded by cedars and spruces where Sulthar had found her after she'd left the Mother's Burning Mountain, and where he'd taught her how to use her mastery of fire to become a firedancer. Each time she returned to it in dream he taught her more of the secret language the animals and spirits used among themselves, and more of the names of power with which they could be commanded.

Each time he taught her more of the healing that she could use to cure or ease the pain of anyone else she might happen to meet, but that could do nothing for her.

That healing she would find only in Kyborash, with her other self's bones.

Chapter Twenty-nine

In her dream she was always only herself, Rafti Shonraleur's-Daughter, and not Rafti Tas Gly's-Daughter, yet at the same time she was also always a green gull, like the malachite green gulls that wheeled over Lake Nal, their white wingtips and tail feathers flashing when they caught the sun. It made no difference what time she fell asleep: in her dream it was always late morning and she would find herself high over the lake, already angling down toward the thick blue-green forest on the shore, the towering spruces, pines, and cedars in whose shade the forest people lived. Sulthar would be waiting for her in the clearing at the center of the forest people's village, and when she flew to him he always caught her in his hands and gently stroked her feathers while he spoke to her, or set her on his shoulder to watch him while he showed her what he wanted her to learn.

But this time his face was grim when he sighted her. As she flew to him he made an abrupt, chopping gesture, and she found herself extending downward, regaining human form. She seemed to be wearing the same clothes she'd fallen asleep in, only they were dry and clean and new again, but when she put her hand to her face she felt only the puckered empty socket where her other self's eye should have been.

"Why did you bring me here, like this?" she asked Sulthar.

But he only gestured at the sky and said, "Casnut demanded it."

She looked up, saw an immense gray hawk with a cruel hooked beak and eyes of burning darkness beating toward her out of the empty blue sky.

"Casnut?" she whispered, suddenly terrified as she remembered the hawk that had attacked Moth after he and Sulthar had brought her back from the dead. Sulthar had told her that that was Casnut, their master, and that Casnut would kill Moth if Moth did not kill him first.

Her hand went back to her empty eye socket again. She wanted the other Rafti, needed her advice, her reassurance.

"Casnut will not harm you," Sulthar said, and she drew confidence from his voice. "He merely wishes to teach you something you will need to know."

"Why me?" she asked, but even as she spoke the gray hawk dived at her and she cringed away, put up her hands involuntarily to shield her face and remaining eye, stepped back.

When she lowered her hands again, Casnut was standing in front of her, examining her.

He was taller than any man she'd seen before, lean but immensely powerful-looking. His thick beard was divided into three braids, the central braid hanging to his waist, while the outside two were looped back over his shoulders and woven into the hair from his scalp to form a single thick braid that fell almost to the back of his knees. Hair and beard were pale yellow shot through with silver, while his skin was a gray so dark it was almost black.

Over breeches and a vest of red-brown leather he wore a caftan of black goatskin, from which hung myriads of living snakes, some with one head, others with two or three heads. The snakes writhed in and out of the confusion of metal objects suspended from the caftan—copper mirrors, a small golden bow and seven tiny golden arrows, the golden skeleton of a hawk that seemed to be watching her with a living intelligence, like the intelligence in the eyes of the brown owl from whose living skin and feathers the shaman's cap had been fashioned—

Like the fierce intelligence in the black eyes with which Casnut himself regarded her. She took an involuntary step back, remembering the shaman who had killed Shulteurtas Jattasteq's-Son and his daughters, then stopped, paralyzed, unable to break the fascination of those eyes.

Casnut held her there a moment, then glanced away, freeing her. She looked down at his feet, afraid to risk meeting his gaze again.

"I won't harm you, Rafti," he said, and his voice was deep and rich, almost gentle. She looked up at his face again, but kept her gaze focused on his mouth and chin, avoiding his eyes.

"What do you want from me?" She tried to make her voice defiant, succeeded only in sounding frightened.

"You call yourself a healer, yet you are unable to ascend the Cosmic Tree, the Tree of All Life, to the heaven beyond the heavens where all truenames and true healing lie. Where you yourself were healed. I can teach you to make that ascent."

"Healed like *this?*" she demanded.

"The healing there lies in the truename. It takes courage to assume a new truename. More courage than you can imagine. But if you wish, you can make yourself whole there."

His voice was so soft, so unexpectedly kind, that she finally dared raise her gaze to his again. "Why?" she asked. "Why are you doing this for me?"

"Because there will be times when I will need you to heal others for me."

"Moth?" she asked, remembering how Sulthar had had

to stay by Moth's side for months helping him regain his strength after they'd brought her back from the dead.

"Among others, yes."

"Why not just heal him yourself? Or have Sulthar do it?"

"Sulthar will not always be there when Moth needs him. And I may be dead, or trying to kill Moth at the time."

Rafti took an involuntary step back. "Why teach me how to heal him if what you really want is to kill him?"

"I don't want to kill him. We are at war, he must learn to defend himself against our enemies, but what that demands of him is more than any sane man would be willing to risk. The only way to force him to change as he must is to make his survival dependent upon it. And so I try to kill him, hoping that he will have mastered the means to prevent me."

"What if you succeed?"

"Then I will have to find someone else."

"And that's all?"

"No. But Moth will need to be strong in ways that neither you nor Sulthar will ever need to be, and he must be forced to develop that strength, however much pain and suffering it costs him. I ask nothing of him that my own master did not demand from me, that I do not still demand of myself."

"Because you're at war?"

"Yes."

"At war with whom?"

"With the Taryaa. The Royal Eunuchs who rule the cities of the Delta, south of Chal."

Rafti shook her head. The names meant nothing to her. "Why?" she asked. "They must be so far away, at the other end of Ashlu. What have they done to you to make you want to sacrifice your life, Moth's life, to destroy them?"

"They want to stop the world. Halt the progression of

life through death and renewal and back to life again, so that what is alive will remain living forevermore, what is dead will never live again. They want to wrest Ashlu from the Mother and the sun, bring it to eternal frozen night, for only then will they find an end to the mutability that threatens them with death and transformation."

"They have that much power?"

"Not yet, though they have been building toward it for ages. When their lives here end they pass from Ashlu to become the stars, frozen Nighteyes, neither dead nor alive, reduced to their immutable vision."

Rafti looked at Sulthar for confirmation. "It's true, Rafti," he said. "They hate us, all shamans, even those of us who are only healers and talkers-to-animals, like me. By our very existence we break down the barriers between the worlds, and the Taryaa need those barriers everlasting and impenetrable if they are to bring the world to a halt. Whenever we ascend to even the lesser heavens or rescue a spirit from the underworld, whenever we so much as heal a child who would otherwise have died, we retard and threaten their dominion."

"What about the Earth Mother?" Rafti asked. "Why doesn't She stop them?"

"The Mother will do nothing, Rafti," Casnut said. "She has no awareness of anything beyond the cycles of birth and death. All that matters to Her is that the world continue, day after day, season after season, year after year, that She play Her part in the eternal cycles of birth and death and rebirth. Nothing that we can do as individual men or women is real to Her, not the way the earth and the seasons are.

"We shamans may seem to defy Her when we snatch people like you back from the dead, yet nothing that we do between our births and our deaths makes any difference to Her, so long as we are born and we die. She is no more aware of us than She is of the Taryaa, yet where they would try to destroy Her works, we would preserve them.

In serving us you would be serving the Mother, Rafti, offering Her far greater service than you would ever have been able to do Her in your valley."

"That's all you'll ever demand of me? To heal Moth and some other people? You won't try to kill me too?"

"I will not attack or harm you, Rafti. I will aid you when I can, as will Sulthar. Yet even so you will find that healing is often no simple task. And remember, now that you are a healer and a shamaness, the Taryaa will consider you as much their enemy as they do Moth or me, whether or not you develop as a healer or do anything to help us. Yet the greater your powers as a healer, the less vulnerable you will be to them."

Rafti thought a moment, finally asked, "What do I have to do?"

"Come with me." He stepped past her. When she turned to follow she saw that the stone hut in which her physical body was sleeping had appeared in the dream, and now filled the clearing in the center of the forest people's village.

Casnut paused an instant before the low entrance. Rafti had an instant's vision of him trying to crawl through and getting stuck in the hole with his snakes writhing and hissing in complaint as he squeezed his way in, his long legs extended out behind him and kicking ridiculously. But as Casnut approached the hut he shrank, so that by the time he reached the entrance he was able to walk through it without bowing his head.

This is a dream. Only a dream, Rafti reminded herself as she followed him. The hut expanded before her. She stepped through the doorway.

Inside, the hut had become immense, a hollow mountain. The villagers were gone. A fire burned in a great pit in the center of a vast plain. A gigantic birch tree with its bark and branches removed extended up out of the fire through the smoke hole in the transfigured hut's roof. Notches for footholds had been carved in the tree trunk's side. The fire licked at the slick wood without consuming it.

Beside the fire pit Rafti's horse was tethered. It was a pure, dazzling white now, its injured leg completely healed.

They walked across the plain to it. The heat from the fire pit beat on Rafti as the horse whinnied, happy to see her, and nuzzled her hand.

"Hold the horse's head," Casnut told her. "Whatever happens, no matter how cruel it may seem to you, don't let go. The horse will not be harmed."

Rafti wrapped her arms tightly around the horse's head and neck, waited.

Casnut stepped back. With his left hand he began tapping out a strange, broken rhythm on the drum hanging from his waistband. The horse began to struggle in silence. Rafti held it tighter, whispered reassuringly to it.

Still drumming with his left hand, Casnut seized one of the three-headed snakes dangling from his caftan with his right hand. He pulled it free, stepped forward again, and began lashing the horse frenziedly.

This is only a dream, a dream, a dream, Rafti told herself desperately as she fought to keep the horse still. He told me he wouldn't hurt it.

There was only the sound of the serpent striking the horse's back, the roaring of the fire behind them. The horse continued to struggle silently, even its hoofs making no sound when they struck the ground.

Suddenly the animal stopped. It stood there, rigid, and began to quiver. Its eyes lost their panic, glazed. Rafti almost lost her hold on it but Casnut shouted at her and she caught hold of it again.

The quivering increased until the animal was quaking, shivering, as though great waves were breaking against its skin from within.

"Get back," Casnut ordered Rafti. She let go of the horse's neck and stepped back just as, with a sound like leather ripping, the horse split open. Great cracks and rents appeared in its skin and spread; from them a quick pink mist began to ooze languidly forth.

Casnut continued to lash the horse until all the mist had been forced from it and was beginning to collect in a vaguely equine cloud. He tossed the serpent he'd been wielding aside, stepped forward, and caught the shivering, shrunken horse up in his arms. Lifting it effortlessly high above his head, he snapped its back with a single powerful twist, then threw the still-screaming animal into the flames.

Rafti closed her eyes, put her hands over her ears, trying to flee the horror of the horse's unending scream. For an instant she saw the tomb in which the other Rafti's skeleton lay chittering to the skeletons of the other handmaidens beginning to take form around her, but she pushed the vision away from her, refused it, and awoke to the clammy darkness of the mountain hut. A hand was sliding her leather pouch smoothly out of her clothing while she could hear her horse—her real horse this time, and no mere dream fragment—screaming with fear and agony, the sound muffled by the walls and the distance and the storm still raging outside.

Chapter Thirty

Rafti grabbed, caught hold of a skinny wrist an instant before it twisted free. She heard the sound of running feet in the darkness.

Make a light, her other self told her.

Rafti summoned the fires within, reached out with them to the fire pit. The coals had been extinguished, were swimming in the water that had been used to douse them, but her anger lashed her inner fires white-hot. She let the fire flow from her into the wet coals and wood. The wettest coals exploded as the fire pit burst into flames, steam roiling up and out to veil the hut in scalding haze. She heard a scream, caught a glimpse through the steam of a whimpering figure scrabbling on hands and knees toward the doorway, dragging Rafti's sacks and saddle behind.

The son. She had been afraid they'd sent the girl she'd cured to rob her.

She started after him.

Wait, her other self warned as she stooped for the door hole. That's what they want you to do. Look.

The ghost opened her perceptions to Rafti. Through the dead eye Rafti saw the villagers, wavering and colorless despite the torches they carried, the bright stolen garments they all wore. What must have been every adult in the village, both men and women, were waiting for her outside, as they must have waited for the chance travelers, the refugees fleeing Kyborash, whom they'd killed for the precious copper swords and knives and copper-headed spears clutched in their hands.

The boy came out of the door hole, sprang to his feet, and ran, heading toward the enclosure where the dead eye showed Rafti her horse lying dead and bleeding as the village children hacked it up for meat with flint knives.

One of the children was the girl she'd cured.

Why didn't you summon me back? Rafti demanded of the ghost. Or—

I tried. You were somewhere I couldn't reach you. I can't use your body without your permission, you know that. But show yourself to them now. Terrify them. It's too late for anything else.

Rafti undid the layers of silk that hid the dead eye. Closing her good eye, she took a deep breath, tried to still herself to everything but her heartbeat, the Festival drum, the Festival song's monotonous rhythms. She loosed the fires within, felt them grow, filling her, encompassing her . . . feeding on her anger as they fed her anger, the two one and the same now, and she was lost within the flames, was the flames, sending out tongues to lick at the stone hut surrounding her, to encompass the stone in turn, feed on it even as it melted and ran, so that the very stone took flame and burned. Her humanity was forgotten, as meaningless as the colorless villagers the dead eye still showed her as they dropped their weapons and ran, screaming, the stone hut around her only ash now, and she stood there on the bare ground, melted rock flowing around her feet, in the night and the rain, burning, the tongues of flame reaching out from her after the fleeing villagers, the boy stumbling along with her saddle and sacks. . . .

There's no need to hurt any of them, the other Rafti told her. They won't threaten you anymore. Show yourself to them now.

The ghost's words brought her back to herself. She let the blaze around her die down, stilled the fires' hungers, and took the burning back out of the ground and air, back into herself, until at last the rain hit the obsidian surface on which she stood without hissing. All that remained was the light of burning that aureoled her still, which showed her unveiled to the villagers as they stared at her from hiding, showed the right side of her face that of a beautiful girl, the left side a puckered purple ruin, whose dead eye fixed them with its unclean stare.

"You! Boy!" she called. "Bring me my things."

The boy just stood huddled behind the hut where he had taken shelter until his mother and one of the village men grabbed him, wrestled him forward toward Rafti, then retreated back into the shadows.

The boy looked around in panic, saw that he was alone with Rafti on the glassy-smooth surface. His face and hands were pink where the steam had scalded them.

He stumbled forward, one, two steps, then suddenly threw everything at Rafti, turned on his heels, and fled panting and gasping into the rain.

Rafti let him go. It was almost dawn. She could feel the villagers still watching her, ready to flee again if she turned her attention to them. She burned the sacks free of the now-useless saddle, bent down, and levered them up onto her shoulders, staggered under their weight.

How much farther? she asked her other self.

Three days, perhaps four with all you're carrying. We should stay here longer, sleep in one of their huts until the rain stops, eat. They won't cause you any trouble now.

No. I can't.

It wasn't the villagers. She knew they were too terrified of her now to be any further danger. But the dream was still there, waiting for her if she let herself fall asleep again. Casnut, and her horse screaming as the shaman broke its back and tossed it into the flames, while here, in this village, they were slaughtering the horse and hacking it up for meat.

Which way? she asked the ghost.

To your right.

Rafti made her way slowly through what remained of the village, along the path winding back and forth down the mountain's far slope.

The rain ceased just after dawn. She was halfway up the far slope, the late-afternoon sun blazing fiercely down on her, when at last she could continue no farther.

There was a large boulder a short ways off the trail. She climbed the loose, shifting rock to it, wedged herself in behind it, where she'd be protected from the sun, hidden from anyone coming upon her in her sleep.

Watch over me, she told her other self and relinquished control of her body. She slept.

Casnut plucked the green gull she'd become from the air. Setting her on the ground, he spoke a single quiet word and Rafti found herself human again, standing as before inside the enormous hut facing the fire pit.

"You lied to me," she said, but he gestured and spoke another word, and suddenly her horse was tethered in front of her, dazzling white, uninjured. Alive. It had no fear of her or of Casnut and tried to nuzzle her hand. At first she pulled back, but at last she let the horse nuzzle her and blow its nostrils into her cupped hands.

"And when I awaken?" she asked.

"This is your horse's spirit. Its body is dead."

The horse continued to nuzzle her, glad to see her, unaware that anything was different. She patted its head.

"To become a true healer you will need to learn the truenames of all those you would heal," Casnut told her. "Each of us is three beings: the spirit, which thinks and acts, dreams and dies and is reborn; the skeleton, our second self, which is born with us and returns to the Earth Mother after our deaths; and the truename, which is eternal and perfect in us and which dwells in the heaven beyond the heavens. But though the truenames are eternal, their relationship with our other selves is not constant: a man can lose his truename as easily as he can lose his soul or body, or the ties between the truename and the other selves can be loosened or distorted. And though the truenames are eternal, immortal, they are not rigid and unchanging like the stars: they are more, not less, alive than we are; they change and grow, mature and alter, and sometimes we are unable to follow them. But it is the name that fits soul to skeleton, that determines whether you are young or old, strong or weak, sick or well. It is the name that determines whether you have two eyes or one, whether you are blind or sighted, whether you are beautiful or hideous.

"To find your truename you will have to ascend the Cosmic Tree, and the only method you are capable of learning to make that ascent is the horse sacrifice. Do you understand?"

Rafti nodded.

"Take the horse's head and hold it," Casnut told her, fixing her with his stare until at last she took the horse's head in her arms and held it tightly for him.

It was only a dream, and Casnut had said that the animal would not be harmed.

Besides, the horse was already dead.

Chapter Thirty-one

Tramu's frightened whimpering took Moth's attention from the distant fishing village on the Nacre's shore that he'd been watching through his horses' eyes from the hillside thicket in which he'd had them hide themselves.

He let fade from his sight the huts of mud-plastered woven yellow reeds built on stilted platforms in the shallow marshes at the river's edge, with the men out casting nets from their round coracles while on the shore their women and children sewed fishskins together to make more coracles or mended the nets. He returned to the kailek, where he lay propped up against the remaining sacks of provisions, pretending to be asleep, the Sword That Was Asp lying sheathed in his lap, where he could feel its faint, hungry thrumming.

Tas Et, he commanded without opening his eyes. Show me what's happening to Tramu.

The shorter boatman was still straining at one of the kailek's twin tillers, managing to keep the raft moving smoothly onward through the churning, muddy waters, here where the Thys emptied into the far greater Nacre, but the other boatman had left his tiller. His hand was over Tramu's mouth and he was holding Moth's struggling cousin securely while he whispered in his ear despite

Tramu's desperate, uncomprehending attempts to escape. Tas Et brought the boatman's words to Moth: he was telling Tramu that either Tramu agreed to help shove Moth off the kailek when they came to the rapids above Kyborash or they would slit his throat.

His threats were without effect: Tramu was incapable of understanding them. The boatman's speech got wilder and wilder. He started shaking Tramu, all the while glancing fearfully back and forth between Moth—still feigning sleep—and Ashanorak, who was sitting at the front of the kailek looking out at the yellow-brown waters as though interested in nothing beyond the occasional drifting leaf or branch, the fish that sometimes darted to the surface in pursuit of fallen insects.

Are they hurting him, potter?

Not yet. He's frightened, nothing more.

Tell me if they begin to hurt him.

Ashanorak was hoping to force Moth into a confrontation with the boatmen that would make him reveal something more about the forces he could command, and so give Ashanorak something to report back to the Taryaa. He undoubtedly thought he was being both cautious and clever, had not yet realized that he was trying to use the boatmen in almost exactly the same way as the Taryaa were using him.

He's hurting Tramu now, the potter's ghost said even as Tramu's whimper once again escaped the hand over his mouth. The sword on Moth's lap began to vibrate angrily before Moth could push his own anger back, isolate it in the depths of his being where Asp could not draw upon it or use it against him.

The boatman glanced nervously at Moth. Moth made an elaborate show of awakening reluctantly: yawning, rubbing at his eyes, stretching, and wincing with unfeigned agony at the pain his movements cost him.

The boatman had let go of Tramu at the first sign of Moth's reawakening. Even as Tramu ran to the protection he had come to know he would find with Moth, the boatman grabbed the second tiller, so that by the time Tramu threw himself down and curled up in a tight, defensive ball next to Moth, there was nothing to show that either boatman had ever been doing anything but guiding the raft through the troubled waters.

"What is it, Tramu?" Moth asked. The question was for Ashanorak and the boatmen, but the warmth in his voice was for Tramu. "It's all right, Tramu."

He tapped out a message of comfort and reassurance on his drum, saw from Tramu's face that the drum-spirit had been able to convey it to him.

Moth shook a few dry leaves and root shavings from the vials the Taryaa had given him out onto his palm and swallowed them. Soon the pain in his leg and side began to recede. He stood up, favoring his good leg, and slipped the sheathed sword into its back harness, then limped over to stand beside Ashanorak and look out with him at the muddy swirling water and the green distant shores.

"We're on the Nacre now?" he asked finally, breaking the silence.

"Yes. We passed the Singing Straits almost a daysixth ago."

"How long did I sleep, then?" He watched some of the tension go out of Ashanorak as the Deltan decided that Moth's questions really were as innocent as they seemed, and thus meant that the shaman had not yet noticed anything.

"A day and a half."

"How much longer until we reach Kyborash?"

"Three days, or so they tell me." Ashanorak looked quizzically up at Moth. "You're from there, aren't you, shaman? So why ask me?"

Moth shook his head. "We weren't a river people. Besides, the river's nothing like this there."

Ashanorak grunted.

"Your friends will be waiting for us when we land?"

Moth asked, letting the pain in his leg and side put a slight quaver in his voice.

"Don't worry, shaman, they'll have the rest of the herbs the Taryaa promised you. The Royal Eunuchs keep their bargains."

"True." Moth hobbled over to Tramu, sat down painfully next to him with his legs stretched out in front of him. He put the Sword That Was Asp on his lap again, with his right hand resting on its pommel, and closed his eyes.

Watch over Tramu for me, he told the potter. Let them frighten him all they want, but call me back if they start causing him any real pain.

I won't let them hurt him, the Ri ghost assured Moth.

Take me back to the village, Moth commanded Tas Et.

And he was there, looking out of the horses' eyes at the village and at the Nacre beyond it glinting silver and orange with the lowering late-afternoon sun.

The fishermen were returning with their catches. Moth studied them, finally chose a stout, powerful-looking man with an oversized coracle who'd had an excellent day and who was returning with more fish than his family would need.

That one, he told Tas Et. Prepare him for tonight.

Chapter Thirty-two

The sun was setting. Moth waited until he was sure Ashanorak was watching him, then opened the Taryaa's vial, shook the few remaining root shavings out into his hand, and tossed the empty vial petulantly over the side.

Ashanorak's gaze followed the vial an instant before returning to Moth, long enough for Moth to trap the shavings under his thumb. He put his open palm to his mouth and licked it clean, swallowed, and grimaced as though trying to force down something so bitter that he was hard put to keep from gagging.

He turned to glare at Ashanorak. "Three more days, you told me?"

A shrug. "So the boatmen say."

"It's too long!" He kept his voice petulant. "I don't have anything left. I can't last till then."

"There is little I can do about that, shaman." In Ashanorak's voice Moth could hear a hint of the contempt that had come to replace the fear in which the Deltan had once held him. "The Royal Eunuch gave you what he had. If you'd been willing to leave when the kailek was ready, you'd be in Kyborash now. As it is, you'll have to wait."

Moth turned away without answering, exaggerated his limp as he stumbled over to sit down and lean back against the provision sacks again. Tramu was waiting for him there, watching him.

"It's all right, Tramu." He accompanied his words with the drum, let the drum-spirit find its way to Tramu's dislodged soul, caught between his body and the spirit-world, and soothe him in his confusion.

No one else was looking at him. He dropped the shavings into a fold in his waistband, where they joined those he'd been saving since the beginning of the trip downriver.

Tas Et? he asked.

Your fisherman will be waiting for you in the center of the river when you pass.

What did you tell him?

That if he does what I demand of him, he will not be harmed.

Good. You didn't have any trouble?

No. Some of the others went after him and tried to make him return to shore until he hit one of them with his paddle. Then they decided to leave him out there until morning in the hope that he'll recover his senses on his own.

Let me know when we're close to him.

Tramu was dozing fitfully now, quivering and mumbling, occasionally jerking awake an instant before falling asleep again. He always slept that way, unable either to escape his dreaming altogether or to find his way fully into the dream realm, where his dreams could develop and complete themselves, liberating him from them and bringing him, perhaps, the peace and strength that would allow him to fully return to his body.

Moth continued drumming, so softly now that Ashanorak and the boatmen wouldn't hear him unless they concentrated on doing so. Gradually Moth altered the rhythms, so that instead of soothing Tramu the drum-spirit was opening the gates to the realm of dreams.

His drumming had little effect on Tramu, but the other men found their spirits loosening their holds on their bodies. Their exhaustion rolled over them like a great, slow wave and they began nodding quietly to themselves, vivid flashes of dream welling up in them as they drifted off.

Moth quieted his drumming even more, so that the men it was affecting could no longer hear it with their ears, but only with their bodies and spirits. He let his own head fall forward, so that it looked as though he'd fallen asleep again, with his hand resting on his drum, where the gathering twilight hid the rapid motion of his fingers.

Let me see them, Tas Et.

The two boatmen were sitting, talking drowsily with each other, their legs dangling over the back of the kailek as they held on to their tillers more to prop themselves up than to control the craft's motion. They had come to a stretch of river where the current was relatively sluggish, and they were in midstream, safely distant from both shores: there was nothing for them to worry about or watch except the water flowing placidly past.

Ashanorak was looking down on Moth and Tramu with the same expression of superiority and disgust that Moth had gone to so much effort to inculcate in him over the course of the voyage. He turned away, stifling a yawn, studied the boatmen for a moment.

The taller boatman was curling up beside his tiller, leaving the other to guide the kailek until the time came to take his place. The second boatman began singing to himself, a song he used to keep himself awake and alert on the river at night, but Moth's drumming was in his song, liquid and flowing like the sound of the river around them, the moon on the rippling water. Every now and then the boatman would dart a glance back at Ashanorak, straighten, and force himself to sing a little louder.

Ashanorak shook his head slowly, trying to clear it, but the boatman's song was in his ears, Moth's drumming in his body and spirit. He took a last look around the kailek, saw nothing threatening, nothing that wasn't as it ought to be, finally took his sword from his harness, and, clutching it the same way as Moth was clutching his own weapon, lay down and drifted into dream.

Without the fear of Ashanorak's anger to keep him fighting his drowsiness, the boatman's song faltered and died. He fell asleep still sitting propped up against the tiller.

Moth let his drumming grow louder, more powerful, as he drummed himself into waking dream after them. In the dream-realm he found Ashanorak dreaming of a Syrr's daughter he had had at Nanlasur; one of the boatmen was dreaming of a girl he had known in childhood, the other of a trip he'd made downriver with his father in his youth, back when Kyborash had been safe within the unconquerable Chaldan Empire.

Moth sealed them in their dreams, safe from fear, secured against any spirits that might speak to them in sleep and try to warn or influence them.

How much longer? he asked Tas Et.

Soon.

He took a pinch of root shavings and another of dried, crumbled leaves from his waistband, swallowed them.

Show me the horses.

They were still there, waiting patiently in the thicket above the fishing village. He guided them around the village, to a cove a short ways downriver.

The fisherman is close now, Tas Et warned him.

Bring him here, but don't let him make any noise.

Moth drummed himself back into the dreams of the others again, made sure that they were safely lost in sleep, then drummed them ever deeper, ever further from awakening, until at last he heard the slap of the fisherman's paddles in the water. He shook Tramu awake and stood, strapping the Sword That Was Asp across his back and shouldering the sack containing the dagger housing Tas Et and his few other possessions. Comforting Tramu with the drum, he led him over to the kailek's side.

The fisherman's terrified face looked up at him in the moonlight.

Tramu recoiled. Tell the fisherman to help me put him into the coracle, Moth told Tas Et, taking hold of Tramu and pulling him forward as gently as he could. Tramu struggled, cried out, but as soon as Moth and the fisherman had wrestled him into the coracle and Moth had wedged himself in beside him, Tramu quieted again.

Have him take us to shore. Downriver from the village, where the horses are waiting, Moth told Tas Et.

The fisherman began paddling, fighting the current until the kailek was lost in the night, then letting the current carry him along as he rowed the rest of the way to shore.

They landed without difficulty in the cove. Moth fixed the fisherman with a stare, then turned away and helped Tramu through the shallow, muddy water and the thick grasses to firm ground. The fisherman stayed behind, seated in his coracle.

Moth called his horses to him with the drum, patted and stroked them, let them blow their nostrils into his cupped hands. He helped Tramu up onto the roan's back and tied him in place, then used the drum to reassure both horse and rider and tell them what they had to do.

The fisherman was still watching from his coracle.

Tell him that if he waits there without moving until dawn, he will be free to go, Moth instructed Tas Et. He used a fallen log to climb up onto his black's back and they rode off. Tas Et had found a mountain trail that would enable them to reach Kyborash before the kailek, which could only follow the Nacre's slow, meandering course, and so would be held back by the sluggishness of the current until it came to the narrows above Kyborash.

Moth had not uttered a word in the fisherman's hearing, had only stared at him with eyes that in the moonlit darkness might easily have been mistaken for the amber yellow eyes of a Chaldan King. The story could only grow in the telling: by the time Ashanorak and the Taryaa traced Moth back to this fisherman and his village—if ever they did—the tale would have changed and developed beyond the point where anything useful could be learned from it. Anything, that is, except that Moth had been able to turn his shaman's abilities to subtlety and stealth when the situation demanded it.

That even if he was not yet powerful enough to be a threat to the Taryaa, he was a potential ally worthy of respect.

Chapter Thirty-three

Shortly before dawn on the second day, their path took them down out of the mountains and into the foothills.

Father buried the dolthe near here, Moth's Ri ghost told him. The ghost led him to a hill higher than the rest, almost a mountain in itself, though it was green all the way to its summit with forests and grasses.

They spiraled and switchbacked up the steep slopes, until, abruptly, the hill leveled off and Moth found himself on a grassy rim, looking down into a broad green bowl-shaped hollow. It had perhaps been the way the bowl's form resembled that of the pots he fashioned that had made Ri Tal choose it for his son's soul-in-clay, but the place reminded Moth more of a volcanic cone sinking slowly beneath the surrounding grasslands, already half buried by them. Within the bowl the ground was grass-covered but treeless, littered with stones of all sizes, from pebbles to boulders. A few naked rock formations still jutted up out of the grass and soil cover.

Over there, the potter's ghost said. Beneath that boulder. The one that looks like some sort of animal's liver.

Moth glanced back at Tramu, saw that he was still sleeping tied to the roan's back. He ordered the roan to follow him, urged his black down the slope into the bowl.

The boulder was dark gray, smooth and triple-lobed; it looked too heavy to move. Moth summoned strength from the spirits of his cap and costume, dismounted. The boulder came halfway up his thigh. Kneeling by it, he braced himself, put his good shoulder to it, and pushed tentatively. The boulder moved slightly before settling back. Perhaps it was lighter than he'd thought. He braced himself again, pushed a little harder, and something ripped in his side.

Shaking some of the Taryaa's medicine out into his hand, he stared at it a long instant, then put it away again. He didn't have enough to waste it on anything less important than a threat to his life.

He walked around the boulder, studying it. The ground on one side sloped slightly away, not enough to let him roll the boulder down it, but still . . . He knelt, felt the earth. It was loose and dry, should be easy enough to dig away.

But that would take time. He untied Tramu and laid him out on the ground, where he could sleep more comfortably. Tramu half-awakened for an instant and looked warily around before dozing off again.

Watching him sleep while he got his breath back, Moth had a sudden urge to send Tas Et into him, use Tramu's strength to move the boulder and have done with it. Moth had felt the urge before, when Tramu was proving unusually recalcitrant, or when he was faced with some obstacle demanding more physical strength than it was safe for him to use. Yet those times, like now, Moth had held back, certain somehow that forcing Tramu to share his body with the frozen-souled thing that had once been his father would be more than his cousin's trapped and atrophied spirit could endure, would be enough to drive him from his life and body for good.

Moth turned away from Tramu, left him to sleep. Using the dagger housing Tas Et, he dug a hole big enough to house the triple-lobed boulder just downslope of it, then carefully undermined it. Walking around to the other side, he put his good shoulder to it and pushed. It wobbled, settled back. He shoved again, harder, feeling that ripping pain in his side again, but this time the boulder rolled away, down into the hole.

A red-brown scorpion as big as his hand that had been hiding under the rock threatened him with its barbed tail as it retreated. Moth waited until it was well gone, then sat down where the boulder had been and began to dig.

Ri Tal had buried the dolthe deep, but it took Moth less time than he'd needed to move the rock before he'd unearthed a stout but gracefully proportioned wheel-turned jar. The jar was glazed a deep orange, with the Ri Sil's mark in black on the side; Ri Tal had rolled the clay with which the jar was sealed with his own cylinder seal. Any Chaldan happening upon the jar would have realized that it could only contain some Ri's soul-in-clay, and so would have returned it to the place where he'd found it.

Moth had dreamed of his dolthe, and used those dreams to fashion the soul-shadow he had once worn around his neck, but he had never actually seen it. He brushed the jar clean with his fingers, put it down on the boulder, looked around for a smaller rock with which he could break it open.

Not yet, his Ri soul advised him. The dolthe cracked when I died. Wait until you have everything else ready.

Moth nodded, thinking about what he'd need. The golden dagger, of course, but after that a forge in which to work, hammers and tongs, beeswax, the proper charcoals . . . He could use the forge he had once shared with his grandfather if it was still standing. Then he would have to search all over Kyborash, find a forge where the smith had been forced to abandon his tools when he fled, or had been killed before he could recover them.

There had been a time when what he planned to do would have demanded months of ritual purifications and prayers to Sartor and the Earth Mother, but no longer. He would do what had to be done with his proper forces, and those of the spirits that were his to command.

He cleaned the pus from the wounds in his leg and side, packed them with fresh snarl leaves and honey grass. He slept then, his cap and costume resting on his wounds so the spirits they housed could help him fight the sickness.

In his dream he tried to find his way to Sulthar, but the northern forests were dark and impenetrable, and when he tried to thread his way through them as a hawk, they closed around him and held him back.

When he awakened at nightfall the pain was so bad that he couldn't wall it off without separating himself so completely from his body as to leave him only half conscious, and he was so weak that he was unable to tie Tramu to the roan and then mount his own horse again before he'd swallowed all the root shavings he'd refused himself earlier.

He sat immobile on his horse a long moment, waiting until he had his breath back and the worst of the dizziness was past.

Tas Et. Can you find Ashanorak for me?

He's in the Siltemple, nephew.

It was pointless to keep on denying the truth any longer. He should have been in Kyborash before Ashanorak, but he'd been too weak to keep up the necessary pace. He had to have the medicine the Taryaa had promised or he would be too feeble to stand against the Necropolis's guardians, too weakened to command the spirits whose aid he'd need for his Ri soul's resurrection.

Is Ashanorak alone?

No. There are seven other men with him. Four Deltan warriors, two Teichi, and a Chaldan.

None of the Taryaa?

Not in the Siltemple itself, but there is one in the godhouse atop the ziggurat.

The Fair where the Deltans, Chaldans, and Nomads had met to trade with one another had always been held near Kyborash. Was that why the eunuch was in Kyborash, because it could make contact with Nomads and Chaldans there with equal ease? Or was it waiting for him?

Does Ashanorak have the medicines? he asked Tas Et.

One of the Deltans is carrying them.

Keep watch on them all. Let me know if the Taryaa awakens or anything changes.

He would have to get the medicines despite the Taryaa, by stealth and subtlety if it was still possible, by violence otherwise. He no longer had any choice.

Chapter Thirty-four

There's a house ahead with some of its roof still intact, Rafti's other self said. You can sleep there.

Rafti let the ghost guide her steps. The moon had already set; dawn was still just a faint hint of rose in the sky ahead. The ground was soft underfoot, marshy-smelling; toads croaked plaintively in the fields around her, and in the distance she could hear a night heron calling. The dead eye showed her the house, colorless and unreal. It was bigger than any house she'd ever been in, though her other self's memories told her that any moderately successful member of a lesser Sil might have owned it.

She staggered in through the doorslit, too exhausted to notice the bones heaped just inside until she tripped over them and went sprawling. The skeletons chittered angrily at her as she got to her feet again and wiped her hands on her cloak.

Let me speak to them, her other self said suddenly. Rafti gave her the use of her voice. The ghost spoke to the bones in the same chittering language they used among themselves and after a moment they quieted.

Give me the use of your body, the ghost said.

Why?

Their bones are all jumbled together. They want me to separate them, then lay their skeletons out correctly.

It seemed ridiculous. She had been walking since dawn of the previous day without pausing to rest for more than a few breaths at a time, and now she was going to spend the time she should have been sleeping rearranging a pile of rotting bones.

Why not wait, do it tomorrow if it's so important? she asked.

You don't understand. They have no tomorrow, no future. Only memories of the flesh that once clothed them and the need to lie in peace as they fade back into the Earth Mother. And—I knew them when they were alive. They were weavers, and always kind to me. It is little enough to do for them. You can sleep afterward.

Rafti gave her other self control, let her thoughts drift as the ghost knelt on the earth floor, disentangling the mossy bones and putting them back together as a man and a woman, two children.

Dilea and her husband, Tarim Nym, their daughters. Rafti recognized them from her other self's memories, remembering their warmth, how they'd always forgiven her the way she kept trying to make them admit the Tarim Sil and all the other craft Sils were inferior to the Tas Sil.

In the years since she'd left her valley, Rafti had given little thought to what she was going to do after recovering her other self's two skeletons. Kyborash had seemed impossibly distant, more something that gave direction to her life than a goal she actually expected to attain. But was this what her life was going to be like after they'd recovered the skeletons—spending the rest of her days surrounded by moldering bones, doing kindnesses to those already dead? She found herself longing for the life she'd had when she'd still expected to become the Earth Mother's Priestess and keep her people safe from harm. The life that her sister, Lashimi, must be living even now.

The comparison was too bitter. She turned away from it,

tried to lose herself in the bright colors of her other self's memories: the caravans making their way out of the city along the Avenue of King Delanipal the Conqueror, the warriors' helmets and breastplates and weapons glinting gold, silver, copper-red in the morning sun; the confusion of merchants, potters, warriors, confectioners, scribes, sellers of songs, and farmers in the Great Square, with the godhouse of bright blue-enameled brick atop the ziggurat, dominating everything; the forge in which her father, Tas Gly, had fashioned the few gold and silver ornaments he received commissions to make—

She remembered how exquisite she had thought the softly glowing gold, the bright silver and gems, he fashioned that first time she had been admitted to his forge, and then it was too late, the memory had caught her, forced itself upon her.

Tas Gly had been without sons and too poor to have an assistant, so she had sometimes been allowed to help him in the forge. At first she had thought his work beautiful, and had been proud to help him—for only in the Tas Sil were women ever allowed to enter even so far as she had into the mysteries of their husbands' or fathers' Sils, so no other girl her age could claim the dignity her responsibilities gave her in her own eyes. But when she was a little older she had seen how the other smiths laughed at him, and she had realized that her father would never be anything more than a goldsmith, never be permitted to work copper or forge weapons. She had cried, then, at the clumsiness of his workmanship, at the way he would emerge defeated from his forge at the end of the day with pieces that were almost beautiful, that could have been as beautiful as anyone else's—and had been, before he ruined them because he was unable to let them alone, to stop trying to rework them, until whatever initial beauty they might have had had been destroyed, and he could only patch and repair them as best he could to offer them up for sale so he could feed his family and buy new gold and silver with which to try again.

But her other self's memories of the father she had loved until he sold her were more bitter than her own, and it was a relief when at last the skeletons had been fitted back together and she could curl up to sleep on a pile of rubble in the corner, where what roof remained would shelter her from the morning light.

It was late afternoon when she awakened and saw the city for the first time through her living eye.

Where her other self's memories had prepared her for beauty, life, color, grandeur beyond anything she had ever seen, there was only ruin. It was impossible to believe that only nine years before Kyborash had been at the height of its splendor, inhabited by more people than she had seen in her entire life, the pride of the vast Chaldan Empire.

Where her memories showed her neat fields and garden plots, outlying houses of sun-dried brick between the river's high-piled earthen banks and the city's walls, now there was only swamp, brightly splotched with the blue reeds the city's children had once spent so much time clearing from the ditches and irrigation canals. The Warrior's Bridge was gone without a trace, both ends of its former span swallowed by the swamp.

And farther from the river, where there should have been more fields, groves of apricot trees and date palms, Rafti could see only blackened ground, charred stumps, the occasional dead fruit tree, its branches black and lifeless as everything surrounding it.

What happened? she asked the ghost.

The Spring Inundation, her other self told her after a moment's thought.

The information was all there, but it was too complicated, too tangled up in memories of things she'd never really seen, never felt, never had to understand.

Explain it to me.

The Nacre rises every spring, and without dikes to keep the waters within its banks, it floods. Without people to keep the mud and reeds from choking the canals and ditches, they must have closed, leaving the land away from the river without irrigation. Even now, the waters have been retreating for a month or more: soon this will all be dry and hard, and then only those plants with roots long enough to pierce through to the water beneath will survive.

Rafti made her way cautiously toward the crumbling city walls, the ruined gate. The tall grass rustled in the wind around her, closed over her, shielding her from the sight of anyone watching from the walls.

Turn away from the river, the ghost told her suddenly. You'll have to circle around and enter through the South Gate.

More scavengers like those villagers?

No. The ghost seemed amused. A lion. She's lying hidden in the grass just outside the gate.

What about inside the city? Are there people living there now?

A few. But not just scavengers. One of the Royal Eunuchs has taken up residence in the godhouse atop the Siltemple's ziggurat with his servitors. There are a few other bands of Nomads and Deltans as well, and some spies reporting back to the King of Chal.

The Royal Eunuchs? The ones that Casnut said he was at war against? Show it to me.

A slim figure lay motionless on its back on a raised platform in a small room of enameled blue bricks atop the ziggurat, its roof open to the sky. He—it—was dressed in loose white robes, with a band of crimson silk hiding its mouth. It might have seemed asleep if its round, pink eyes had not been open, staring sightlessly at the stars above. There was a thin coating of dust on its eyeballs, and yet its chest was still rising and falling steadily; it was still alive.

It's in some sort of trance, she realized. But why? What's it doing here?

They rule the cities of the Delta League, the ghost told her. We sometimes saw them when they came for the Fair, when Nomads, Chaldans, and Deltans all came together to trade with one another. But I don't know anything about a war between the Nomads and them.

Rafti let the ghost share her memories of the dream in which Casnut and Sulthar had told her about the Taryaa, asked again, What's one of them doing here?

I don't know. Its spirit seems—absent. As though it's asleep or . . . I don't know. But it doesn't seem to be any danger to us now, at least so long as we don't do anything to attract its attention to us.

No, Rafti agreed. She circled around, slipped into the city through the South Gate.

Within the walls it was even worse. Thick yellow mud covered the ground, squishy underfoot. Rafti realized that the city was being slowly buried, year after year, beneath successive layers of silt.

Fire had destroyed the few buildings with wooden or partially wooden frames. The sun-dried brick from which most of the others had been constructed was crumbling, dissolving back into mud, unable to resist the dampness. Plants had rooted themselves in the bricks and were splitting them apart; a tangle of nettles and purplish-green weeds choked the streets; and in the shade of a ruined house Rafti glimpsed a great bulbous yellow fungus growing sticky and pale.

Rafti looked around again, fighting to keep from being overwhelmed by her other self's sense of loss and anger. She attempted to fit what she saw to the ghost's memories of the Kyborash she'd known when she had been alive. Something like a white stick caught her eye and she realized abruptly that everywhere she looked, jutting from the mud or thinly covered by it, were bones. And now that she knew them for what they were, she could feel them whispering to one another, could feel the confused muttering of their speech as a wet vibration in the mud underfoot.

Can you understand what they're saying?

They're remembering who they were.

Rafti waited, but the ghost said nothing more.

Which way should we go? she finally asked.

They buried her body beneath a house on the far side of the city. The bones tell me there are people all around the Siltemple and the Great Square; we'll be safer if we avoid the center, circle around just inside the wall.

Left or right?

Left.

Rafti took a street as dead and rotting as the rest, while her other self fed her memories of the time when the fallen buildings had housed chisel workers, leather crafters, a family of scribes, even a few Warriors of the Hand.

Someone's coming! the ghost warned her suddenly. Hide!

Rafti glanced hurriedly around. One of the houses she'd just passed had an almost intact facade. She ran back and slipped in through its doorslit.

The roof had fallen in. She climbed a pile of loose rubble to the lightslit set high in the wall and peered out.

She could see the street clearly—could even see the line of small footprints leading to the house that would give her hiding place away to anyone who noticed them. She turned away from the street, examined the house. There was nowhere inside she could hide. The only other way out would be to climb one of the walls, but if she did, she'd be seen by anyone looking in her direction.

She heard voices, an onager's protest, somebody yelling at the animal. She put her eye back to the lightslit, squinted.

There were three men, dark-skinned with brown hair and beards. The first was tall and skinny, tugging on the onager's rope and wearing a scribe's ragged gray siltunic, but where the eye of the King should have been blazoned on his breast in gold there was now only a clumsily sewn patch of what looked like lionskin, with one corner flapping free. The others wore black siltunics in good repair. One was young, perhaps only a year or so older than Rafti, with a narrow gash of a mouth in a smug, plump face. The third man was old, small and twisted, and his right eye—like Rafti's left—was blind and milky.

Lapp Wur. The exorcist. Rafti felt the urge building to strike out at the bent man, burn him where he stood. She caught hold of her feelings, fought her other self's revulsion and hatred, damped the fires that had begun to flame in her before they could leap to Lapp Wur and destroy him.

Her other self's memories came welling up and she remembered the way her father had come gloating to her in those last days before she'd died. He'd boasted to her of how he'd bribed Lapp Wur to believe him when he accused Moth of sending spirits to torment him, and of how the exorcist was going to torture Moth until he admitted it. She had hated her father then, hated him worse than she had ever hated anyone before. She had died hating him, and it had only been in Sartor's Royal Realm, during the eternity she had spent reliving her life over and over again, that she had come to recognize the father she had loved so much in that greedy, ferretlike, lying little man who had so smugly sold her to her death. Only then had she realized that she had hated him as much for the way he had failed both her and himself as for what he'd actually done to her.

Rafti tore herself free of her other self's pain, forced herself to concentrate on the street outside again.

Lapp Wur stumbled, swore. He reached down into the muck beneath his feet and picked up a mud-filled skull, suddenly hurled it with a jerky, almost insectile motion to shatter like an egg against a nearby wall, splattering the tall man leading the onager with yellow mud.

The tall man glared angrily back at Lapp Wur, opened his mouth, then clamped it shut again. There was a faint smile on Lapp Wur's lips. The tall man lowered his head and turned back to gaze at the street in front of him once more—but by then both he and the onager had trampled Rafti's footprints, obliterating them.

Why didn't you warn me earlier? Rafti asked the ghost when they were gone. They might have found me.

There are too many skeletons here, too many broken bones crying out their confused memories . . . it is hard to know when they are speaking of things happening right now and when they are only remembering what they have known before.

But they're gone now, those three men? And no one else is coming?

You're safe again. But go slowly, and keep close to places you can hide in.

Twice Rafti had to detour to avoid buildings the ghost told her were inhabited; once she was forced to take shelter in a fire-gutted shrine while seven mounted men galloped by. They all looked like Nomads, but the ghost told her that they were the Royal Eunuch's servitors and that five of them were really Deltans.

It was well into the night by the time she reached the house beneath which the stillborn child had been buried. The house had been built on low ground, in a quarter of the city that had been almost completely razed and that was now flooded, and what remained of it was little more than a heap of crumbling and dissolving clay bricks jutting from the muddy water.

The child had been buried beside one of the interior walls. Even when Rafti had dragged away the rubble over it, the spot was still covered with three or four fingerwidths of foul-smelling stagnant water.

Rafti moved some of the rubble around to make a flat place, then unrolled one of the lengths of crimson silk she'd brought from the northern forests and spread it out, anchoring the corners with fragments of brick.

Crouching down, she tried to use her dagger to dig, but the mud was so wet it might as well have been liquid. The only thing she could do was scoop it up in her cupped hands, throw it away before it could drain through her fingers, then start over again. The walls of the hole kept collapsing inward, but she kept on trying until the rubble around the cleared area began sliding in as well.

Pausing an instant to catch her breath, she flattened out another spot a little farther away and spread the silk out there. She cleared more rubble and started over, trying to dig through to the firmer ground beneath the silt before it sifted over her work and buried it again, but the task seemed hopeless until finally, with dawn approaching, she thought of lining the hole with broken bricks. Though they didn't stop the mud's inward progress altogether, they did slow it to the point where she could dig mud out faster than the hole filled up.

Day came and she saw that there were no walls still standing anywhere near her, only low mounds of rubble, like the one she was working in. She was completely exposed, visible to anyone within a hundred twenty or more bodylengths, but there was no reason for anyone to come where she was and she was almost down to the child's bones, so she continued digging frantically until she realized that she had to be visible not only to anyone near her but to the Royal Eunuch in the godhouse of enameled blue bricks atop the Temple ziggurat.

What about the Taryaa? she asked the ghost. Is it awake? Can it see me?

I don't know. The ghost sounded abruptly worried. Its spirit still seems as absent as before but it's sitting up as if it were completely awake and aware now, questioning Lapp Wur about strangers in the city. . . .

And?

Lapp Wur is telling it that he hasn't seen anyone new in the city except a few scavengers, though it looks as though somebody might have ridden through on a horse a few days ago. The Taryaa is telling him to find out if anyone saw who it was, and if they did, where he came from and what happened to him. . . .

Is it looking in our direction?

It doesn't seem to be, but I don't know what it can perceive, what it can or can't do. We'll be safer if we hide until dark again.

Rafti put the silk back in her sack, took refuge for the day in a house just outside the flooded quarter. Sleep was a long time coming, but when at last she drifted off, she found herself back in the forest people's village. Sulthar was there alone this time, and it was good to see him, good to be a green gull in the forest's freshness and forget Kyborash's mud-choked desolation.

There's a Taryaa in Kyborash, she told him, after her first moments of delight had passed. In the godhouse on top of the ziggurat.

Has it seen you, or does it have any reason to know you're there?

I don't think so.

Then so long as you can keep it from noticing you, you should have nothing to fear from it. The Deltans and their Taryaan masters used to come to the Fair outside Kyborash to trade with the Nomads. Now they keep one of their number here to maintain contact with the Teichi and the others who serve them in Chal and in the north, and to keep the Chaldans from rebuilding the city. But none of that should make any difference to you, unless you do something to make it realize you're not just another scavenger.

Reassured, she gave herself back up to being the gull and to the joy of learning to use her wings, of soaring and swooping, gliding effortlessly above Lake Nal's clear, still waters.

When she awakened, the day had passed and the night was already half gone. But she had already cleared the rubble from the grave and most of the pieces of broken brick she'd used to line the hole were still in place, so the work was far easier even though the hole had filled back up with mud while she slept. She dug as fast as she could, scooping the mud up and hurling it away, and it was only a short while before her other self told her that they had reached the skeleton.

Rafti surrendered control. Working with the same rapid precision she'd displayed disentangling the weavers' bones, the other Rafti dug out the tiny, soft-tipped bones that had never had the chance to grow to their full length, the bony plates that would never fuse together to make a baby's skull, and laid them out on the silk.

As the skeleton began to take shape the ghost spoke to it in the chittering whispers the skeletons used among themselves, but the bones remained silent. The other Rafti was digging much more carefully now, sifting the mud delicately through her fingers as she searched for a sliver or flake or jagged fragment of shattered bone she could fit to one of the bones on the silk, for scattered carpals and metacarpals she could put together to make hands or feet.

Finally she seemed to have finished. She sat back on her haunches in the mud, staring at the tiny reassembled skeleton, then asked it a question. There was no answer. She repeated her question, waited, then rapped out a sharp command.

What's wrong? Rafti asked. Why doesn't it answer?

Perhaps some of the bones are still missing. . . . Her other self sounded hesitant, unsure for almost the first time since they'd left the Mother's Burning Mountain. She groped in the mud some more, letting the fine silt sift through her fingers again and again, finally went over to where she'd thrown the mud she'd flung away earlier and examined it carefully.

What is it? Rafti asked. Are any of the bones missing?

Not missing, exactly, but . . . some of the cervical vertebrae have been too badly crushed. I have all the larger pieces, but the rest are too tiny, like dust, and there are too many of them, they're all mixed in with the mud or water or washed away. . . .

Then it's—dead? Destroyed? You can't put it back together somehow, find a way to heal it?

No. Maybe. I don't know. I can't do anything now, but there might be a chance, after we get my other skeleton back—

What about my eye? My face? Can you heal me without the child's skeleton?

I don't know. I won't know anything until we recover my other skeleton.

Rafti carefully wrapped the child's bones and put them away in one of her sacks. The ghost guided her back to the house in which she'd spent the previous day.

She dreamed again of the forest village, of Sulthar and Casnut, her horse screaming in agony as she held it prisoner and stared at the betrayal in its liquid brown eyes, but the dream was merely a dream, without message or meaning.

Until it changed, and she dreamed she was trapped in her other self's bones in SarVas's Necropolis. Suddenly Moth burst through the burial chamber's wall struggling against unseen spirits, the Sword That Was Asp glowing a malevolent red in his hands, only to collapse bleeding and unconscious to the floor.

When Rafti awakened, the dead eye showed her that he was lying there still, bleeding from his eyes and forehead, from what seemed to be hundreds of wounds both great and small.

Unconscious, he still clutched the Sword That Was Asp in his hands, and with every instant it drank more of his fading life.

Chapter Thirty-five

Their route took them up out of the foothills and back into the mountains again. At midday they came to a village—or what remained of a village, for in its center, surrounded by half-melted stone huts, was only a smooth glassy expanse, like obsidian, but banded and striated with oranges and red-browns that made it look like an enormous piece of polished jasper set flat into the ground.

Moth approached the smooth expanse. His horse nosed at it, nostrils flaring. Moth could smell a faint but pervasive odor of burned rock, slag, and ashes, underlying the heavier stenches of goats and human filth.

Tramu also recognized the smell, remembering it from the mines. He began to whine desperately, struggling to escape the bonds holding him on the roan's back.

Can you calm him? Moth asked his Ri ghost.

I'll try. The ghost separated itself from Moth, and for a moment Moth could see it clearly: a boy of fourteen, with brown hair and soft black eyes alive in his dead face; his skin was dry and leathery, pierced everywhere except around the mouth and eyes with small triple-lipped wounds. Then the ghost faded into Tramu's dreams and was gone.

Tramu quieted again. Moth went back to studying the village.

A Master of Fire had been here. Probably a Tas weaponsmith who'd been attacked by the villagers and who'd discovered he could use his mastery of fire to defend himself outside the sacred confines of the forge despite the vows he had sworn and everything the Tas Sil had taught him.

Moth could see a goat behind one of the intact huts, hear others bleating in some sort of enclosure, but there was no sign of the village's inhabitants.

Where are they? he asked Tas Et.

Huddled in their huts watching you through the chinks in their walls.

Is there any danger?

No. They've seen the red in your hair; they're too terrified to attack you.

Could the weaponsmith have been Tas No? Moth turned the idea over in his mind a moment, examining it. His grandfather had been old when Kyborash had been conquered, and Moth had always assumed he'd been killed, but was there any chance he might have escaped? If he'd broken his vows like this Tas, he would have been able to use his mastery of fire to defend himself—

But Tas No would have died rather than break his vows. Whoever the Tas who had done this had been, he was only a stranger, and Moth had no time to waste on him or this village. He urged the horses on again.

By evening he was close enough to Kyborash to look down upon it from the mountain he was descending and see it spread out below him like a half-buried corpse.

It was the first time Moth had seen Kyborash since Casnut had chosen him from the captives lined up for his inspection in the Great Square. Moth could sense his Ri soul mourning the city, but he closed himself to the ghost's emotions: that part of him was dead. And even if it had not been, he had died too many times on Tvil's stake to mourn anything Chaldan.

We are going to Kyborash to resurrect me, the potter

reminded him. To bring me back to life so you too can live.

It was true, but it changed nothing. Moth kept himself closed off.

They reached a deserted guard post shortly after sunset, paused for a few moments' rest, then rode on. By moonrise they were within the city walls.

Are they still in the Siltemple? Moth asked Tas Et.

Yes.

Show them to me.

Five men were sleeping on water-stained purple and crimson silken cushions in what had been the Hall of Hierodules. One of them was Ashanorak. The rest were also Deltan, though they were dressed as Teichi warriors.

The only real Nomad sat on a stone bench behind his sleeping companions, watching the entranceway, his recurving bow resting comfortably on his knees. A Teichi.

Which one has the medicine?

The one lying to the left of Ashanorak, with the gray streaks in his beard. The medicine is in a pouch he wears slung beneath his left shoulder.

I see it. Where's the other Nomad?

Standing watch with the horses.

Show him to me.

A dozen horses were gathered around a dry fountain in the Siltemple's outer courtyard, sleeping. Propped up against the fountain's mud-crusted marble rim sat a second Teichi. He too was sleeping, but his weapons were ready at hand.

As Moth watched, one of the horses stirred. The Teichi opened his eyes and grasped his bow without making any other movement that might have betrayed his presence to an enemy. He remained there, immobile and alert, for a few moments before he put his bow down again and went back to sleep.

What about the Taryaa?

Tas Et showed Moth the godhouse. The Taryaa was lying on his back on a raised platform, staring up at the stars. Sartor's Nighteyes, shining cold through the god-house's open roof. Moth recognized the platform as that upon which every year, during the Spring Inundation, the King, or the Kyborash Syrr Sil in his absence, celebrated the hierogamos with a girl of the Syrr Sil newly come to womanhood. The Taryaa's face was vacant and hard, like something carved from ice or stone.

It's communing with the stars, he realized, and then, I've never seen them without their disguises before. Like the one that told Tramu and me we could think of it as someone's aunt. All their politeness and delicate laughter, never looking you in the eyes, never saying anything directly. This is what they're really like. Hard, empty, cold.

Are there any other Deltans or Nomads nearby? he asked Tas Et.

Another Nomad party on the far side of the city.

Show them to me.

Three Nomad warriors sitting talking quietly around a fire in the courtyard of what had once been the Kyborash Syrr Sil's house. Their tattoos and scars proclaimed them Dzantzir, a tribe with little liking for either Casnut or the Teichi. They were unlikely to help Moth, but would pose him no threat.

Unless they were there because of the Taryaa? But that would change little, if anything: he would still have to find and prepare the forge he was going to use while his strength lasted, before anyone learned he was in the city.

Take me back to my body, Moth told Tas Et. He made his way through the dark, twisting streets, skirting fallen walls and pools of stagnant water, to the house he had once shared with his grandfather. The roof had fallen in, but the forge compound behind the house was undamaged, its hearth still usable, though everything of seeming value had long been stolen from it. But when Moth dug in a spot he remembered, he came upon not only the copper, bridesmetal, and gold ingots he had once helped Tas No bury there, but also upon a hastily sealed wide-mouthed jar of the sort used to store barley. When he broke the seal he found it contained Tas No's hammer, tongs, files, and other tools.

Tas No could only have hidden them there while the city was under attack, hoping to escape and return for them later. Moth had always assumed he'd died then, and the fact that he had never come back for his tools was proof, if proof were needed, that he was indeed dead.

There was enough charcoal and beeswax left, but the clay used by smiths was inadequate. Moth needed the same white mountain clay from which, when he was only Sartor-ban-i-Tresh and a potter's son, he had fashioned his darsath: the soul-shadow he had worn around his neck, its form modeled after that of his dolthe as he had glimpsed it in dream. The white clay produced ware of great strength and delicacy, but was too rare and difficult to work for utilitarian objects, like the molds smiths used.

He would need glazes as well: the dolthe he had dreamed so many times was brightly colored. Try Ri Cer Sil's house, Moth's ghost suggested. Moth nodded, glancing up from the pile he'd been putting together. Tramu was asleep again, twisting and jerking uneasily. Moth buried his dolthe, tied Tramu to a post by his ankle to keep him from wandering off if he awakened.

Watch over him, he told his Ri ghost.

I'll keep him safe, the ghost promised.

Moth slipped out into the street. The skeletons were whispering to one another in the mud underfoot, but none of them spoke with his grandfather's voice: he ignored them as he made his way to the house in which Ri Cer Sil, the Sil potter, had once lived, keeping when he could to dry ground, clumps of weeds, or heaps of rubble, where he would not leave any footprints to lead someone back to the forge when morning came.

As he had hoped, Ri Cer Sil's potting compound held

not only the clay and glazes he needed but also digging tools he could use to gain access to the Necropolis.

Tramu was still asleep when he returned. Moth cleaned out the hearth and laid the fire, set out the hammer, tongs, and crucibles, prepared the clay and everything else he might need when he returned with the dagger.

Strapping the Sword That Was Asp to his back, Deltan-style, Moth felt its insatiable hunger even through the protection of its sheath. He left his Ri ghost watching over Tramu and retraced the route they had taken to the house, brushing away their footprints with a dry palm frond he'd found in Tas No's inner courtyard. When he reached a crossroads he threw the frond away. Using a pile of rubble as a mounting block, he climbed on the black's back and rode painfully through the labyrinth of narrow, moon-shadowed streets toward the Great Square.

The night was too bright to risk showing himself on the broad Avenue of King Delanipal the Conqueror, or to try crossing the Great Square on horseback. He left the horse in the courtyard of a house off one of the lesser streets debouching into the square, gulped down his remaining root shavings, and continued on foot.

As he drew nearer, the sound the bones in the mud around him made grew louder, more pervasive, like the muttering of a vast multitude, and when finally he turned the final corner and looked out upon the square, the sound was almost deafening.

When last he had seen the Great Square, it had been filled with captives, starving and delirious but all still alive. Now a low white rounded mound, almost a small hill, gleamed in the moonlight at the center of the square, with smaller mounds jutting from the mud around it: heaps of whitened skulls, chittering their past lives to one another, all that remained of the pyramid of ten thousand severed heads the Nomads had left piled in the square when they left the city.

Somewhere in that vast whispering murmur Moth thought

he heard his grandfather's voice, and with it other voices he remembered, men, women, and children, their individuality lost in the chittering confusion but almost distinguishable, almost clear. He strained, trying to recognize them, abruptly realized that he'd been standing frozen, in plain sight, as he listened.

He caught himself, blocked the voices out, and refused to hear them as he darted back into the shadows. They were dead, gone, even their ghosts long vanished. These were only their bones, and it made no difference who they might have once been, or even if Tas No were among them.

Tas Et, Moth asked, is there anyone else here who might have seen me?

There are four men sleeping in the Warriors' Temple.

Chaldans?

Scavengers.

What about the Taryaa?

Tas Et showed him the eunuch still lying motionless on its back, staring up at the stars.

Is it aware of me?

Its awareness is turned in upon itself. Do you want me to take possession of it?

No. Show me the others.

The Deltans lay sleeping on their stained silken cushions. One was snoring loudly. The Nomad inside the Hall of Hierodules with them had changed position, moving to another dark recess from which to watch the entryway, but he too was sleeping lightly now.

Outside in the courtyard, the guard shifted slightly in his sleep, still dozing against the fountain.

If the guard hears me, take possession of him and keep him from crying out. Warn me if any of the others awaken, or if the Taryaa does anything.

He smeared his face, hands, and hair with mud. Staying close to the walls to keep his silhouette from being outlined against the sky, and moving with a broken, uneven motion, freezing immobile at intervals, he circled around until the heaped skulls hid him from the Siltemple's gate.

The mud made small sucking noises as he ran to the mound and crouched down behind it but nothing that could have been heard from a distance.

Show me the courtyard again.

The guard was still sleeping.

Let me hear what he can hear, Moth commanded, taking his drum from his waistband. He began tapping it, beating out a very faint rhythm at first, then letting it get gradually louder, until he was drumming as loudly as he could. Yet no sound reached the courtyard, none of the horses so much as pricked up its ears.

One of the smaller mounds of skulls was closer to the Siltemple. Moth ran for it, sprinting hard despite the agony in his leg and side. The skulls in the mud beneath his feet cracked, groaned, sometimes shattered with wet, muffled retorts. He threw himself down on his stomach behind the mound, lay there until he had gotten some of his breath back and the pain from his wounds had subsided a little, then tried his drum again.

This time the sound reached the outer courtyard. A horse whinnied, bringing the Teichi instantly awake. Moth waited, totally motionless, while the guard searched the courtyard and went to the gate to stare out at the Great Square, finally glanced into the Hall of Hierodules to make sure everything there was also as it should be.

Moth waited until the guard was satisfied and had gone back to dozing against the fountain before he allowed himself to shift to a more comfortable position. The Nomad's eyes were closed, but Moth waited until his breathing had settled into a slow, steady rhythm to start drumming again. He kept the sound low, insistent, directing it this time to the horses, using the drum to make sure they wouldn't awaken when he turned his attention to the guard.

Then he changed the rhythm, drumming harder now,

and eased the guard from his light sleep into a deeper slumber, trapping him there as he'd trapped Ashanorak and the boatmen.

Show me the Taryaa and the Hall of Hierodules again.

The Taryaa still lay immobile in its trance. Ashanorak and the others were all still asleep. Getting painfully to his feet, Moth hung his drum from his waistband and limped slowly up to the Siltemple gate. Standing over the sleeping guard, he drummed him even further from the world of waking. Just before he entered the Hall of Hierodules he paused again and drummed those within still deeper into sleep, imprisoning them carefully one by one in their own dreams.

It was utterly dark beyond the threshold. Let me see through your eyes, he commanded Tas Et, and picked his way between the sleeping Deltans to the man with the medicine, his left hand never pausing in the soft, insistent rhythm it was tapping out on the drum even when he eased himself painfully down onto his knees and turned the Deltan over.

He found the pouch on its thong and pulled it out from under the Deltan's vest. He was about to cut the pouch free when it struck him that the longer the Deltans took to discover the herbs were gone, the longer before he'd have to worry about them looking for him.

Loosening the pouch's drawstrings with his right hand, he groped inside. His fingers encountered something smooth and he pulled out two packets tightly wrapped in black silk. He sniffed them, recognized the root shavings and dried leaves by their odors.

Still using only his right hand, Moth transferred the herbs to his belt pouch, then ceased drumming long enough to rip two pieces of silk from a cushion. Wadding part of each piece up and wrapping the rest around the wadded-up part, he made two imitation packets and put them in the pouch, then slipped it back into place.

With luck he'd have finished his work in the forge and be far from the city before anyone discovered the substitution.

He pushed himself to his feet, fighting back a groan, stood there trembling but still drumming softly, before he stepped over the Deltan he'd just relieved of the herbs.

His bad leg collapsed under him as soon as he put his weight on it and he fell. The Deltan he landed on gave a startled "Ooof!" in his sleep, but didn't awaken. Moth lay across him an instant, gathering his strength, then dragged himself off the sleeping man and got to his feet again, supporting his weight as best he could on his good leg. His fingers went to his drum, only to discover a slack, lifeless drumskin.

He clutched frantically at the drum, already knowing it was hopeless: he'd shattered the wooden rim when he fell and the drum-spirit had abandoned the drum. It was only dead wood and painted leather now, without power. Useless.

The Sword That Was Asp throbbed on his back, feeding on his rage and despair, urging him to murder the Deltans in their sleep. Moth stood shaking, fighting back the fear and anger that rendered him vulnerable to the sword, forcing himself to calmness.

Show me the Taryaa.

The Taryaa was still in its trance.

Drawing what little strength he could from the spirits of his cap and costume, he turned his back on the sleeping men and limped out of the Siltemple, dragging his bad leg past the guard and horses without awakening them.

Outside in the Great Square he retraced his steps meticulously, blurring the footprints he'd left behind in the mud.

It was almost dawn when he arrived back at the forge. Tramu was awake. Moth untied him and let him stretch and relieve himself while Moth sealed the broken drum in the grain jar Tas No had used for his tools, then buried the jar beside his dolthe.

He started to unhook the sheathed Sword That Was Asp, hesitated, finally left it strapped to his back. Without the strength to command the sword it might well devour him as it devoured those he killed with it. Yet Asp had been King of Chal, and should still hold dominion over the spirits guarding the Necropolis: if all else failed, perhaps the Taryaa's herbs would give him the strength to wield the sword long enough to overcome the guardians.

Moth mixed up some of the horse's blood and milk mixture, gave most of it to Tramu and forced himself to drink the rest. When Tramu finished, Moth tied him back to the post. Tramu made no move to resist, but Moth could see the fear and anger, the betrayal, in his eyes.

"I'll be back for you soon, Tramu," he said, trying to make his tone of voice convey the reassurance that Tramu was incapable of comprehending from his words, but Tramu's expression remained unchanged.

Make him understand, potter.

There is nothing I can do.

He spent months like that in the mines, Moth reminded himself. In the dark, without food or water. One more day won't hurt him.

"I'll be back for you tomorrow night, Tramu," he said, speaking as much for himself as for Tramu. "I swear it to you."

He could feel Tramu's gaze like a weight on the back of his neck as he left.

Chapter Thirty-six

How much farther? Moth asked.

There, his Ri ghost told him. Between those two hills.

Moth squinted into the rising sun, urged his horse forward. Though he had seen the Necropolis twice before in his body, he would never have been able to find it again without the ghost's help: during the years since it had been sealed and buried, the grasses had reclaimed the site, so that now, even looking directly down on it from his horse's back, Moth could see only a slight hollow filled with brittle yellow-brown grasses.

Where is the blade? he asked the ghost.

Directly below Princess Daersa's chamber. It has been working its way deeper, seeking the Earth Mother ever since you left it there.

Moth dismounted, let his horse graze while he unwrapped and cleaned his wounds, packed them with fresh honey grass and snarl leaves. He sat on the hill slope, staring down at the hollow, trying to remember.

When he had retrieved the northern Rafti's soul, he had entered the Princess's chamber from the ways beneath the earth and passed through it without difficulty. It had been easy enough then to avoid the Roads of the Dead and the tomb's guardians. But he had little strength or life with which to oppose the Roads of the Dead now, no drum with which to summon and command spirits, and he would have to enter the Necropolis in his infinitely more vulnerable physical body.

Unless he could just dig down, tunnel under the Necropolis without ever entering it at all?

No. The pit in which it had been constructed had been well over six bodylengths deep. Even if he somehow managed to dig that far without arousing the tomb's guardians before his strength failed him, the Necropolis's brick floor would almost certainly collapse on him if he tried to tunnel directly under it. In his weakened condition that alone might be enough to kill him, even without the retribution of the Necropolis's guardians, which was sure to follow. So he had no choice but to go through the Necropolis itself.

Show me the interior of the Necropolis, Moth commanded Tas Et.

I cannot.

Why?

It is forbidden. I am Tas, bound by the laws of my Sil. I cannot profane the grave of a Prince of Chal.

But you have sworn vengeance on the Kings of Chal and on all of their descendants!

Yes. But I am Tas. I cannot profane the grave of a Prince of Chal.

It was hopeless. Sometimes Moth forgot that Tas Et was no longer a man or his uncle, that he was less, even, than a ghost, frozen in the eternal and impossible contradictions of the smith's curse that, dying, he had called down in Sartor's name on Sartor's earthly husbandman.

Moth closed his eyes, summoning back memories of the day he had seen Rafti buried. After the ten-year-old Princess had made her way down the ramp into darkness, the Sil Herald had described her progress through the handmaidens' chamber to her own resting place, then cried out that her chamber had been walled up behind her. Rafti and the other handmaidens had followed the Princess down the ramp and taken their place in their chamber. The tomb had been sealed with immense slabs of rough-hewn white marble.

It will be easier to dig down beside the Princess's chamber and break through the wall, the Ri ghost suggested.

Moth considered it. The marble slabs covering the Necropolis were too massive to be broken through or removed easily, but the brick walls were ghost-guarded: a dead Chaldan warrior's powdered bones had been mixed into the clay used for each brick, and the warriors' spirits were bound to the defense of the walls.

Are there any weak points in the walls? Moth asked.

No. But they are still weaker than the roof. You don't have the time or strength to try anything else.

Moth nodded. The ghost was right, and even without his drum to aid him he was still a shaman, still a spirit master: he would have a better chance against the dead warriors than against the marble slabs' brute materiality.

Unstrapping the sheathed sword, he put it down on the ground within easy reach, but distant enough so he need not waste his strength fighting the dead King's spirit. He measured out herbs and swallowed them, then stretched out flat on the ground with his eyes closed, trying to empty his mind and rest while he waited for the medicine to work. But his thoughts kept returning to the broken drum, and when he pushed them aside there was nothing to distract him from the pain that kept seeping through the barriers he'd built against it.

When he felt a little stronger he set to work, using a short-handled pick with a flint blade to loosen the earth, then removing it with a fire-hardened blackwood trowel.

It was agonizing work, crouched over trying to keep his weight off his bad leg; each time he swung the pick he could feel his side ripping a little more. He worked slowly, methodically, almost chipping away at the hard ground, using the trowel as much as possible, trying to save himself for the assault on the Necropolis and its guardian spirits.

The sun had passed its zenith and begun to descend again when the pick's flint blade struck a fragment of particularly hard rock and shattered.

Moth stared in shock at the useless pick, then hurled it away with a cry of fury. Squatting in the shallow, useless hole he'd made, he scrabbled at the earth with his trowel, the agony in his side only goading him on, until finally even his rage could drive him no deeper through the rock-hard ground.

His rage. He suddenly remembered the unknown Tas who had broken his oaths and burned his way to freedom. "Your anger is Raburr's life-flame burning within you," the Tas Sil had taught him when he'd been initiated. Moth was no longer Tas, his shaman's drum was dead and useless, but he had been a smith before he had become a shaman: he was still a Master of Fire.

He summoned back memory: Tas Et impaled while Tramu and Pyota watched, Rafti killed and Kyborash destroyed, Casnut and the Taryaa, his broken drum and his body's betrayal. With memory came anger, his smith's rage, opening his hassa to him—the flame slumbering in the thread-thin canal running the length of his spine suddenly turbulent, pulsing green, blue, white, hotter with every breath he took, every hated memory, surging brighter until his hassa exploded outward to engulf him, so that he was Moth no longer, but only flame.

The blackwood trowel caught fire in his hand and he hurled it away. He could feel the Sword That Was Asp responding to his anger, but the sword no longer frightened him. He picked it up, strapped it to his back again, its futile attempts to turn his rage against him only further fueling his fury.

Around him the grass caught flame. With the last of his conscious control he contained the burning, kept it from spreading inward, directed it down at the ground beneath his feet.

The roof! the ghost was screaming at him. Burn through the roof!

He ignored the ghost as he ignored the sound of his horse, somewhere far away, whinnying in terror. Around him the earth smoked, fused, melted, ran. Molten, it eddied sluggishly, caught fire, and burned. Moth sank slowly down through it as it bubbled and boiled away around him, a white-hot cloud of vaporized rock and soil that blinded him as he burned a sloping trench down through the ground to the Necropolis.

For an instant the thick brick wall resisted him. He sensed the spirits of the dead Chaldan warriors trying to bring their individual strength to bear against him, each trying to defend the individual brick to whose defense his bones had bound him, but they were too slow, sluggish with the torpor of the long dead, and before they could stop or harm him he had lashed out at the wall with a final paroxysm of flame and violence.

The bricks before him exploded into white-hot vapor and were gone. The spirits that had been bound to their defense were freed when the bricks containing their bones were destroyed, while the others could do nothing against him so long as the bricks housing their proper bones remained unharmed.

The Necropolis was open to him.

Chapter Thirty-seven

There were no more attacks, no more barriers. Without opposition to fuel Moth's rage, it died. Moth was only himself again, fighting the agony in his leg and side, the avid hunger of the sword on his back.

He shook his head to clear it. The early-afternoon sun slanting in over his shoulder showed him the Princess: a ten-year-old child's small skeleton lying in state on a great tawny wooden bier with the carved legs and claws of a lion, surrounded by heaped copper mirrors and precious gold and copper implements. She was still dressed in cloth of gold and half covered by a robe of charred white eagle feathers, and she still wore the immense headdress of lapis lazuli beads with tiny stylized copper and gold birds sporting on it in which she had been buried. One side of the headdress had come loose and allowed a few long strands of lank gray hair to escape.

Scattered over robe and bier and floor were myriads of cylindrical beads of lapis lazuli, carnelian, gold, copper, amber, and jade from the Princess's burial necklaces. Her skeletal hands were still clutching at the last remaining necklace, a thick rope woven from dozens of strands of tiny green pearls.

Drugged and unconscious, the Princess must still have

felt herself suffocating in the sealed, airless tomb, must have tried to save herself, gasping for air as, in her confused sleep, she tore the tightly wrapped necklaces she thought were choking her from her neck until at last her strength failed her and she died, still fighting to free herself from her rope of green pearls.

Moth remembered the way she'd walked unflinchingly down the ramp to her death, how young and proud she'd seemed, how brave.

But now everything seemed quiet, calm, at peace. The only movements to be seen were the faint breeze Moth had let into the tomb disturbing the Princess's lank hair, the drifting dust motes caught in the slanting sunlight, the light winking from beads and mirrors, one or two flapping scraps of still-smoldering cloth. The warriors guarding the Necropolis's brick walls remained trapped within them, within the laws that had been laid down for them at their deaths, as Tas Et had been trapped and bound by his smith's death curse. Moth could detect no further guardians, no other traps or dangers.

Potter, Moth asked, is there anything else here I need fear?

The Roads of the Dead open here, his Ri ghost reminded him. And there are other powers bound here. They are still dormant, but may yet awaken.

What sort of powers?

I cannot be certain. Remember the Harg, how helpless I was there. I am Ri, consecrated to the Mother; where She holds no dominion I can do nothing.

Moth squinted into the burial chamber, remembering the Roads of the Dead. But he'd been free of his physical body when he'd traveled them, his senses unobscured by his body's limitations, and he'd had his spirit-drum to aid him. Now, calling on all the lesser spirits of his cap and costume to aid him, he could perceive only a faint, cloudy hint of turbulence, not so much within the air as somehow beneath or beyond it, an impression of vortices that for all their violence did not so much as disturb the lazily drifting dust motes.

I can show you the Roads of the Dead, the potter said unexpectedly. Not what they really are, or where they lead, unless they lead to realms in which the Mother has a share of dominion. But I can see their gaping mouths; you can look at them through my eyes and avoid them.

Tell me where they are, what I have to do to keep away from them.

Look at them through my eyes.

Tell me!

You're afraid because I'm dead.

That's ridiculous. I'm not afraid of Tas Et—

Because he's only your uncle. Less than your uncle, just what his death curse has made of him. I'm *you*, and I'm dead. Tas Et can force his agony on you but he can't touch *you*, the real you, the way I can. You're afraid of being trapped in my death with me. That if you get too close to me you'll die too.

That's not true, you— Moth made himself stop. It was true.

You need me to survive, the ghost insisted. You don't have any other choice.

Moth finally nodded. Show me, he told the ghost.

It was not like looking through Tas Et's disembodied eyes, perceiving everything on all sides at once. Rather, it was as though much of the world had turned to perfectly transparent ice—yet ice that was paradoxically warm and glowing with subtle colors that did nothing to hinder its transparency—while the rest of the world had grown darker. The sky overhead was shadowed and sunless; in the Necropolis he could see the Roads of the Dead now, turbulent clouds of swirling darkness, their vortices like hungry mouths. Yet at the same time he could see, with a vision that was neither truly the ghost's nor truly his own but somehow born of the union of the two, that the vortices were in fact gaping mouths lined with serrated rows of flat, triangular fangs—like the maw of Tua-Li, the World-Eel, though Tua-Li's fangs were of flashing silver, and these of what seemed like black ivory.

Yet for all their resemblance to the voracious World-Eel, the mouths were passive, waiting; they would not attack Moth so long as he kept away from them. He wrenched his gaze from them, studied the rest of the Necropolis. Through the transparent walls he could see Prince SarVas on his bier, guarded by his retinue of dead warriors and by other guardians whose shadowed forms Moth could only half-glimpse, even with his doubled vision, and through the walled-up doorway he could see the long chamber in which the skeletal remains of Rafti and the other handmaidens lay chittering softly to themselves.

Looking down he saw the golden dagger almost directly in front of him, buried only perhaps a half bodylength beneath the floor. The bricks flooring the tomb had been fitted tightly together and only lightly mortared: if Moth could pry them up without damaging them, he should be able to get at the dagger without arousing the wrath of the dead warriors whose bones the bricks contained. The tomb's other guardians seemed to be concerned solely with protecting the Prince's remains. If he could keep away from the Roads of the Dead and avoid arousing the tomb's other guardians, he might be able to get the dagger and leave with it without any further danger.

Moth swallowed half his remaining herbs, shook his head a final time to clear it, and started forward, only to jerk to an abrupt halt once again just before he stepped through the hole in the wall and into the tomb.

The Princess's skeleton lay silent and unmoving on her bier, without even the signs of life and awareness that the handmaidens' second selves in the other chamber were manifesting, but it could do Moth no harm now to take every precaution he could.

He prostrated himself to the skeleton and said, "Princess, I apologize for the damage I have done your resting place, and for the intrusion I am about to commit. I swear to you on my truename, which is Sartor-ban-ea-Sar, and upon this sword, the Sword That Is Asp, that I am here only to recover something that is mine and of no value to you, not to rob your tomb or desecrate your remains."

There was no reaction he could see or sense, but he had expected none.

Potter? he asked.

I can perceive nothing you have not already sensed yourself.

Moth put aside his uneasiness and entered the chamber.

As he crossed the threshold his back flared with pain where the sheathed Sword That Was Asp rested against it. All around him he felt the Necropolis and its guardians coming alive.

Chapter Thirty-eight

Moth froze, ready to fight or flee. He could feel himself being watched now, sense forces gathering, see, with his Ri ghost's vision, dark turbulence seeping forth from the Roads of the Dead, bringing with it confused visions of the realms to which they led—

On his back the sword surged and pulsed with the forces that had been awakened when Moth entered the tomb. Moth felt Asp probing him for weakness, for fear or anger the spirit could use against him.

Hurry! his other self urged him. Get the dagger!

Moth ran forward, yanked the carpet from the spot beneath which the golden dagger was buried. He needed something to pry the bricks up with. A slender copper lady's dagger, its hilt set with topaz and carbuncles, was lying on the floor beside the Princess's bier. Grabbing it with a hurried promise to the Princess to return it as soon as he finished, he jammed it down between two bricks. The mortar came away easily. The blade flexed when he tried to pry the bricks apart but did not break; yet each time he tried, the two bricks would move almost imperceptibly apart only to settle back into position again.

He needed another knife. After a moment's search he located a similar knife on the far side of the Princess's bier, behind one of the Road-mouths. With his normal vision he could see the dagger clearly, but to his ghost-sight it was invisible, lost in the dark turbulence spilling forth from the Road.

The only way to get to it was to go over the Princess's bier, wedge himself between the Road-mouth and the wall, and try to snatch the dagger from the turbulence without being eaten.

With a mumbled apology for disturbing the Princess's bones Moth scrambled awkwardly up onto the bier and over her legs.

As he jumped down on the other side one of her skeletal hands clutched weakly at him. He easily twisted free of its grip, but lost his balance, and, trying to avoid landing on his bad leg, came down instead on an ivory ball inlaid with golden crickets and malachite-winged day moths. He tottered an instant, trying to keep to his feet, but once again his bad leg betrayed him and he fell.

Into the Road of the Dead's gaping mouth.

The mouth closed over him, both a cloud of swirling darkness and a hungry maw. The knife-edged triangular teeth could have shredded him, ripped him apart; instead, they gripped him with curious gentleness, holding him firmly, yet scarcely penetrating his skin—until, suddenly, with a single convulsive motion of the thing's great throat muscles, it swallowed him, and he found himself drowning in the Nacre's sunless waters, blood from the shallow wounds the fangs had opened in his flesh drifting forth to join the rivulets of Neetir's flaming blood that coursed and twined through the icy river around him, their brilliance painful to his eyes yet shedding no heat.

The Sword That Was Asp was a chill malignancy on his back, numbing him, dragging him down into darkness. He fought the cold and the currents that caught him and crushed him, tried to bring his numbed arms up so he could grasp the sword and draw it without having it plucked from his hands by the ever more furious violence of the currents.

The sword fought him as he spun tumbling through depths so cold they stole his very smith's rage from him, while the currents wrapped themselves ever tighter around him, trying to crush the air from his bursting lungs.

At last he forced his numbed muscles to obey him and caught a grip on the sword's pommel, managed to hold on to it long enough to draw the sword forth with all the strength of both his arms.

With his final gasp of air he cried, "In the name of Asp, King of Chal, I command you to return me to the world of the living!"

Water flooded into his mouth and throat, choking him. He was drowning . . . and then, suddenly, he was lying on the tomb's brick floor vomiting up great gouts of freezing water, which turned to clouds of gray dust as they burst from his mouth and nostrils.

The Sword That Was Asp was still clutched tightly in his hands. He was cold, colder than he had ever been, colder than anything living could long remain and survive. Asp was gnawing at his spirit, trying to drain him of what life he still had.

Moth tried to summon up strength, the smith's rage and burning that would free him, but there was nothing left, everything had been stolen from him. It was all he could do to prevent the sword from taking complete control of him.

He wanted to fling it away, be free of it, but he knew that once it was out of his control, it would use the forces of the Necropolis to destroy him. His only hope was to keep on clutching it, keep on trying to use it against the Necropolis and its guardians until he could win his way out again.

The dagger! his Ri ghost was screaming in his head. *Get the dagger!*

Still clutching the sword in both hands, pushing it in

front of him, he crawled to the cleared spot on the floor, raised himself up onto his knees, and stabbed down at the narrow crack he'd opened between two of the bricks.

His hands were trembling and he missed the crack altogether, but the sword cut through the kiln-dried bricks as easily as if he'd been trying to slice soft cheese. As soon as Moth realized what had happened, he yanked the sword out again and hacked a hole through the bricks. The earth beneath was hard-packed and the sword had no special power over it, so Moth used it like any other digging tool, stabbing down with the point, working the blade back and forth to loosen the dirt, then scooping it out with the flat of the blade.

It took him only moments to retrieve the dagger. He had what he'd come for, what he needed to become a whole man again. Too tired to feel more than a vague relief, a sense of completion, he stuck the dagger in his waistband and staggered to his feet, turned to leave through the hole he'd burned through the wall.

Tas Et hung there impaled on King Tvil's stake, barring his path.

"Get out of my way!" Moth screamed.

No. I am Tas, nephew. Ras Syrr. Sworn to the service of the King of Chal. I cannot allow you to leave.

Moth just stared at him, fighting back an urge to break down into hysterical laughter.

He isn't really there, Moth thought confusedly. He's just his death curse, not even a real ghost. He can't stop me if I don't let him.

I can walk right through him.

He was hanging impaled on Tvil's stake, pink foam dripping from his nose and mouth as he swore his death curse against King Tvil and his line. He could see Tepes Ban and the King laughing together, Tramu and Pyota huddled with the blowpipers in the cage at his feet.

The Necropolis, his proper body, everything else was gone. There was only the sharpened stake Tepes Ban had pushed up through his body to emerge from his shoulder, only the Great Square and the laughing spectators, the musicians playing for King Tvil's delight.

I'm still in the Necropolis, Moth told himself. All I have to do is walk out of here.

I still have the sword even if I can't feel it. They want me to drop it, or blunder into one of the Roads of the Dead again.

"Asp!" he tried to scream. "Free me! I command you!" But nothing changed; his words were only in his mind; he could not feel his lips or throat moving.

Potter! Sartor-ban-i-Tresh! Lead me out of here!

But the Ri ghost too was gone, hidden from him.

I can walk out of here. Asp won't be able to use Tas Et against me anymore when I'm out of here.

He tried to remember how he'd been holding the sword, willed his muscles to obey as he pictured himself raising the sword, walking forward, willed himself to swing the sword from side to side in front of him and clear the way—

He thought he felt something resisting him. Forcing himself to concentrate even harder despite Tas Et's agony, he tried to feel his cap and costume on his body, learn from their spirits what it was he was confronting.

A wall. Something blocking him. His bad leg must have thrown him off, kept him from walking straight. He willed himself to bring the sword up, pictured himself slicing through the bricks in the wall beside the hole just as he had sliced through the floor bricks, then using the flat of the blade to clear the fallen bricks out of his path. He imagined himself stepping through the hole he had created, out into the sloping trench he'd burned through the ground.

He tried to feel himself walking up the slope, tried to block out the Great Square, the stake on which Tas Et was dying impaled. He willed himself forward, making himself feel the fresh air, the afternoon sun on his face.

He should be there by now. Out of the tomb and the

trench, on the hillside outside. Free. He willed himself free, pictured it, believed it.

Leave me, he commanded Tas Et, and felt the instant of his uncle's death wavering around him, weakening, the pain from the stake fading into distance.

He willed himself to swing the sword in a great, two-handed arc and fling it as far away from him as he could, made himself see it go spinning over and over and away, gleaming with deceptive beauty in the late-afternoon sun, to land far enough from him and from the Necropolis so that Asp had no further control over either the Necropolis's guardians or himself.

He willed Tas Et gone, and at last his uncle's spirit withdrew. The stake was gone altogether. There was only the familiar pain in his leg and side.

He was lying on a cool surface with his eyes closed.

He opened his eyes to almost perfect darkness. Yet with what little light there was he could see that he had not fought his way to the freedom he had pictured, but only deeper into the Necropolis, through the wall separating Princess Daersa's chamber from that of her handmaidens.

He still held the Sword That Was Asp gripped in both hands, and the sword was throbbing, burning, as it drank the last of his fading life and strength.

He made a final, convulsive effort to pry his hands from the pommel and free himself.

Not so much as a finger twitched. He closed his eyes again in defeat and let himself slide away into sleep and darkness.

Chapter Thirty-nine

Rafti's dead eye showed Moth lying bleeding at the far end of the chamber, before a ragged hole in the wall, the faded silks and loose bones of one of the handmaidens crushed unheeded beneath him. Even unconscious, he was still clutching the Sword That Was Asp's jeweled pommel with both hands.

Everything about the sword—the long copper blade, the pommel wound with copper wire, the jewels set into it—was shiny and dark, blacker than the blackest obsidian. Moth's hands were a livid gray that even as Rafti stared was slowly fading toward black.

He's dying, Rafti told the ghost.

The sword is killing him. We have to get it away from him and get him out of there.

How?

My skeleton. Asp has dominion over it, as he has over everything else in the Necropolis—but you were never of Chal, Shonraleur's-Daughter. He had no dominion over *you*.

What am I to do?

Animate the skeleton for me. Make it a part of your body here. Burn anything or anyone who tries to stop you.

Rafti hesitated, memories of fear caught in her throat

and choking her. But she was no longer the girl who had been so terrified at being stolen from the Mother and her proper rebirth, and she let the fear wash through her and away.

She closed her good eye. She could feel the disjointed bones composing her body now, feel them coming together, fitting themselves, somehow, to the bones safely encased in that living body of which she was still dimly aware, so that these dry bones were coming to share the muscles, the tendons, the fleshy armor of that distant other self. . . .

Knowledge was seeping into her from the skeleton, knowledge of the earth and stillness, of fading and death and the Mother. But it was dangerous to let herself know too much; she had to animate the skeleton with her separate self, make it wholly a part of her distant body, or Asp could reach her through it. She refused the skeleton's knowledge, imposed her life and limitations on its dry form.

She found the channel in the skeleton's spine, the vertebrae fitting tightly back together again so that the narrow canal ran the length of the spine without blockage or interruption. But there was no flame within it, only an emptiness like a well leading into the depths of the earth. Rafti reached back into that other body, sleeping now curled up on its side, into that other skeleton that was this skeleton as well, and found the column of flame burning there. She fed the flames with her fear and anger, her desperate need, and as the flames leapt higher in that distant body, they were here with her as well . . . at first only the barest feeble flickering, a hint of orange warmth, then growing, expanding, until a pillar of ascending flame filled this dry spinal canal and she could at last let the flames in that sleeping body die back to quiescence.

Rafti willed herself to see, and though she was bare bone, looking out of a skull's empty eye sockets, she could see. The long, low chamber was a tapestry of strangely interwoven clarities and obscurities, of meanings and senselessnesses. . . . Her vision was not hindered by the brick walls or stone roof, but only, in some way she was unable to grasp, different when she looked through them.

She could see the Roads of the Dead opening like hungry mouths into the tomb, see the hole Moth had burned in the outer wall, the sloping, glassy-walled trench leading to the outer air.

She got to her feet. The ceiling was too low for her to stand upright, so she hunched forward, concentrating on feeling the play of her body's muscles and sinews as she made her laborious way through the heaped bones and riches toward Moth.

The other handmaidens' bones had ceased their dry whispering. Hands were clutching feebly at Rafti now, skeletons were trying to crawl forward to bar her way, but they were all weak, as light and substanceless as dry twigs, nothing even remotely capable of standing against the strength of Rafti's hardened muscles.

I'm Rafti Shonraleur's-Daughter, Rafti kept repeating to herself. I have no place here. None of these pitiful heaps of bones can stop me.

A hand clutched at her ankle. When she reached down to pull it away a skull snapped its stubby-toothed jaw shut on her thumb, bit down, and clung even after Rafti tried, with mounting horror, to shake it off.

Burn them, the ghost commanded. Rafti burned them, the dry bones catching fire and blazing as though they were really nothing more than the dry kindling they so resembled.

More bones were hunching across the floor at Rafti like bleached, awkward insects, trying to clutch and bite, turn her aside. She waited until just before the first bones actually got close enough to touch her before lashing out and burning them, but their destruction did nothing to halt the scuttling attack of the other bones. In an instant of what might have been either overwhelming rage or fear, Rafti burned them all, destroyed all the other handmaidens' remains.

The smoke and ash from the burning bones and silks did not settle or drift away, but hung, a vaguely man-shaped cloud, over Moth's body, as if the handmaidens were even now still trying to keep her from him.

Rafti suddenly recognized the shape into which the cloud was struggling to condense: that of Tas Et, Moth's uncle. He was dying impaled on the stake, but his hands were reaching for her, she could see his bloody lips moving, hear him whispering to her to stop, go back, leave Moth to the fate he had brought upon himself by desecrating the tomb of a Prince of Chal.

Tas Et can't stop you, Rafti, a boy's soft voice said. She saw Moth's third self now, the dead boy, standing protectively over the body, weaving in and out of the smoke.

Not even Asp can hurt you, so long as you don't touch the sword and avoid the Roads of the Dead, the ghost continued. The desiccated mask of his face was strangely serene; his black eyes seemed bright and alive.

What should I do? Rafti asked, trusting him.

Pry his hands from the sword without touching it, then carry him out of here to safety.

Rafti looked around for something she could use to pry the sword out of Moth's hands. She found an ornamental dagger, picked it up clumsily, and was reaching for what she thought was another when she heard the dead boy cry out, Rafti! Behind you!

She spun around. Moth was getting slowly to his feet, still gripping the sword. The cloud of smoke and ash that had been hovering over him clung to him now, enshrouding him, blurring his form and features so that sometimes he seemed to be Tas Et, at other times only himself, but most often a broad powerful man with green pearls gleaming in his full beard, his avid amber eyes full of hate.

King Asp, Rafti's other self told her.

Rafti backed away as the figure came at her, swinging the sword in short vicious arcs that for all their clumsiness would be more than adequate to shatter her other self's frail skeleton.

The dagger she was still clutching was a useless toy. She threw it at him in panic anyway, only to miss completely and hear it clatter against a wall.

The sword. Her only hope was to burn the sword, destroy it with fire as she had destroyed the goatherds' village. She reached into the skeleton's spinal canal, found the fires she had ignited there, fed them with her fear and need, shaped them as they leapt higher. . . .

No! her other self screamed at her. Asp will drink your fires and devour us! You can't—

But it was too late. The fires she'd summoned exploded out of her, and she had only just enough time to deflect them away from the sword and at the hands with which Moth was clutching it.

His hands caught flame and burned, yet on his face she could see only Asp's implacable hatred. For an instant Rafti thought that Asp's will would be enough to animate the carbonized flesh and bone and make it continue to serve him, but then, even as Moth continued to advance on her, his hands crumbled to ash and let fall the sword.

Moth's body had been braced against the great sword's weight. Now, with that abruptly gone and Asp's control over him ended, he toppled backward, to lie unmoving, his eyes open but sightless.

Get him out of here, the dead boy said. Quickly, before Asp can stop you.

Rafti grasped Moth by the ankles, dragged him through the ragged hole in the wall into the Princess's chamber, then across its floor in little jerks. Her other self's skeleton had little strength but never tired: she could repeat the same motions over and over again forever if necessary.

The Princess's skeleton stirred as Rafti dragged Moth

past it, but Rafti burned it to ash before it could do anything to try to stop them.

There was no further resistance from any of the Necropolis's guardians as she jerked Moth slowly up the sloping trench into the late-afternoon sunlight.

Moth's black stallion whinnied nervously and backed away, its nostrils quivering, when it saw Rafti with Moth. The dead boy patted it gently and said something that seemed to calm it. It began cropping grass placidly a little farther up one of the hills.

It was a handsome horse, sleek and graceful, with a long glossy dark mane and beautiful eyes. She didn't want to kill it.

You have to, her other self told her.

I know.

Rafti continued pulling Moth through the tall grass until her other self told her, That's far enough away. He'll be safe here.

Rafti let go of Moth's ankles, stepped back to look at him better.

Blood and pus were oozing from his leg and side. His arms ended in blackened stumps. His breathing was shallow and irregular, while his eyes had rolled so far back in his head that only the whites showed.

Can you help him? Rafti's other self asked.

I don't know. I can try.

The dead boy watched in silence as she knelt by Moth's body and unwrapped the cloths binding his leg and side. She kneaded the edges of his wounds to force the pus from them, then wiped them clean with dry grass.

The pressure of her fleshless fingers on his wounds should have been agonizing, but Moth just lay there unmoving. The dry grass with which she'd wiped the pus from his wounds seemed to writhe where she'd thrown it, as though alive with squirming malignance.

Rafti laid her hand lightly on Moth's wounded leg. Blocking out all other sight and sound, she searched the sickness.

It was there in him, a thick sullen cloud of roiling darkness. The dead, eating him from within. She tried to penetrate the darkness, pierce through it to Moth's spirit, but found only the sickness, the hungry gnawing. She had come to him too late—Asp had already stolen his spirit or devoured it.

No, her other self told her, I can still sense him. But he is so weakened and obscure that I can't make him aware of me.

Rafti tried to draw on Moth's inner heat, use it to drive the sickness from his body. But Moth's life-fires were almost extinguished, and when she tried to feed her own flames into the canal in his spine, they had no effect. The sickness was everywhere within him, pervading his body; there was no way she could burn it out of him without destroying him at the same time.

The healing Sulthar had taught her was useless.

Casnut had forced her to learn the horse sacrifice despite her revulsion, and the horse sacrifice might have enabled her to save Moth. But she would have to wait until just before dawn to begin, and it was not yet sunset. He would be dead long before then.

He's dying, she told the Ri ghost.

You can't do anything for him?

No.

The dead boy just looked at her.

I'm sorry, she said.

There's a copper box in his belt pouch, the ghost said. Put a little of each herb you find in it into his mouth. That should give him enough strength to keep him alive until we get back to Kyborash.

Rafti fumbled with the drawstrings, finally managed to get the pouch open despite the clumsiness of her fleshless fingers. She took out the box and opened it. It was divided into two compartments, one containing crumbled reddish-brown leaves, the other full of waxy purplish-black shavings.

What are these?

Taryaan medicines. They can't heal him but they'll give him the strength to survive a little longer. He would have been dead weeks ago without them.

How much longer?

I don't know. He's dying because he can't heal himself. He hasn't been able to heal himself without outside help since we were split from each other and I died. We were going to take the dagger in his belt, the one he killed me with, and use it to construct a new soul figurine for me, to house both of us together so we could be reunited. If you help us, it may still be possible.

What good would that do?

When we are whole again we will be a single person once more. That single person should have the strength to conquer this sickness and survive. But even if he dies, we will have died reunited, we will return to the Earth Mother's womb together, to be reborn as the single person we should always have remained.

Rafti? Rafti asked her other self.

I don't know. Maybe. King Asp would have returned from the dead at the Seven-Year Festival if the sword hadn't been stolen before it could be reforged. And even if this doesn't entirely heal him, it might still keep him alive long enough for the horse sacrifice.

What do you need me to do? Rafti asked the dead boy.

Be my hands while I work the clay and forge the metal for the new dolthe.

How long will it take?

Less than a daysixth. Everything is already ready.

Rafti touched a finger bone to Moth's side, searching the sickness. The dead were still gnawing at him, but they seemed weaker, somehow, as though something was holding them back, keeping them from doing Moth any great harm while the herbs were working in him.

I'll try, Rafti told the dead boy, and blocked the afternoon hills from her sight, to open her good eye in the ruined house where she'd slept the day before.

Chapter Forty

Rafti wrestled the sapling she'd cut down through the narrow doorslit to Tas No's house and stumbled over a pile of rubble just inside. Without her other self to aid her, her night vision was poor. She left the sapling just inside the house, groped her way in the moon-shadowed darkness across the central courtyard and to the doorslit leading to the forge behind the house.

Satisfied that she knew the way, she turned to go back for the sapling when she heard something like a strangled cry behind her.

She shrank against the wall, waited an instant, immobile, her hand on the handle of the long knife she'd used to hack through the tree's slender but resilient trunk, listening. After a moment she heard a long, whuffling snort, recognized it as coming from a sleeping horse, but heard nothing more.

She slipped through the doorslit, then sideways along the wall and froze again, the knife in her hand and her back against the coolness of the wall. Finally after long moments of poised immobility, she brought her left hand up in front of her. Fire flared in her cupped palm, sun-bright, to dazzle anyone lying in wait watching her.

She saw a roan horse leap to its feet and try to escape,

only to be held in by the forge compound's walls. Something moved to her left and she turned, saw a pitiful half-starved-looking man tied by his ankle to a post. He was whimpering as he tried to hide behind the slim post. There was something wrong with one of his arms.

There was no one else in the forge.

Feeling furious with the dead boy for not having warned her he'd left a prisoner in the forge, Rafti approached the man, letting the light in her cupped palm die down to a glow. He looked harmless but she remained prudently out of his reach as she studied him.

His filthy matted hair and beard were as red as her own hair, and there was something about him that told her she should know him. She searched first her own memories, then those her other self had bequeathed her, abruptly remembered how the other Rafti's father had forced her to watch Tas Et dying on the stake in the Great Square with his wife and son and assistants huddled in the cage at his feet.

His son. Tramu. This was Tramu. She stared at him, at his tangled hair and twisted arm, remembering him, remembering the years she'd lain awake nights wanting him when she'd been Tas Gly's daughter, how she'd admired him and would have done anything to have him for a husband. How she had known from the way he sometimes looked at her, even before he'd come to her during her time as a hierodule, that she would have been able to have him for her husband had she been the daughter of any other smith in Kyborash but Tas Gly.

Rafti? she asked in sudden panic, afraid of being overwhelmed by the torrent of memories not her own. Tas Gly's-Daughter?

There was no answer. She was alone. The memories had come from her other self's life, but they were her memories as much as the ghost's now.

"Tramu?" she asked gently, remembering him in the cage, how she would have done anything to take his pain from him and how there had been nothing she could do. "You don't have to be afraid of me, Tramu."

"Tramu?" she asked again, but it was hopeless, he was like a terrified child or animal, and the Nomads had cut out his tongue—he would never be able to answer her.

He was still cowering. Without conscious intent she put her hand to her face, assured herself that the silk wrapped around its left side still hid the dead eye.

She realized what she was doing and yanked her hand away, all the anger that had been driven out of her by the realization that this was Tramu sweeping over her again.

She closed her good eye. Through the dead eye she could see that her other self was approaching the city. She concentrated until she heard the wind whistling through the open bones of her skull, felt her right hand clutching the stallion's glossy mane while her left held the golden dagger Moth had recovered from the Necropolis. Moth's body was draped over the horse in front of her. The dead boy was seated there as well, somehow sharing the same space.

What is it, Shonraleur's-Daughter? the other Rafti asked, sensing her presence. What's wrong?

Opening her good eye again, Rafti let the ghost look through it at Tramu and the post he was trying to hide behind.

That's Tramu, she said, feeling the ghost's horrified anger, so much like her own.

What happened to Tramu? her other self demanded of the dead boy before Rafti could continue. What did you do to him?

He went mad in the mines at Nanlasur. We rescued him.

Then why is he tied there, like an animal?

For his own protection. To keep him from wandering away and endangering himself before we were whole enough again to try and heal him.

What if you'd died? Rafti asked.

Then he would have died anyway, with no one to protect him or take care of him.

The dead boy hesitated, then continued: We had no one else we could trust. Our only hope of healing him was to get the dagger from the Necropolis and heal ourselves first.

What happened to Pyota? Tas Gly's daughter asked.

I found her charred bones in the pit where they burned the bodies of the slaves who died in the mines.

I'll watch over Tramu and find a way to heal his spirit if you cannot, Rafti said. If Moth dies.

Thank you, the ghost told her.

Rafti concentrated on the forge compound, let the hills fade from her sight.

She made soothing noises as she freed Tramu, as though she were reassuring a baby, and kept watch on him while she worked.

She cut the sapling's branches off, leaving only the seven roots for which she had chosen this particular tree still attached to the trunk, then stripped it of bark. She cut seven notches in the trunk where the seven slimmest and most supple branches had been, then lashed those branches together and put them aside. Taking the straightest remaining branch, she cut a section as long as her arm from it and, shaping the wood as Casnut had shown her, carved a heavy cane from it with a horse's head on one end and its hoof on the other, the ends connected by a tight helical groove.

She studied the finished horse-stick. The work was crude, but the best she could do: it would have to suffice. She wrapped it in silk, then began digging the fire pit.

When that too was finished, she braced the naked trunk upside down in it, with what had once been the crown of the tree buried in the earth and four ropes leading to four heavy stones, one for each of the four cardinal directions. The seven roots extended up toward the sky.

After she'd piled the remaining bark and branches in the fire pit around the tree, she stepped back. There was nothing more she could do without Moth's horse, or until just before dawn.

Rafti sat before the furnace, studying the hammer and its family, the crucibles and the wet white clay in its broad-mouthed jar, letting her other self's memories of Tas Gly's forge help her understand the tools, what they were and how to use them.

Something moved. She glanced up, saw that the roan horse was nibbling at the bark she'd piled in the fire pit.

She jumped up, yelling, and drove the horse away from the fire pit, then went over to it and patted its side, spoke soothingly to it for a moment.

She was a healer, not a killer; she had no desire to ever hurt anything the way Casnut had hurt her horse when he'd taught her the horse sacrifice.

But she would do it if she had to. For Moth and, if need be, for Tramu.

Chapter Forty-one

Rafti was awakened by the sound of her other self leading Moth's horse through the house.

She got out of the doorway where she'd been lying to keep Tramu from wandering away while she slept and went over to stand beside him as they came in.

Even in the moonlit darkness it was worse seeing Moth through the good eye and smelling the rot eating him from within.

Help me get him down, the other Rafti told her. Through Rafti's good eye her other self was only an ivory and brown skeleton with some scraps of leathery skin still clinging to the bone here and there, but through the dead eye Rafti could still see the ghost as the fourteen-year-old girl she had once been, still dressed in the silks and jewels in which she had gone to her death.

Tramu was whimpering, terrified. Rafti left him to cower in a dark corner while she eased Moth down off the horse and stretched him out on the ground.

Her other self went to the furnace and put the gold dagger down by the other tools, then returned to watch as Rafti touched her fingertips to Moth's wounded side and closed her good eye.

The sickness was worse. She took the copper box from his belt pouch and opened it. The box was almost empty.

We had to give him most of the herbs for the ride here, her other self said.

Rafti put a pinch of each herb in Moth's mouth, waited, then searched the sickness in him again. This time the Taryaan medicines had made no difference that she could detect. She hesitated, then gave him most of what remained.

"He's weakening," she told the dead boy aloud.

I know. We don't have much time left.

"Tell me what to do."

Do you see that silver blade on the chain around his neck? His soul silver?

Rafti nodded.

Get it, then dig up the jar I buried in the back of the compound. Bring them both to the hearth.

Now, sit down and listen, the dead boy told her when she'd done as he'd asked. There are things you will need to understand before you can start.

When I became RiTas–a potter-smith, sealed to both the Ri and the Tas Sils—my soul was sundered. Before, when I was only Ri, my truename was Sartor-ban-i-Tresh, but when my soul was split by my initiation as a Tas, I became Sartor-ban-ea-Sar as well. My two souls shared my body for a time and might eventually have learned to live in harmony with each other. But my uncle's ghost forced my death—Sartor-ban-i-Tresh's death—so that Sartor-ban-ea-Sar would be freed of the Ri Sil. Thus, he could become a weaponsmith capable of carrying out the vengeance my uncle had sworn on the King of Chal—

"Moth killed you," Rafti said.

We are both Moth. We both had our part in my death. It was suicide, not murder.

The ghost paused, looked at her. Do you understand? he asked.

"Enough," Rafti said. "Go on."

A Ri fashions his own life into the pots he shapes, just

as a Tas fashions *his* life into his metalwork. I killed myself—or rather Sartor-ban-ea-Sar killed me—by killing the creations into which I had breathed my self and my essence with his gold dagger, which Sartor-ban-ea-Sar forged for the task.

"He—killed pots? I don't understand."

In a sense. We destroyed that part of me that I put into the pots I fashioned.

Rafti nodded.

Now, break open the jar. Use the dagger's hilt.

Rafti cleared a space on the stone slab beside the tools and put the jar down on its side. She tapped it cautiously.

A little harder, the ghost said.

She hit it harder, then harder still, and broke open a hole in the base.

Take out what you find inside, he told her. Be careful not to lose or damage any of it.

Reaching in through the hole she'd made, Rafti brought out a long, slim, sharp-edged fragment glazed a shiny copper color, then a small statuette with one arm missing, finally two gently curved red things almost like flattened ceramic clam shells. She laid the pieces out on the slab, studied them an instant, then fitted them together.

The soul figurine had the form of a man with a bright copper blade where his right forearm should have been and, jutting from his shoulders, wings suggesting those of a butterfly, but still crumpled and unfolding, as though the butterfly had just emerged from its chrysalis.

Rafti bent closer, studied the dolthe in the bright moonlight. Exquisitely fashioned, it depicted the face and form of the dead boy, but it was pierced everywhere with the same triple-lipped wounds she could see on him. The wounds were as perfectly rendered as the face and body; they did not look like the finished dolthe had been damaged, but rather as though the artisan shaping the clay had pierced it himself while it was still damp and malleable, before firing and glazing it.

Looking at it, Rafti was irresistibly reminded of how crude the horse's head she had just finished carving was.

"I can't do this for you," she said. "This is a perfect likeness. I'm not a potter, I can't shape clay like this."

You need not worry about making the dolthe look like me so long as it *is* me, the dead boy said. My dolthe took this form only after it was buried. It grew and changed in the ground as I grew and changed; when I shaped my darsath, the shaping altered my dolthe, as my dolthe directed the shaping.

His darsath: her other self's memories showed her the clay soul-shadows that Chaldan potters wore on thongs around their necks.

First, the dead boy continued, you must dream the dolthe . . . share the dream that came to me as I was shaping my darsath. . . .

"Share your dream?"

Yes. So it can guide your hands as it guided mine, as my father's dreams guided his hands when first he fashioned the dolthe. Lie back against the forge and close your eyes. Let yourself drift. It will be only a waking dream, nothing to fear.

Closing her good eye, Rafti saw an island of bare, wet clay rising from the waters of creation, and knew it to be Baalkunti, the primeval island, the first land . . . but Baalkunti continued to thrust itself upward out of the waters and toward the clear, empty sky, until she could see that it was not an island but a head, a head of clay on a neck that grew ever longer while red and black grasses sprouted from the head's crown . . .

She realized that it was her head. She was Moth and it was her head.

. . . but yellow grasses were sprouting among the red and black blades, and all the grasses were lengthening, growing, until the grass had completely hidden the head, until it fell to Ocean itself.

Suddenly there were birds, the infinite sky black with

their numbers, though they were so far away that they were only clouds of tiny, darting specks. . . .

One speck grew larger, blacker, became a hawk *diving* straight down into her eyes. . . .

Like a flower unfolding to greet the dawn, the clay head opened and became the world.

She saw Kyborash, and it was a living city under attack by a horde of Nomads on horseback led by a man of fire-hardened clay. In his left hand he held the horse's reins, while where his right forearm should have been a blade gleamed.

The man of clay was Moth. He was dressed in a caftan of black goat hide and breeches of red leather. From the caftan hung copper mirrors and the golden skeletons of many hawks; his hair was tied back from his face in separate strands of red and black with a serpent the color of amber. The snake hissed and coiled, dripping yellow venom from its fangs, and Moth's eyes—her eyes—blazed with hatred.

Yet all this was only a small cylinder of red, black, and yellow glazed clay with wings of red copper. Only a clay cylinder, but gazing on it she could see everything she'd witnessed somehow contained within it.

Do you understand? the dead boy asked her. The dream was ended; she was herself again.

"That was what it looked like before your father buried it?"

Yes.

"And you want me to make you another one just like it?"

No. That dream is over, ended. Everything it has prophesied has come to pass. You must create a new dolthe, one that will contain not only our past but our present and future as well.

"How?"

The dead boy gestured at the gold dagger.

When Sartor-ban-ea-Sar forged this dagger, he forged

our lives and deaths into it; when he killed me he invested it with my spirit; and though it no longer houses me as once it did, I can reenter it again. His life—what remains of his separate life—is contained in the soul silver you took from around his neck. You must melt them together, return them to their embryonic state, and alloy them before they can be differentiated again. Then you must shape the alloy you have produced, and after you have given it form, shape clay around it so as to create from their union a new and living dolthe.

"But I don't know how to shape any of it!"

Do you remember how, when you were still in your valley, you would open yourself to the Earth Mother and She would guide you unharmed across the coals?

"Yes."

Open yourself to the dolthe that was, to the clay and the metal and the truenames we bore. Let the forms sleeping in all of them flow through you and guide your hands, as once the Mother guided your dance. Then whatever shapes you mold will be true shapes, and the dolthe a true embodiment.

"That's all?" Rafti demanded, unbelieving. "I just do whatever feels best to me at the time, just like that, and you're alive and whole again?"

You know better than that. This is not just any metal, just any clay: my life is already in them. And you are both a healer and a Master of Fire.

"You trust me with a great responsibility," Rafti said finally. "To reshape your very soul. Too great a responsibility."

I have no choice, or I would not have asked this of you. But I loved you when I was alive. I would trust you in any case.

"You loved my other self," Rafti said. "The ghost. Not me. And though she was your friend, she never loved you, not the way you loved her."

Then I would trust in her friendship, and in yours.

Rafti hesitated a moment longer, then said, "Tell me what to do."

Ignite the charcoal in the furnace with your inner fires, so the hearth flames will be part of you and remain subject to your will. Melt the soul silver and this dagger together in a crucible, then shape them with your hands.

"What about the hammer and the other tools?"

If you were Tas, they would have become part of you, and they would have participated in the shaping with you. But as it is, they would only hinder you.

Rafti nodded.

When the metal is ready, work some dust from the former dolthe into the clay you have prepared, then mold that clay around the metal core.

Drying and firing the dolthe would take a potter many days, but you are a Master of Fire: it will only take you instants for what nature would require months to do. Make sure not to allow the metal to lose its form when you fire the clay. You will *know* when the clay is dry, when the fire has hardened it, when to bleed the heat from it to keep it from cracking.

After you have finished the rest, glaze the clay and fire it again, then bury it in a jar like the one my father used.

Is there anything I can do? Rafti's other self asked.

You can give her your eye to see with, but nothing more. Life can only come from life.

Now, the dead boy told Rafti, hold the soul silver in your hands. Can you feel it—its rigidity, the sharpness of its edge, the blunt end's weight?

"Yes."

Look at it through the ghost's eye. Can you *see* its form, how it *means* that shape and could take no other without changing what it is?

"Yes."

Put it in the crucible, and put the crucible in the furnace. Ignite the flames with your hassa but keep the fire from the crucible.

The charcoal burst into flame. Rafti felt it burning, breaking down, becoming the flame whose dance she danced for it, keeping the heat from the crucible.

Let the fire begin heating the silver now, the dead boy told her. Slowly, evenly, so that no part of it ever becomes hotter than any other.

Rafti felt the heat reaching through the clay crucible for the silver, entering it, softening it. She could sense the silver fighting to retain its form.

Heat it until it is all ready to melt at the same time, but keep it from melting yet, the ghost instructed her.

The silver trembled on the verge of dissolution.

Now. Rafti let the heat reach through to the silver. The blade lost all form and fell in a silver pool to the rounded bottom of the crucible.

Rafti heard a sound like someone sighing, glanced over at Moth's body. The pain lines on his face were smoothing out, as though every experience that had marked him since he had first cast his soul silver was gone, had never been.

Suddenly she glimpsed Tas Et standing over him and thought she saw a reflection of his dying agony on Moth's face.

"What about Tas Et?" she asked.

Ignore him. He is no threat without the sword to turn him against us. He has no part in our coming change and resurrection.

The ghost stepped forward, somehow slipped into the dagger, like smoke drawn back into a fire. Staring at the dagger through the dead eye, Rafti could see the dead boy within it, as she'd seen Moth's life in the clay cylinder she'd dreamed.

Put me in the fire, the dagger told her.

Rafti laid the dagger in the crucible, where it stretched over the silver in the rounded bottom without actually touching it, like a bridge over a pool of water.

Backing away, she knelt down, closed her eyes. She found the dagger in her mind, sensed it with the heat beginning to seep through the crucible to it. She warmed its gold slowly, evenly, feeling the metal soften, tremble, yet keeping it from breaking down and liquefying, holding its rigidity until she truly knew its form, felt the conflict between form and dissolution in herself, and then she let the form go. The liquid gold fell into the pool of silver.

Rafti opened herself further to the two metals, letting them heat and cool separately and together so she could feel the potential structures, the embryonic forms, lying hidden in them. Reaching into the furnace, she took the crucible out, holding the metals in fusion with her inner fires alone. She increased the heat and began shaking the crucible rhythmically, as Sulthar had sometimes shaken the leather cup full of the rounded gemstones and sharp-sided quartz crystals he cast for divination. With each shake Rafti could feel the metals cascading into each other, spreading, fusing, and melding.

She let a single drop of amber-colored alloy, no larger than a dust mote, cool to rigidity. It hung suspended in the molten metal pool's turbulent heart. With each shake of the crucible, each movement, heavy currents of gold or silver or their alloys swirled against the rigid mote. When the moment felt right, Rafti would cool the metal sloshing past the mote and allow it to adhere, melting the new accretions away when she sensed they were wrong. Gradually, the seed mote grew, accreting strata of gold and silver, amber-colored electrum, like an embryo taking on form in the sustaining inner ocean of its mother's womb.

Rafti was shaking the crucible ever more gently now, careful not to injure the shape taking form within it, making sure that the tides of metal washing over and through it did not melt it or carry any of its substance away.

At last she realized that there was nothing further she could do with it in the crucible. She let the remaining metal cool to butter-hardness around the more rigid shape, closed her eyes again, and lifted the soft mass out.

Proceeding by touch alone, she molded it. She felt no uncertainty, no need for decision or experiment. It was as though she were merely smoothing the surface of something already existent, even as the form grew and evolved in her hands.

Finally, she knew that there was nothing more she could do with the metal alone. She opened her eyes and looked at it.

She knew it with a knowledge as profound and intimate as that with which she knew her own body, yet she was surprised by what she saw.

The metal had formed what seemed the stylized skeleton of a man with the wings of a great bird instead of arms, made up of knobby gold masses and delicate wires, thickenings and hollownesses, mostly amber-colored but occasionally breaking into swirls or protrusions of pure gold or silver.

Rafti closed her good eye again, stared at the form through the dead eye. The metal was swathed in clouds of bright mistiness that somehow *meant* Moth to her, though she could never have translated that meaning into words. And yet, his two names were there, their sound resonating in that shape she could feel, could sense. . . .

She turned to the stone slab and reached for one of the copper files, intending to grate some dust from the former dolthe to mix with the fresh clay, as the dead boy had instructed her to do. But where the dolthe had been there was only a mass of soft, damp, undifferentiated clay.

She looked over at Moth. He was lying curled up tightly, his face smooth and empty. Inhuman.

For a moment she was terrified, all concentration and purpose lost. The clay was only a pile of drying mud; the golden skeleton, so like a hawk's, only a confusion of yellow metal.

It's all right, her other self reassured her, and she felt the ghost's presence within her again for the first time since she had returned to the city. Take the clay in your hands again and begin kneading it.

Rafti picked up the clay. She rolled it between her hands and suddenly everything was right again; she could sense the clay, feel its meaning struggling toward her, guiding her hands.

She felt something that was almost a hunger, a need, in the clay she was working. She took some wet clay from the jar and worked it in. It helped but it still wasn't enough.

Turning toward the metal skeleton she'd shaped, she suddenly realized that this was the form she'd felt in the clay, struggling to realize itself.

She began molding clay to the metal, working with desperate speed as she pressed it into place between the ribs, filling in the spaces between the wire-thin wing bones. When at last she was finished almost the entire metal surface had been covered, with only two tiny golden balls left exposed on the head—the eyes—and a larger ball of amber-colored electrum on the end of one of what she now realized were taloned feet.

The heat came boiling up in her without any conscious effort to summon it. She took the statuette her hands had molded and caressed it carefully, chafing it, heating it until the water rose from the drying clay in a cloud of steam.

She continued heating the dolthe until the clay was hard as leather, then increased the heat and let the figurine bake in her living fires, finally took the projecting ball of electrum and softened it between her fingers to a thin paste, spread it with swift, sure strokes over the entire surface of the dolthe, except the two eyes, which remained their harsher gold.

It was done. She felt the overwhelming tide of rightness leave her, stared dumbly at the dolthe in its perfection.

But then that perfection, too, seemed to recede, fade. The dolthe was just a statuette of a man-shaped figure with Moth's face, veined wings something between those of a moth and those of a bird, and the taloned feet of a bird of prey.

Rafti heard a stifled groan from Moth. She went to him and knelt, put her hand to his wounded side.

He was still dying. His body had at last begun fighting against the dead eating him from within, but it was too late and he was too weak.

She looked back at the dolthe, saw the electrum dulling, tarnish spreading over it.

Moth was dying and she had no choices left.

She made soothing sounds as she led Tramu back to the post and tied him to it again, then attached the roan nearby.

Help me hold the horse, she told her other self.

Chapter Forty-two

Rafti held the stallion's head as Casnut had shown her, the horse-stick and the switches she had cut ready at hand.

"I apologize for the pain I must cause you," she told the stallion in the secret language, sincerely meaning the words the ritual demanded, hating what she had to do.

She began lashing the horse's back with the switches, careful not to break the animal's skin: not a drop of blood could be allowed to escape. The horse screamed its pain and fear, but she held on to its head with her left arm, her other self aiding her, and between them they kept the horse immobile long enough for Rafti to lash its spirit free of its body.

The spirit tried to flee. Rafti let go of the horse's head and pursued it. As she caught hold of the spirit's form and color, her other self whispered its truename to her: Maryssat. With the power of the truename Rafti compelled the spirit into the horse-stick and bound it there.

The horse's body was still standing by the fire pit, staring with warm, wet, empty eyes. Rafti positioned it over the pit and gripped its neck again.

Casnut had killed Rafti's horse by picking it up and breaking its back, but Rafti did not have that kind of strength. She was a firedancer; what she had to do, she would do with fire.

Help me see, she asked the other Rafti. The dead eye showed her the interior of the horse's body, the great heart still beating sluggishly, the muscles, bones, sinews all in their proper places.

Placing her hand in the horse's mouth, she summoned the fires within. Flame leapt from her clenched fist, obedient to her will, leaving the bones and blood vessels unharmed, taking muscles, nerves, and brain and burning them all with a heat so sudden and intense, yet so perfectly contained, that even after the muscles had been reduced to ash, the blood continued to circulate through the intact vessels, only slowly seeping forth to fill the intact skin.

Holding the loose sack of skin with the drenched ashes and bare bones slopping around inside so as to make sure no blood spilled out of the mouth or nostrils, the holes where the eyes had been, Rafti lashed it to the sapling to wait for dawn and the ascending sun.

She put the switches in the fire pit, glanced over at Tramu and the remaining horse. The moonlight had not been bright enough for them to truly see what she had done. Tramu was already asleep again, while the roan stood immobile, still cautious, but no longer terrified.

The roan, at least, had nothing farther to fear. Rafti went over to it, patted and calmed it as best she could.

The eastern sky was paling with the first hint of dawn. Rafti could delay no longer.

She put Moth's dolthe in a leather sack, tied it to her horse-stick. Her other self offered her the silk-wrapped fragments of bone from the stillborn child's spine, then lay down. Rafti felt the ghost's presence enter her again as the dry bones lost their cohesion and fell apart. She wrapped the cervical vertebrae in silk, put both packets in a second leather sack, and tied that as well to the horse-stick.

Tramu was still sleeping. Rafti stood behind him, brought the horse-stick up over her head.

No. I can't.

She stayed there, paralyzed, a long instant before she lowered the stick and started to turn away, then suddenly brought it up again and smashed it down as hard as she could on the base of his spine. There was a sharp crack as the vertebrae she had struck shattered, louder by far than Tramu's short, startled cry of agony, and then it was over and Tramu's spirit was oozing forth, still tiny and confused, like a snail from its broken shell. Rafti grabbed it and shoved it into a third sack, tied it to the horse-stick with the others.

She took off her clothes and laid them aside. Their weight would hold her back during the ascent.

The moon and stars were still bright overhead but the sun was beginning to appear. Moving with cautious haste, Rafti took the stallion's blood-filled skin and laid it on the twigs and bark in the fire pit, making sure that no blood spilled and that the skin itself never touched the earth. With the horse-stick tucked under her arm she shinnied up the slick barkless trunk to where the four ropes bracing it were tied. Letting her legs dangle, she used her arms alone to pull herself up past the ropes without disturbing them, then caught hold of the pole with her legs again and shinnied the rest of the way up to the first notch.

Over the compound wall she could see the street getting light. She looked back up, searched the sun.

The pole was swaying dangerously. If the rocks she'd braced it with weren't heavy enough and it fell over before she completed her ascent, Moth would die, she would have murdered Tramu and killed his horse, and all for nothing.

She held herself absolutely motionless, gripping the pole with aching arms and legs until at last it stopped swaying.

She heard male voices behind her. The men could be looking right at her, seeing her head projecting over the wall, coming for her or aiming an arrow at her, but she could do nothing, not even turn to see if they'd discovered her. Only wait, summoning her internal fires as she watched for the rising sun. . . .

Now! her other self shouted in her head as the sun broke free of the horizon. Rafti ignited the bark and branches.

"Keep your breathing steady, your eyes and ears open," Casnut had said. "Remember everything, every sight and sound and smell. A true shaman can recognize the cracks between the worlds and knows how to find them anywhere."

As the flames licked the horse's skin, the pole began to bend and twist, supple as a serpent, trying to shake Rafti off. She clung to it as the world reeled below, stretching and contorting, twisting like the pole itself, as though the very world were a living creature trying to escape the lance pinning it to the ground. Then the fires burned through the skin and the blood inside came streaming out in a congealing cascade to hit the fire and explode upward in a great cloud of choking smoke.

There was an angry shout behind her.

The smoke burned her nose and throat, stung her eyes. She couldn't keep herself from blinking.

The sky was still blue but the sun was gone. The shout had been cut off in mid-cry.

The skinny pole whipping back and forth was abruptly still, had changed, become an immense tree rooted in the heavens yet branching and flowering there as well. The tree extended downward through the world's flat disk to the burning red-orange magma of the Mother's Inner Ocean, and there it *became* the Mother, its rough bark merging with Her mottled skin where She grew thousand-armed, heavy-breasted, and legless from the sucking yellow mud of Her Ocean's floor, with Tua-Li, the World-Eel, wrapped in endless looping coils of flashing ice and silver around her buried roots, his great dorsal fin rippling a dull burning red—

No. The pole had not changed. It was she, Rafti, who

was different now, able at last to see that which had always been there, visible had she only known what to look for, had she only known it was there to be seen.

The horse-stick was a horse again, eight-legged and black, the soul sacks dangling from his neck. The smoke from the burning blood was making Rafti lighter, pushing her upward, toward the sky.

Looking down, she could see six Nomad warriors on horseback clustered together behind the compound's rear wall. A seventh was yelling something as he started around the side. They were frozen totally immobile, like statues rather than living men, and Rafti knew that whatever happened to her during her ascent, whether she succeeded or failed, it would all be over before the yelling man completed his shout.

She dismissed them from her mind. Far, far below them Tua-Li was thrusting himself out from beneath the Mother's roots. His blind, vaguely equine head wove back and forth as he searched the cause of his disturbance, then his great coils came pouring out of the mud in seemingly endless loops as he came streaking up through the Inner Ocean.

Rafti? Rafti demanded, uneasy though not yet truly afraid: Tua-Li was a creature of the earth, not the sky, and the ground was already so distant, so far below. But there was no answer, only a peaceful drowsiness in her head, a fuzzy blur when she tried to look out of the dead eye. The ghost was asleep for the first time since she'd stolen Rafti's soul from the Mother, and nothing Rafti could do would rouse her. Even so, Rafti still felt only a dreamlike certainty as she climbed onto the stallion's back, to find it as hard and slick as the green wood of the horse-stick had been. Wrapping her arms tightly around his neck, gripping his smooth sides with her knees, she clung to him as he carried her higher, toward the single bright star now hanging directly overhead, a point of searing brightness where the World-Tree pierced the sky.

Maryssat rapidly climbed the rough scarps in the fissures between the great irregular sheets of fibrous green and brown bark, galloping when he could, at other times forced to cling like some gigantic beetle to the sheer tree face with all eight of his legs while Rafti fought to keep from slipping from his unyielding back. When no other path presented itself, Maryssat would leap what seemed like impossible distances, held up by the smoke still rising in thick clouds from the fire pit so far below.

Though the smoke was warm, the air was bitterly cold. Something made Rafti look back, down through the smoke at Tas No's forge, where Moth's and Tramu's bodies were still perfectly visible, despite the thick smoke and the immense distance separating her from them. She saw the ground part as Tua-Li's enormous head came thrusting forth on his long, serpentine body. The eel sniffed at the roan, which remained paralyzed with terror even after the long head moved on, to hover over Moth and Tramu.

He's sniffing for their souls! Rafti realized, suddenly afraid for them.

Rafti! she cried to her other self. Help me! But though her other self could not be awakened, the World-Eel had already forgotten Moth's and Tramu's soulless bodies and resumed his search.

Tua-Li thrust his long, narrow snout into the fire pit, investigating the embers, tasting the smoke. The long dorsal fin running from behind his blind bulging forehead down his back like a ribbon of burning mane rippled with languid fire as slowly, ponderously, but with implacable grace, the great head lifted to point at Rafti, so that had the World-Eel been sighted, he would have been looking at her.

Yet even blind he had still somehow sensed her, found her.

He can't get to me here, this far from the ground, Rafti told herself uneasily. He'll find the Nomads soon, attack them instead.

But even as she tried to make herself believe it, the World-Eel's great coils came pouring up out of the ground and Tua-Li was rearing, weaving himself into the smoke, swimming up it with sinuous, impossible strength, like some monstrous fish fighting its way up a mountain cascade.

Coming after her.

"Faster!" she screamed at Maryssat, knowing it was hopeless, that he was already climbing as fast as he could. She was still closer to the second notch than the eel was to her, but fast though Maryssat was, the World-Eel was far faster. As Tua-Li drew closer, stretching ever farther upward from the seemingly endless coils still looping out of the bottom of the Mother's Inner Ocean, Rafti saw for the first time how truly enormous he was, how truly terrifying.

Casnut should have warned her, told her what to do. With helpless rage she realized how little he had really taught her, how utterly unprepared she was for the dangers she was confronting.

For Tua-Li, the guardian of the Mother's Inner Ocean, and of the dead who went there to find rebirth– and Rafti was carrying off the souls of Moth, Tramu, and her other self, all of whom should have been the Mother's.

What if Tua-Li wasn't really coming after *her* at all? What if all he really wanted was their souls?

She could drop them, that might satisfy him—and even if it didn't, it might still distract him long enough for her to reach the notch.

Except that she couldn't do it, couldn't bring herself to throw any of them to Tua-Li.

Maybe she could trick him with an empty sack.

She transferred Moth's dolthe to the sack holding her other self's bones, looked around for something to weight down the empty sack more convincingly. But there was nothing she could use: for all the seeming raggedness of the World-Tree's bark, no loose splinters or sheets or flakes ever broke free or sloughed off, there was never anything that was not still alive and growing, still part of the tree.

The tree and the Mother were one. It would have been unthinkable to tear a piece from it with which to distract Tua-Li, even if she could do so without further enraging him.

She wadded up the leather sack, hurled it at Tua-Li.

It hung in the air below her, bobbing up and down in the smoke, finally listed to one side and began drifting down with agonizing slowness.

She glanced up, saw that the notch in the tree, just below where it pierced the sky, was closer than she'd dared hope. The sky itself rippled and shone, as though agitated by currents beneath its surface, with jets of azure cloud spurting from it like upside-down geysers.

The sack was a tiny speck far below when at last it glanced off one of the huge undulating streaks of burning red that crossed Tua-Li's bulging forehead where a sighted creature's eyes would have been. Yet tiny though it was, it caught the World-Eel's attention. He twisted back, his great head looping around to investigate the sack before he dismissed it and came after Rafti again.

The stallion reached the top of a scarp and leapt. As they hung in the air, Rafti could see the notch's distorted image, like a great puckered mouth, reflected in the rippling blue of the sky overhead. The rising smoke curled in over the smooth, mottled bark of the lower lip, vanished inside.

The stallion landed, scrambled for footing, leapt again . . . and once more the distances stretched and shrank around her, so she was closer to the notch than Maryssat's unaided efforts could have ever brought her.

She opened the sack holding Tramu's soul. The spirit had collapsed in upon itself and looked like an iridescent pink pearl with a sleeping man's reflected image somehow trapped in it. She put it in with Moth's dolthe and the ghost's bones, weighed the empty sack in her hand.

Maryssat leapt again. The sky was so close Rafti could feel its weight on the back of her neck. A tendril of churning azure mist brushed her bare shoulder with coolness.

But below her Tua-Li's blind, uprushing face blocked out the disk of the world, his mouth gaping open to reveal fangs like jagged silver cliffs, a red-burning maw that could have swallowed the world whole.

Rafti tried to summon her inner fires, but she was too desperately afraid, too panic-stricken, to command them.

She threw the empty sack at Tua-Li. It vanished into his maw without slowing him. She needed something else to distract him with.

Something alive. But she could never give him the souls she was carrying, and without Maryssat she would never reach the heaven beyond the heavens.

That left only herself.

Trying to keep herself from thinking about what she was doing, she jammed the little finger of her left hand into her mouth up to the knuckle, bit down as hard as she could. She had to force herself to swallow to keep from choking on the blood, on her scream, but no matter how much it hurt, how hard she clamped her teeth down, worrying the bone, the finger was still part of her, still attached.

She spat blood, opened her jaws wide and slammed them shut as hard as she could, bit down again and again, twisting and grinding at the bone as though trying to rip a wing from a poorly cooked fowl, finally yanked her hand from her mouth and twisted and tore off what remained of her dangling little finger with her other hand.

Only then, as she hurled it down into Tua-Li's mouth, did she allow herself to scream.

The stallion leapt again. His leap arced farther and farther upward, so that he was flying, the World-Tree shrinking and foreshortening above them as at last they gave themselves entirely over to the smoke-road.

Rafti could see the sky pressing down on her clearly for

the first time, as though sacrificing her finger had removed some impediment to her vision. For an instant the beauty of it caught her, almost blotting out the pain, all thought of Tua-Li. Above the notch the World-Tree altered, became a pure, glorious turquoise, yet glowing with life where the stone she had known was only dead and shiny. A great branch reached out toward infinity in each of the four cardinal directions, branching and rebranching, and all the myriads of branches were covered with broad, furling azure leaves, through which lapis-blue mists drifted.

Rafti lost sight of the sky as the stallion banked. She clung desperately to his neck as, far below, Tua-Li snapped his great jaws shut on her severed finger.

He began to shrink, until he was only an eel a few times the length of a human body, rearing from a hole in the ground in Tas No's forge. For an instant Rafti was back on the pole, shinnying up the last few palmwidths separating her from the second notch, then, soaring effortlessly, Maryssat glided in through the great mouth in the World-Tree's side and Rafti found herself in the second of the realms separating her from the heaven beyond the heavens and the healing awaiting her there.

Chapter Forty-three

Great masses of gray and white clouds were churning angrily around Rafti, veiling the tree, while the winds tried to snatch the horse-stick and leather sack from her hands, pluck her from the surface on which she stood. There were half-formed figures in the clouds, their faces suffused with what might have been lust, might have been anger.

Lightning struck at her feet, and she saw that she was standing on a broad, translucent green leaf growing from a transparent crystal vine coiled around the World-Tree's turquoise trunk. Rafti caught a glimpse of a great transparent flower a little higher up the vine before the light was gone and the clouds obscured her view again.

Lightning struck again, and she realized that the storm-spirits were attacking her. But the flash was incredibly slow: she could see it starting, stretching jerkily toward her, building up speed as it came—yet even at its fastest the bolt was no more rapid than a thrown stone, and she sidestepped it easily.

More lightning bolts came streaking slowly at her from the clouds around, yet they were not only slow, but feeble, and for all the storm's seeming violence, the winds were less powerful than those she had met with in the mountain passes on her way south. The spirits seemed drained, powerless for all their malice, as though something had stolen their proper strength and force.

The World-Tree's turquoise trunk was a sheer pillar, unscalable. The crystal vine looked too fragile to bear her weight for long, but there wasn't any other way upward. Clutching the horse-stick in her right hand, her left shoulder braced against the tree, she groped her way higher, using the vine's gnarled tendrils and leaf stems as handholds and footholds. The vine swayed under her, swung whenever a particularly violent gust threatened to blow her off, but showed no sign of breaking or pulling loose.

Even clinging to the swinging vine, it was still almost easy to avoid the dim, sluggish lightning bolts. The winds were too enfeebled to blow her off or snatch the horse-stick and bag of souls away, the sleet and rain only a discomfort like so many others, the cold that bit at her not even chill enough to make her call up her inner fires.

Even the distance she had to climb before the vine led her into an opening in the tree's side seemed shrunken, trivial, as though not only the storm-spirits but their very realm had been drained of its substance. Within, she followed the vine up a slight incline to find herself in a palace of polished turquoise, surrounded by bare, beautifully shaped chambers and halls, delicate arches, vast empty rooms radiating away in all directions.

This can't all still be within the World-Tree, she decided. This is the sky. I'm inside the sky.

Light shone through walls, floors, and ceilings, reflected off them again in a thousand shades of blue, as though the entire palace had been carved from a single gigantic block of ice. Rafti continued to follow the vine, which had become a glowing emerald green and now sometimes grew along the floor, at other times clung to walls or ceilings or vanished into the rock, only to emerge a little farther along. Sometimes the walls and floors were so highly polished that Rafti could see her blue-tinged reflection perfectly in them; at other times they were as thin as the ice on a pool the first night of winter, which cracks if you so much as touch it. She would find herself walking into immense, almost transparent sheets of rock before she realized they were there, feel a moment's utter panic as they shattered around her. She began advancing more cautiously, testing the floor beneath her feet before putting her weight on it, but though the vine wound through caverns and halls, up inclines and natural stairways, between pillars that looked as though sculptured forms were hidden just below their surfaces, it always avoided the gulfs she saw yawning open in the floors of other chambers and corridors, it always took her higher.

As she climbed, the stone became more transparent, shinier, so that she moved in a constant welter of multiple reflections. At times she saw what might have been other vines, but they were blurred by the thicknesses of translucent stone separating her from them. Sometimes she could hear water flowing and, peering through the luminous walls, see it dropping past her at enormous speeds. Sometimes, too, she glimpsed strange, empty shapes in the walls and ceilings, as though she were looking at bubbles caught in the rock, yet bubbles reproducing perfectly the forms of living men and fish, and, once, a great bird.

She had paused to examine the bird shape when she noticed that something strange was happening to her reflections. Though she was standing still, the blue-tinged images continued to move with a life of their own, jumping from wall to wall, splitting and recombining, distorting as they changed shape, going from flat to curved, concave to convex, surfaces, sometimes even sinking through transparent walls to emerge in the chambers she could see beyond them. And the reflected chambers and halls themselves continued to shift, altering and flowing as though she were still walking past them.

She started walking again, slowly, and the reflected images followed her, preceded her, clustered around her mockingly. By now she could see that not all of the distortions were natural. Some had all ten of their fingers, others were missing thumbs and toes, still others had shapes or faces that could never have originated in any reflection of her own form, no matter how distorted by the surface mirroring her.

"Who are you?" she demanded, halting. "What do you want?" Her voice reverberated off the walls around her, changing before the echoes died away into jerky, almost inaudible music that seemed to mock her fear as the reflections mocked her form.

There was no other answer. She set off again, the reflections gamboling and flowing around her. The turquoise palace had lost its beauty; even her echoing footfalls sounded derisive now. And the vine was getting harder to follow, burying itself in the stone for long stretches, its reflections twisting and writhing away from her down false paths, taking her through long corridors only to disappear and leave her to find her way back through the labyrinth to where she'd lost the vine and start over again. The corridors and rooms were constantly changing as altered reflections flowed over and through their walls; often she would find herself following the vine down what she thought was a new corridor only to discover that not only was she following just another reflection, but that she had followed it down the same corridor as before. Or, worse, to suspect that that was what had happened without ever being certain. It seemed more of an annoyance, a petty aggravation, than anything else . . . until, three times in a row, following what seemed to be three different paths, she found herself teetering on the brink of the same gulf and realized that the reflections were doing their best not only to lead her astray but to kill her.

She tried running her hands over the smooth walls, feeling for something that would enable her to distinguish one direction from another, finally closed her eyes to shut out the reflections.

As soon as they were shut the horse-stick altered. She

could still feel it, unchanged, in her right hand, but with her eyes closed she saw it transform itself into a tiny green gull, like the gull she herself became in the dreams when Sulthar summoned her.

She opened her eyes. The gull was gone. She closed them and the gull was there again, glowing in the shimmering darkness. It flew before her, leading the way, and she groped blindly after it.

The air was changing. It was cooler and fresher-smelling, soothing to her lungs yet somehow thicker, resisting her progress while at the same time buoying her up, supporting her as the smoke from the horse's burning blood had supported her, and easing the ache of her tired lungs.

Long before the gull disappeared, folding its wings and diving upward, and Rafti opened her eyes, she had realized she was underwater, breathing water as naturally as she had ever breathed air.

She was still in the turquoise labyrinth, but the reflections were gone. The stone was only stone again, while the light that had shone from it now suffused the water itself.

The vine had become an immense ropy blue-green waterweed, with blade-shaped trailing leaves longer than her body. Other plants drifted by in little clumps, puffy blue and green things with bloated bladders and rippling tendrils, all carried along by the current that was beginning to catch Rafti up.

She fought it until she noticed that it always paralleled the waterweed, always carried her higher. She gave herself up to it, cautiously, then with increasing trust as it wound through the maze of passageways like a living thing. It swept her through vaulted chambers and narrow tunnels, up immense chimneys in the darkening rock, the water glowing brightly around her. It was all she could do now to keep from being dashed against the walls, yet there was no malevolence here: if the current was itself alive, aware of her as the storm-spirits had been, it was indifferent to her and wished her no particular harm.

At last Rafti was swept up a final rock chimney and out of the caverns altogether. The current was a whirlpool, spinning her around and around the waterweed at the center of its vortex as it lifted her through the waters of an immense ocean, then up out of it in a gigantic waterspout.

Below her as she spun she caught dizzying glimpses of a vast winter sea in which chunks of ice as big as the world's disk floated. The waterspout carried her spinning through an unbounded sky, the waterweed around which it whirled growing suddenly huge, sending out leaves, branches, flowers, as Rafti was carried ever higher, until at last she reached the moon and was deposited with sudden, inexplicable gentleness on its undulating silver surface.

Chapter Forty-four

The hills shimmered silver-soft around her, and though she knew she was in a place of the dead, that knowledge brought no fear. There was nothing fearsome about the moon. The thick tangled grass looked like twisted metal blades but was as soft beneath her as gray silk; the tarnished silver mists drifting over the hills drifted through her as well, cool and moist, so that she was a soft swirling of silver-gray, nothing more. She felt she had only to wait a little longer and she would melt into the hillside, sink down roots, become like the soft grasses.

There was something she had to do.

She tried to put the thought out of her mind but it worried at her until she remembered the bag of souls. This was a place for the dead. A place for them.

She sat up, looking around for the horse-stick with the soul sack tied to it, found it in her left hand. The bag's drawstrings were undone. She must have already opened it.

She took out the stillborn child's bones, unwrapped the packet, and let the bones slide out, a tiny shower of white dust and small rounded fragments.

The breeze caught the dust up and it was gone. The bones lay in a pale heap on the hillside, slowly soaking up silver until they were the same silver-gray as everything else, and even their forms were softening, sinking in, becoming absorbed.

A single new blade of silver grass pushed its way out of the vanishing mound and grew until it was indistinguishable from the others, swaying gently with them in the moist breeze.

Rafti reached into the sack again and brought out Moth's dolthe. The statuette was leaden; only portions of the head and wings were still amber-colored, and the eyes still their fierce gold.

Even as Rafti watched, the wings faded a little more.

She started to set the dolthe down, but the golden eyes caught her gaze, held her, implored her, until suddenly she realized: he isn't dead yet!

They were still alive. They shouldn't be here.

She put the dolthe back in the sack, but the child's bones were gone and there was no way to distinguish the blade of grass that had grown from them from the others.

She stood up and looked around, but there were still only the silver hills, the mist-filled valleys. There was no sign of the World-Tree, or anything else she could use to continue her ascent.

She tried to remember how she had come to be on the hillside, but the mists were still drifting through her thoughts, veiling her memories.

Perhaps if she shut her good eye, the dead eye would show her her route.

She tried to shut her good eye, only to find that it was already closed: everything she had seen here, she had seen through the dead eye alone.

When she tried to open her living eye it resisted her, as though the skin had closed over it, but even as her hand went to her face, she managed to pry her lid open.

The moon was a stagnant silver sea, tarnishing to night in its depths. The World-Tree jutted from the oily silver waters, black and immense, bare, dead. The hills she had found so inviting were only the World-Tree's twisted branches breaking the surface of that too-calm, too-still sea.

In the depths she could glimpse pale, naked hybrid creatures without skin or eyes, neither men nor fish, swimming blindly. A memory returned to her, something her grandmother had taught her, and she recognized them: the souls of the dead who had been unable to draw their birth labyrinths again after the Mother effaced them, and whom She had eaten. They were blind, almost maggotlike, yet there was something about their half-seen forms that drew Rafti's gaze, that fascinated her and awed her at the same time that it horrified her.

She wrenched her eyes away, looked up.

Crowning the World-Tree like an immense golden flower on a withered black stalk hung the sun. She could feel its heat on her upturned face, hear the roaring of its fires.

Calling to her. To the fires slumbering within her.

Ecstatic fury sang through her as the serpent of flame in her spine awakened. The moon faded from her awareness. Through her eyes, through the skin of her face and shoulders and body, the sun's fires entered her. She breathed in its burning, the solar flame ever hotter within her, until the very hatred and anger that had kindled her inner fires had been burned away.

On a pillar of flame she rose to the sun and was lost within it.

All forgetfulness had been burned from her. Everything she had ever seen or felt or known or been was clear to her, every memory she had ever had was limned in imperishable flame . . . and Rafti was that flame, encompassing all that she had ever been, yet soaring above it without longing or regret.

And yet, she still had the horse-stick gripped in her left hand. The horse-stick was a thing of bloated blackness, feeding on her will to keep the sun's burning from the bag of souls tied to it, pulling her through the sun. The fires parted before it, a black mouth gaping open to engulf her.

She emerged to chill night. She wanted to cling to the sun's warmth, the brightness of its fires, but the horse-stick was pulling her deeper into the darkness, and the sun was drooping away from her on its long stalk, falling toward the lunar sea. Then the moon's tarnished waters closed over the sun, and it was only a fading glow in the abyss, was gone.

Stars were all around her, swarms of staring, hate-filled frozen eyes, leeching the warmth from her soul. Black ice was building up on her body and limbs. She flailed around helplessly, trying to crack and claw it away, but her efforts only drained her. The sun had burned all fear and hatred from her, she had lost the route to her inner fires. Perhaps the fires themselves were dead.

Her hair had frozen into a single, solid mass. The ice crawled up her ears and nostrils and other orifices, threatened to fuse her teeth together. She ground them from side to side, the ice gritty between them, wrenched her jaws apart, and tried to spit the ice out, but her frozen spittle clung to her lips, crept back down her throat.

Dark frost spider-webbed both the living and the dead eye, thickened, until she no longer dared so much as blink for fear that her eyes would freeze shut forever. The frost gave her vision a spiteful clarity, so she could see the earth's disk so far below the lunar sea. She longed to be there, for warmth and sleep, for all that was familiar and precious to her. Yet the ice contaminated her vision, showing her the earth as the stars saw it, rotting from within, the whole disk twitching with maggot-eaten foulness. Plant or animal, man, bird, fish, or scuttling, burrowing thing, it made no difference: all was foul beyond redemption with disease and suppurating growth, inexorable mutability, it all cried out to be stopped, halted, the whole of creation frozen into clean certainty, immobilized in an eternal moment that would replace life and change, banish the birth that led only to death.

Rafti fought the ice taking root in her soul; she called up memories of human warmth, her father's kindnesses, Cama's generosity, the tenderness and longing in Moth's voice that first time he'd spoken to her. But it was all hollow, false; every hope led to another betrayal; below, she could see men and animals slaughtering each other even as they themselves rotted and died; she remembered how her father had thrust her from him, how Manlaiteq Manmoutin's-Son had turned against her, how Cama had wanted to use her and Sulthar had given her to Casnut—

Casnut. The stars were his enemies. She searched the earth's disk until she found him.

He was sitting before a campfire in the midst of an arid northern waste, sharing water from a goatskin bottle while he spoke with three Nomad warriors she had never seen before. She wanted to cry out to him, tried to force words from her frozen throat as if, somehow, she could make him hear them despite the impossible distance separating them, but seeing him now with the cold clarity of the stars' vision, she saw him as he was: empty, self-serving, contemptible. There was no hope to be had from him, and her cry died in her throat.

Yet before she could look away he glanced up at the sky and saw her. Saw her, through the sky's blue vault and across the void separating them, and his gaze caught hers, held her, forced her to look at the image of herself reflected in his eyes, forced her to see herself in that image as he saw her despite the black ice contaminating her vision, and in his eyes she was not contemptible, not self-serving or empty or false. She remembered her revulsion at the way he'd broken her horse's back, how his attempts to kill Moth had outraged and horrified her even after he'd made her see the reasons behind his actions, made her believe he was asking nothing of Moth that he himself had not endured. But she had not seen the world through the stars' cold contemptuous eyes then, she hadn't known who his enemies were, what he was struggling against. Now that she knew, she saw that what truly outraged and horrified her was not Casnut but the necessity that dictated his actions.

Casnut looked away, back at the other men around the fire, and the link that had bound Rafti to him as closely as if they had been face to face with each other was gone. Yet the revulsion she remembered, her outrage and horror, were still there, had not been burned from her by the sun's fires as her petty personal fears and angers had been. Recognizing them, knowing and accepting them at last for what they were, she discovered in herself a dispassionate hatred whose existence she had never suspected, and it was not chill and deadly like the stars' spiteful contempt for the living, but as pure and clean as the sun's cleansing fires had been, asking nothing for itself but only that the object of its hatred no longer mar the world she loved.

She felt the flame of her hatred rising in her, through her, through her entire body and being, and it was cold, far colder than the ice in which the stars sought to imprison her, so cold that it was no negation of warmth and life, but only of death.

The stars fought to contain her, turn her hatred back against herself as she burned the ice from her soul and body, reached out to encompass the stars around her.

A star shattered, another, and then an entire constellation exploded into glittering dust, frozen, disintegrating images, before at last their massed strength overwhelmed her and she was cast from the sky.

Chapter Forty-five

Still clutching the horse-stick with the bag of souls tied to it to her breast, she fell screaming in fear and confusion through earth and sky and sea. Until, suddenly, there was no more earth, no more sky or sea, no more falling, and the sound of her voice was lost in an onslaught of shrieks and giggles, whispers and shouts, cries, murmurs . . . the cooing of mothers soothing infants, the wheedling of sycophants . . . every voice in the universe speaking every tongue, uttering every truename, and all at the same time.

There were only the voices, no mothers, no infants, no sycophants. She was drowning in voices, in a babble of confused sound. Yet she could see, she could feel and smell, for as each truename was spoken, it took on material form, flared into substance before fading back into the primordial chaos again, only to be re-created anew the next time it was uttered.

She caught the sound of a voice saying, "Valinor Shonraleur's-Son," and her long-dead grandfather took form, smiled lovingly at her before he faded again. She knew then that she had reached the heaven beyond the heavens, the center where everything that had ever had or ever would have a name still existed, where all that was lost could be found, where all that had died could find rebirth.

There was a name she had to speak but it fled her, was lost in the infinite chorus, only one name among so many. For an instant her own name fled her as well and she felt panic rising in her until suddenly she remembered it again.

"Rafti!" she cried. She had no lips, no throat, no lungs, but she had a voice, she was her voice, was her cry, her truename, she was Rafti. An infinity of Raftis taking on substance and form, all the people she had ever been—the little girl who had first dared to walk the coals, the older girl lying dead on them, the infant her mother had just named, and the old woman she would someday become—but she was not only them, she was Rafti her mother's mother, mourning the death of her husband in the cell carved out of the mountain's rock behind the Temple, she was the ghost who would soon become her second self, awakening panic-stricken to her dry bones in the Necropolis, she was all of them, all her ancestors, all the other Raftis in the other valleys, in Kyborash and Chal, she was everyone who ever had or ever would share her truename, her essence, she was every Rafti who had ever been or who would ever be. . . .

As the sound of her voice died away they all started to fade, die back into the confused welter of potentiality. She tried to find the rest of her truename, the name that made her herself alone, but she was only a voice among all the other voices, she no longer knew whose voice it was, and when she tried to cry her name again she no longer recognized it, she was only part of a continuous stream of sound that flowed through her to spill into brilliance and substance, then fade again.

Names came to her or she picked them from the babble, and she cried them: "Moth! Kyborash! Tramu! Cama! Maryssat! Father!" As the names spilled through her voice to flare into substance she became them, she was Kyborash, she was the horse-spirit, she was all the Moths, all the

Tramus, Camas, Sulthars, and Fathers that had ever been, that would ever be. Yet as they lost their substance and faded again she realized that there was one name she had not uttered, one name she had to remember. She could be anything, anyone, but she had to remember this one name, the name that could be spoken nowhere but here, in the heaven beyond the heavens.

She cried out name after name, every name she could find or invent, and as she cried them she became them, and then they passed from her again.

Until, at last, she cried "Casnut!" and as all the Casnuts spilled through her to return to potentiality, she remembered the World-Eel, whose truename Sulthar had taught her long ago.

"Tua-Li!" she cried. Yet here, in this place, his name was no longer as Sulthar had taught it to her. As it resonated through her she realized that all the other names, all the other voices, were ordered by this one voice, one name, her name. She was Tua-Li, and all the other names were only echoes of her one name, fusing and dividing in the infinite silence.

She was everything that had ever been or that would ever be. Yet there was no confusion, no incoherence, no loss of herself in primordial chaos. There was only herself, only Tua-Li, and Tua-Li was Moth, was Tramu, was Maryssat, Rafti the daughter of Tas Gly and Rafti Shonraleur's-Daughter, was the Mother Herself.

From the infinite possibilities her names, their names, offered her she chose the syllables and resonances Rafti had come to the heaven beyond the heavens seeking. Then the heaven beyond the heavens was gone and she was only Rafti once more. Only Rafti, yet she was whole—she had two living eyes again and her face was perfect and unscarred—as she and Moth and Tramu burst from the yellow mud at the bottom of the Mother's Inner Ocean and soared upward on Maryssat's back through the glowing magma with its swirling currents and scarlet fires, climbing toward the skin of the world.

She felt free, joyous, unconstrained, fully herself and no other for the first time in her existence.

The ghost was gone. There was only Rafti, only Shonraleur's daughter. And yet, she remembered Tas Gly's daughter's life, her death and imprisonment in Sartor's Royal Realm, the panic she had felt when she realized that the child as whom she'd been meant to be reborn had died in the womb.

She was alive, but she had been dead. What she had known as a ghost she knew still, what she had been able to do she could still do.

She glanced over at Moth and Tramu, remembering them. How she'd loved Tramu, hated him, envied him and been humiliated by him. How her father had forced her to accompany him to the Great Square and she'd seen the hatred in Tramu's eyes as he stared out at the cruel, mocking faces surrounding him only to see her weeping, and how his face had softened for an instant, just long enough to let his anguish and despair show through, before he turned away from her. How she would have forgiven him anything then, done anything to help him, and there had been nothing she could do.

She remembered, too, how she'd slowly come to care for Moth, almost love him, until that too ended in tragedy and her father sold her to Prince SarVas's Necropolis. She remembered everything, what it had been to be the other Rafti, and the memories were *hers*, not borrowed, not another's. She was Shonraleur's daughter and yet she was Tas Gly's daughter as well: her two selves' truenames had fused in the heaven beyond the heavens, where time and sequence had no meaning, where present, past, and future were continually born anew, and she, Rafti, daughter to Tas Gly the goldsmith, had been reborn as herself, Rafti Shonraleur's-Daughter.

When Moth's and Sulthar's attempts to summon her back

from the dead had liberated Tas Gly's daughter, there had been no chance confusion of similar names, no coincidence involved. She had always been Tas Gly's reborn daughter, though it was only now that she had finally learned to know herself for who she was.

And, knowing herself, she knew there was nothing more for her in Kyborash, or on the Nomad plains. She had left the Mother's Burning Mountain in search of healing, of renewal, and she had found it, found more than she could have ever hoped for. Now the time had come for her to return.

Beside her, Tramu was coming out of the daze he'd been in since they'd begun the ascent. He was looking around him with growing uneasiness, lost, beginning to panic.

Reaching over, Rafti grasped his shoulder, steadied him before he could lose his grip on the horse and fall. He stared at Moth and at her, rigid with terror, until she said, It's all right, Tramu. Then, abruptly, he seemed to recognize them and slumped back with relief, though his face was still closed and wary.

He studied Rafti, Moth, Maryssat, the burning magma flowing around them, with a bewilderment and fear he tried to hide behind the impassive mask he must have shown the overseers at the mines, though Rafti could see it in the throbbing of veins in his neck and temple, and the tension in his hands, knotted tight in Maryssat's mane, in the way his eyes darted back and forth, never quite meeting her own.

It's all right, Tramu, she said again. There's nothing to be afraid of here. How do you feel?

He shook his head, pointed at his mouth, then suddenly stopped, shock and wonder clear on his face. His hand went to his mouth, felt his tongue.

You don't have to worry about that anymore, Rafti said. You can talk again now.

He put his hand slowly back down again, his face working, finally asked, Rafti?

Yes. You're safe here with us.

There was nothing more for him in Kyborash or Chal now either, no more than there was for her, and her people's forges had been cold for too many generations.

They were of the Children of Raburr, as Tramu was of the Children of Raburr. They would honor a smith.

Chapter Forty-six

Maryssat burst from the ground into the dawning day and came to an abrupt halt. They were back in Tas No's forge compound. Everything was just as that part of Moth that had been his Ri ghost remembered it—and he could still see it all as his ghost had seen it, his vision stretching unhindered by walls or obstacles to encompass the courtyard and the darkness inside the house, Ashanorak and the others on their horses behind the rear wall, the Taryaa still lying entranced in the godhouse atop the Siltemple's ziggurat. The fierce flames from the dead horse's burning skin and bones were shiny faience; the smoke wreathing the body Rafti had left clinging to the upside-down tree trunk hung in motionless coils. There was only stillness, silence, the sun hanging immobile on the horizon, a few stars still faintly visible in the pale sky overhead.

For a moment Moth felt confused, overwhelmed by the chaotic visions flooding into him. But the ghost was part of him again: the knowledge and skills he needed to master the visions were there for him to use, and he narrowed his attention down to what he could comprehend.

Stay here, Moth told Tramu as he and Rafti helped him down off Maryssat's back. They won't be able to see you until we—

Tramu? Do you understand what I'm saying?

But Tramu was staring at Rafti as she walked confidently toward the fire, and at the other Rafti, clinging motionless to the pole jutting from it, the dead eye gleaming wet and white in her scarred face. He looked back and forth between the two, his face twisting.

You're not the only one who's suffered, Moth told him roughly, suddenly angry. She had to endure far worse than the mines to become someone who could rescue you.

Remembering the cringing creature he'd rescued, he expected Tramu to deny that anything could be worse than the mines, mumble something self-pitying and evasive. But Tramu only nodded slowly, still staring at the two Raftis, and Moth felt his anger leave him. It would be hard enough for anyone to face what Tramu had to face unprepared.

He looked around. Beyond the fire pit lay a small human skeleton, still wearing a handmaiden's gold ribbons and jewelry: all that remained of the Rafti Tramu had known. And behind the skeleton lay two dead bodies, one half hidden behind the other.

Do you see that? Moth said, pointing at the first body.

Tramu stared at it. His face twitched, then went impassive and closed again as he finally recognized the body in its Nomad shaman's garb with its arms ending in charred stumps.

That was me, Moth told him. I was dying, before Rafti rescued me.

What about me? Tramu finally found the courage to ask. What was I like—before?

You don't remember?

I remember when the Nomads cut my tongue out. . . . And my arm. At the mines. They broke my arm when I tried to keep them from stealing Mother's food after her coughing got too bad—

And then? Moth asked, more gently.

Just dreams, nightmares . . .

What kind of dreams?

Everybody was dead, all around me. I was in the mines but at the same time I was in Kyborash too. The whole city was dead, bones everywhere, and then I was trapped in a tomb, underground, and a Nomad was trying to get at me to rip my tongue out again. . . . Then I woke up with you.

The mines and the city were real, Moth told him. Come over here.

Rafti was watching them from the fire pit. Tramu started toward Moth. He hesitated an instant by the fire, staring down at the horse's body burning so fiercely without being consumed, at the frozen, silent flames and the smoke hanging immobile in the air, then glanced back and forth between the Rafti on the pole and the Rafti standing watching him.

We'll keep you safe, she assured him.

I'm not afraid.

He tried to force a smile, couldn't keep himself from looking up one last time at the body on the pole as he walked away from the fire pit, obviously frightened but as unwilling to give in to his fear as the Tramu Moth had known before he'd been sent to the mines would have been.

He joined Moth by the two bodies. Moth reached down and turned the second body over. Tramu stared at it in silence.

That's me, he said at last.

Moth nodded, still waiting.

Does that mean—we're all dead now? Ghosts?

No. Rafti didn't take our souls to the heaven beyond the heavens just to let us remain crippled or dead.

I don't understand. If I'm dead . . . You said I was dead. That's my body.

It was your body, and it's dead. But it doesn't have to stay dead. You're still here with me, *you're* still alive. If you've got the courage to do what I tell you, *this*—Moth reached over and tapped Tramu on the chest—and not that dead meat on the ground will be real again.

I'll be alive again? he asked uncertainly. I mean, like I am now, but just me again, in my own real body, not—

Yes. Just you, cousin, the way you always were.

Tramu shook his head in frustration. I don't understand!

We'll explain when we can, Rafti said. After you have your body back.

Moth waited until Tramu finally nodded.

This is where it all begins, he said. Remember, they won't be able to see you at first—and later, when they can, they'll be too afraid of angering me to hurt you.

What if they're not afraid? Tramu asked, half challenging.

They will be. Watch Rafti.

Rafti jumped with inhuman ease up to the disfigured Rafti clinging motionless to the pole and vanished into her semblance. When she leapt down from the pole again Tramu gaped at her in astonishment. Her face was whole again, no longer scarred and hideous, but the face of the Rafti who had made the ascent from the netherworld, and only a single leather sack now hung from the carved baton in her hand where before there had been three.

Watch, Moth said again. He lay down beside the dead Moth's body and rolled over into it. There was an instant of total disorientation as his two bodies merged, a searing flash of almost unbearable agony, and then he had hands again and his wounds were gone, though his arms and throat were still covered with tiny, long-healed scars. The flames in the fire pit were leaping and crackling, and Moth could hear Ashanorak yelling angrily in Deltan behind the compound's rear wall as all the senses he had forgotten he was lacking for so long came alive again simultaneously. For a moment it was all he could do to lie there with his fists clenched in the dirt and the breeze playing over his face, overwhelmed by the smell of the earth and smoke. He grabbed a handful of loose dirt and pebbles, ground them together in his fist.

Rafti was wrapping herself in a gray woolen cloak. There was a beauty to her, to Tramu and the ruined forge compound and the sky above it, that was totally new, that Moth had never noticed before.

No, he thought as he got slowly to his feet, feeling the play of the muscles in his legs, listening to the metal bones and ornaments on his Nomad shaman's costume jangling as he moved, it's not new. I'd just forgotten what it was to be truly alive. I'd forgotten how precious life really is.

He turned to face the doorslit just as Ashanorak came through it dressed as a Nomad warrior, his long copper sword gleaming in his hand, the two Teichi directly behind him. A moment later three more Deltans dressed as Nomads followed.

Tramu shrank back against the compound wall, behind Maryssat, steadied himself with one arm against the eight-legged horse's hard flank, his other hand half up as if to protect his mouth. Moth knew he'd recognized Ashanorak as the Nomad from his dreams, the one who'd been trying to cut his tongue out again.

The warriors looked right past Tramu and Maryssat without seeing them, glanced at Rafti, only to look away again, dismissing her. They took up a grim-faced defensive formation facing Moth.

Tramu straightened and let the hand shielding his face drop to his side again. He had his fear under control and Moth knew then that he was once more truly the Tramu he'd known before, that not only his body but his spirit had been healed in the heaven beyond the heavens.

Tramu was studying Ashanorak and the others with a look of fierce concentration. He's realized that they really can't see him, Moth thought. And how much more afraid of me they are than I am of them.

"Ashanorak," Moth said with a mocking grin.

"Moth," Ashanorak said, acknowledging him. He put his sword back in the sheath he wore slung Deltan-style across his back. "I've brought you your medicine."

"You're too late. As you can see, I no longer need it."

Ashanorak gestured at Tramu's dead and twisted body. "What did you do, sacrifice that poor madman's life to get your own back?"

Moth laughed outright, and this time his laughter was sunny, joyous, the way he remembered laughing when he and Tramu had been boys together. He was pleased to see that for an instant Tramu joined him with an uncertain smile.

Ashanorak followed Moth's gaze to look directly at Tramu, not seeing him, then turned back to Moth.

"You demanded medicines and safe-conduct to Kyborash for yourself and your madman," Ashanorak said, with a glance back at the two Teichi to make sure they heard him. "You swore an oath to my master in return. If you ignore the safe-conduct, refuse the medicine, it is no affair of ours. My master's oath to you has been fulfilled. Your oath still binds you."

"Show me this medicine," Moth said. "If it is truly what your master promised me, then I agree that my oath still binds me and I will fulfill it."

Ashanorak thought that over an instant, nodded, yelled, "Cimarduras!"

Another Nomad came through the doorslit.

"Give him the medicine."

Cimarduras took out the silk-wrapped packets, held them out to Moth.

"No," Moth said, his face impassive again but with an almost imperceptible hint of mockery on his face and in his voice, just enough so Ashanorak could feel and resent it, but not enough so he could be certain it had really been there. "Let Ashanorak open them, so you all can bear witness."

Ashanorak hesitated, then reluctantly took the packets from Cimarduras.

"Open them. Let us all see what's inside."

Ashanorak opened first one, then the other, to discover that they were only wads of mildewed silk.

Cimarduras took a step back. He babbled, "But—but they were there. I saw them. They can't be gone."

"They are, you fool." A sudden breeze snatched one piece of silk from Ashanorak's hand. He snatched it back, began ripping it in half.

"Wait!" Moth said. Ashanorak paused, looked up at him. "Your master's medicine is more valuable than you realize. Give it to me. Now!"

The words were a command. Ashanorak started to hand the flapping pieces of silk over, abruptly checked himself. "No. You won't make a fool of me again, shaman."

"You have little choice. I command you, and so does your master. Will you tell your Taryaa that I asked you for the medicine promised me and that you refused to give it to me? Give it to me!"

Ashanorak's hand went to his sword. Before he could draw it Moth cried, "Tas Et!"

Suddenly Tas Et was dying impaled on the stake where a moment before Ashanorak had stood—yet Ashanorak was still there, writhing in Tas Et's agony with him.

"Leave him," Moth said quietly, and Tas Et was gone. He glanced over at Tramu, was glad to see that Rafti had walked over to him and, ignored by the Nomads, was reassuring him quietly.

"Have you forgotten Nanlasur?" he asked Ashanorak scornfully, and held out his hand.

Ashanorak looked at the others. They kept their faces impassive, or looked away. He took a reluctant step forward, handed Moth the silk.

Moth smiled fiercely. "As I said, I have no further need for the Taryaa's medicines, but there are others who might. My dead cousin here, for instance." Moth gestured to Tramu with a quick movement of his head.

"Go to your body and lie down beside it the way Moth did," Rafti whispered to him. Then, facing the warriors and pretending to address them, she said in a louder, commanding voice, "Have no fear."

They looked at her in surprise, registering her presence and the fact that she might be a potential danger for the first time.

Tramu walked over to his dead body, standing straight, keeping himself from flinching or even so much as looking at Ashanorak and his men when he crossed in front of them. They were all still watching Moth, though glancing at Rafti now and again as well.

When he reached the body, Tramu looked back to Moth for approval. Moth nodded his head almost imperceptibly. His face working with fear, Tramu knelt down beside the corpse.

Only then did he see that the body's back was broken.

He jerked back, then forced himself to reach over, touch the cool flesh. For an instant the fear on his face vanished, replaced by intense pleasure. He pulled back again, even more frightened than before, looked to Moth and Rafti for reassurance again.

Rafti smiled at him. Turning his back on Ashanorak and his men, Moth walked over to join Tramu, grinned at him as soon as he was sure Ashanorak and his men couldn't see his face, and nodded. Tramu relaxed a little. Moth wadded the larger piece of silk back up and opened the corpse's mouth, stuffed it inside. He was close enough to Tramu now that only Tramu could hear his murmured words.

"Lie down flat beside your body and roll yourself into it, as I did. There will be pain, but it will pass in an instant and then you will be whole again. Ashanorak and the others will be too afraid of you to try to harm you."

Tramu lay down beside his dead body, closed his eyes.

"*Now,* if you want to be alive and well again."

Tramu rolled over and into his dead body.

"Awaken, Tramu," Moth said dramatically, pulling the silk from his mouth. An ecstatic, astounded smile on his face, Tramu opened his eyes and got slowly to his feet, looked around him in unfeigned wonder, like a child seeing the world for the first time.

Moth turned back to Ashanorak. "It would seem that the first of the medicines your master sent me is very powerful indeed," he told the Deltan. Ashanorak was trembling visibly now. "The other seems less so, but I should still be able to find some use for it. . . ."

While Moth was talking, Rafti had removed the leather sack from the horse-stick. She handed him the stick and he walked over to the fire pit, both pieces of silk flapping weakly in his other hand. Staring down at the burning horse's bones and skin, he cried, "Maryssat!" and tossed stick and silk into the pit.

The fire pit exploded into crimson flame. One of the Deltans screamed. When they could see again, a black horse stood in the cloud of settling ashes that was all that remained of the fire and the tree trunk that had been jutting from it—Moth's horse, though now it had only four legs again.

"Maryssat," Moth called again, gently this time, and the black came to him and nuzzled his hand.

He turned back to Ashanorak. "You can tell your master that I thank him for his safe-conduct here and for the power of his medicines. I will fulfill my oath to him. Now, leave us."

His voice was fierce, hard, triumphant: there was no way Ashanorak or the others could do anything but obey him.

He felt pleased with the unflinching way Tramu looked after them as they slunk away, ridiculous in their terror. With the vision he had inherited from his Ri ghost he watched them through the wall as they mounted their horses and rode off. Let me know when they reach the Siltemple, he commanded Tas Et silently.

Tramu had turned to study Moth and Rafti with the same intense concentration with which he'd been studying

Ashanorak and the others. "Who are you, really?" he finally asked.

"Moth. Your cousin Moth."

"Here? Like this?"

"I'm a shaman now, Tramu. Do you remember Casnut, the Nomad shaman when we went with Father to the Fair?"

Tramu nodded, frowning.

"Like him."

"You're a Nomad, then."

"Like the ones who cut out your tongue? No. They were mercenaries in the Taryaa's pay, like the two Teichi you saw with Ashanorak. The Taryaa who pay the Nomads are your true enemies, not the Nomads themselves."

"What difference does it make?"

"Much has changed since they sent you to the mines, cousin. You spent years in your dreams. You have a lot to learn."

"What about you?" Tramu asked Rafti. "Are you really Rafti?"

"The Rafti you knew died and was reborn. I am the person she was reborn as. Yet I still remember what it was to be her, Tramu. I still remember you."

Tramu stared at her intensely again, nodded slowly. "You're taller than she was. Slimmer, and there's something about your nose, the way you hold yourself. . . . Yet—"

"Yet I'm still her."

"Yes." He was silent a moment. "I should be terrified of both of you," he said at last. "As terrified as they were."

"But you're not," Moth said. "We saved you from the mines, brought you back to life and health, gave you your tongue again. And you know us, you've known us all your life. You know you would never have anything to fear from us."

"What about Father? You called on him and he came. I saw him, still dying on the stake. . . . The Moth and Rafti

I knew would have never left him in agony like that, not if they could have brought him back to life.''

Moth hesitated. ''We can't bring him back, Tramu. But the choice was his, not ours. As he was dying he called down his smith's death-curse on King Tvil. Now he's trapped in it until the curse has run its course.''

Tramu looked at Rafti. ''He's telling the truth,'' she said. ''We'd free him if we could.''

''But you—used him,'' Tramu told Moth. ''Even if you can't free him, you shouldn't just make him serve you like he was your slave, or—''

''We use each other, cousin. I have sworn to aid him in his vengeance against Tvil. And it was when he forced me to become the instrument of that vengeance that he put me on the road that led me to become what I am now. Yet if I can ever free him of his curse, I will.''

''Will you swear to that, on your truename?''

''Yes. I swear on my truename that if ever I can free Tas Et from his curse and his death agony, then I, Moth who was Sartor-ban-i-Tresh and Sartor-ban-ea-Sar, will do so.''

Ashanorak has reached the Siltemple, Tas Et told Moth.

Moth closed his eyes, concentrated, saw Ashanorak climbing the ziggurat's steep steps, the Taryaa, free of its trance now, watching him silently from the godhouse's door.

''We have to leave now,'' Moth said, opening his eyes again. ''I want to be gone before Ashanorak reports back to his master.''

''Why?'' Tramu asked, almost challenging him again. Provoking him to see how he'd react. ''If they're so afraid of you.''

Moth forced himself to remain patient. ''Ashanorak's afraid of me. The Taryaa he serves aren't, and they are far more dangerous than he could ever be.''

''Then why did you let him leave?'' Tramu asked.

''Because I need to show the Taryaa that I have enough power to be a useful ally to them, though not enough to be a threat to them. So long as they think they can use me safely, they'll leave me alone. Help me, even. Now that they know you're with me and under my protection, you won't be in any immediate danger from them."

He saw the frustrated incomprehension on Tramu's face, continued trying to explain anyway. "But I can't trust them. They hate shamans and they'll turn on me as soon as they realize I've become strong enough to threaten them. Now that they know you're with me, the less additional information they learn about either of you, the safer we'll all be. That's why we have to leave Kyborash before the Taryaa has had a chance to do anything."

"I'm not going with you," Rafti said. "I'm going back to my valley."

"You're going back?" Moth realized he was standing there gaping at her as stupidly and awkwardly as he'd so often gaped at the other Rafti when they'd been children together. "Why?"

"My people need me. And—there's nothing for me here, skulking through the ruins, trying to betray the Taryaa before they betray you, or—"

"I'm here," Moth said. "You could stay with me. People always need a healer, as much here as in your valley."

"No. I can't. I'd like to stay with you, be your friend and companion—but that's all it would be, can't you see? It wouldn't be enough. It wouldn't change anything."

"But I need you too," Moth said, and this time he couldn't keep the longing out of his voice. "To help me against the Taryaa and the stars. . . . They are as much your enemies as they are mine."

Rafti glanced up at the sky. Low on the horizon, a last few stars were still visible. "I know. They almost destroyed me during my ascent—would have destroyed me without Casnut's help. I know why you're fighting them. But—you don't need me to help you. Not *me,* Rafti Shonraleur's-Daughter who was Tas Gly's daughter. My people really do need me. I used to think they needed me to be the Mother's Priestess, and I was wrong, but now . . . It's not just that I'm a healer. They've been isolated in their separate valleys too long. I can teach them to be Masters of Fire so they can cross the Mother's Burning Mountain and become a single people again.

"Do you understand, Moth? I know who I am now. I know what I have to do."

Tramu had been listening silently, studying their faces, frowning. "What about me?" he asked angrily. "You saved me from the mines, you gave me back my tongue and healed me, but I'm still just an escaped mine slave. I don't even understand what you're talking about. It doesn't have anything to do with me. As soon as somebody recognizes me they'll put me back in the cage."

Rafti turned to him. "You could come with me, Tramu. My people would welcome a smith to rekindle their cold forge fires for them."

There was compassion in her voice and the way she was smiling at him, but there was a hint as well of the same warmth and fascination, the same longing, with which her former self had always regarded Tramu, back when Moth had been only Tramu's Ri cousin . . . and Moth knew, abruptly, that it was hopeless, that whatever his own feelings about her were, neither the Rafti he would have married had her father not sold her to die in SarVas's Necropolis nor this Rafti she had become would ever have felt anything more for him than the friendship she was offering him.

"Your people?" Tramu asked her.

"The Children of Raburr who fled to the north rather than submit to the King of Chal," Rafti told him.

Moth forced himself to look away from them, let them talk to each other. He concentrated on the Siltemple.

Ashanorak was telling the Taryaa how he'd seen a girl clinging to an upside-down tree trunk . . .

"Are they smiths?" Tramu was asking.

"They once were, but they've lost their forge lore. They—"

"Rafti," Moth said suddenly, "you can't go back. Either of you."

"Why?"

"I didn't know you'd already fought against the stars when I let Ashanorak go. Without Ashanorak to tell them what you looked like in the flesh the Taryaa wouldn't have known how to recognize you as the shamaness who'd been powerful enough to defy the stars and defeat them—"

"I didn't defeat them. Casnut helped me."

"It doesn't make any difference. Now that Ashanorak's told them, they'll hunt you down, no matter where you go. Even in your valley."

"I have to go back."

"You won't be safe there!" He gestured angrily up at the sky. "They're almost blind now, but at night—"

In the godhouse on top of the ziggurat the Taryaa had motioned Ashanorak to silence. It was staring fixedly up at the last star still visible through the opening in the roof.

Tas Et! Moth commanded. Hold the Taryaa's body and spirit for me. Break its trance!

The Taryaa's body convulsed and went rigid. It fell back onto the dais, its globular pink eyes bulging even farther from its head, then slumped limply forward.

I cannot hold it much longer, nephew. It's letting itself die.

"What's happening?" Rafti demanded. "What's wrong?"

"The Taryaa's trying to contact the stars. I'm trying to hold it back, but it's making itself die so its spirit can join them."

"Can you stop it?"

"I don't know. Maybe, if you help me."

"Where is it?"

"The Siltemple. On top of the ziggurat."

Rafti closed her eyes. "I see it. What do you need me to do?"

"Just keep its body alive while I try to find how to stop it."

"Let the Mother have it," Rafti said.

"What?" Moth glanced over at her in surprise. Her eyes were still squeezed shut.

"Give its spirit to the Mother. If it can't draw its birth labyrinth perfectly, it'll lose all memory of ever having been a Taryaa and be reborn as someone else."

Moth nodded. "Good. How long can you keep it alive?"

Rafti concentrated again. "A while. Not very long."

To Tramu, who was looking on in frustrated incomprehension, Moth said, "We're in danger—"

"Because you let him go?"

"Yes. But we can save ourselves if we act quickly enough. Go watch the street, make sure nobody gets in."

Tramu just stood there looking at him.

"Hurry!"

"I don't have anything to stop anyone with."

"Here." Moth threw Tramu a knife. He caught it clumsily and squeezed through the doorslit into the house.

"Ready?" Moth asked Rafti.

She nodded.

Moth straightened, let his breathing settle into a slow, steady rhythm. He began to chant. The chant grew, filled him, and he started to dance, slowly at first, then faster, so that the sound of his chanting was lost in the clashing and jangling of the heavy metal bones and ornaments on his costume. He reached down for his drum—only to remember abruptly that it was broken and useless, buried in the back of the compound.

He let his chant die, stopped dancing. He wouldn't be able to summon enough strength that way now, not without the drum-spirit's aid.

"What's wrong?" Rafti asked, opening her eyes.

"Nothing. Forget about me, go back to keeping it alive!"

Put me in its body, he commanded Tas Et.

He felt the agony of the stake, tasted salty blood on his

lips, and heard King Tvil's laughter. He wrenched himself free of the Great Square, blocked the pain, but a confusion had come over his spirit. He was lying on the dais in the godhouse. He tried to stand, straining for the pale sky overhead, lost control of his muscles, and fell back, his vision blurring.

"I can't keep it alive much longer," he heard Rafti's distant voice say. "It's dying."

His sexless body felt boneless and soft, shaken by tiny tremors, spasms, as muscles and sphincter let go. Moth could feel the heart beating ever more sluggishly, faltering despite Rafti's efforts to keep it going, could feel the lungs collapsing in on themselves, refusing to draw air, the life-flame in the Taryaa's spine no more than a memory of warmth now despite the fires Rafti fed it from her own hassa. The dais beneath him, his white robes, the band of silk hiding his toothless mouth, everything felt smooth, slick, without purchase. As though both he himself and the world around him had already been masticated and coated with saliva, were ready to be swallowed. Ashanorak leaning over and shaking him was disappearing into a chill mist, the fear and rage on the warrior's bearded face smoothing out as the shoulder he was gripping faded, the questions he was screaming receded, were lost in silence. Somewhere, immeasurably distant yet still closer than Ashanorak or the vague contours of the godhouse around him, Moth could see the night sky, the stars gleaming bright and cold.

Moth sensed the Taryaa's spirit trying to hide from him in its slippery dying flesh, yet afraid to retreat too far into the realms of sleep and risk trapping itself there, where it would be unable to escape the death of its body. Moth pursued the spirit, tried to read the truename it had renounced in its color and aspect, but the spirit was only vaguely man-shaped, bulging and shrinking half liquidly, without constant form or definition except for a single transparent crystalline eye in its center.

Once, when Moth thought he had it trapped, he tried to communicate with it, tell it he wouldn't hurt it if it obeyed him, but it showed no sign that it retained enough humanity to understand him. When Moth seized it, it squirmed from his grasp like a fish underwater, slipped away, battering at the prisoning wall of its fading flesh until Moth caught up with it again and it fled him once more.

Every moment took them farther from the worlds of sleep and waking alike, weakened the barriers keeping them from the avid stars in the cold night beyond the sky. The spirit was shrinking in upon itself, solidifying around the central eye, the last of its human semblance fading. The stars were pulling at them, trying to draw them both up through the blue dome of the sky to the night beyond. The sky was like a waterspout, sucking him in with ever increasing strength as the Taryaa's sheltering flesh faded and he was drawn closer, but he held himself between the spirit and the vortex, kept trying to force it back into the realm of dreams, where he could seize it even without its truename.

Moth! I can't hold it any longer!

Moth cried a word in the secret language and became a hawk. As the Taryaa's spirit leapt free of its flesh and was drawn up toward the early-morning sky, Moth quit fighting the stars' pull, flung himself into the sky.

The sky was pale azure, growing brighter. The Taryaa's soul fled upward, trying to escape the sun's blinding light, pierce the sky to the night beyond. Moth climbed desperately after the spirit through the chill air, slowly narrowing the distance between them.

Just below the sky's pale dome, he overtook it with a final powerful beat of his wings, twisted back and seized it in his talons.

The Taryaa tried to escape, but its transformation had continued as it rose ever higher until it was little more than a compact crystalline mass now, and the sun's heat had stolen what little strength it still possessed. Moth had no trouble keeping it clutched securely against his breast. He tried to bank, halt his upward flight, but he was going too fast, the stars' grip on the Taryaa's struggling spirit and on his own spirit-flesh was too strong.

Together, Moth and the Taryaa struck the sky and slipped without resistance through its smooth azure surface into a maelstrom of churning turquoise and chrysoprase-green winds. For an instant the World-Tree's immense canopy of interlaced branches seemed to take on substance around them, but before Moth could seek their shelter they faded back into the darkening colors of the storm.

Still struggling, they passed from the storm into the night beyond.

A wall of lapis lazuli hid the earth. The stars surrounded him, swarms of hate-filled frozen eyes, leeching the warmth from his soul.

The Taryaa too had become a star. Moth clasped it tighter to his breast, wrapped his wings around it, kept it from communion with the others. They were trying to reach it through him, ice probing through his feathers to his skin and spreading throughout his body while the Taryaa's chill invaded his breast. The stars drew in closer around him. He could no longer feel the talons with which he was grasping the Taryaa.

With a final effort, he burst free of the ice imprisoning him, spread his wings, and dived back into the lapis wall, keeping his body between the Taryaa and the stars. The stars tried to draw him back, their pull on him like myriads of tiny hooks embedded in his flesh, tearing at him as he forced his wings to continue beating, dragged himself laboriously down through the blue-green storms and out of the sky's shell into the day beneath.

The pull seemed to ease a little once he felt the sun's heat on him again. The earth was coming up below. Just before he struck it he cried another word in the secret language.

The earth's skin parted before him as easily as the

waters of Lake Nal would have parted before the green gull whose form he'd taken. The stars' grip on him was even weaker beneath the earth than it had been in the day above, but whenever he ceased struggling against the pull, tried to let his wings rest and just glide deeper, he found himself slowing, his trajectory turning upward again. And though the force the stars were exerting on him diminished, it never really ceased, not even after he had passed from the dark depths of the earth's skin into the burning orange-red currents of the Mother's Inner Ocean.

Yet everything else was peaceful, still. He could see for immense distances, see the buried roots of mountains, the ripening veins of ore groping their way upward to flower just beneath the skin of the earth. The Ocean's gentle heat spread through him, soothed some of the pain. Even the Taryaa's frozen soul seemed warmer, less rigid, almost like flesh again.

Blue-white brilliance flared in the distance, shone from the flashing scales and fins of the cloud of blind silver fish surrounding the Mother.

She was beautiful and terrible beyond all comprehension, heavy-breasted and legless, growing from the Ocean's floor like the World-Tree that was another of Her forms. Moth fought against the absolute dread She inspired, the paralysis of will that was as much awe and overwhelming fascination as it was fear, and that never diminished but only seemed to grow stronger each time he was forced to confront Her.

The Taryaa had regained the vaguely human form it had lost during its ascent and was beginning to struggle again, feebly and in total silence. Moth gripped it tighter, continued down through the Ocean's languid, burning currents, the shimmering cloud of fish, toward the Mother.

As he settled to the burning yellow mud of the ocean floor before one of Her immense gnarled green and brown roots, he spoke his truename and regained human form. He kept his arms wrapped tightly around the Taryaa's tallow-soft, melting form, but the stars' pull on the two of them was still almost strong enough to carry him off; he dug his feet into the sucking mud, used it to anchor him there.

The Mother towered over him, thousand-armed, mountain-huge, Her brown eyes infinitely gentle and loving, Her mouth filled with innumerable jagged and discolored tusks. She was waiting for the soul whose death had brought it before Her to stick the longest finger of its right hand into the burning mud at its feet and leave there the personal labyrinth it carried marked in the fine lines and whorls of its fingertips, the pattern that would determine the nature of its rebirth.

Moth felt the mud beneath his feet shudder. Tua-Li had sensed their presence and was streaking up toward them from his lair beneath the Mother's roots, to devour them if they failed to comply.

But though the Taryaa had regained quasi-human form, its limbs ended in amorphous lumps: the Taryaa had no fingers, no personal labyrinth. Moth grabbed one of the feebly struggling limbs and pressed it into the mud, then stood back, watching to see what the Mother did. But She ignored the slight hollow he'd made, continued watching them in silence, while the ocean floor beneath them shook ever more violently with Tua-Li's approach.

Could he just leave, abandon the Taryaa to Tua-Li?

No. The Taryaa was light, almost buoyant. As soon as Moth let go of it, it would be drawn upward again, back to the stars. The only way to make sure the Taryaa would still be there when Tua-Li arrived would be to keep holding onto it until the World-Eel arrived, but it was one thing to provoke the World-Eel's anger when you were above the world's skin, another to defy it here. He would be devoured along with the Taryaa.

He pressed the Taryaa's tallow-soft arm into the mud again, harder, but it was hopeless; the hollow was a little bigger but nothing else had changed, there was no way he could give the Taryaa fingerprints. . . .

Unless he gave it his own. But then he, and not the Taryaa, would be the one trapped in the Mother's labyrinth, forced on to a new rebirth.

Not if he altered the whorls so they were no longer his.

He grabbed the Taryaa's waxy arm again, pressed his own fingertip into the malleable lump on the end of its right arm where its hand should have been. Using his nails, he quickly altered a few lines, scored some of the other whorls and lines deeper. Even before he'd finished the crude new birth labyrinth he'd created, it was beginning to lose definition, melt back into the Taryaa's shapelessness; but before it could be entirely reabsorbed and lost, he pushed the lumpy end of the spirit's arm as deeply as he could into the sucking yellow mud.

And the ocean floor beneath him stopped shuddering as the Mother's thousands of graceful hands came snaking toward them on the ends of Her long, sinuous arms.

Chapter Forty-seven

Moth yanked the Taryaa's flaccid arm from the mud, took an involuntary step back. He tried to step forward again, grab onto the Taryaa and keep the stars from pulling it back up to them, but the Mother was staring straight at them, She saw *him* now, and he could no longer resist Her fascination. All thought of escape and survival, of the way the force with which the stars were trying to draw him back to them hurt like myriads of tiny barbed hooks tugging at his flesh, ripping at it, was forgotten as he was caught and held by Her gaze, by the sinuous interweavings of Her thousands of arms, the dance of Her exquisitely tapering hands.

The Mother slipped Her hands into the burning yellow mud around the hollow the Taryaa's arm had left, grasped the ocean floor on every side and pulled it away. As the sea bottom stretched, the hollow was pulled larger, until finally it was an arm's length in diameter.

The Mother lifted her many hands, held them hovering over the hollow an instant longer to give the Taryaa a final chance to contemplate its birth labyrinth and fix it in its memory. The spirit just lay there, a quivering, amorphous, vaguely human mass.

The Mother patted the left side of the design flat. Her

blind silver fish were suddenly all around Moth and the Taryaa, darting over and between them. Moth felt something like a confused passage of wings behind his eyes, as though some great bird had brushed against his spirit only to be gone again before he could even realize it had been there. The Taryaa's spirit twisted and roiled in the mud, made a deep low moaning noise, the first sound of any sort Moth had ever heard it make.

Moth knew that whatever happened now, the Taryaa could not escape the Mother, would never return to tell the stars about Rafti. It was time to escape, go back to the surface. But the sinuous movements of the Mother's hands and arms were opening out onto vast cycles of growth and death unfolding like flowers blossoming over the eons, unendingly fascinating as grassland succeeded forest and withered into desert, seas rose and receded, races of men or beasts were born and flourished and died, no two cycles identical yet all following the same invariable course, all manifest in the Mother's inhuman grace.

Yet even staring in tranced rapture at the Mother, Moth remained aware of the Taryaa. It should be bending forward now, trying to use its half-melted limbs to complete the pattern. But it just stayed there, oblivious, whimpering, doing nothing. Helpless.

Unexpectedly, Moth found himself pitying the spirit. Whatever it had been before its death had been destroyed when the Mother had effaced half its memories by rubbing out the left side of the birth labyrinth Moth had fashioned. It was no longer his enemy, no longer a threat to Rafti or anyone else, and it would lose what remained of its proper self when it followed that false labyrinth's meaningless turnings toward annihilation, or at best a monstrous birth.

It was his victim now. But he was whole again; he felt its pain, his responsibility for its suffering, in a way that he had lost while his Ri self had been dead. And here, in the Mother's presence, that seemed far more important than whether or not he might be forced to play his own part in the cycle of death and renewal a little sooner than he had expected.

He stepped forward, through the cloud of darting fish, the Mother's hands weaving all around him without ever touching him, and knelt beside the half-erased labyrinth. The Taryaa's arm looked solider, the lump that was its hand a little better defined, but when Moth tried to guide it through the motions of completing the labyrinth, he only succeeded in rubbing out still more of the design.

The Mother was still watching impassively. Moth dragged his own forefinger through the clay, carving shallow channels, filling in the blank left side of the pattern with as close a duplicate as he could draw of what remained on the right side, so as to make a single, roughly symmetrical, twin-lobed pattern. At the same time he smoothed out those parts of the right side that he could see had been badly damaged when he'd used his nails on the imprint he'd left in the Taryaa's flesh.

When he'd done all he could, he stood up and looked at the Taryaa.

The spirit had changed. It was human again now, yet nothing like it had been in life: it had taken on the appearance of a young boy with red and black hair, like Moth's own. The boy had yellow eyes in an open, trusting face that reminded Moth of the face his Ri ghost had shown him for so many years, though where Moth's eyes were sun-fire yellow the boy's were the dull amber of a Chaldan King.

When their gazes met, Moth felt a confused shock, as though for a brief instant he had been looking at his own face through the boy's eyes.

The boy struggled to his feet, and Moth saw that he was deformed, his right leg much shorter than his left, and twisted. He tried to speak, but could only babble garbled, imploring sounds that seemed to infuriate and bewilder him.

Almost sobbing now, but still trying to make himself

speak, the boy raised his arm and gestured awkwardly upward, in the direction from which Moth could feel the stars' pull coming, and as he gestured, Moth saw that there was something wrong with his chest and shoulders as well.

It might have been kinder to have let Tua-Li devour him, Moth thought.

Working his feet loose from the sucking yellow mud, he took a step toward the boy, opened his mouth to say something reassuring.

Four of the Mother's hands ceased their dance and closed on the boy, plucked him from the mud. The Mother held him suspended there, struggling, while the silver fish darted around him in a blind frenzy. She pulled the birth labyrinth larger as She hurled the boy into the pit She'd created. He shrank as he tumbled head over heels into the pit, so that by the time he finally struck the mud at the bottom, he was no larger than Moth's littlest finger, far too tiny to be able to see over the ridges.

The Mother's hands wove back and forth over the pit, shielding it from all interference as the boy got laboriously to his feet and lurched forward through the maze toward whatever rebirth awaited him, dragging his bad leg behind him. With each step the boy took, Moth felt a faint twinge in his own right leg, until at last the tiny, stumbling figure reached the center of the maze and faded.

The pain in Moth's leg swelled, burst over him like a wave and was gone. For an instant he was aware of his shadow-self lying on the ground in Tas No's forge, Tramu and Rafti bending over it, then that too was gone and there was only the Mother's Inner Ocean, the pain from the stars' hooks in his spirit-flesh.

The sea bottom closed back over the hole where the Taryaa's birth labyrinth had been.

Rafti and Tramu were safe, or would be as soon as he could deal with Ashanorak and his men. Rafti could help him fashion a new drum with which to free himself from the stars. There was no reason to delay his return any longer.

He felt the Mother watching him. She was aware of *him* now, the way She'd been aware of the Taryaa. Waiting for him to kneel, press his labyrinth into the mud, make his way through whatever he could reconstruct of it to rebirth.

The silver fish were darting madly back and forth all around him again now. He could sense Tua-Li stirring once more in the mud beneath the Mother's roots, feel the World-Eel's chill silver coils sliding over one another, the mud shuddering beneath his feet as it parted, closed behind Tua-Li again.

Moth kept himself from looking directly at the Mother, but he could feel Her awareness on him, and he could not keep himself from seeing Her with the directionless sense of perception he had inherited from his Ri ghost. He felt his will, his strength, draining from him, lost in the endless round of death and resurrection, the cycling eons.

No. Rafti and Tramu needed him. He would walk his birth labyrinth for the Mother soon enough.

He concentrated on the force with which the stars were still trying to draw him to them, the pain of it, like hooks ripping at his flesh, let it fill his awareness and blot out some of the Mother's fascination.

Crying a name of power in the secret language, he became a hawk. The Inner Ocean felt leaden and thick, an immense weight pressing down on him, and he still felt the Mother's gaze on him, but he forced himself to beat weakly upward through the silver fish and the red-burning depths, letting the stars drag him toward the skin of the world when he no longer had the strength to force his wings to beat any further. When he ceased fighting the stars the pain diminished, but his awareness of the Mother's gaze on him remained with him, paralyzing his will, until at last he passed from the Inner Ocean, and the darkness of its stone sky hid Her from him.

He tried to break free of the stars' hold on him then, but

the dark rock around him disintegrated into choking gray dust and he found himself in Nanlasur's Great Square, surrounded by heaped, rotting bodies, pyramids of severed heads grinning at him with the slack-lipped, empty-eyed faces of all the men and women he had ever betrayed to their deaths. Even as he realized that the stars had drawn him not back up to the night sky but into the Roads of the Dead, the Great Square too vanished and he found himself back in human form, drowning in a fetid icy sea.

Chapter Forty-eight

The waters seethed around him, burning with the chill fires of Neetir's flaming blood. He strained against the force that was dragging him through the depths and fought his way to the surface, gasped for air. He had just enough time to see the lapis lazuli citadel looming stark and sheer from the ocean ahead of him, Sartor's Eighty-four Aspects glaring down from the dust clouds overhead, before the citadel began to spin, sending the bloody waters churning madly around it.

A huge swell struck Moth and knocked the breath from him. Before he could recover, the whirlpool forming around the spinning citadel had pulled him in, was hurling him at the citadel at its center.

Just before he was dashed against its walls he managed to lift his head out of the water long enough to cry, Sartor-ban-ea-Sar!

To become Sartor-ban-ea-Sar the Tas weaponsmith, Moth had had to kill Sartor-ban-i-Tresh the potter. Now that Sartor-ban-i-Tresh was alive again, neither name was truly his, neither could contain him. He was Moth, only Moth. Yet his Tas name still retained its power: the citadel stood abruptly motionless, while the moving waters lashed him in toward the gaping jaws of one of its eighty-four obsidian gates.

A final wave lifted him almost gently from the sea as the stars pulled him forward. He found himself suspended on nothingness beneath the gate's jagged arch, where a dead warrior barred his way with a great copper sword drawn and darkly gleaming in the netherworld's burning twilight. Yet this was no Warrior of the Voice like the one who had barred Moth's passage when he had entered the Tepes Realm, but a short, dark-haired muscular man with faceted copper mirrors for eyes, wearing a smith's siltunic open over the gaping wound in his chest.

Moth knew him: the first man he had ever murdered, the slave he had killed at the Harg in the rites that had made Sartor-ban-i-Tresh the potter's son truly Sartor-ban-ea-Sar, a Tas weaponsmith capable of carrying out his uncle's vengeance.

"Sartor has tasted your life's blood, grandson," Tas No had told him over the slave's body, his eyes hot, his face flushed and excited. "Your life is His now, your blood His and His alone to drink."

That had been when Moth had first truly seen the lie at the heart of the Tas Mysteries, first known that the kindly grandfather he had always respected and loved had a hidden face, and that that face was loathsome.

Behind the guardian Moth could see a confusion of dark, tangled lapis corridors that twisted and coiled over and through one another even as he watched. He caught a faint, cold hint of the burning-eggs stench he remembered from the Harg.

This could only be the entrance to the Tas Realm. The force pulling him on was stronger than ever, dragging him forward.

The guardian raised its sword. Moth felt the sword's greed to drink his soul, knew it for another blade like the Sword That Was Asp.

Guardian, Moth said quickly, unable to tear his gaze

from the darkly gleaming blade, its reflections in the faceted mirrors where the dead man's eyes should have been, I am Tas, Ras Syrr, I was initiated as a weaponsmith in the Tower of Three Levels at the Harg—

Moth hesitated. He had traveled the Roads of the Dead many times, but he had never dared enter the Tas Realm and risk confronting whatever power it still might have over him. Yet without his drum to help him fight the stars' grip on him the only possible way back lay through the citadel, and he had no sacrificial animal or Tepes's son with which to buy safe passage through another realm.

He remembered how the Tepes's son had been plucked from the spirit-boat as soon as they'd entered the Tepes Realm.

My truename is Sartor-ban-ea-Sar, he said. And though he lied, though he was Sartor-ban-ea-Sar no more, his hassa flared into sudden brilliance with his words and burst from his lips like a bird of multicolored fires.

The firebird struck out over the ocean, but the forces that had dragged Moth through the Roads of the Dead had it still, and it was pulled inexorably back through the jagged-toothed obsidian gate.

The guardian's sword lashed out, struck the firebird and drank its flames. As it died Moth felt the cold blade cleave his skull, slice with surgical precision down the length of his spine, leaving the severed vertebrae dead and dry and empty in his icy unmarked flesh.

Enter, the guardian commanded, drawing back to let him pass.

Too numb to do anything but obey, Moth staggered past into the labyrinth of coiling lapis lazuli corridors.

It was dark there, and cold, yet for an instant healing fire flickered in his empty spine. An instant only and then the fires died away, but not before his spine was whole again and he could sense the flames of his hassa banked but ready, awaiting his command.

He had forgotten Rafti. She must have sensed the body

he had left back in Tas No's forge dying, reignited its failing life-flames with her own.

He tried to reach out to Rafti then, draw on her for strength to escape the netherworld, but without the spirits of his drum and costume to aid him he couldn't penetrate the burning twilight.

Yet when the stars had destroyed the firebird, they had lost their hold on him as well. Though he dared not betray that he was still free by heating his cold bone to life again before he was ready to escape, it was hard to keep his exultation from his face as the shifting confusion around him began to take on solid form.

The coiling corridors were gone. He was on a frozen plain, surrounded by the shattered ruins of an immense dead city.

"A warrior dies and is gone, never to return," Tas No had told Moth during his initiation. "But a weaponsmith who forges a blade that delights Sartor is granted life eternal in a land of undying fire. A life as sharp and shining as any sword."

There was nothing like the Realm of Undying Fire his grandfather had promised him here, nothing, even, like the Tepes Realm with Sartor's Tepes Aspect glaring down from overhead at its jagged wilderness of splintered bone and Neetir's monstrous decomposing flesh. Only a faint stale reek of sulfur, icy ruins stretching away to infinity in the starlit darkness.

And the dead. The dead lay everywhere, beyond numbering, dull with the dust and frost that coated them. Warriors of Chal and the Delta and a thousand other nations long vanished, with stars burning a chill blue-white in their fleshless eye sockets.

At first Moth thought that, crazily, there had been some impossible mistake and he'd blundered into the Syrr Realm. Then he realized that many of the dead had the red hair of smiths. Yet all of them, smiths and warriors alike, were clutching copper swords like the one the dead slave guarding the gate had held, and all the swords burned with the same dark soul-devouring fires as the Sword That Was Asp, while the warriors clutching them were not merely dead but annihilated, empty husks serving the swords.

"The blade a warrior carries with him into battle is death," Tas No had told Moth when he had taught him the smith secrets. "If a smith forges his own death into the blades he makes, the warriors wielding them will achieve heroic feats of arms and Sartor will be delighted."

"And how does one forge one's death into a blade?" Moth had asked.

"I can tell you only this now: the blade is Sartor's tongue with which he tastes death. . . ."

This is what Asp would have done to me, Moth realized. I'd be here with the rest of them if Rafti hadn't taken the sword away from me.

He had been dead once already, and though his memories of the time he had spent as a ghost were blurred and distant, he had no great fear of dying again. Yet the warriors' dry emptied corpses horrified him. It was nothing like the terror he felt in the Mother's presence: not awe but revulsion, welling up uncontrollably in him at the sight of something that should never have been, death leading only to death, to emptiness and eternal hunger.

Moth heard slow footsteps behind him, turned. Tas No was there, dressed as he had been when Moth had last seen him, the day before Kyborash had fallen, in his finest siltunic. The siltunic was still new-looking, unspotted beneath the frost and dust coating it, but the old man's forehead had been split open, and in the deep fissure over his left eye Moth could see fragments of whitish skull and frozen clumps of pinkish-gray brain matter, crystals of frozen blood like clotted rubies.

Grandfather? he asked, trying to conquer the outrage the shambling corpse aroused in him. Do you recognize me, Grandfather?

Your sword, grandson, Tas No said in the same flat

tones the guardian had used, ignoring Moth's question entirely. But the voice was still his voice, and there was something about the way he was looking at Moth that was the same. And Moth, who had been hoping for some sign that the grandfather he had once loved had not been totally annihilated, realized then that something of him *had* survived and was perhaps conscious of who he had been and what he had become—and that that was far worse than if all that remained of him had been an empty husk animated by some other's will. Yet hearing him speak, Moth also finally understood the way his grandfather had changed at the end, as the death he had forged into the swords he made ate him from within, leaving little but Sartor's soul-devouring hunger to peer out of his eyes, speak with his quavering voice.

Sartor has delighted in the killing your bright blade has brought Him, Tas No continued. In His generosity, He now grants you the blade itself, to wear for all eternity as token of your loyal service.

Moth dropped his gaze for the first time from his grandfather's face to the blade he was holding out.

It was the Sword That Was Asp.

Rafti had left the sword in the hills by the Necropolis when she rescued him, yet the sword Tas No was presenting him was the Sword That Was Asp nonetheless. Moth knew that if it so much as touched him now, it would devour him as it had devoured all those he had killed with it, leave whatever remained of him its eternal slave.

Grandfather, I am unworthy, he said, taking a step back.

Wherever this realm truly was he could see the night sky overhead. The stars had lost their hold on him; he could take hawk-form and fly free.

He tried to summon up his rage, ignite his hassa, and give himself the force to transform himself. He felt the first flickerings of renewed warmth, a tentative tendril of flame shooting up his spine.

Crying a name in the secret language, he became a hawk. He beat his wings, trying to gain altitude, but the cold had eaten far more deeply into him than he had known, and as he tried to draw on his inner fires they wavered and died.

He summoned up the memories that had always brought anger, and fed them to his hassa: all the agony and betrayals, Tas Et dying on the stake, the things that had been done to those he loved, that they had done to themselves or that he had done to them. But though the memories were as painful as ever, they brought with them no instantaneous rush of rage and heat, no strength, and he fell back to the frozen plain, lay there stunned.

He realized he was back in human form again, struggled to his feet.

Take your sword, Tas No said, still holding it out to him. Nothing in his toneless voice or unaltered stance revealed any awareness that Moth had tried to escape.

Grandfather, Moth repeated, retreating slowly, I am unworthy.

That decision is not yours to make. Sartor commands you.

Moth turned and ran, looking desperately for somewhere he'd be safe long enough to summon back his hassa's strength.

The dead were rising up all around him, covering the plain, emerging from the ruins, cold stars burning in their fleshless faces as they closed in around him.

He kept on running anyway, but there were too many of them, they were everywhere, there was nowhere he could hide. Any one of them could have annihilated him, used its sword to drink his soul, but those closest to him laid their blades aside, clutched at him with chill worm-eaten hands, and hugged him to their odorless corpses.

They held him prisoner as Tas No came limping slowly toward him with the Sword That Was Asp and the death he had forged into it.

Warmth flickered in the base of his spine again.

Rafti. He tried to break through to her before the fires died, but she was still beyond his reach, or incapable of hearing him.

He tried to summon Casnut, putting all the power Rafti had given him into the summoning, but there was no more response than there had been from her.

The dead drew aside, left a corridor open for Tas No and the sword. Yet even the sight of what his grandfather had become ignited no cleansing anger. Moth had lost his smith's ready fury. Some of what he had been as Sartor-ban-ea-Sar had been lost, perhaps when Rafti had healed him, perhaps only now: he was too cold for anger now, too cold for rage, and he had no time to find a new way to nurse his hassa's faint flickerings to the blaze he needed.

He had no rage, no fury—and yet, searching desperately for some strength in himself he could use against the dead, he found the revulsion Tas No and the others inspired in him. He was afraid of them still, yet this dispassionate, almost pristine hatred was a thing apart from his fear, a cold, impersonal force. It did not draw its strength from his fear and frustration, his anger at the way life had cheated him and all those he'd loved, to overwhelm him with an ecstasy of passionate fury, raging power, but neither was it chill and spiteful like the hatred the stars directed at the living, and at everything that might threaten their eternal frozen stasis. There was nothing he envied or desired for himself, not even the satisfaction of revenge, but only that the world be cleansed of the Taryaa and the stars and of all their works, that they cease to threaten and corrupt all that which he loved.

The chill flame burned the weakness from his soul, from his spirit-body. He cloaked himself in it, reached out with it to the dead, found within them the feeble sparks of trapped heat and force that were all that remained of their enslaved trueselves, and those he destroyed.

The warriors who had been holding him scrambled back

in clumsy panic, stumbling against one another, some falling to shatter like icicles, the cold stars in their eye sockets exploding into splintered fragments. But the others crowded forward with their swords raised, and behind them waited Tas No with the Sword That Was Asp, and the death that was for Moth and Moth alone.

Moth held them off, the chill flame a protective wall, shattered and broken bodies heaped ever higher around him: a ring over which the others came stumbling at him, only to fall and add their bodies to the pile.

The ring of broken bodies was a mound seven or eight bodylengths wide and as high as his shoulders now, slowly creeping inward toward him as heads, bodies, limbs, and internal organs frozen hard and smooth as quartz crystals, shards of flesh of all sorts, came rolling down the ring's inner slope, and still the dead came inexorably on, clambering clumsily up and over the fallen to hurl themselves at him. To escape, Moth needed only to transform himself into a hawk and fly free, but he had to keep track of all of the dead with his sense of perception as they came at him from every side; he had to be ready to strike out at them before they reached the top of the mound and became visible to his eyes; he dared not risk the instant of total inward concentration shape-changing demanded. Even if he managed to complete his transformation, they would be on him before the hawk he had become could gain enough altitude to escape, and if even one of their swords so much as touched him, it would drink his soul.

A dead warrior made it over the top, hurled itself down at Moth. Moth lashed out at it with the chill flame, but the body continued on its trajectory, the sword still clenched in its frozen hand. Moth dodged aside, barely avoiding the sword, but the warrior's outflung left arm struck him a glancing blow and knocked him off balance as it shattered.

Before he could pick himself up two more dead warriors had thrown themselves at him, while more came running clumsily down behind them. Moth lashed out at them with the chill flame, annihilating the feeble sparks of life-warmth animating them, but there was no time to get out from under them as they fell, no way he could escape the swords in their frozen hands.

A great gray hawk with burning eyes swooped from the darkness overhead and caught the two warriors in its talons, carried them off.

Casnut. Casnut had saved him.

Moth stared after the hawk an instant, bewildered. Why now, after Casnut had tried to kill him so many times before?

He suddenly realized he'd let his concentration falter. The dead were flooding over the top of the mound now, hurling themselves at him. He struck out at them with the chill flame, but there were too many of them now, crowding in around him; he couldn't deal with them all at once. The ground around his feet was littered with frozen bodies, swords. One wrong step would destroy him.

The hawk let the bodies drop, was wheeling back. Abruptly Moth realized the dead had changed their tactics. They were still crowding in, still rushing him as before, but it was all a feint now. While he'd been distracted Tas No had reached the top of the mound unnoticed and, shielded by the others, had made his way down the inner slope, always hanging back a little to keep from attracting Moth's attention while the others attacked him until now, at last, he was close enough to make his move.

For an instant Moth was paralyzed by the sight of Tas No running at him, the Sword That Was Asp gleaming darkly in his hands, the mutilated face that was still that of the grandfather he had loved distorted in a rictus of ecstasy. He was less than a bodylength away before Moth finally recovered, lashed out, and annihilated what little remained of his grandfather's trueself, but by then the other dead warriors were upon him.

They could have destroyed him easily with their swords, but they came at him so slowly he knew it was just another feint. One of the other warriors bent over Tas No's body, snatched up the Sword That Was Asp.

They were saving him for the sword. None of the warriors counted, only the sword. Moth lashed out at it with the full force of his revulsion, the absolute cold of the flame he wielded.

The sword fell from the dead warrior's hand to shatter like glass at Moth's feet.

The dead warriors, the ruined city, the very frozen plain, all cried out their agony in a single voice.

And in the sky above, Sartor opened His Nighteyes. The whole plain was flooded with the harsh golden glare of His gaze. Everything stopped. Almost directly above Moth now, Casnut hung motionless in the sky, like a dragonfly in amber. The dead were frozen immobile in mid-gesture.

Moth tried to move, transform himself, cry out and break the silence, but it was hopeless; he was totally paralyzed, he could only watch as, wherever the chill golden light fell on the dead, their bodies shriveled and cracked open.

Things like blind groping grubs or maggots, but hard and segmented, their smooth limbless black bodies glistening like ice, were emerging from the dead warriors' desiccated husks.

In the Tas shrine in Kyborash, Sartor had been portrayed as a many-armed warrior of idealized beauty and ferocity, ten of whose twelve arms ended in gleaming copper blades. There was nothing of that idealized humanity in the things Moth was seeing now. And yet they were beautiful, their individual motions combining like the inexorable unfolding of some crystalline flower as they fitted themselves to the blades the warriors had carried, fused with them in the absolute silence to create a dark crystalline latticework spider-webbing across the plain, covering the ruined city and incorporating it into itself. Not beautiful as the Mother was beautiful, with a terrible beauty surpassing human understanding; beautiful, rather, in the precision of their movements, the geometric perfection of the lattice that was forming: the horrible fascination of a limitlessly replicating order, a single action and pattern duplicated to infinity in a mirror grown vast enough to encompass the universe, yet reflecting nothing but its own image, emptied of all but itself.

The very air was crystallizing around Moth and Casnut as the lattice reached from the plain up to the sky where Sartor's Eighty-four Aspects glared down in cold golden-eyed fury, but they too were only part of the lattice, facets of a single crystalline Face. Trapped in the lattice, Moth could glimpse an endless succession of frozen human faces, their rigid, tormented features only masks for the single Face that stared blindly out through them.

Already the ruined city, the plain itself, were becoming transparent, hollow, fading, as they were drained of their substance, until there was only the lattice, a single infinitely replicating crystal of dark ice with the Nighteyes glaring blindly out of it in mad, frozen hate. Moth was embedded in it, part of it; the lattice was rooting itself in him like some monstrous plant, draining him of his reality.

Moth made a final effort to bring the cold flame of his revulsion to bear on the lattice, free himself, but it was too late—all he could feel was an overwhelming disgust that was as much for himself as it was for anything else. Everything was foul and suppurating, diseased, contemptible, rotting. Nothing he could do would ever change any of that.

The Tas Realm was gone. There was only the lattice, his face staring back at him in pointless rage or terror from a thousand reflecting surfaces.

In the silence, he heard Casnut singing.

A faint, wordless chant, little more than rhythmically modulated breathing, and yet it penetrated the crystal walls, freed him of the paralyzing horror of Sartor's vision.

He tried to twist around. The crystals that had grown into his flesh shattered into shards delicate as broken eggshells but sharper than any knife. Every movement he made ground the fragments deeper into his wounds, and the other shards cut him whenever he so much as brushed against them, yet he neither bled nor felt any pain.

He looked up. Through the crystal separating them he could see that Casnut was in human form again, naked, using his fists and feet and forearms to batter his way through the lattice. The crystal walls burst in utter silence; the only sound Moth could hear was Casnut's low, unvarying chant.

Moth's wounds were bloodless but Casnut was bleeding badly. Each time he crawled through a hole he had broken open, over shards already slippery with his streaming blood, he slashed open new wounds. Moth could see white bone peering out through the severed muscles of his arms, see organs soft and slippery in his opened belly.

Casnut worked his way methodically down to Moth, ignoring the damage he was doing to himself. When he had almost reached Moth, Moth managed to bring his own hands up, battered feebly at his side of the crystal walls separating them.

They shattered. For a long instant Moth and Casnut stared at each other without saying anything.

Only one of us can return to life from here, Casnut told Moth finally. You.

Why? Moth asked. Why sacrifice yourself for me?

Because you're finally ready to fulfill your vow to the Taryaa and take my place. Do you remember how I once told you that no sane man would endure what my successor would have to endure by choice, but only because there was no other alternative except death? Yet I also told you that no one could be forced to do what would be required of you, that it could only be chosen willingly.

So?

To make that choice you had to know who you truly were, what Sartor and the Taryaa were. You had to heal your sundered spirit, and you had to face the Tas Realm.

Before you entered it you were still a smith like your grandfather. Sartor's creature, though unaware of it.

But the forces you were wielding here told me you had finally learned to hate Sartor and the stars as I hate them, not with a smith's hot-blooded, weak, self-indulgent rage but with your very self. I knew then that you had chosen. That you were ready to take my place.

But I don't have your power. I can't—

You will have it.

Casnut resumed chanting. His chant was wilder now, unlike anything Moth had ever heard before, with the voices of many different men and women weaving in and out of the wordless song.

Still chanting, Casnut held up his right arm. Where his hand had been his arm now ended in a hawk's shiny black talons. He plunged the taloned hand in through one of the rents in his side. Moth could see the muscles in his arm straining as he grabbed something deep within him and twisted. Yet his chant never faltered, even when he pulled out a vertebra and held it forth for Moth to see.

It was not bone at all, but stone: a single sculptured piece of midnight blue lapis lazuli, slick with blood.

My power, he told Moth, his voice no different than it had been before. Yet though he was still standing as straight as ever, he had always been taller than Moth and now they were the same height.

Turn your back to me, he told Moth.

Moth turned away. Casnut slit open the flesh over Moth's lower spine with a slash of his taloned hand, but there was still no pain, not even when Casnut parted the flesh and reached in to grip Moth's spine with both his normal and taloned hands.

Suddenly he yanked the vertebrae apart. Moth felt an explosion of agony, and then the lapis was in place in his spine, smooth and cool, and he was two people.

He was Moth, himself, and he was back in Tas No's forge again. Rafti was holding him in her arms while she and Tramu stared at Casnut's mutilated and bloodless body writhing feebly on the ground before them. And yet at the same time he was Casnut, not the bloodless body in its heavy shaman's costume but the naked, bleeding Casnut collapsing in the shrinking hollow his chant had carved out for him as the lattice claimed him at last, drained him of the pain of his wounds as it drained him of himself.

Casnut's body was gone. His costume was empty. Moth could no longer sense the lattice.

He opened his eyes, got to his feet. Rafti and Tramu were staring at him. He turned his back on them, walked over to Casnut's empty costume, and took the drum from the waistband and stroked it softly, sensing its power.

"You're safe now," he said, turning back to face them. "Both of you. I stopped the Taryaa before it could let the stars know who you were."

"You were dead," Rafti said. "I tried to bring you back, but it wasn't enough. And then Casnut came, but he—"

"I was trapped in the Tas Realm," Moth told her, feeling the twin fires of his hassa, the one of burning and the other of absolute cold, twining together in his spine. "Casnut had to sacrifice himself to rescue me."

"Why?" Rafti asked. Tramu was looking on in baffled silence. "Why would he die for you now after he tried to kill you for so many years?"

"I don't know. Not really. He told me it was because he knew I'd realized I was ready to carry on his war against the Taryaa and the stars for him."

Besides, Casnut asked in his head, what makes you think I'm going to stop trying to kill you now?

Tramu started to say something. Moth gestured him abruptly to silence.

You're still alive? he demanded. It was all another trick?

The soundless voice was amused: No. Not alive. I'm a

ghost now, like all those who passed their power on to me. All that Sartor has ever had of any of us is our bodies.

What do you mean, you're not going to stop trying to kill me?

You only had me to deal with before, Casnut told him. Now you have all those who went before me to contend with as well. The dead have little patience with the weaknesses of the living.

We all died trying to destroy the Taryaa and the stars, another voice said. Moth realized he could hear them all now, a multitude murmuring within him. As you will. But your initiation is over. Your death will mean something now.

What choice do I have this time? Moth demanded of Casnut.

He heard their laughter within him. The same choice we had, one of the others told him.

Part Four: Tramu

Chapter Forty-nine

The roan balked. Tramu patted its side, spoke soothingly to it while he readjusted the stout leather sacks draped over its back and heavy with Tas No's tools, with copper and gold ingots.

He glanced up again at Moth, standing watching them from the top of the broad stairway cut from the Mother's Burning Mountain's basalt slope, then looked back down at the lush green valley with its neatly tended fields below, at the crowd looking up at them, the six members of the Council standing behind the Temple, waiting for Tramu and Rafti to complete their descent. He could see that all the people had the same flame-red hair as Rafti, and none of them seemed to be carrying any weapons.

"My people would honor a smith," Rafti had told him, and they had no need of a weaponsmith, it wouldn't make any difference to them that he had never been to the Harg or learned to work the secret copper.

Rafti paused a little below him, soothing Maryssat while she waited for Tramu to catch up with her. Some of the people in the crowd had recognized her now; Tramu could see them pointing up at her, and the wind carried her name to him. An old woman in ragged red rags had shoved her way through the crowd and was trying to force her way into the Temple, though she was not being allowed past the thorn barrier surrounding it. He recognized her from Rafti's description: the village shamaness, Cama.

He glanced back up toward the volcano's rim a final time, but Moth was gone. There was only a great black hawk soaring away over the Mother's Burning Mountain.

They continued leading the horses slowly down the basalt stairs until they were close enough to distinguish the Council members awaiting them. "My father," Rafti said, pointing to a stern-faced man wearing a vest of greening copper links who was standing rigidly erect, holding his rod of office in front of him like a ceremonial spear.

"That's your mother beside him?"

"Yes."

As they made their way down the final stretch of stairs Tramu saw that the Council was gazing in wonder at Rafti's unscarred face. Only Rafti's father's face remained stern and hostile, but the joy so clear on Rafti's mother's face and the rest of the Council's awed astonishment were enough for Tramu to know that they would find the home here that Rafti had promised him.

Soon he would have to speak to them, present Rafti's father with the horses, and tell them all who he was, beg a place for himself among them. But for the moment he was content just to be whole and free and alive, smelling the valley's clean air, so pure after the foulness of the mines, Kyborash's dank rot.

As though all the pain and horror had never happened, had only been a dream of dying from which he had been born anew.